P9-APC-197

# TRAPDOOR

BOOKS BY BERNARD J. O'KEEFE

*Shooting Ourselves in the Foot*

*Nuclear Hostages*

*Trapdoor*

BERNARD J. O'KEEFE

# TRAPDOOR

HOUGHTON MIFFLIN COMPANY

BOSTON 1988

For information about permission to reproduce selections from
this book, write to Permissions, Houghton Mifflin Company,
2 Park Street, Boston, Massachusetts 02108.

Library of Congress Cataloging-in-Publication Data

O'Keefe, Bernard J.
Trapdoor / Bernard J. O'Keefe.
p.  cm.
ISBN 0-395-48353-0
I. Title.
PS3565.K38T74  1988  88-12835
813'.54—dc19  CIP

Printed in the United States of America

P 10 9 8 7 6 5 4 3 2 1

*To Geri, Tom,*
*Kathi, and Carol*

# TRAPDOOR

# PROLOGUE

---

FROM HIS POSITION AT THE SIDE OF THE SUNLIT pool, Kane watched the toes of the five swimmers. Those of the Britons in lanes 1 and 5 were flat and listless, almost resigned, as they awaited the crack of the starter's gun. The Greek in lane 2 had the smallest feet and the smallest toes, well scaled to the lithe, diminutive, swarthy body which wiggled those toes constantly, knowing that they had to be first off the edge to have any chance against their more powerful competitors.

Kane could see, in lane 4, that the Dutchman's toes were already squeezed against the rounded tiles, that he had made his commitment, decided his course of action, that his mind would remain blank and his large body rigid in the fraction of a second before that plan could be put into action. The Hungarian in lane 3 was still calculating, shifting, perhaps noticing from the ripples that a puff of wind had caused a slight crosscurrent he would have to adjust for in his initial thrust. The powerful muscles in his supple Slavic torso gave one last involuntary ripple of their own, a ripple of readiness for come what may. But his toes were motionless, stretched out straight and slightly splayed for maximum contact area, held a half inch off the tile, prepared to trade a few milliseconds of starting time for the greater efficiency of a powerful coordinated thrust.

Behind the swimmers stood the starter, a little to the right of center to avoid the puddles left on the tiles by the swimmers from previous races on their way to the locker rooms. Immaculate in crisp whites, he had quieted the hundreds of spectators with his shout of *"Ready."* When the warning *"On your mark"* came through the hand-held megaphone, the crowd surged to its feet in unison. Those men who still wore straw hats had instinctively removed them. The women were a contrast: the Americans wore the straight knee-length skirts that had been almost a uniform during the war; the Europeans, even at sporting events, were already sporting Christian Dior's "New Look," with long, full, billowy skirts that fluttered like banners as they rose to their feet.

Kane was in high spirits. Here he was, a college sophomore, guest of the American ambassador, on his first visit to London, his first voyage abroad, present at the 1948 summer Olympics — the first Olympic games in twelve years, the first peaceful coming together of the nations of the world, the first outward manifestation that the sacrifices of the war years had not been in vain. He knew little about the competitors in this final heat of the four-hundred-meter freestyle, but as a fine athlete in his own right, he was fascinated by all athletic contests.

He smiled as he remembered what his high school football coach had drilled into him: "Watch their feet, boy, watch their feet. If you're going to be a running back, you've got to get the tacklers to commit before you do. It doesn't make any difference how they wiggle their hips or turn their shoulders or tilt their heads; there's only one place where they make contact with good old terra firma, and that's through the bottoms of their feet. When they turn into their arches or rise on their toes or dig back on their heels, that tells you where they're going to go. That's when you make your move."

Kane realized that this was the first athletic contest he had been to where the competitors didn't wear shoes, so he had decided to watch their toes. On the basis of his coach's advice, he would root for the Hungarian.

"Two bits on number three, Apples." He nudged his companion.

"Even money?" Appleby asked.

"Yep."

"You got it, jerk."

Kane's athletic instincts were good, but his eighteen-year-old's impression of the 1948 Olympics was far from the mark. London was patched and scrubbed from its wartime destruction, but the patching and the scrubbing had formed a thin veneer over the psychological and physical scars of the previous decade.

England was no longer a world power; the United States was dominant, but the ease and arrogance with which the Americans swept up the preponderance of gold medals made the new alignment difficult to bear. Germany and Japan were forbidden to compete; Stalin, in one of the first manifestations of the cold war, had boycotted the events to demonstrate, for all the world to understand, the Soviet Union's displeasure with the actions of his former allies.

But even the four-hundred-meter freestyle was not what it appeared on the surface, for the Dutchman was not a Dutchman, the Greek was not a Greek, and the Hungarian was not a Hungarian. The deceptions of that day would reach far into their lives, entwining them inextricably with one another, and with Kane, the spectator who watched them so intently in the soft sunlight of the summer day.

The Dutchman, Ludwig Schultz, was a product of the Hitlerjugend, the son of an embittered German storm trooper who had slipped into Holland with a forged identity in the confusion of the Nazi collapse and had imbued his young son with a soul-searing hatred of all his conquerors, Communist and capitalist alike. The Greek, Salom al Emir, was a Lebanese youth whose family had been wiped out in the three successive British invasions of Beirut in the past twelve years. His maternal uncle, Elia Malik, a Greek swimming coach, had adopted him and developed him into the best athlete on the Greek swimming team. The Hungarian, Pyotr Ivanovitch Rostov, was an outstanding Soviet athlete who had received secret dispensation to compete under the Hungarian flag after Stalin had announced his boycott.

Al Emir's toes squeezed as the gun went off, as though they had pulled the trigger; he was first into the air and first into the water with a good lead. Schultz was next, ponderously propelling himself from the balls of his feet. The Britons came after, flying off in unison at either end, like a pair of moving bookends. Rostov's toes surveyed the situation for an instant, then sent him off gracefully and powerfully, in a flat arc to maximize air distance and at a slight angle to the latest gust of wind. Kane was impressed, even though his favorite was three meters in the rear.

For the first few laps the Hungarian-Russian gained on the leaders, his strong arms cutting the gap like slices from a length of salami, a few centimeters at a time. Midway into the race, the five were virtually tied, their heads and shoulders dipping simultaneously below the surface to make the turn, like water nymphs in a ballet. But when they surfaced in the opposite direction, Kane noticed that his favorite, instead of breaking first as he had expected, had fallen behind. Relentlessly, number three made up the distance. For the next several laps, the handsome blond Slav swam strongly, coming even with the pack, and in some laps slightly ahead, but each time he lost his advantage at the turn. Something was amiss. Kane's favorite was too good an athlete to be making faulty turns. Could there be interference? The big man in lane 4 did seem to be a little too close as they dipped beneath the surface.

Appleby nudged Kane's shoulder. "Give up, turkey," he taunted him. "Your guy doesn't even know how to turn around."

Kane ignored him, concentrating on the swimmers as they went into the last turn. The Englishmen were tiring, falling significantly behind. It was a three-man race, with Rostov again slightly in the lead and swimming smoothly. Kane couldn't understand what happened next.

Instead of dipping below the surface to make his somersault, Rostov came out of the water like a trained porpoise, straight up. Kane could see his swimming trunks, his thighs, his knees, his shins, almost his ankles. Raising his arms quickly to propel himself downward, he twisted his body and dropped into the water like a stone. For a fraction of a second, there was nothing to be seen on the surface, only the frothy churning from the somersaulting bodies below. Then, in lane 2, the head and arms of the Lebanese-Greek completed a perfect turn and started effortlessly down the home stretch. Next came the Englishmen, head and head, as they had been from the start. Trailing significantly, Rostov leaped from the end of the pool in a powerful thrust. Kane could see nothing in lane 4.

What he could not see, what he could not sense, was Schultz's determination to control the race. Schultz knew what he wanted to do, what he had to do: he had to prevent the enemies of his homeland from winning. He couldn't win himself; the swimmers to his left were too good for him. He was proud that he had beaten the Americans in the previous heat; he looked at the Englishmen with scorn. He knew that Rostov was the favorite and had heard him speak Russian in the locker room. This was his enemy. Schultz was indifferent about his other opponents, caring more about who should lose than who should win.

He kept a meter ahead of his enemy for the first few laps, making no move. Midway in the race, he brushed the other's ankle with his arm, making it appear an accident as they came out of the turn. At each succeeding turn he was forced to become bolder, eventually gripping his enemy's ankle to throw him off the pace. As they entered the final turn, he sensed that his opponent was on to his game and would take evasive action. Schultz would be ready for the Russian pig.

He moved his body into the third lane, stretching his arm at full length to be ready when those reaching feet arrived. His middle fingers gripped the short crossbar of an empty ring holder for balance. But when the feet arrived, they came from above, not below. They came with blinding speed and with the full weight of the heavily muscled body providing the thrust. Schultz felt the heel contact his outstretched fingers, felt them grind against the short metal crossbar, felt the crack and the pain of the breaking bones. He opened his mouth in a gurgling scream of anguish, but no sound, only bubbles, rose to the surface. He struggled to the ladder at the far end of the pool, climbed painfully to the top, and half stumbled, half crawled to the locker room, his curses unheeded by the cheering crowd. He toweled himself without showering and dressed as best he could, but was unable to tie his shoelaces. Still cursing, he rushed out into the summer sunshine and vanished in the crowd.

Kane saw him leave but paid no heed. All he saw was his favorite, two meters behind, churning in a fury to reach the leader, who seemed to have the race won handily. But Rostov was not to be denied. He seemed to skim the surface as his arms drove like paddle wheels and his feet performed an entrechat, in water rather than air. "Watch those feet," Kane whispered as the excitement rose. The arms reached the Englishmen, then drove past them.

The leader could hear the roar of the crowd, could see him coming, could feel his power somehow transmitted through the roiling waters. Al Emir broke rhythm to speed up his own pace; that was his undoing. Rostov caught him in the last five meters and finished with a massive lunge that pushed him half a length ahead as he touched the edge of the pool.

Kane was delighted when Rostov showed up at the cocktail party the Australians gave for their hosts, the British.

It was a Gatsbyesque gala, not the kind of affair one would normally expect to see in staid old Britain. But what the hell, this was the last day of the Olympics, and it was an international group. The English would not have run so splashy a party, even before the war, and certainly not in these days of extended austerity. The Australians ran the show for that reason, and because they wanted the Russians to attend, a diplomatic impossibility had it been an official British function. The weather was perfect, the sky soft well into the night with the long summer twilight.

The party was held at a golf club in undamaged Hertford, since the Australians were rebuilding their embassy. In the ash-paneled ballroom a string band played waltzes, which barely deflected off the massive chandeliers before they were absorbed by the soft tapestries on the walls, while beside the swimming pool, jazz from a brass band fought its way over the murmuring of voices and the click of high heels against tiles. Liquor flowed freely, and the buffets reflected every ethnic cuisine except Japanese sushi and German wurst. The guest mix was eclectic: military uniforms in lest-we-forget profusion, diplomats in full ribbon, clean-looking, crew-cut athletes, the international hope for the future, bright-eyed and shiny-faced. As it had in the pool that afternoon, everything looked smooth and tranquil on the surface, but below the surface tension of the pool and the politics, the struggles went on.

"Hey, Brad, there's the guy that won the four hundred," Kane said, pointing out Rostov to Appleby. "Who's that he's with?"

"I don't know." Appleby shrugged. "Let's ask Dad."

Shorter than Kane, who was six foot one, and about the same age, Rostov was not a big man. His blond crew cut and sinewy neck suggested a Slavic Cossack heritage that was modified by the more delicate, slightly flattened face of his mother's Magyar origin. His shoulders were sloping and his arms long; you could almost see him in motion, pulling that sleek body through the water with ease.

Appleby touched his father's shoulder. "That blond fellow just arriving did a beautiful job coming from behind to win the four hundred freestyle. We'd like to meet him. Do you know those people he's with?"

"I sure do. That's the Russian ambassador, Molotov," Mr. Appleby said. "He's a tough cookie, but fair. He's a lot easier to do business with than his uncle, the foreign minister. The young girl must be his daughter or his niece. I've never seen her before. Come on, I'll introduce you."

Kane was puzzled. "I'm surprised that he'd show up at an Olympics party when they've boycotted the games. Besides, that swimmer, Rostov, is a Hungarian."

The elder Appleby was amused. "Oh, it doesn't bother Molotov. His job is to get out and meet people, not to sit home and sulk. Besides, they've snuck in a few of their better athletes to get them some competitive practice for the next Olympics. The Soviets are very pragmatic and competitive. They only want to play when they can win. I think that was one of the reasons for the boycott. I understand that they and the East Germans are putting a lot of effort into training young athletes. It will be a big propaganda deal for them in a few years. Even now, I wouldn't be surprised if your Hungarian turns out to be a Russian in sheep's clothing. Come on."

He introduced them to Ambassador Molotov, who in turn introduced them to his daughter, Anna, who was attending school in London, and to Rostov.

"That was a great last lap you swam," Kane said. "What was that maneuver you used, coming out of the water at the turn, and what happened to the man in lane four?"

"Thank you," Rostov said. He ignored the first question and replied truthfully to the second. "I don't know. I had never seen him before. I suppose he picked up a cramp or something and had to drop out."

Kane barged right along, ignoring diplomacy. "You all speak such excellent English. I hadn't expected that."

Anna Molotova handled the comment with a smoothness beyond her fourteen years. Even the braces on her teeth and the teenager's long skinny legs could not hide the natural grace of the developing black-haired beauty. "My father is a student of languages. It helps a diplomat, you know. He's actually colloquial in half a dozen. As for me, I spent the war years in English schools. In fact, I had difficulty getting back into Russian when I went home. Peter can speak for himself."

She turned to Rostov, who was taking soft drinks from a waiter and handing one to her.

"Yes, Peter. Are you actually Hungarian, or are you Russian?" asked Kane.

Rostov ignored the gaffe. "I'm both." He smiled. "My mother is Hungarian. She is a nurse who met my father when he was wounded in the First World War. She learned her English during the British occupation of our native Georgia in 1920. Fortunately, we are all allies now."

Oh, oh, I blew that one, Kane thought. He moved to change the conversation. He was rescued by a newcomer hurrying to shake Rostov's hand.

"It was a great race, young man. I'm Elia Malik, coach of the Greek swimming team. It was really quite exciting. You've met my man, Salom al Emir, of course. We tried, but you were just too good for us."

The young Lebanese looked tiny beside Rostov and the two Americans, but he handled himself well. "Unfortunately, with the unrest in our area, there has not been much time for sports." Emir spread his hands and gave a slight bow. "I am pleased to have gotten as far as we did. I congratulate you again, Mr. Rostov, on your victory."

Malik turned to the Americans. "I work for an American oil company in Athens. I only do this in my spare time," he said, then ducked under a waiter's tray of drinks and moved on to the next group. Salom al Emir moved his head in what was halfway between a condescending nod and a bow, then followed Malik.

The crowd became more boisterous, the noise level rising to compensate for the band that had started to play and the shouting crescendos of a group of Aussies singing down-under songs. The ambassadors drifted away, but the four youngsters drew into a tighter group and talked athletics, oblivious to the political innuendoes parried around them.

The young people chattered on. Brad Appleby talked baseball — Ted Williams and the Red Sox — and the prospects for the university team, of which he had been freshman captain. He talked about Kane's prospects after being elected to the high school All-America as a running back, and said it was a pity that neither sport had been accepted by the Olympic committee. Rostov politely interjected that Kane and Appleby would both be gold medal winners if their sports had been included.

Kane was fascinated by Rostov's aplomb. Having only a vague idea of where it was, he was astonished to hear that the climate of Rostov's Georgia was mild enough for year-round outdoor swimming. And Kane was chagrined that his country and Great Britain had occupied large parts of the Russian Empire after Russia surrendered to the Germans with the Treaty of Brest-Litovsk. Rostov shrugged it off and did not seem the least bit embarrassed that he had competed under the Hungarian flag in spite of the Russian boycott. Anna, wide-eyed, listened to it all.

The evening was a microcosm of a world to come. The diplomats, in all their regalia, were older, senior people with the grace and ease and small talk of a generation bygone, a world of kings and queens and princesses, a world of diplomacy in which the crowned heads of Europe were all cousins who might send hordes of troops crashing into one another's territory, but who would not be so gauche as to spoil the evening by referring to the carnage. Two wars had killed that world. The diplomats knew this; their conversations were slow and languid and ethereal as they conjured up the spirits of the past to give them a decent burial before their own expiration.

The military were lean and lithe and confident. Now, they thought, it was their world and they had won it fair and square. They knew how to run armies and navies and air forces; they knew how to protect their friends and punish their enemies; they had been to all corners of the globe and had met with all its peoples; they knew how to win wars and to keep the peace.

Although they didn't realize it, their new world had ended before it began. It had ended on a tower in the wilds of a desert in New Mexico, in the Jornada del Muerto, the Journey of Death, at a place called Alamogordo.

The athletes were the youngest, but a new breed among youth. Within a decade, the rapid march of technology would bring forth the age of communication, an age in which television would make athletes and entertainers instant celebrities and instant millionaires and powerful politicians, an age in which the ability to perform and to communicate would give these talented individuals a power transcending that of the kings and generals of old.

The former supreme commander of the Allied forces was at the party; marking time as a university president, he was still fawned on by the diplomats, revered by the soldiers, and idolized by the athletes. He was to live and even to reign during this transition, at times concerned about the complex and mutually supporting technological collaboration between the military and its industry, at times concerned about the growing influence of television over international politics. At one point he was heard to grumble, "If this keeps up, someday we'll have an actor as president."

Nuclear weapons were not discussed. To some, they were just another piece of ordnance, large, to be sure, but not conclusive to the inevitable surrender of the Japanese, and certainly not threatening to the world reorganization now evolving. To others, they were unsportsmanlike and threatening, as gunpowder had been to bowmen, tanks to cavalry, and bombers to battleships. They took the glory and the chivalry out of warfare. To a third group, they were a disturbing reminder of the dominance of the United States, which would possess the secret for a generation to come, more than enough time for it to put the world in order, once and for all. The secret whispers of nuclear parity, of megatons and ICBMs, were not in the lexicon of these groups. Those whispers were still confined to the faraway laboratories of the United States of America and the Union of Soviet Socialist Republics.

1

THE BOEING 707 SURROUNDED BY SYRIAN PEACE-
keeping troops on the end of the runway at the Beirut Airport
was the pride of Middle East Airlines, the Lebanese national
carrier. An ominous stillness hung over the airport and the
whole of Beirut's Moslem western sector as the sun rose in a
cloudless sky. But the telephone lines between Beirut and Damascus were anything but quiet.

The cities were a mere fifty miles apart, but in the Middle
East, a few miles make an enormous political difference. President Assad, comfortably in control of his country as the years
rolled by in the last decade of the twentieth century, was irritated but well in control of himself as he lectured the new
president of Lebanon in this first crisis of his tenure. Assad's
plush quarters on the edge of Damascus were quietly elegant
and discreetly guarded. Assad nodded to the maidservant who
came to refill his coffee cup, lowering her eyes and bowing as
she received the wordless instruction, then backing away from
his presence and disappearing behind the heavy brocades of the
entryway.

"If you don't tell Abu Nidal to have his men surrender within
the hour, I'll order my troops to destroy the aircraft. Syria is
responsible for the safety of your city," said Assad.

"By Allah, Assad, it's my aircraft and my airline and my city.

There will be no violence. I can handle the situation. I am not a man of violence, you know that." The new president of Lebanon spoke calmly, but the rasp of exasperation was obvious in his tone. "Abu Nidal is a patriot. He is not the terrorist that the Western press makes him out to be."

"You may not be a man of violence, but Abu Nidal is, and the Israelis are," the Syrian leader replied. "My people tell me that Israeli aircraft are on the runways, poised to take off and retaliate against your own PLO camps if anything happens to their man."

"I've spoken to Nidal. He intends no violence. He merely wants to hold the man for an exchange of prisoners."

"I think you're naive, Emir. I'll believe that when I see it."

Salom al Emir's office, a blend of Eastern opulence and Western efficiency, was in the center of a bombed-out ruin. On the outskirts of Beirut, it had been the library of a wealthy Arab merchant, left intact when he, his ladies, and the main buildings of his forty-room palace had been wiped out by a Mark VII demolition device that had worked its way loose from the wing tip of an Israeli Phantom fighter, many raids ago. Two walls held tapestries interwoven with Lebanese flags, the dark green foliage of the cedars of Lebanon accentuated by the faint redolence of the native cedar paneling behind. The other two carried rows of books, their neatly ordered deep-tooled leather and unsullied gold leaf–bordered pages attesting that their formidable phalanxes had never been breached by human hands. The deep, rich tones of the small Iranian rugs, askew on the hardwood floors, reflected shifting kaleidoscopic patterns of light from the small panes of stained glass in the windows.

It was not only the gray metal desk that shattered the serenity of the library; four matching filing cabinets and a hulking Mosler safe with an ominous black dial circled a battered mahogany-veneer table heaped with papers, pamphlets, and spare rolls of paper for the crank-handled National Cash Register adding machine at one end. Emir, like Arafat before him, was not a man for amenities.

He called himself a moonlighter. Recently installed as the

compromise president of Lebanon, he recognized that there was no power in the job, that the conflicting interests of Syrians, Soviets, Iraqis, Iranians, and Egyptians made it impossible to deal with the Israelis and their American supporters in a unified manner. Still, the title gave him credibility, afforded him opportunity to come out of the closet, to show himself to the public, to make speeches and pleas for support, but, most of all, it strengthened his ability to carry out his primary responsibility as the accepted, but unannounced, leader of the Palestine Liberation Organization.

Above all, Salom al Emir considered himself a pragmatist. Trained in terrorism, surrounded by violence, steeped in an atmosphere of rage and despair, faced with the conflicts of high-minded motives and scurrilous acts, Emir had remained aloof from the passions and prejudices of his associates, preferring to deal with the world as it was, to obtain his objectives by working within systems and without violence.

He was a terrorist who had never committed a terrorist act.

For Emir's purposes, the office in the bombed-out palace better fitted his dealing with his PLO associates than did the more conspicuous downtown quarters reserved for him as the president of Lebanon. He knew what he had to do in this instance — hold off Assad until he could get to Nidal. The PLO had the power of the underground purse. It was a billion-dollar business, assessing nations throughout the Middle East and disbursing funds to militant groups as well as to unfortunates in the concentration camps. It controlled banks and businesses in several nations. All Emir needed was a few hours to put the pressure on Nidal, who was already boasting of the capture of the aircraft.

Emir's train of thought began to wander when he heard the unmistakable murmur of helicopter engines approaching from the west. Within seconds, the murmur became a roar, drowning out Assad's quiet, slightly supercilious remarks on the other end of the line.

Assad could hear it over the phone. He raised his voice to a shout. "What's that noise? . . . Aircraft? . . . Everything's supposed to be grounded."

Emir cut off the conversation. "I'll call you back."

The door to the office opened suddenly as his aide, Hassan, broke into the room. "It's Israeli helicopters, sahib. They're headed for the airport."

"Call a general alert and get the airport commander on the telephone."

On the Boeing 707 the three hundred passengers plus six terrorists heard the noise also. The passengers, a diverse group of businessmen, families, and a few tourists, were too bewildered by their frightening experience to attach significance to another noise; the terrorists were too jittery to pay attention until the aircraft came into view outside their windows. Only one of the passengers deduced its significance; he tensed to be ready for action.

The six Sikorsky attack helicopters swooped down, surrounding the 707, two on each side and one on either end. The Israeli commandos hit the tarmac running, AK47s and Uzis waving in all directions. The lieutenant commanding the small Syrian detachment ran forward, firing a warning shot in the air. He was cut down instantaneously by AK47s shooting from two directions. Leaderless, the remaining Syrian troops discarded their weapons and raised their arms. At a gesture from their commander, six of the Israelis rounded up the Syrians, expertly trussed their arms behind their backs, and forced them to lie face-down on the asphalt, guarded by two of the commandos. The whole action had been executed crisply. No more than four minutes had passed.

There was complete silence for another two minutes. The sun glinted off the side of the 707, forcing the Israelis to shield their eyes until the angle had changed. Then the left window of the cockpit opened. The head of Israeli Colonel Benjamin Shapiro appeared in the opening, a pistol pressed against his temple. A few seconds later, the leering visage of one of his captors was visible, one arm around Shapiro's neck, the other hand holding the gun. The message was clear: one move against the hijackers and the colonel would be executed. Time stood still for seconds as the antagonists glared at each other.

Suddenly, the terrorist was dead before his eyes and his brain could register the sight of the flash or the sound of the single rifle shot reached his ears. The sharpshooter had positioned himself in the doorway of the nearest helicopter as soon as the blades stopped turning, waiting for this gesture of defiance characteristic of Abu Nidal's Islamic Jihad. A small round hole appeared in the forehead of the terrorist as the force of the bullet's impact drove his head back out of the sight of the poised Israeli commandos. Colonel Shapiro could be seen grasping the pistol from the dead man's hand and turning to confront his other captors.

His motions were lost in the roar of the blast from the rear of the aircraft.

Demolition experts from the helicopters had rushed to attach shaped charges to the sides and underfuselage of the 707. Mission accomplished, they had run back twenty paces and thrown themselves face-down on the ground while a helicopter commando closed the switch that detonated the charges and neatly blew the complete tail assembly clear of the transport. Two men came running with an aluminum ladder, propping it against the smoking, gaping, almost circular hole in the fuselage of the huge plane. A third, laden with smoke and tear gas grenades, swiftly climbed the ladder. He lobbed the grenades into the main cabin, then stepped aside and leaped the twenty feet to the tarmac, stumbling to catch his balance. Two more commandos, gas masks on their faces and submachine guns in their hands, followed him up the ladder and dashed into the cabin. There were three bursts of gunfire. Bullet holes stitched the glinting aluminum skin of the aircraft from within. Screams of terror mingled with angry shouts of authority. Silence again, then a single pistol shot, and Shapiro appeared once more, this time in the hole where the tail had been. He dropped to the ground, followed by the two machine gunners, who discarded their gas masks as they ran. The three climbed into the nearest helicopter, ducking the accelerating rotor blades. At a common signal, all six helicopters rose quickly into the air and headed toward the Israeli border fifty miles away.

From the windows of the library-office, Emir and Hassan heard the gunfire and watched helplessly as the aircraft flew south, almost over their heads. His shoulders slumped and Emir cursed softly as he walked back to his desk to face the telephonic wrath of the president of Syria.

Abu Nidal's shoulders were in a permanent shrug. Unceremoniously hustled to Emir's office by security guards, Nidal sat quietly, his body slumped over the small folding chair, his crossed ankles reaching nakedly into his sandals from the frayed hem of his robe. He half listened to Emir's denunciations. "Look what you've done. Six civilians killed, two of them Syrians, four of your own stupid people dead, the tail blown off a multimillion-dollar airplane, Assad furious, the Israelis looking like heroes, all for nothing. What were you trying to accomplish?"

Emir jumped to his feet from behind the metal desk and placed his hands on the table, his chin jutting out as he continued the tirade.

Nidal pushed some papers aside, slid his feet onto the mahogany table, and leaned back onto two legs of the rickety chair. "I've told you three times now. The pig Shapiro is a killer. He has wiped out at least a dozen of my people. We spotted him in civilian clothes in Athens and figured out that he was on some sort of secret mission. When he had the arrogance to book a flight to Tehran stopping off here, we figured we had better pick him up while we could. It's as simple as that. If the stupid Syrians had let us alone and permitted us to take him off quietly, we'd have done so with no fuss. Then we could have exchanged him for some of our people or sent his testicles to Tel Aviv on a saucer."

"Shapiro doesn't matter. He's a small-time operator. What matters is to get away from this senseless violence which infuriates the rest of the world and sets them against us."

Nidal rose from his chair to confront the Lebanese president.

"You may be president of this country and head of the PLO, but how many troops do you have? You don't even have control of your own territory. You can't move without kissing Assad's ass. Syrian peacekeeping force. What does that mean? It just means that they want to keep us in submission forever. Look at all those people starving and dying in the refugee camps while the fucking Israelis continue to build settlements in our homeland. What kind of justice is that? What can we do but keep fighting for our cause?"

"Slow it down, Nidal," said Emir, retreating behind his desk as Hassan slipped quietly into the office. "Let's forget about Shapiro. There are more subtle ways of accomplishing our objectives. You can be helpful to me."

"How?"

"Do you know anyone who is familiar with nuclear weapons — where they are stored, how to handle them?"

Nidal, sensing an opening, grinned slightly and sat down. "What do you want to do, blow up Tel Aviv? Nuclear weapons don't sound very nonviolent to me."

"Never mind what I want to do. Do you know anyone or don't you?"

Nidal sparred. "Those things are tightly guarded. The Sikhs tell me that even if you get hold of one, you have to know a code to make it operate. The Americans keep close tabs on them, they tell me. Muammar's been trying to buy or steal one for years. He thinks he can get one in Turkey or Italy, where the security is pretty lax."

Emir brushed the objections aside with a wave of his hand. "Qaddafi's a fool. I want no part of him. I'm looking for someone who knows how to handle them, to transport them. I'll worry about the rest. Answer my question."

"I probably do. Let me think a minute. Yes, I do know one man, a German. He's been obsessed for years with the idea of stealing a nuclear weapon and selling it to someone. So far, he hasn't succeeded, but he might be worth talking to. I should be able to find him. What's in it for me?"

"What's in it for you is to keep your head on top of your

neck. Assad's on a tear. He'll wipe out both of us if we don't do something to make up for that stupid hijacking. What's the man's name? I want to talk to him."

"Ludwig Schultz."

Hassan wrote down the name on a small pad and slipped quietly out of the room.

Abu Nidal found Schultz in Milan, working with the Red Brigade on a labor uprising that would topple the Italian government for the umpteenth time in the last forty years. Schultz, who was receiving a pittance for his activities, was still suspicious of the Palestinian when he inquired about knowledge of nuclear weapons. But he agreed to meet with Hassan in the Milan airport for a thousand dollars.

Hassan was inconspicuous in Western business clothes as he led Schultz to the empty first class lounge. Schultz, in seedy brown trousers, soiled white shirt with open collar, and a well-worn gray sweater was uncomfortable even with no one to observe him.

Hassan had an hour's worth of questions about Schultz's background but little to say about his own objectives. Schultz answered the questions in a soft monotone with no emotion showing on his stolid Teutonic face and no curiosity as to why the questions were being asked. Hassan was particularly curious about Schultz's employment at the nuclear testing grounds of Bikini and Eniwetok in the Pacific Marshall Islands and his work at the Nevada Test Site. "How did you get a job there?" he asked.

"False credentials."

"Why did you leave Bikini before your contract was up?"

"I got bored with the small islands. They were too confining."

"And Nevada?"

Schultz gazed at him blankly and shrugged. "Same thing, I guess. I wanted to get back home to Germany. What do you want of me?"

Hassan could see that he was not going to get much more

from the German. He explained that his superior was interested in nuclear weapons and would like to get some information on their size and portability, but he would not go beyond that. They both sensed an impasse and broke off the meeting with an agreement by Schultz to meet Hassan's principal in Beirut.

When Hassan ushered Schultz into Emir's presence at the library office, the conversation was more direct. Emir stepped forward to meet them, smiling, with his hand extended. "I know you."

"From the forty-eight Olympics," Schultz replied. "The Russian caught you."

"He was a very powerful swimmer."

"The bastards. I hate them all. Communists, capitalists, they're all the same. Some day . . . What do you want with me?"

Emir ignored the question and motioned Schultz to a seat at the table. The hulking Schultz, still in the same gray sweater, soiled shirt, and brown trousers, again looked out of place and uncomfortable beside Hassan and Emir, who were dressed in expensive Western suits and sipping coffee, which Schultz had refused.

The stolid look on Schultz's face indicated that there would be no small talk, so Emir came right to the point: "I want a nuclear weapon from the American stockpile," he said.

"It has to be from the stockpile?"

"Yes, and one of the newer ones. Ten million deutsche marks, in the currency of your choosing."

Schultz's expression changed. The stolid look was replaced by a gaze of sly cunning. He admitted to the two Lebanese that he had worked at the nuclear test sites with the intention of stealing a weapon, but would give no details. He had been evaluating the possibility of stealing a weapon from the European stockpile, was convinced that it could be done, and had a plan for it, but had been constrained by lack of funds. Emir assured him that money was no problem. They agreed that Emir would provide an advance fee of two hundred thousand deutsche marks and that Hassan would be the contact man.

"Anything else?" asked Emir.

"Yes. I'll need a United States passport, and I'll need to make contact with an American protest group called Makepeace."

"Done."

They did not shake hands. Schultz stood up and walked silently to the door. Hassan joined him to make the detailed arrangements.

"One more thing," Emir called after Schultz. "I want no violence."

Schultz shrugged, nodded once, then proceeded through the doorway.

"Bullshit," screamed June. "You're just like every other goddamned man. Take a woman for every goddamned thing you can get, then you dump her. I built that department up, made you look like a hero. I'm the best software designer in California, and you know it, and everyone else in this company knows it. Herb Goldstein knows it. All your customers know it. And the first time a real promotion opportunity comes up, what do you do? You give it to a man, that's what you do. I knew that's what you were going to do. Give it to a man. That's typical of your macho, football-jock mentality."

June's breasts almost bounced out of her bra as she strode back and forth across the living room rug in front of the astonished Kane. He started to get up from the sofa, but she pinned him there with the force of her gaze.

"I know you've got another woman — your administrative assistant. Administrative assistant, my ass. It's just an excuse to tramp that bitch all over the country with you. I'm going to sue you for discrimination. And I'm going to tell them everything. All about us, too. I don't care if it all comes out in the papers. The TV people will love it. The great football hero. The great scientist. The great tycoon. The founder of an industry, the idol of Silicon Valley, buddy-buddy with pols and presidents, taking advantage of a poor little female software designer. TV will love it." She paused for breath.

She had decorated the apartment herself; now he could see that it irritated her. The contrasts that gave it vigor exacerbated her frustration. He had been living in hotels whenever he left corporate headquarters in L.A. to visit the semiconductor plant, but she had twitted him, saying that he could not be a true Silicon Valley high-tech hot rock without a pad in Palo Alto, so he turned the problem over to her. The kitchen was a masterpiece of modern microwavery, the brushed stainless steel of the implements and the shiny beige plastic counters unadorned and unabashed, poised to challenge McDonald's or Burger King in a competition for efficiency. The study, too, had all the bells and whistles, but the VCR, the compact disc player, the TVs, and the shortwave radio were hidden under or between dark walnut-paneled bookcases that covered three walls; they were controlled by a row of buttons recessed into the side of a large desk in front of the window.

The living room was modern, with Picasso and Klee prints breaking the starkness of the plain white wall; two free-form chrome sculptures sat on the polystyrene tables. But the rug had been made thick and soft for sound absorption, and she almost stumbled on it in her exasperation.

"Knock it off, June. Take it easy, slow down." Kane interrupted her, pulling himself out of the plush armchair. "Nobody's trying to discriminate against you, least of all me. It's Herb's recommendation, not mine. You know I wouldn't overrule a division head. You're the best software designer I've ever seen. You're the top professional in your field. It's Herb's opinion that making you an administrator would be a waste of your talents. If there's anything I've learned in business —"

She stalked across the room to face him, her chin a few inches from his. "If there's anything you've learned in business —" She was mocking him. "That's the standard line of bullshit when you don't want to promote somebody. Especially a woman. Maybe I should take a course in stenotype. Then I could get reports out quickly if some of your gay young men should come up with a new application for the chip."

"That hurts, June," Kane replied, turning away sadly. From the first day he'd met her he had been impressed — no, not just impressed, but astounded at her design capability. He couldn't believe what she had gotten out of the KA9090. He'd built Kane Industries on his ability as a microchip inventor, and he knew his products. The KA9090 was his crowning achievement, probably his last contribution as a technologist, now that he was spending so much time on administration. She had gotten more out of it than even he had thought was achievable. "You're good. There's no denying that."

June bore in. "You are a scientist, you are an inventor, but you are also a manager. Don't tell me I can't make the switch. That's just an excuse."

He tried to explain to her that the switch from technology was possible, but that very few were able to succeed. He pointed out that there were big successes — Ken Olsen at Digital, Bob Noyce at Intel, but that these were the exceptions. For every Olsen and every Noyce, there were hundreds of would-be technology gurus strung out all over the landscape. "They never even bother to go bankrupt; they don't have enough money to hire a lawyer. They just disappear.

"I don't know where I learned it. Maybe it was from sports. Maybe it was just instinctive. I've always been able to handle men. But not women, I guess."

"Oh, you can handle women, all right," she said. "And I'm a prime example of that — up until now, that is. Look at you. Over sixty, you look thirty-five. More hair than Reagan. And you're a smooth-talking son of a bitch, I know that. Don't tell me you can't handle women."

"That's not what I'm talking about. Being a professional and being a manager are two different things. Einstein was the greatest theoretical physicist of all time but he couldn't have fought his way out of a paper bag as a manager. Hey, I grew up in Los Alamos. I watched Oppenheimer. He was no Einstein, but he could lead men and women and get more out of them than they ever thought they could produce."

June was disgusted. "Look, I'm not talking about winning a Nobel Prize or being the director of Los Alamos, for Christ's sake. All I want is to run a lousy little software division which is so far down in your organization that you would never even know who the hell I was if you hadn't slept with me."

"You're hitting below the belt again, June. I was impressed by you the first time I saw you, at that trade show."

"Don't try to kid me. I know what you were impressed by." Her tone was a little less raucous.

The first thing anyone noticed about June Malik was the size of her boobs. The second thing anyone noticed about June Malik was the size of her boobs. Kane was no exception. Wherever she went, whatever she did, she drew open stares from the men and sly looks from the women. A further assessment of her velvety black hair, deep brown eyes, narrow waist, and shapely legs revealed a truly beautiful woman of exquisite proportion, but the first impression was always the same. In June's mind, it was her misfortune to be born both brilliant and beautiful.

Kane stepped back and threw out his arms. "Okay, I'll admit it. I didn't know who you were, but that was understandable," he said. "Why don't you relax. I'll make us a couple of drinks. I have to go to Washington in the morning for that testimony on plant security, but I'll be back in a few days. I'll get hold of Herb and see what kind of compromise we can work out. I'm sure you'll be treated well financially."

Her face hardened and the raucousness came back into her voice. "I don't give a damn about money," she said, "and I'm not going to any drink. I'm not going to be put off by any sweet talk from you or Herb Goldstein. I'm getting the hell out of here."

She turned and ran across the plush carpet and disappeared into the foyer. Kane heard the door of the apartment slam with a reverberation that rattled the glasses in the dining room cabinet.

He rubbed his chin in amazement. He went out and poured himself a stiff scotch. Herb had said he was making her a senior scientist. That's a much better deal than division manager, and it paid more, too. She could come and go as she pleased, which she likes, he thought. And she's much too smart to be wasted as a middle-level manager. There must be something else. Come to think of it, she's been acting pretty itchy lately. It goes back to when she finished that PAL job.

Kane had long been a maverick in the high-tech business. Although he had over a billion dollars in defense contracts, he was both uneasy and outspoken about the complexity of the new weapons systems. He had opposed the deployment of Cruise and Pershing missiles in Europe and was a staunch opponent of the Strategic Defense Initiative, or "Star Wars," program. This had provoked considerable skepticism in the press and some strong warnings from his customers in the Defense Department. The *Wall Street Journal* remarked that these were strange words from "a card-carrying member of the military-industrial establishment." One assistant secretary of Defense had reminded him of an old political maxim, "If you want to get along, you have to go along." But Kane would not back off.

He felt that a strong economy was the best deterrent to totalitarian and Communist expansion and stated that he'd be willing to forgo defense business if it would lower the budget deficit. Not all his stockholders agreed with him.

But his real concern was the complexity of the new weaponry. The tanks, the bombers, the fighter planes, were getting so complicated that they were difficult to keep in service. The Bradley tank regularly broke down after a couple of hours of operation. The B1 bomber radars were incompatible with their navigation systems, and naval frigates kept their Phoenix defense systems turned off for fear of firing on friendly aircraft or spurious land masses. And one microchip could throw out an entire submarine defense system. "The only country that can compete with us is the USSR," he had argued at a recent congressional hearing. "If we get into a war with the Russians, it's the end of civilization."

He worried endlessly about an accidental or terrorist detonation of a nuclear weapon. He remembered a report put out by an international task force on nuclear terrorism, warning that all nuclear weapons should have locks, called Permissive Action Links, or PALs, to prevent their accidental or unauthorized use; he agreed with it thoroughly. He was somewhat familiar with the locks on United States weapons, but he hadn't worked on that problem for years. He was aware that an officer followed the President around with the so-called football which contains the code for unlocking the devices in the event of a nuclear war alert. He was also aware that, since Reagan, the officers he'd seen on television had always been pretty young ladies, rotated among the services. A little macabre, but a nice touch, he thought.

What he didn't know was that the task force report had caused a considerable stir in Washington and at NATO, with the usual resultant flurry from the bureaucracy to do something to protect their backsides.

The call that had changed everything had come directly from the secretary of Energy on a Sunday afternoon, almost two years ago. The secretary had gone right to the point. The President wanted the PAL devices upgraded on a top-priority basis. Experts had reported that Kane's new microchip, the KA9090, was the most powerful processor on the market, and the most compact. Kane remembered being puzzled — Why all that power for such a simple application?

"We want to change the code in each device periodically," the secretary said. He wouldn't say more.

"Wow." Kane whistled. "That's a pretty tall order. And you must know I think weapons are too damn complex already. There's a tradeoff between availability and security that should be examined carefully."

The secretary was not impressed. "I'm afraid that decision has already been made," he said. "The Sandia laboratory weapons design people will be in touch with you in the morning."

Kane remembered deciding to bring June in on the problem from the beginning, even though he didn't know if she had a military clearance. He'd worry about that later. The decision had been a good one, but now his lover and the best software designer in the company had just walked out of his life. He shook his head, unable to admit to himself which was more important.

The telephone rang. Kane jumped up, hoping that June had changed her mind, but it was Goldstein wanting to know if he'd talked to her. Kane told him what had happened, expressing irritation that Goldstein hadn't handled the situation more smoothly.

Goldstein went on the defensive. "I didn't do anything, for Christ's sake. I just told her that I was making her a senior scientist and that Dick Martin would be the new Software Division manager." He went on to explain that he thought he was doing her a favor, since she'd make more money and have a great deal more independence. He said that he was astounded when she just up and quit. Was there anything he could do to rescue the situation?

"Nothing right now. I'm going to Washington this weekend. Let's give her a few days off so she can cool down. Then I'll talk to her."

"I don't know, boss. That lady has awfully strong opinions and doesn't change her mind very easily, but you know her better than I do and you're calling the shots," Goldstein said. "Good luck."

June went immediately to a pay phone after checking her baggage at the airport. She dialed a Washington number and heard the phone on the other end ring four times before the answering machine clicked in. There was no announcement, just the beep of the machine signifying readiness to receive the message. She gave the number of the pay phone, omitting the area code, and hung up. Exactly thirty seconds elapsed before her phone rang.

"He went for it, completely," she said into the receiver.

"Good" was the answer. "I'll relay it."

# 2

ASSIM MAHMOUD WAS NOT HAPPY WITH HIS NEW assignment. He had been quite content in Damascus, analyzing American intelligence reports. His superior, President Assad, was furious with the Lebanese president's performance in the Beirut hijacking incident; Assad had threatened to move more peacekeeping troops into Lebanon, and in particular, to take over the airport. But Salom al Emir had argued persuasively for a month's time to carry off a new plan of major importance to the whole Middle East. Emir wouldn't divulge the nature of the plan, but he agreed to accept a personal representative of the president of Syria to participate in the effort.

"Keep your eye on him," Assad had warned Mahmoud. "Emir has been a good manager in the PLO, but he may be out of his depth as president of Lebanon. He has some weird ideas on how to deal with the Israelis and the Americans."

As the black Mercedes worked its way into the Anti-Lebanon mountains, Mahmoud looked back at the beautiful, old, undamaged city of Damascus and envisioned with distaste the prospects of an assignment in the ruins of Beirut. He was a solid, swarthy man whose sour visage framed in the depths of a heavy mustache and full beard made him look sinister in the seedy Western suit he was wearing. He knew he had been selected partly because of his proficiency in English, but he had hated his days in the West and was resentful that he was required to wear American business clothing.

He had allowed two hours for the trip, even though the cities were only fifty miles apart. There were two mountain ranges to traverse: the first was stony, dry, and bleak; all the moisture from the Mediterranean was captured by the higher Lebanon Mountains to the west. The countryside grew more interesting as the driver came down the slope into the fertile Bekáa Valley, fed with water from the west. This was the source of all Lebanon's agriculture, but Mahmoud could see that the infrastructure, the roads, bridges, and dams were already growing dilapidated with inattention and that the farmers and travelers moved with listless resignation.

He'd had no difficulty crossing the border. His Mercedes had official Syrian plates and bore two flags on its hood — the black, white, and red banner of Syria with its two green stars, plus the red and white flag of Lebanon with its prominent green cedar. But there were very few cedars of Lebanon to be seen as they worked their way down the coastal side of the Lebanon Mountains toward Beirut. Most had long since gone to feed the ferocious energy demands of war.

Beirut was in shambles. The city that had been the pearl of the Mediterranean was like a sun-bleached shell, the pearl extracted, cast aside, and crushed by the animosities of its inhabitants. The odor of decay was pervasive. From time to time they ran into barricades. Once they were stopped by a Syrian detachment whose officious captain insisted on looking at their papers, but for the most part they were waved along into the section still under Emir's control. There the troops were diffident and casual, passing the Syrian vehicle along with surly, antagonistic stares.

The Mercedes picked its way through the littered streets until it came to the bombed-out palace. Although Emir's library-office was set back from the road, it was still made conspicuous by the guards surrounding it. Hassan came quickly to escort the

Syrian into the building, where he gave him an incomplete description of his mission.

Mahmoud, uncomfortable in his Western clothes, clearly irritated at having had to take instructions from Hassan before he could see Emir, paced restlessly around the office, stumbling once on a small rug. The Lebanese president sat calmly behind the steel desk, oblivious to the Syrian's complaints.

"You'll have to tell me what this is all about, Emir. I'm the personal representative of the president of Syria, and I demand appropriate treatment. You are shunting me aside by sending me to the United States. I am not going to —"

Emir stared at him coldly. He raised his hand to forestall the objections. "You will receive every courtesy as the personal representative of President Assad," said Emir. "I'm sending you to the United States as liaison because of your command of the language. Soon you will be given a complete briefing. For the time being, the operation is too delicate to be entrusted to anyone who does not have a need to know. President Assad has agreed that you will remain under my orders for the duration of the project."

Mahmoud leaned forward to speak again, but he recognized the implied threat and was silent.

After a slight pause, Emir continued. "You have your tickets. You will take the afternoon plane to New York. There you will check with my consulate, who will know the whereabouts of a Mr. E. Bradford Appleby. You are to make Mr. Appleby's acquaintance at the earliest opportunity and stand by for further orders."

Emir stood up and nodded to end the interview.

The encounter took place in Washington.

Mahmoud's plane to Athens was delayed two hours, allowing him only fifteen minutes to make his connection to New York. After an exhaustive sprint through the corridors, he made it as the doors to the plane were closing. When he arrived in New York, there was no one to meet him, and he found that his baggage had not made the connection in Athens. He took a taxi to the Lebanese consulate and furiously confronted a surprised consul. He blasted him for not having been at the airport, reminded him of the importance of this secret mission, then inquired about Appleby. His irritation mounted when he found that Appleby had gone to Washington to attend a cocktail party at the Lebanese embassy.

It took until noon the next day to find that his luggage had ended up in Paris. He had time only to buy a clean shirt before taking the shuttle to the District of Columbia. When he arrived at the embassy at six o'clock, he was greeted by an affable ambassador, very pleased with himself for having put the cocktail party together at the last minute, ostensibly in honor of an Egyptian diplomat who was being reassigned. He knew that the diplomat had been a close friend of Appleby's and was able to lure him to Washington for the occasion. He had no idea who Mahmoud was or what he was about, other than that his mission was important and that he was anxious to meet Appleby. When he found that the meeting was supposed to have been arranged for New York, he was devastated at the mix-up, apologizing profusely.

Mahmoud angrily dressed down the ambassador, pointing out that he was not only the personal representative of the president of Lebanon, but also of the president of Syria, and was on an assignment of crucial importance to both their countries. Then, in rumpled suit, jet-lagged, and with a brain spinning trying to think in the English he hadn't spoken in five years, he made every attempt to keep his fatigue and his temper in control while the ambassador, determined not to antagonize this unusual person any further, made it a point to introduce him to as many guests as possible. Slowly, he made the rounds, his hand on Mahmoud's back.

"Here are two people you should meet. The beautiful woman is Anna Rostova, wife of the Soviet ambassador to the United Nations. The man is Bradford Appleby."

Mahmoud looked over Appleby, tall, cool, light-haired, smooth-featured, impeccably dressed, the model diplomat. He

was conscious of the contrast with his own unkempt appearance. A sense of frustrating inferiority welled up in him, but
with it a determination to best this man, and all his kind. As
they approached the couple, someone jostled Mahmoud from
behind, sending him stumbling into Appleby and spilling his
drink over both of them.

"I'm terribly sorry," said the startled Appleby. "Did
I . . ."

Mahmoud ignored the apology, turning to curse the offender,
while the woman deftly plucked a towel from a passing waiter
to wipe their lapels.

The red-faced ambassador stuttered over the introductions
while Mahmoud glowered at everyone. The sense of his un-
recognized importance brought the bile of frustration and fatigue into his throat. He could contain himself no longer.
"That's the trouble with Americans. Always trying to push
people around," he said.

Appleby's deprecating laugh increased the Syrian's anger.
"Oh, come on, old fellow," Appleby said. "We're both all dry,
thanks to Anna. You shouldn't make such sweeping generaliza-
tions. In fact, I think the man who accidentally pushed you is
a Spaniard."

"It doesn't matter. It's something that seems to happen when
people get around Americans. When people get pushed, their
natural reaction is to push back."

He launched into a diatribe about America and its foreign
policy, which Appleby listened to with a mixture of irritation
and amusement until Anna Rostova, attempting to change the
subject, called her husband over to be introduced.

Mahmoud was not to be mollified. "You Russians are just as
bad," he told the astonished Soviet. "You and the Americans
try to squeeze us from both sides as though we were lemons.
You —"

"Just a minute," replied Rostov. "If you think —"

Anna broke it up.

"Excuse us, Mr. Mahmoud," she said. "Peter and Brad are
old friends who have not seen each other recently and have

much to talk about." She took the two by the arms and led them away from the still sputtering Mahmoud.

Mahmoud slumped, cursing himself, realizing that his mission had gotten off to a disastrous start. Then he straightened, glared at the Lebanese ambassador with an implied threat of retribution if any of the incident was reported back to Damascus or Beirut, turned, and rushed out of the room.

Pyotr Ivanovitch Rostov woke up worried. This was unusual; Pyotr Ivanovitch was not a worrier. What worried him most was that he didn't know what he was worried about.

Instinctively, as it did to all Soviet diplomats stationed in capitalistic countries, the thought came that he might be in some sort of trouble at home. He was followed, of course, and his phones were tapped, but that was standard, good intelligence practice; he would have done the same if he were in charge. There was no telling when any normal human being would be unduly attracted by the temporary capitalistic temptations of the fleshpots and of the flesh. No, that couldn't be it. He dismissed the thought. As ambassador from the Union of Soviet Socialist Republics to the United Nations, trusted confidant and personal representative of the General Secretary, he had a solid home base. Maybe it had something to do with the American, Appleby, whom he was meeting for lunch. That couldn't be, either; he'd known Appleby since the 1948 Olympics, the day of his first big win. Certainly he had no domestic problems. He had felt his wife stirring as he was awakening and knew that the tea would be brewed and the simple breakfast ready when he walked out of the bedroom. Put it in the back of your mind, he thought, donning his robe. It will come.

All worries vanished when he walked out of the bedroom into the small kitchen.

"*Dobroe ootra*, Petya darling," Anna greeted him.

When they had arrived for his assignment, he'd had Anna set up an apartment separate from the sumptuous quarters normally occupied by the ambassador, off limits to both staff and servants. This was their little hideaway, where they could talk the talk of the long-married, of the boys in school in Moscow, of the chitchat of the day before, of the schedule for the day to come.

After half an hour of small talk, Rostov asked Anna about her schedule for the day. She outlined her routine of United Nations committee meetings, including a lunch for the Romanian ambassador's daughter. "And you?" she asked.

"I'm going down to the screen room for a senior staff meeting, then off to a lunch with Appleby," he responded.

"Appleby? You're seeing a lot of him lately. Couldn't it be misunderstood?"

"Not on our side. They think I'm converting him to the faith," he said. "There are a few noses out of joint in his shop, since he is without portfolio, but their UN staff is pretty well accustomed to being bypassed. As for the press . . ."

He stopped, deciding he'd better not carry that one any further.

Next he dressed and went to the screen room. All over the world, every embassy has at least one such room, electrically, mechanically, and acoustically isolated from the ultrasensitivity of modern detecting devices. This one was large enough to contain a conference table seating twelve, six filing cabinets, a secretary's desk, a bank of batteries for electrical isolation, and some tanks of chemicals. The room was elevated on shock absorbers high enough to allow crawl space below it, with the ceiling raised to protrude into the floor above. Encompassing the floor, ceiling, and walls was a fine metal screening, soldered at the joints. Separated by two-inch rubber insulators was another covering of heavy, coarse mesh, also soldered at the joints. The door was soundproofed, fitted carefully with sheet metal inside and out, the edges provided with spring-loaded feelers to make electrical contact with the rest of the room when closed.

Every morning at seven o'clock, two technicians, one with acoustic and electronic sound generators on the outside and one with ultrasensitive detectors on the inside, went over the entire room, checking its acoustic and electronic integrity and searching for bugs. The batteries and an alternator supplied heat, power, and light, so that the room was completely isolated, except for support through the shocks, from the rest of the world. Even the two steps leading to the elevated room were separated from it. The room had contained shredders, but all embassies had learned from the American experience at Tehran not to depend on them. Most embassies now shipped their dead-storage documents home to be retrieved by cable if needed for reference. The few classified current files in the screen room were equipped with simple incendiary devices in case of surprise attack. One small tank of chemicals contained enough plastic foam to fill the room, while another was connected to a ceiling spray that would coat all exposed surfaces with a sticky, unwashable goo if security was breached. In case of emergency, these destructive devices could be actuated from the guard's desk or from the ambassador's office.

Pyotr Ivanovitch's deputy and two briefing officers from Intelligence were waiting when he identified himself to the guard and entered the room. They snapped smartly to attention. He waved them down with a gesture. "What's new?" he asked crisply, settling himself.

"Not too much," replied the deputy. He reviewed the China situation — Deng Xiaoping's successor had fired two of the older generals and confirmed Deng's contention that Marxist planning is no longer practical in a modern technological world economy. Rostov snorted but made no reply. In Central America, Nicaragua was as confused as ever. The KGB reported an opportunity to trump up a charge of misappropriated funds on Duarte in Salvador. The finance ministers of the Latin-American countries were meeting in Peru, and Captain Kuragin from Finance was there to brief him.

"Go ahead, Captain," Rostov said.

"Thank you, Comrade Ambassador," said the captain stiffly. "We understand that the Peruvians are pushing for repudiation of the American debts. Of course, we don't expect them to go that far, but we are pretty well connected in the Peruvian delegation, and our people feel that we can get a consensus of the meeting to tie repayments to a percentage of exports."

"What percentage?"

"I hope not more than fifteen percent."

Pyotr Ivanovitch whistled. "That's pretty close to repudiation. It could topple a number of the big banks, if they can make it stick. Anything on the Middle East?"

"Major Denisov of the Middle Eastern desk is here for that," replied the deputy.

"Major?"

"Thank you, sir. There's only one thing worth mentioning. You recall that when five of our men were taken hostage in Beirut, there was a terrible fuss back home. The conservatives complained to the General Secretary, saying that he was too soft and it would not have happened in the old days. So he called in the Enforcement branch of KGB, who went to Assad of Syria. The Syrians got the men back, then went in and quietly wiped out the section of the Jihad who were responsible for the stupid act. But they've been having trouble finding someone to keep the lid on. Now that the Americans and the Israelis are out of there, we'd like it to quiet down. It's not easy to find a Lebanese president acceptable to the Syrians themselves, to us, to the Iranians, the Iraqis, and the PLO. They finally came up with this man, Salom al Emir. He's an unknown quantity. We're watching him, and we're worried that he's too close to the PLO. We don't give a damn about the PLO or the Israelis; we just want the place to quiet down. Now we find an unusual number of PLO troops snuggling up to the Israeli border. Emir assures us that there's no problem, that he has everything under control. There's nothing particular to be done about it; my boss thought you should be aware of it."

"Al Emir." Rostov nodded. "I swam against someone with that name in 'forty-eight. Beat him, too. He was swimming as a Greek, but he talked Arabic. Nationalities weren't too clear in those days. About the right age. I wonder if it's the same fellow."

Pyotr Ivanovitch's brows knitted, and he held a frown for a moment. PLO troops on the Israeli border. They couldn't do that without the acquiescence of the new president. Pretty cheeky for al Emir to start out this way. He has to be close to the PLO. Still, it's nervy. What was that about Lebanon at the cocktail party the other night? Have to ask Anna. He dismissed the meeting and went on with his paper work.

As they prepared to leave for their respective engagements, there was a contrast between them. Anna, tall, her dark-haired beauty reminiscent of Tolstoy or the Petrograd court, dressed simply and elegantly. A lifetime of association with the diplomatic corps in cities throughout the world, coupled with an evanescent but dignified charm, had given her an élan in dress and bearing that she had had to subdue somewhat until the arrival of Raisa Gorbachev on the international diplomatic scene. Now, she was careful to walk that fine line in overall deportment between the traditional background Russian wife and the object of the gushy adulation of the New York fashion press. She handled the delicate distinction well. "Now I only have to walk one step behind you," she told her husband.

Pyotr Ivanovitch's style could be described as "emergent Russian." The Soviet diplomats had never adopted the baggy uniforms of Mao Zedong or Castro, but their style until recently had been reminiscent of Henry Ford's dictum for the Model A Ford — "Any color as long as it's black." With their crew cuts and ashes dangling from cigarettes held between thumb and index finger, they would never have been mistaken for bloated capitalists. Now, with their new look and public relations consciousness, they grew their hair a little longer and were somewhere between the Japanese and Western Europeans in the cut of their clothes. Pyotr Ivanovitch had always had more style than the others. For one thing, he had never smoked and did not have the smoker's unkempt look, and his slope-shouldered athletic body allowed him to carry himself with flair. Only a little taller than his stately wife, his blond hair fading a little at the temples, he matched his springy stride to her graceful glide, and they drew admiring smiles even in the splashy crowds of midtown Manhattan.

They didn't take the limousine; he felt it was too conspicuous and ordered the Chevrolet. But they might just as well have taken a fire engine for the commotion they caused. As the car pulled out of the garage to go downtown, the American box of automobiles moved with it, one a block ahead, one a block behind, one on either side street, crackling up their radios to monitor their progress. Simultaneously, the Russian tail did likewise, each aware of the other's existence and monitoring their radios, but pretending they didn't see one another in the prevailing practice of intelligence professionals. To the pilot of the helicopter, lagging at a discreet distance, there was the sensation one gets on a moving train, that the nine vehicles of the impromptu convoy were fixed in space with the streets of New York scrolling northward beneath them.

The couple, aware but oblivious to it all, chatted languidly, reminiscing about the Olympics in England where they had first met Appleby. Rostov laughed. "You were a scrawny teenager then," he said. "I never thought I'd end up marrying you."

His wife looked into his eyes and smiled. "I did," she replied.

As the chauffeur pulled up in front of the Four Seasons, Anna said, "Remember me to Brad. That Lebanese or Syrian, or whatever he was, gave him a hard time at the cocktail party the other night."

"I've been meaning to ask you about that. Who was he, anyhow?" her husband asked. "You whisked me away so fast, I never really understood what was happening."

"I'm not sure myself. I think he was drunk, which is unusual for those people. But he was obviously new. Don't they have a new administration or something over there?"

"Yes, but go on."

"Well, Brad and I were talking and this character butted right in and started berating Brad about the United States and its policies in the Middle East. I guess Appleby's pretty used to this, but it was obviously beginning to bother him when you came along. Then he started off on the Soviet Union — I've never heard one of those people so arrogantly critical of us before. If he was not drunk he was certainly confused, so I pulled you away in a hurry. Ask Brad. He can fill you in. See you, Petya darling."

Now he knew what had been bothering him when he woke up that morning. The man was a Syrian, yet he was representing the president of Lebanon. That didn't make sense. Rostov mulled over the incident. He had the trained diplomat's ability to pick up the slightest innuendo, the merest scrap of conversation, and file it away in his subconscious for days until he connected it with another event. The appointment was obviously a recent one. He knew that Assad was furious with Emir over the Beirut Airport hijacking. Why would he loan him a senior executive, clearly not a diplomat, and why would Emir suddenly send him to the United States? He would have to look into this further, but his instinct told him not to mention it to Appleby.

As Kane walked into his hotel room in Washington, the phone was ringing. It was Goldstein.

"Do you know where June is? I want to talk some sense into her, but I can't find her. Did she say where she was going when she left you?"

Kane laughed. "She was so mad, I would have been the last one she would have told where she was going. Did you check her apartment?"

"I did, but she's not there. I talked to her housekeeper, who told me that June gave her a big check and left with a couple of suitcases full of clothes. I'm really getting concerned."

"Don't worry about it. She'll cool down and show up on Monday. Forget about it till then, and have a good weekend."

"If you say so, boss."

# 3

SCHULTZ WATCHED THE FIRING PARTY THROUGH strong binoculars, one cylindrical binocular barrel resting on his two crooked fingers for steadiness. He looked at a slight angle to focus away from the blind spots in his eyes. Steady as he was, the images blurred as the shimmering heat from the afternoon sun in Yucca Flat caused the subjects to dance and shimmy as though they had Saint Vitus' dance. They jiggled like marionettes on strings as they rolled their oversize dice in the vast Nevada desert.

"What are they doing now?" asked Foster Martin, lowering his own binoculars.

"They are setting up their code," Schultz announced flatly.

"What does that mean?" Martin persisted.

Schultz's six companions looked remarkably similar in the searing sunshine. They were wispy, their hair sandy and insipid, their faces and arms white with a pallor that would be blistery and sore by the morning. The men had droopy mustaches or scraggly beards or both; the females, with their severe, short-cropped hairstyles, were distinguishable from the men only by their lack of facial adornment.

Martin was their leader. He and his companion, Penelope, were a cut above the others in appearance. They were founders of the Makepeace group and organizers of this protest movement against nuclear weapons testing. Abu Nidal, through his friends in the Baderhof gang, had arranged for Schultz to be their guide.

It was an effort for Schultz to conceal his scorn; he had been over this so many times before. His chest heaved in a deep sigh as he explained that the device would remain unattended for several hours while the firing party returned to Control and Security swept the area. As he spoke, he could tell that the details were making several members of the group nervous. He went on to say that to prevent anyone from detonating it in the meantime, the firing party inserted a one-time code into the circuitry of the firing mechanism. One person from each laboratory rolls a number. He shook his fist as if he were rolling dice. All eyes were on him now. He told them how the other lab follows and then they record the four-digit code in the inner circuitry to be deciphered at the last stages of the firing sequence. He shook his fist again and rolled his deadly imaginary dice. "That way no one can know the code in advance," he said, looking around at the nervous group. "If it wasn't for that, we could blow it up when it wasn't ready and embarrass the hell out of them."

"Isn't there any way of stealing it?" one of the young women asked, edging closer to Schultz. She was restless, impatient with the waiting, uncomfortable in the hot sun, shuffling from one sandaled foot to the other.

"Look, sweetheart, the thing is fifteen hundred feet under the ground." He shook his head at her and again explained, more annoyance in his voice than before, that all the firing cables went underground from a container. He pointed. The container was locked and alarmed and monitored by remote television. There was no way of getting to it. He pointed again, this time to a wide arc of trailers ringing the zero point. "Those are instrumentation laboratories. When the device is detonated, there are detectors in the test package which monitor the reaction and send the data up fiber optic light pipes to the trailers, where it is recorded on oscilloscope cameras."

"What happens to the detectors?"

"They are only a few feet away from the device and are evaporated within millionths of a second, but that's all it takes to measure the history of the reaction. Most of the fiber optic cables are destroyed also, but the signals travel up at the speed of light and stay ahead of the shock wave until they are recorded."

"The trailers look like covered wagons circling the campfire as protection against the Indians," said Penelope.

"Yeah, we're the Indians." Martin laughed. "What do they do with the trailers afterward?"

"They are hauled off to the next experimental site, which will probably be a number of miles away. Then a new hole is drilled and the process is repeated," Schultz explained patiently. He felt like a tour guide talking to a group of sightseers.

In a way he was. This was not his kind of activity and these were not his kind of people. These were negative people, passive, unaggressive, unhappy spectators, sitting in the grandstands, observing the unfolding game of international affairs, protesting, objecting, catcalling, derisive of the efforts of the players on the field, full of advice as to how the game should be played, but lacking the knowledge, the stamina, the skills, the experience, or the will to suit up, leap the barriers, make the choices, choose the sides, and engage directly in the fray. They were outside the power structure and powerless to change its direction, hoping somehow to delay the game, but no more effective in the long run than the beer-drinking sports fan sitting in his living room on a Sunday afternoon, yelling instructions into the television for the quarterback to throw the ball.

To Schultz, the shimmering figures at the other end of his binoculars were his enemies. They were the developers, the owners of these powerful weapons he longed to possess; he knew that no amount of protest would deter them from their capitalistic objective of world domination. To him they were a powerful enemy, a ruthless enemy, but a respected enemy. He visualized himself as a scout, seeking to determine the weaknesses in his enemy's game, so that in the next encounter, when he would be on the playing field, he would be victorious. He needed to use these protestors, these detested spectators, to achieve his purpose. But, feeling his years, he was an aging terrorist with little to show for his lifetime. So he had asked Emir to arrange through Abu Nidal for him to help the Makepeace group stage a protest at this underground nuclear weapons test at the Nevada Test Site. This group would be helpful to him when he pulled off his big coup, which, this time, was going to be successful.

Schultz was a perennial loser, a modern Miniver Cheevy. His happy days had been in his midteens, when he was a leader of the Hitlerjugend. He had loved the uniforms, the marching, the discipline. He had prospered in the environment, learning to hate capitalists and Communists and Jews with equal fervor. He was big, slightly stocky but fast, and his athletic skills and industriousness had brought him to the top of the movement as a protégé of Goebbels. The crowning achievement of his lifetime had been an award for excellence pinned to his breast by Der Führer himself. He was like the high school football hero whose reminiscences of the good old days served to cushion a lifetime of failure.

When his father had smuggled him into Holland, he was capable enough to make the Dutch Olympic swimming team. He realized later that his impetuous action in the four-hundred-meter finals had been foolish, but his hatred of the Communists was intense, and he would probably do the same thing again. He had never even looked back to see who won. He knew that his coach would discharge him in disgrace, so he couldn't have gone back. He had headed for the docks, shaking his fingers in pain.

The broken bones were treated by an alcoholic quack in the slums of Soho and never did heal properly. With his Dutch passport and a string of lies, he had managed to sign on as an able seaman aboard a short-handed Dutch freighter leaving for the Orient the next morning. The newspaper reports of the Russian's victory had only deepened his frustration.

There followed years of wandering, of fighting whatever government system there was to fight. He served with terrorists in Spain, with the PLO in Palestine, with the Red Brigades in Italy. In the early fifties, when it was safe to do so, he returned to Germany and joined an anti-Communist group. His obsession was the return of fascism, his fantasy to steal an atomic bomb and hold the world at bay. Unfortunately, there were no nuclear weapons to steal in Europe in those days, so he went where the action was.

In the spring of 1958, Schultz and four other zealots signed up with Holmes and Narver, a California construction contractor building concrete bunkers for the United States nuclear weapons test series at Bikini atoll. Fritz Braun and Gregory Wagner were explosive experts from the Baderhofs. Harold Kramer was an electrician who had designed the electric timing circuits for an Austrian terrorist group, and Hans Miller was a soldier of fortune who had worked with the Islamic Jihad and the Italian Red Brigades.

Bikini atoll seemed like an ideal place to steal a nuclear weapon. The atoll was in the Marshall Islands, eighteen hundred miles southwest of Hawaii, tropical in character, but comfortably cooled most of the year by steady trade winds. The atoll was almost circular, about twenty miles in diameter. None of the islands was more than half a mile wide; they varied in length from sandpits to three miles. The shallow lagoon diluted the deep blue of the surrounding mile-deep ocean into tints ranging from fire opal to a creamy white. From the air the tiny islands looked like oval-shaped pearls strung on a pale blue cord against a violet velvet background. The Teutonic precision of the few remaining rectangular coconut pine groves was the only remnant of the German occupation prior to World War I. The Japanese had left few marks during their thirty-year occupation; the atoll had been skipped over by the Americans, who hopped from the bloody battles of Kwajelein one hundred eighty miles east to the naval base of Eniwetok, an equal distance to the west.

A decade of testing had leveled the palms and poisoned the fish by the time Schultz and his associates arrived to live in tents erected on the barren sand. But the prospects of stealing a weapon seemed ideal to them. A weapon test was a ponderous effort, involving a military task force of hundreds of ships, boats, and aircraft, with twenty thousand scientists, construction workers, soldiers, sailors, Marines, and Air Force flight crews. All of these had to be evacuated by ship prior to a test. After the evacuation, a small scientific party would arm the device and proceed by small boat to a concrete firing bunker twenty miles across the lagoon. This meant that the nuclear explosive was left unattended for six hours as the final preparations were completed. Schultz's idea was to evade the evacuation screen, steal a small landing craft, load the device aboard, and head for a neighboring unoccupied atoll.

By destroying their personnel records, they devised a scheme for evading the evacuation checklist while Hans Miller managed to repair and fit out an abandoned landing craft that Fritz Braun learned how to operate. But they reckoned without the United States Navy.

The Navy probably hadn't given a thought to terrorists, but they were quite conscious of the Russian submarines observing the tests from a safe distance, and the Navy was not about to have a submarine land a small boat to steal a device during those six hours of vulnerability. As the first test drew near, the conspirators discovered to their dismay that the atoll was ringed for a hundred miles with patrol ships and aircraft. Try as they might, they could not figure out any means to evade this blockade. They made one foray outside the atoll but were promptly picked up on radar. They convinced the Navy that they had merely been fishing and drifted into the open sea. After this close call they decided to give up and return to the mainland.

Their next focus was on the continental test site that had recently been established on an eighteen-hundred-square-mile gunnery range ninety miles outside of Las Vegas, Nevada. Hans Miller became restless and wanted to return to Europe, but Schultz talked him out of it. Instead, by day they lounged

around the small gambling house where they had taken temporary jobs as shills and by night they continued to plan.

Schultz explained the difference between the two sites. "In
the Pacific, we had the United States Navy worrying about
Russian submarines. There was no place to hide. Here, the test
site is eighteen hundred square miles — bigger than Bavaria.
It's full of caves and holes where we can conceal a device. We
might be able to get it off site the first day, camouflage it, and
store it in a warehouse. When we strip off all the nonessentials,
the basic weapon is small enough to be stored in a trunk. It will
be easy to get out of the country. It will be worth millions and
millions of deutsche marks to the Libyans or the Syrians."

The reluctant Miller was persuaded, while Kramer was en-
thusiastic, feeling that they had learned enough from their previous failure to be successful this time. Braun and Wagner were
content to take orders from Schultz. Kramer had joined the
electrical workers' union while he was in the Pacific and had
no trouble getting a job with one of the subcontractors to the
government. Miller was hired as a crane operator by REECo,
the construction and site maintenance contractor for the
Atomic Energy Commission, while the others signed on as
laborers. They bought a four-wheel-drive pickup and spent
weekends roaming around the area until they knew it thoroughly. They found a small cave in the side of a mesa overlooking Yucca Flat, a cave which could contain the pickup and
be camouflaged to blend into the mountainside to escape detection.

The five men rehearsed for weeks. In that year, 1959, the
Eisenhower administration was still going full blast with atmospheric tests, ignoring world opinion and putting off underground testing until Kennedy insisted on it the succeeding year.
Most of the devices were fired from two-hundred-foot towers
in Yucca Flat.

To avoid suspicion, they did not mingle with one another,
fearing that their German accents would make them more conspicuous. Wagner and Kramer, beer drinkers, spent a good deal

of time in the bars listening to the wide variety of rumors and gossip that pervade every construction camp. There was little talk of politics or radiation; most of the conversation revolved around test schedules and the prospects for overtime. Braun, a ladies' man, flirted with the female clerks and secretaries who were outnumbered ten to one by the men, but who were attracted by his blond hair, Teutonic physique, and soft accent. When the odds against picking up a girl became too great and he had the money, he would drive off in the pickup with a group of buddies to visit the bordello in the nearby town of Beatty or the "Chicken Ranch" in Indian Springs, both in counties with legalized prostitution. The prostitutes were an excellent source of rumor.

Miller was the athlete. He participated in the softball games and the bowling leagues. Although schedules and yields and types of experiments were classified, people treated them casually, using a jargon and a series of code words quite transparent to the astute observer. Schultz was the quiet one, listening, listening, content to spend hours sitting around the reading room or dawdling in the cafeteria, hoping to pick up that little piece of intelligence which would improve his prospects of success.

On the evening before the test they had targeted, Schultz watched the red, searing sun sink over the mountain to the west as the work crews finished the cleanup of D minus one. There were reels of cable, generators, portable toilets, and the usual debris of a construction site to be hauled away. Darkness fell rapidly on the dry lakebed. The tower was awash in light from spotlights ringing the area, but the vans and trucks and flatbeds snaked their way westward through the vast desert to the next oasis of light, the control point, twenty miles away. There they stopped for the roll call and security check necessary to assure that no one was left behind. The caravan passed "Newsmen's Nob," the press area on a hillock below the Control building, where already half a dozen of the fifty invited observers drank and smoked around a campfire lit to ward off the desert chill rapidly descending on the area. The caravan wound on past

Control, where the test directors, the senior scientists from the laboratories, and the heads of the contractor companies finished their last-minute preparations. The bigwigs, the inevitable assorted VIP collection of politicians and admirals and generals, on official duty as observers, whiled away the evening with bridge and poker games. Then the lights of the caravan dipped from sight as it drove another fifteen miles to the base camp for the monotonous routine of beer and supper, movies and bed.

By eight o'clock the lakebed was empty, except for a small detachment of security guards who were nervously smoking and pacing the small area in the glare of the spotlights, looking up every few minutes to the sheet metal cab containing the multikiloton monster, wondering if it was leaking radiation, fearful that it might somehow self-detonate, counting the seconds until they would be relieved by the arming party.

Schultz and his men were silent and nervous as they listened to the babble on the radio, primarily of security guards making sweeps and remote experimental stations checking in, interspersed with time checks and weather reports from Control.

Braun broke the silence. "What time do we start?" He asked the question primarily to hear himself talk.

Schultz was patient. "Let's go over it all one more time. The last security sweep will be at midnight. The arming party will arrive at one and should be gone by two. You will start walking at two-thirty. It should only take you about an hour and a half to walk the eight kilometers at a leisurely pace, even carrying the tools. That should put you there about four. You will have the better part of an hour to get into the cab and disconnect the device. Kramer and Miller will remain on the ground. You, Braun, and you, Wagner, will enter the cab. If it is locked, you can saw the lock off. The cab is only made of sheet metal, so if worst comes to worst, you have time to saw a hole in it.

"I'll start out in the vehicle at zero time and be there in fifteen minutes. When the device does not detonate, it will take them at least an hour to check the circuitry, then half an hour for the arming party to get back to disarm. No security forces would be allowed into the area until the disarming is complete, so we don't have to worry about them. I am quite certain that the hoist is intact and that you merely have to lift the floor panels in the cab to lower it after you disconnect the cables. An hour and a half should be plenty of time to lower the device into the truck. We can hide out here for a week until the furor dies down and then leave quietly."

"What if the disarming party comes sooner and surprises us?" Miller asked.

"We'll shoot them. There won't be more than three in the party, and they're not likely to be armed. We'll take the bodies with us. That will give us an extra hour to get away in the confusion."

At 11:30, they could see the lights of the security patrol leaving the remote stations, stopping periodically at experimental stations to see that no one was left. Flashlights probed and winked and disappeared as the invisible bodies behind them tried locks and looked over buildings to see that the area was clear. As they came closer Schultz could hear the sound — first faint, then raucous — of loudspeakers warning all personnel to leave the area. At midnight they pulled up to the barbed wire fence surrounding the bomb tower to have a cigarette and exchange greetings with their buddies guarding the zero area, then on to the control point, speakers blaring and lights probing as they completed the final sweep of the day.

Silence descended on the desert.

At 12:45, three double pinpricks of light gradually resolved into three vehicles approaching the zero point. The vehicles pulled up to the gate in the barbed wire fence. All the members of the arming party were well known to the security guards, but every badge was examined meticulously and every face was probed by flashlights. The arming party strolled around the area, chatting with the guards and trying to appear casual but careful. Four in number, they were dressed identically in well-worn khakis, heavy workmen's steel-toed boots, and plastic hard hats. They were veteran scientists all, well aware that the ferociously powerful device sitting peacefully two hundred feet above their heads was quite harmless now, but that in a few minutes it would be connected to twenty-five miles of buried cable leading to the Control building. Realistically, they knew that the circuitry was as safely designed as human skill could conceive, but in their hearts there was a fear that some stray streak of lightning, the teeth of one of the hundreds of burrowing animals along that twenty-five-mile path, or some overlooked quirk in the design would impress a fleeting voltage on the four key wires that would instantaneously send them all to kingdom come.

Two of the scientists climbed into the elevator. Loaded with tools and meters, they clanked their way to the top of the tower and opened the sheet metal door. Schultz could not see what they were doing, but they were in constant telephone communication with the test director at the foot of the tower. After about fifteen minutes the two emerged, secured the door in some fashion, and descended unhurriedly to the base. There was a confusion of people in the spotlight's glare as last-minute preparations were made. Then the security guards left and roared their way to the safety of distance. The arming party watched their departure, then leisurely entered their vehicles and also drove away into the darkness. It was exactly two o'clock when the arming party left the site.

Fifty minutes later, Schultz's men, loaded with gear, started out at a brisk pace. "Slowly, slowly," Schultz yelled after them. "You have plenty of time. Don't wear yourselves out."

"Why don't you give us a ride down, Schultz." Wagner complained, hanging back a bit. "There's no one out here."

"No," Schultz replied. "Already the weather aircraft will be coming into position at ten thousand meters, and within an hour the first cloud-sampling planes will be passing over the area to calibrate the atmospherics. They all have radars which could pick up the metal in a vehicle. When I start down at zero time, they will be too confused by the lack of an explosion to pay any attention. When we leave the tower, we will have plenty of time to drive from the lakebed in an easterly direction and double back through the hills where radar will not pick us up."

Wagner grumbled a bit, then hoisted the backpack containing his tools across his broad shoulders and hurried to join the others.

The hour and a half of inactivity was an eternity for Schultz. Many things could still go wrong. The four men could not lose their way, for the floodlights of the tower made it stand out for tens of kilometers on the ground and for tens of thousands of meters into the sky. But they could stumble and take nasty falls on the hard colichi of the desert hills. The weather could take a turn for the worse and the shot would be postponed, bringing the disarming party back. For a moment he panicked, realizing that they had not rehearsed for this possibility. Then he relaxed. Weather postponements had never occurred after the device was armed. Weather did not change that rapidly; the authorities were very careful to postpone before arming if there was any question. Also, they would plan carefully and unhurriedly before coming back. He also knew that certain critical experiments were interlocked, to prevent the device from detonating if the experimental instrumentation was not ready. But he knew that all crucial experiments had considerable backup and would not lock out the firing signal unless something catastrophic happened in the last few seconds. Still, an aircraft could crash or some drunk could wake up and climb out from a hiding place in the cleared area and start pulling wires or yelling on the radio in his panic. The radio — he had been listening to it for so many hours that it had retreated into his subconscious like a youngster doing his homework in the blare of rock-and-roll.

"Able Charlie to Dumpster."

"Come in, Able Charlie."

"Able Charlie to Dumpster. Moving in to first leg of holding pattern. Altitude, ten thousand five hundred meters. Bearing, zero-nine-zero. Not a cloud in the sky."

A ceaseless chatter emanated from the aircraft. To Schultz, immersed in his own thoughts, the conversations sounded casual, but tension was everywhere. The pilots had flown these missions before, but they could never become accustomed to them. The intense white glare, reflecting from the windows even as they turned away, penetrating the dark goggles they would don at minus fifteen seconds and whip away as quickly as possible, would pulse at their retinas as they watched the blue, green, yellow, red, gray, mushrooming cloud climb quickly past five thousand meters, ten thousand meters, then twenty and thirty, and spread in an ever-widening circle toward them. The shock wave would be like no other, the first sharp crack pushing them away, then the second phase more slowly sucking them back into the vacuum of displaced air. They were nervous. They had a right to be.

Soon the measured voice of the countdown announcer cut in from the control point, overriding conversations on all frequencies.

"In one minute, the time will be — minus two hours. Thirty seconds . . . twenty seconds . . . ten . . . nine . . . eight . . . seven . . . six . . . five . . . four . . . three . . . two . . . one . . . now. Minus two hours. The next time check will be at minus one hour and thirty minutes."

The chatter on the radio subsided. Scientists manning remote stations completed their readiness checks and settled in with blankets to ward off the decreasing temperature. Security guards had finished their sweeps and gone off for coffee. The aircraft had settled into the elliptical holding patterns designed to place each at its assigned bearing and attitude in the final split second before the blast. By the time the announcer gave the hour-and-thirty-minute signal, all conversations had ceased.

Schultz could see the first opal of dawn flicker between the mountain peaks. There was an occasional glint of light from the circling aircraft, reflecting the morning sun, but all was still black on the desert floor. Schultz decided that it was time to test the walkie-talkies.

The World War II–vintage walkie-talkies had a maximum range of twelve kilometers on the ground, but a little farther from his altitude.

"Can you hear me, Fritz?" Schultz asked without preamble.

*"Ja, Ludwig, sie sind klar. Nur zwei kilometers jetzt."*

"No, no, speak English," Schultz said. They were out of hearing, but some freak echo from a mesa might be overheard, and the foreign language could excite suspicion.

A different voice came up from the distance. "Hans here. We are moving well. Another ten minutes."

"Another ten minutes." This was the longest time of all. Schultz was on the verge of success after all these years. A success that would be his, and his alone, for the others were urged on only by the millions that Nasser or the shah or the PLO would pay for the weapon. But for him it was not just the money, not even the prestige among his peers. It was revenge, revenge against the superpowers for crushing his nation, the rape, the pillage, the poverty, the ignominy, the humiliation of his fatherland cleaved into two parts, the one a craven, Communist cur, the other a boot-licking capitalist lackey, writhing separately in their death throes like the two parts of a severed animal. Between the still crew-cut scalp and the powerful neck, with the solitude, the silence, the inactivity, the lack of visual focus, his brain raced from fantasy to fantasy, from elation to depression, from fear to overconfidence, chewing up the time and lack of signal input with idling fantasies of its own.

Schultz stepped outside the cave to urinate, but nothing would come out. As he ducked back in, the exultant voice of his coconspirator split the silence.

"Ludwig, Hans here."

Almost simultaneously, the dull voice from Control marked the one-hour time check. Plenty of time. No one within twenty-five miles.

"How does it look?"

He could hear the panting, elated voices of the four as they put down their tools and rested after the long walk.

"Fine. They even cleaned up the area. Maybe they wanted it to look nice when we got here. Not even a cigarette butt."

The joking went on for a full three minutes, as they moved to their respective tasks.

"Ludwig, Hans. Do you realize we are seventy meters away

from ten million marks. The Fräuleins —" Schultz could hear excited shouts in German, contrary to his orders. He cursed. Hans came up on the radio again, this time his voice shrill.

"*Mein Gott,* Ludwig, they've removed the elevator. We're getting the hell out of here."

A chill went down Schultz's spine, but he recovered quickly. "Hans, no. Be calm. I have thought about the elevator not working." He lied. "You have over fifty minutes. Braun and Wagner can climb the ladder in twenty minutes, easily. Then they have thirty minutes to enter the cab and disconnect the firing cables. Even if the cab is locked, they can saw through the lock or the cab itself. It's only sheet metal. Then we have at least an hour and a half before anyone comes back in. Longer, if we want to wait and kill the disarming crew."

Wagner came on, voice quavering with fear. "We're going to run for it, Ludwig."

Schultz's brain was focused now, clear and ready. Wagner was the weak one. He'd influence the others. They'd never come back a second time.

"It's too late, Wagner," he replied coolly. "You're out on the lakebed. No matter how fast you run, you can't get far enough away. There's no protection. If the heat and the shock wave don't get you, you will die a slow death from the radiation. Proceed, quickly."

"Can't you call for a postponement?"

"Our radios don't have enough range. Tell them to climb. Quickly. Quickly."

There was a pause.

"You bastard."

Then silence.

He knew he was the only one close enough to see, even with high-powered binoculars. He could see them bustling about in their indecision, two apparently ready to run, the other two trying to talk sense into them. He called on the radio, but they would not answer. For now, he was the enemy. He could see one, probably Wagner, taking control and gesticulating forcefully, pointing up at the cab.

The bustle subsided. Some decision had been made, but minutes had been lost. Two men — he couldn't tell who, probably Braun and Wagner — were strapping packs on their backs. The tempo speeded up, now that the decision had been made. The two rushed to the base of the tower, the taller one, who must be Braun, starting the climb, with Wagner three rungs behind.

"In one minute, the time will be . . . minus thirty-five minutes."

For the first fifty feet, they climbed like men possessed. The two on the ground jumped up and down in excitement, reaching their hands over their heads and pulling down in a climbing motion as though to help. The men then paused, realizing that they would run out of energy if they didn't slow down. The climb became slower and more methodical. By the hundred-foot mark, the energy drain of the eight-kilometer hike was taking its toll. They were pausing more often, Wagner practically at Braun's feet, probably wishing he had led the way. Schultz tried to raise them on the radio. There was no reply.

"In one minute, the time will be . . . minus twenty-five minutes."

Schultz wondered if they were aware of the time. He decided that they must have the speaker of the radio at the base of the tower turned up full blast. They still had ample time.

Two thirds of the way up, Braun's foot slipped. Wagner was so close behind that Braun's feet hit the top of his hard hat, almost dislodging him. The impact swung Braun wildly to the side so that one hand lost its grip. Wagner's mouth hit a rung of the ladder, stunning him. Braun pulled himself up, almost chinning himself with one arm so that the other could grab hold. They paused, obviously exhausted. They seemed to hang in both space and time, the seconds circling away around them. Wagner recovered first and made a move as though to climb around Braun, but the ladder was too narrow and he waited until Braun could open up three rungs on him again. Agonizingly, they hauled themselves up the remaining rungs. Almost at the top, Braun was so exhausted that he had to remove his backpack and sling it onto the walkway around the cab before he could take the last few steps.

"In one minute, the time will be . . . minus fifteen minutes."

Fifteen minutes, Schultz thought. Still enough time. He rushed out to start the pickup. He was gone two minutes. As he dashed back to the tripod, he heard the radio silence break.

"The goddamned thing's locked. Give me the hacksaw."

The two bodies blended into one in Schultz's binoculars as Wagner held the padlock steady. Braun sawed steadily against the tempered steel, wearing the blade down as it cut through the lock. The microphone key on the discarded radio had jammed open on the deck of the catwalk. Schultz could hear their labored breathing.

"You have most of it, but the blade is worn out," said one, calmly. "It will be faster if you change blades." They broke apart.

"Ten . . . nine . . . eight . . . seven . . . six . . . five . . . four . . . three . . . two . . . one . . . now. Minus six minutes."

Schultz longed to choke the man who was uttering those words — anything to hold back the sequence — but the voice droned on.

There was a clang over the speaker as something fell and reverberated against the catwalk. Schultz saw one of the men lunge, but heard a succession of ever-fainter clangs as the object bounced through the girders of the tower to land at the feet of Kramer at the base.

"*Mein Gott,*" shouted Wagner. "He's dropped the saw."

There was a shocked silence. Then the voice of Braun. "The hammer, the hammer. The lock is almost sawed through."

A series of sharp cracks announced that they were trying to break the partially severed shank of the lock.

"Five . . . four . . . three . . . two . . . one . . . now. Minus four minutes."

"It won't break," came the plaintive cry.

A voice cut in from below. "Take the hatchet. Cut a hole in the wall. It's sheet metal, only a quarter-inch thick. Hurry, hurry."

Dawn would break into the valley in another ten minutes. Schultz could see the first glow of the sun from his elevated position. The cab was silhouetted against the predawn. Schultz could see more plainly now, the hatchet glittering in the heavy arm of Wagner as it bounced and ricocheted off the vibrating surface of the corrugated sheet metal.

"You have a break. Make it bigger so I can crawl through." The voice was Braun's.

"Four . . . three . . . two . . . one . . . now. Minus three minutes."

"You cut and I'll hammer. A little bit more and I can squeeze through." Two metal objects could be seen flashing.

"Three . . . two . . . one . . . now. Minus two minutes."

Braun's head and shoulders disappeared into the hole. "He can make it," Schultz spoke aloud. But another pause. Braun's belt had apparently caught on the jagged sheet metal.

"Two . . . one . . . now. Minus one minute."

Wagner's hatchet flashed, cutting through the belt, the pants, the underwear, and deep into the flesh.

"Minus thirty seconds."

*

Braun's body jerked, then wriggled rapidly.

"Minus fifteen seconds."

Braun's body and legs disappeared from sight, one shoe falling to the catwalk as the feet went through.

"Minus ten seconds . . . nine . . . eight . . . seven . . . six . . . five . . ."

If Schultz had not tripped over the tripod and dropped the binoculars at that moment, the intense light focused through the powerful lenses would have burned a hole through the backs of his eyes and seared into his brain.

As it was, even though his head was turned and his eyes slightly averted, the reflection from the soft gray rock of the cave burned millimeter-size spots on each of his retinas, causing him to reel backward in pain and the shock of blindness. The intense heat blistered the skin on his unprotected face and arms, and he had no protection from the shock wave when it hit. It threw him against the back of the cave, knocking his head against the rock so that he was not conscious of the suction of the second phase as it pulled him from the wall with a sickening sucking sound and deposited him in a heap on the cavern floor.

Never in the history of mankind did human beings die as quickly as Braun and Wagner and Miller and Kramer. At Hiroshima and Nagasaki, the weapons had been detonated thousands of feet in the air and the primary fireballs did not touch the ground, so that even the victims directly under the explosions lived for seconds before succumbing to the combined effects of heat, blast, and radiation. For Braun and Wagner, only millionths of a second passed before their bodies were stripped down to their basic molecules and then to atoms, and then those atoms, billions of billions of billions of them, disassociated into radioactive nuclei and protons and neutrons and free electrons. For the other two, it was milliseconds.

The energy in that softball-size core was so great that what millionths of a second before had been living, breathing human beings became primordial matter, mixing with the neutrons and protons and electrons of the casing, the cab, the tower, and the surrounding soil to become the energy carriers for the heat and blast and the radioactive cloud that rose roiling into the stratosphere. The energy for the images on the film of the cameras of the photographer on Mount Charleston came from that matter. The radioactive particles collected by the sampling aircraft at thirty thousand feet were that matter. Those radioactive nuclei fell upon the midwestern grain ingested by cattle whose radioactive milk was drunk by schoolchildren and dusted the meters of the laboratories that tracked the cloud around the world. So great was the energy from even that relatively small, ten-kiloton explosion, that many days later, those negligible but measurable particles which softly sifted down from the skies onto their native Germany, to be breathed in the air, drunk with the water, and ingested from the soil, contained neutrons and protons and electrons and atoms that had, less than a week earlier, been parts of the bodies of Braun and Wagner and Miller and Kramer.

Such thoughts, although they were to come many years later, were far from the mind of Ludwig Schultz when he regained consciousness six hours after the explosion. At first he thought it was midday, but then he realized, to his horror, that the sensations of light fed to his brain by the damaged nerve cells of his retinas were indications of blindness, temporary or permanent he knew not. He did not even know what blindness was like, whether it should be light or dark, but he knew that with his eyelids open he could resolve nothing.

There was total silence except for an automobile engine running. He remembered that he had started the pickup and left it idling just before zero time. With the extra tanks it must be still running. He crawled in the direction of the sound and stood to reach the ignition key and turn it off. The springs were sticking through the charred upholstery of the seat; he could feel the blistered paint on the hood. He circled and found that although the blast had thrown the vehicle against the rock wall, it had survived with only a dented bumper and one flat tire.

Schultz sighed, relieved. He had a spare tire, plenty of gasoline, and food enough to last indefinitely for one person. No one would know of the failed coup. What was there to see? he asked himself. Even if he were discovered, which was highly unlikely, he had committed no offense and would merely be run off the test site as a trespasser.

After three days, his vision had recovered enough so he could drive. But since he was in no hurry and had no place to go, he stayed ten days, loaded the pickup, and drove off the site into obscurity. No one missed the five Germans. They were transients; after a decent interval, their accumulated pay was turned over to the state as unclaimed funds.

Schultz was a loser, but he was a survivor.

Now, more than thirty years later, Schultz was shepherding a group of protestors, hardly wet behind the ears, around the same Nevada Test Site. As he looked at the dry lakebed of Yucca Flat, he flicked his binoculars toward that distant mesa where he had hidden for those ten days. He felt the hair bristle at the nape of his neck and the sweat break out on his forehead. He had sworn never to come back, hoping someday to drive the horror to the back of his brain, but when the opportunity came to join the Makepeace group, Schultz, like a moth returning to a flame, could not refuse. Besides, he needed them for his big coup.

This time the testing was different. There were no towers, no cloud-sampling aircraft, no remote photographic stations. There would be no visible fireball, no blast of heat, no airborne shock wave, no radioactive cloud to be tracked around the earth. The world had become complacent about nuclear weapons, about their energy, about their destructiveness. No one had seen a nuclear explosion in more than thirty years. Most of those who had witnessed the massive power of these tiny devices had died or retired. The new generation worried about Three Mile Island or Chernobyl, mere sputtering fuses compared to what Schultz had witnessed.

The preparations went on in spite of Makepeace, with only a half dozen security guards carefully eyeing the small group. As the arming party prepared to withdraw, a larger contingent of guards rounded up the protestors and forced them to pull back to a safe distance.

"We could have hidden, you know," said Schultz, "and forced them to postpone the test."

"But suppose they didn't know we were here and set it off."

"Those are the chances you take in support of the cause." Schultz laughed, breaking his sober demeanor for the first time.

"Not me," said one of the males nervously. "We're nonviolent. We've done our job. Let's get out of here."

The government people allowed them to witness the test from a safe distance near the control point. Through binoculars, with no concerns this time, Schultz watched a slight puff of dust as the shock wave from the warhead hit the surface of the lakebed. An ever-widening circle of dust puffs looked like ripples from a still pond in which a stone had been thrown. A few startled rabbits darted aimlessly about, but other than that, the surface of Yucca Flat was undisturbed. A few minutes later, the cavity caused by the explosion collapsed, leaving a shallow circular depression like a fingerprint in an unbaked pie crust. It would sit there for posterity to count the many fingerprints in that pock-marked landscape, each attesting to a different test, one an MX primary, another a "Star Wars" laser, another a 155-millimeter tactical warhead, this one a Cruise missile.

The Makepeace group were delighted. "We've made our point," said Penelope. "Off to the next event."

"I've enjoyed working with you, Schultz," Martin said, shaking Schultz's hand. "See you in Europe."

"You sure will," Schultz replied.

# 4

AFTER DROPPING OFF ANNA AT THE FOUR SEA-
sons, the chauffeur turned his head inquiringly toward Pyotr
Ivanovitch.

"The Helmsley Palace," he was told.

As the Chevrolet moved in the midtown traffic, the impromptu convoy scurried to cope with one-way streets while
maintaining its distance. As they drew up to the hotel, Pyotr
Ivanovitch saw the familiar tall figure of Appleby standing
under the marquee. Recognizing the automobile, Appleby
waved.

"Where to, Brad?" asked Rostov.

"Let's try Central Park South today," Appleby said, ready
for the question. As the vehicle moved north, approaching the
park, the two exchanged pleasantries. The chauffeur turned his
head again as they pulled up to a red light.

"The Park Lane," said Rostov.

They alighted and walked briskly through the lobby. "Where
are we going?" asked Rostov.

"The main dining room," Appleby answered.

The maître d'hotel recognized Appleby immediately. That
recognition and a large bill entitled them to the small quiet table
in the corner always kept in reserve for unexpected special
guests. They grinned at each other as they sat down.

They had developed a special technique for their luncheon meetings. They didn't want to meet in secret. By the perverse code of the media and whatever intelligence services were tailing them, secret meetings would be too conspicuous. So Rostov picked up Appleby from whatever hotel he might be staying at, Appleby picked a street that had a large variety of restaurants and clubs, Rostov picked the location, then Appleby the room. The technique was not foolproof, but it ensured against bugging and the natural tendency of either to pick a favorite restaurant in advance. Each took note of the occupants of adjacent tables as he sat down and would be quick to spot changes during the meal.

The meetings were an outgrowth of an idea that had occurred to both the General Secretary and the President after the third summit in 1989. Both men prided themselves on being excellent communicators, as indeed they were, but they were frustrated by the language barrier and the presence of interpreters. They felt that if each could designate a trusted associate, skilled in both languages, to talk without inhibitions or implied commitment, they might better get their respective points across. They understood that the meetings could not be held in the Soviet Union and that neutral cities presented security problems on a long-term basis, so the talks would be held in the United States. Since Washington was too full of press and diplomats, New York was the choice. The President was happy with a personal representative, but, in the Soviet system, a title was imperative.

Pyotr Ivanovitch Rostov was ideal for the General Secretary. He had worked his way up in the hierarchy as a stern opponent of corruption, and, with Eduard Shevardnadze, had made the Georgian Republic into a productive economic unit. He had come to Andropov's attention in his attempts to improve the Soviet economy, and, after a year of marking time under Chernenko, he had moved into prominence with the new General Secretary and his foreign minister. His appointment as ambassador to the United Nations raised no eyebrows.

Bill Kane described his friend Appleby as a "healthy Harry Hopkins." The resemblance between Edward Bradford Ap-

pleby and Franklin Roosevelt's trusted confidant was un-
canny; both had the same lanky looseness, the same diffident,
disarming smile, the same lack of cant or conceit. With Roosevelt's lack of mobility, Hopkins had been the President's
eyes, ears, and legs in foreign capitals during World War II.
Appleby performed a similar function. Born into a Boston
Brahmin, public service family, Appleby was bred for diplomacy. After college, he had specialized in Russian at George-
town. He then worked his way up in the State Department,
spending a number of bleak years in the embassy at Moscow during the cold war. In his firsthand studies of Soviet agriculture, he met and was impressed by the opinions of Shevardnadze and Rostov.

The lunches had been pleasant, the two feeling each other
out, the dialogue primarily exchanges of viewpoints on history,
politics, and philosophy. They had ranged from the Romanovs
and Rasputin to King George and George Washington, from
geography and climate to agriculture and economics.

"Well, Pete, where do we start today?" Appleby asked with
a smile.

Rostov was somber. He hesitated, started to speak a couple
of times, unfolded his napkin on his lap, then went right to the
point. "Brad, we've been sparring around for three weeks now,
and I've enjoyed it, but I think it's time we got down to some
substantive issues."

Appleby's smile faded a bit and he instinctively looked from
side to side before moving his face closer to Rostov's. "Like?"

"Like when the hell are you going to get those Cruises and
Pershings out of Europe?"

Appleby leaned back. The smile, a little wary now, returned.
"That's substantive, for sure," he said. "Do you want the party
line, or what?"

Rostov shook his head. "No, I don't want the party line. Let
me tell you what's bothering me. We made a good start with
the intermediate-range missiles, but now we're stalled again.
We each have twenty-five thousand nuclear warheads deployed. One hundred are enough to destroy civilization, so

taking out a few thousand more on either side is not going to make a damned bit of difference. Right?"

Appleby nodded.

Rostov emphasized again that, throughout history, the fear of warfare on their homeland had been paramount in Russian minds. War had always caught them unprepared, and they did not intend to have it happen again. The nuclear weapons almost on their border were the biggest stumbling block to further disarmament progress. He felt that their presence meant that an accidental war could break out at any time.

"Look at World War One," Rostov said. "I've never understood how World War One started. I've read about Sarajevo and the assassination of the archduke, but that has never seemed to me to be a reason to plunge a planet into near suicide. You are a historian, Brad. What's your explanation?"

"Funny you should ask, as the saying goes," replied Appleby. "I've never understood either. One day there was peace, and the next day a continent had erupted. It was not caused by one person or one country, like Hitler's Germany. It broke out simultaneously with Britain, France, Germany, Russia, Austria, Serbia, all ready for war, for no apparent reason. Do you suppose it could happen again, that way?"

Rostov frowned. "We worry about that more than you do. You have a Pearl Harbor complex — you believe war will start by a premeditated strike of massive proportions by our country. We don't think that way. We know you are not going to strike first — that is, the realists in our country know it. We have more of a Sarajevo complex, that the war will start with some irresponsible action by a small country or an individual and envelop us all. That's why we try to keep our hands in governments wherever we can, all over the world.

"That's the jazziest explanation I've heard yet," said Appleby.

They paused while the waiter removed the dishes, then Rostov resumed. "Look, Brad, the purpose of these meetings is to sit down and talk to each other head to head to see how the other one thinks. Maybe it's a rationalization, I don't know, but this is how we think."

"Go ahead."

Rostov went on. He pointed out that these missiles were on the soil of sovereign NATO nations and could not be controlled properly by the United States, that a change in government or poor surveillance by one of the weaker nations could lead to the kind of deliberate or accidental act that ended up as another Sarajevo.

Appleby bristled. "What about your own tactical missiles?" he asked. "One of those could be set off. What's the difference?"

Rostov raised his hand to calm the objector. "The difference is that we don't let our warheads out of our own hands. The missiles are under the control of Warsaw Pact nations, but the warheads with the nuclear explosives are kept in the Soviet Union."

"But we keep the firing circuits locked up with some kind of electronic devices. The only people who have the codes are American citizens." Appleby was angry now.

Rostov was scornful. It didn't seem at all credible to him that the Germans or the Turks or a terrorist group would not be able to steal the codes or that the Americans would not have to divulge them in the event of tension in Europe. He pointed out that field commanders would require advance information just at the time when the tension was at a maximum.

Appleby backed off. He controlled himself, breaking out the diplomatic smile again. Rostov had a point, he thought. He promised to look into the security measures in Europe, but explained that it would probably take a month to get an unclassified explanation. Then he changed the subject.

"How do you like the UN job, now that you've been in it for a while?" he asked.

"Oh, I like it pretty well," Rostov replied. "We don't get many choices in our country — you just have to learn to like the things that are assigned to you. I don't like the formality, the cocktail parties, the chitchat. On the other hand, Anna likes it, even though she misses the boys. She grew up in this world, you know."

"She is a charming woman. I thought she handled that boorish clod at the Lebanese embassy very well the other night," said Appleby.

Rostov was surprised that Appleby recalled the incident. "I never did get that man straightened out. Anna whisked me away too fast. Who was he, anyhow?"

Appleby laughed. "That's Anna's skill. She knew you would blow your stack at some Middle Eastern wimp taking on the Soviet ambassador to the United Nations. Us Americans, we're used to it. We get it all the time."

"What do you mean?"

"I had never seen him before. I don't even remember his name," Appleby explained. "He is a plenipotentiary of some kind from the new president of Lebanon. Anna and I were talking about nothing in particular, when this pompous ass strutted up and started berating me about the U.S. presence in the Middle East. This is pretty routine stuff for me. I didn't pay much attention to him. Anna was slightly amused until you came along and he started on you and the Soviet Union. Then she decided to get you out of there.

"The thing that puzzles me is why this guy would start to belittle the Soviet Union. They are usually pretty careful about alienating you people. He wasn't drinking, but he had a patronizing, supercilious air about him. Do you know our saying 'He looked like the cat that swallowed the canary'?"

"Yes, I do," said Rostov, pronouncing each word slowly and distinctly. So it had been bothering Appleby, too, or he wouldn't have brought it up. Rostov decided to say nothing. He looked at his watch. "It's been a good session, Brad. I've got to get going. See you in a few days."

"*Do svedoneya,* my friend."


"*Salaam aleikum,*" said the aide, bowing stiffly before the gray metal desk. Hassan was tall for a Lebanese, but he was slim, dark, and graceful. He had the ability to move so quietly that he startled people by suddenly appearing, as from nowhere. Emir had felt his presence before he spoke.

"*Aleikum salaam,*" came the annoyed response. Emir remained bent over a sheaf of papers, his head motionless as he drew a lime-colored fluorescent marker over a line of text to emphasize its contents.

"*Sabah il-xeir, aleikum, sahib,*" continued the aide, his expression obsequious as he touched his fingers to his forehead.

Emir looked up, annoyed, his features contracting into a grimace. "Look, Hassan, I've told you to knock off the formalities when we don't have visitors. We have a lot of work to do and we are never going to get it done if we spend half an hour saying hello. What did gold close at last night in the States?"

"Up eleven cents." Hassan straightened up, almost at attention, as his features sharpened.

"You hedged?" It was more a statement than a question.

"Oh, yes, sir. We have some healthy pension payments to the Druze this week and an oil payment is due Thursday to the Ayatollah Khouri. The Sudanese drought shows no sign of letting up; they are a considerable cash drain on us. These people are completely dependent on us, but none of them want anything but gold — It's a nuisance, but we try to accommodate them when we can. I hedged ninety days in London."

"Good work." Salom al Emir beamed at his assistant. "I'll make a businessman out of you yet."

He turned back to his work while Hassan melted away. He was anxious for the meeting with June. She was the key to all his plans, but he found it difficult to visualize her in this new role.

After the Olympics, Emir had lived with the Maliks in Athens for a while, until, homesick even without a family, he drifted back to his native Beirut, there to share in the prosperous years of that pearl of the Mediterranean. He was hired by a Kuwaiti oil brokerage firm and became head of the Beirut office. But in Lebanon, business and politics were inseparable. One naturally followed the other. Almost automatically, he became a member of the PLO. The ability to travel in his job was an important asset, and as he journeyed throughout the Middle East, his opposition to the Western nations and their Israeli allies grew stronger and stronger. His was not a hatred that would erupt into violence, the usual outlet of his Islamic associates. It was more of a sense of injustice, a feeling that his people had been wronged and that those wrongs must be remedied. The West was his enemy and that enemy must be defeated, but he bore no ill will to individuals, nor did he particularly wish them harm. They were a product of their system as he was a product of his. Although his family had been wiped out by the fighting with the British, he could sit across the table from an Englishman or pass a British soldier on the street with no feelings of enmity. He remembered the statement of a member of the IRA to whom the PLO had given refuge after the bombing of a Belfast government building: "I have never met an Englishman I didn't like, nor an English government I could tolerate."

He had similar feelings with respect to Israel. He had great sympathy for the sufferings of the Jews and a personal empathy for any group forced to leave their homeland. In fact, he could not understand how the Jews could live in peace with the Christians. After all, it was in the name of Christ that they had been persecuted for two thousand years, not in the name of Allah. He did not see the justice of uprooting Arabs to give Jews a home. They had no more right to the land than his people did.

As the West's dependency on Middle Eastern oil grew in the fifties and sixties, Emir had also developed a sense of outrage at the economic injustice of relations with the Western democracies. The big oil companies lifted the oil from the desert for ten cents per barrel and sold it for three dollars per barrel. He cast aside the argument that the Westerners owned it because they had found it. They deserved compensation for their efforts but, basically, it was part of the soil of the sovereign nations whose borders contained it, and it was those sovereign nations who were the rightful owners. Working initially with the Kuwaitis and then with King Faisal and Sheik Yamani of Saudi Arabia, he was instrumental in the formation of OPEC, that crisp acronym for the Organization of Petroleum Exporting Countries. By the time the oil crisis hit, he had purchased calls on a huge inventory of prime crude, which he cashed in for a considerable fortune when the price of oil rose abruptly. He invested most of his money abroad, then devoted his time exclusively to politics, in the PLO and in Lebanon.

The disastrous involvement of Israel's Menachem Begin regime and the Americans in Lebanon strengthened his position in both areas. In the PLO, he emphasized building up the organization's finances, leaving the publicity to Arafat. By the time he secretly took over, the PLO was a powerful billion-dollar organization, supporting refugee camps and resistance organizations all over the Middle East. In Lebanese politics, he was more prominent. He was not a man to make enemies. When the Gamal regime fell, and the Syrian peacekeeping force came in, the various factions haggled for months before settling on him as a compromise choice for the presidency. He had consolidated power smoothly and quietly until the plane hijacking. That had been a setback, but now he had the plan to recover, and June would be key to its success.

June stepped off the conveyor onto the escalator at the Los Angeles airport, her mind half paying attention to the cartoon greetings of grade-school students pictured along the jetway, the other half unfocused, unwilling to grasp the enormity of the decision she was about to make. She dawdled, bought magazines at the newsstand, although she knew that there would be plenty on the aircraft, moved listlessly through the lounge, then sat down on a bench just as her flight was being called.

This was the crucial time. She could still get up and walk back through the gates, possibly even retrieve her baggage. She could call the secret number and tell them it was all off, then report back to Kane Industries on Monday morning. Bill would be delighted to have her back, and the type of job was not all that important. Her heart sank as she thought of him. You always hurt the one you love. The refrain kept repeating in the back of her mind. But could she go back and did she want to?

She had burned a lot of bridges. What would the authorities say? Would there be retribution from overseas? But, more important, what would happen to the grand plan? What would happen to the thousands of refugees, rotting for generations in the camps? Would there ever be an opportunity again for justice without bloodshed? Would she, could she, let Emir down at this point? No she could not. She had a sense of foreboding, of inevitable personal tragedy, but she shrugged it off with the resolution that her own destiny was unimportant.

The public address system boomed out last call for flight 763 to New York. June leaned over, picked up her handbags and newspapers, then walked resolutely onto the airplane.

She slept fitfully during the flight to New York, trying to watch the movie or read, anything to put the decision out of her mind, now that it was made. She had no difficulty changing airplanes at Kennedy Airport. She arrived on time with an hour and a half to catch the flight to Rome, which was going on to Athens.

The young couple in the seats across from her looked Lebanese, but she couldn't tell. During cocktails, they introduced themselves as Joseph and Alice Naggar. They were pleased to learn that she was going on to Athens, where they talked vaguely about having some export business. They spoke perfect English. She wanted to try Greek or Arabic but was embarrassed that she might offend them. They spoke in generalities during the cocktail period, but after dinner was served, they leaned back in their seats and seemed to take turns sleeping for the rest of the flight.

She bumped into them a couple of times in the shops at the Rome airport, and they seemed happy to be seated across from her again on the flight to Athens. When the seat belt sign went off, Joe immediately got up to stretch, heading to the rear of the aircraft. When he returned, he rang the bell for a flight attendant and handed her a note. June watched the attendant take the note and hurry with it to the cockpit. In less than a minute, the copilot came sauntering back into the cabin; he leaned over to talk to Naggar, then walked slowly to the cockpit. June thought it strange that the copilot would leave the cockpit before they had reached cruising altitude, even though the seat belt sign had been turned off. An air of electric, almost palpable tension began to build. The attendants looked nervous, whispering to one another as they congregated around the galley.

It happened so suddenly that she had difficulty recalling the events. There was a scream from the rear of the aircraft, then a single shot. A man waving a large pistol and shouting in Italian came rushing up the aisle. June instinctively ducked in her seat as the man went by, headed for the cockpit. She peeked up to see Joe Naggar stand, take out a small revolver, and put two bullets into the back of the terrorist, who plunged headlong onto the aisle, three feet from the cockpit.

There was pandemonium in the aircraft. It vibrated heavily as the pilot fought the controls to balance the shifting load with passengers milling about. The copilot came rushing back, turned the body over, and told the attendant not to bother calling for a doctor. The man was dead.

The pilot's voice came over the public address system, first in English, then Italian. "Ladies and gentlemen. Please remain seated with your seat belts fastened. We have been cleared for an immediate descent to the Athens airport and we may encounter some turbulence on the way down. All meal and beverage service has been discontinued for the remainder of the flight. I will give you further information on the incident you have just witnessed as soon as I receive it."

June held her head in her arms and sobbed uncontrollably. Had the man been out to get her? Were there others? Why had she started this awful business anyhow? Why had she not walked out of the L.A. airport at the last minute? It was too much for her. She slumped against the back of the seat and lost consciousness in fear, apprehension, and weariness.

She felt someone beside her, placing a cool, wet towel on her forehead and massaging her wrists. She opened her eyes and recognized Alice Naggar. "Miss Malik," Alice said in Arabic, "everything's all right. You're safe and we'll be on the ground in ten minutes."

She explained that she and her husband were from the Lebanese secret police, assigned as escorts from New York to Beirut. When Joe had walked back to the rear of the aircraft, he had recognized a member of the Italian Red Brigade. The man was sitting quietly, and not to make him suspicious, Joe had sent a note to the pilot via the flight attendant. The pilot had alerted an officer of the Italian Secret Service detailed to ride flights between Rome and Athens. When the officer went forward to question the man, he had pulled out a pistol, shot the officer, and went screaming toward the cockpit.

"Joe was ready for him when he went by," Alice said succinctly. She went on to explain that they had found a note in the terrorist's pocket, demanding release of two Red Brigade prisoners held captive in Greece. So far as they could tell, the man was operating alone.

Thank God, thought June. Bad as it is, it's not aimed at me. The sense of foreboding returned but with it a renewed resolution to proceed, whatever her fate.

The Athens airport was in turmoil. Joe Naggar went off with the flight crew and the Greek authorities to file reports on the shooting, but Alice stuck with June. She was a very calming influence as they transferred to Kuwait Airways flight 436 from Athens to Riyadh with an intermediate stop in Beirut. June had no idea that the flight had been delayed an hour and a half to receive transfer passengers from Rome. Nor was she aware of the two fighter aircraft that picked up the Boeing 737 just outside the Athens airspace and escorted it until it turned onto the taxiway in Beirut, the pilots rolling their wings in a gesture of farewell to the flight crew while maintaining radio silence.

Alice Naggar had called Hassan from the Athens airport to notify him of the shootings. Emir was distressed. After the hijacking experience in Beirut, he had been worried about June's journey. At first, he had thought to charter a plane from Los Angeles, but he was afraid to arouse American suspicions. He settled for escorts from New York, and now was glad he had done so. The Naggars had handled their assignment well.

He had decided not to meet June at the airport himself but

to send Hassan. There was no security problem, but he didn't want to link her with him just yet. "She's bound to be very upset after this experience," he had said to Hassan. "I wouldn't want a scene at the airport. If the Americans don't, the Israelis will certainly have someone assigned to the airport to see who's coming and going. Is she traveling under her own name?"

"Yes, sahib, for two reasons. We want the Americans to trace her ultimately. It will strengthen Mahmoud's position when he contacts the President. The other is that we felt that she'd be pretty nervous and that to give her a false passport would only have made her more concerned."

That made sense to Emir, but he was still worried about her arrival. He decided to have her brought directly to his office before she went to the safe house. He didn't want it to look as if she were being put under lock and key.

Hassan assured him that the safe house would give no such impression. He described the twenty-room villa up on the hill. It belonged to Prince Fahd and was where President Assad stayed when he was in Beirut. The prince would be in Egypt for the next six months, so Emir had it available. There was a beautiful garden and a pool. The security guards would be kept completely out of sight.

Hassan took the limousine with just the chauffeur, no flags. Security police, all dressed in Western clothes, traveled in a Porsche in front and a Citroën in the rear. The additional guard detail at the airport wore robes. The only visible sign of VIP treatment was to have her bypass customs and passport control.

With Alice's help, June had composed and freshened herself on the flight, changing from the sweater and slacks she had worn while traveling. As soon as the ringing of the bell announced that the seat belt sign had been turned off, she rose and walked resolutely forward to be the first passenger to depart.

Hassan spotted June immediately as she strode briskly out of the jetway, her magnificent figure contrasting with her severe navy blue skirt and jacket and the white tailored blouse. She could have been posing for an airline ad as she swung her well-worn briefcase from her left arm. He observed the glares of disapproval in the eyes of the veiled women and the surreptitious lascivious lip-licking of their husbands, their attention diverted momentarily from scanning the faces of the other passengers.

"Hassan, it's so long since I've seen you," June said, stepping aside so as not to block the path of the other passengers, throwing her arms around him and kissing him on both cheeks. The security guards started in surprise. But June was oblivious to it all as she hugged the embarrassed Hassan, who stooped to reach for her briefcase and hide his blushing face.

The driver held the door open for her as Hassan started to walk around the car to the front seat, but June slid across the seat to make room for him.

When the door was closed and the limousine pulled away, June dropped all pretense and collapsed in tears. "Oh, Hassan, I was so worried. I was afraid that the FBI or the CIA or somebody was going to pick me up. And when that awful man came screaming up the aisle . . . I still don't know if I'm . . ." She made an effort to compose herself, but the words would not come. They rode the rest of the way in silence.

Soon they pulled up the long driveway to the library-office, the area suddenly ablaze with lights as they approached the building. Emir was in the doorway to greet her. He could feel the tears streaming down her cheek as she held him for a full minute before speaking.

"Oh, Sal, Sal, I hope I'm doing the right thing," she sobbed as she broke the embrace and looked pleadingly at him.

For an instant, he had a qualm. He was confident of his cause and willing to take his own risks, but as he held her he could remember the young girl who used to come dashing into her uncle's arms for comfort and reassurance when she was hurt or frightened. Now he felt from her the same total abandon, the same confidence and trust that a child places in her protector. Was he doing the right thing, taking her from her friends and her adopted country, endangering her life? Would he be able to protect her from danger if the plan went wrong, or from vengeance if it went right? He embraced her, seeking his own reassurance from the warmth and pliancy of her trust. She gave him that reassurance by kissing him eagerly and collapsing in his arms. He suddenly realized where he was, standing on the steps with a dozen silent witnesses looking on. He pulled her up and kissed her lightly on the forehead.

"Come inside. Of course you're doing the right thing. You're just tired after the long journey."

She chattered nervously as they walked into the office and he sat her down in the only armchair. "I feel so proud of you, Sal, when I see you on television or in the newspapers. Just think, the president of Lebanon used to bounce me on his knee and read me bedtime stories. Mom would have been so happy if she had only lived another year to see this come about."

"I never forget, June, that if your parents hadn't befriended me at the end of the war, I would have ended up on the city streets," Emir said, again putting his arm around her shoulders.

"Well, you became the president of Lebanon without our help. I've always treasured the days in Athens when you lived with us. Do you remember bringing home the little Greek cakes and the American candy bars, and I would be waiting with flowers I had picked from the garden? I can still see my white communion dress and how you threw a kiss to me as I came up the aisle. When you went away, I always cried and hoped that on your next visit you would stay forever. Those were the happiest days of my life.

"I've never felt comfortable in the States. Greece and Lebanon have always been my home. I suppose that's why I'm doing what I'm doing." She gently pushed his arm from her shoulder, stood up, and gave him a mock salute, but he heard the tremor in her voice.

"The first thing is for you to get some rest. We have prepared a lovely villa for you. Nick and Sophia Mitropoulos are in town and so are the Frangos. If you'd like, Hassan could arrange a small dinner party at your villa for tomorrow or the next night."

"Tomorrow would be perfect. I recover quickly."

When she had left, Emir called in Hassan and asked, "What do you think?"

Hassan described how she had acted at the airport, cool and collected as she left the airplane, but collapsing into tears in the limousine when no one could see her. She was obviously high strung and would need time to collect herself. After all, he pointed out, that incident in the airplane alone could have put a weaker person into shock. Then, seeing him and finally realizing that she had cut all her ties must have hit her very hard. He thought that a dinner party with old friends would do a lot to occupy her mind and provide diversion.

Emir demurred. He reminded Hassan that only she had the crucial numbers, and that she could back out at any time by revealing them.

"I hate to say this, sahib," said Hassan, "but the stakes are high, and when some of your associates realize what your plan is, they may want to put her aside, as a precautionary measure."

"You mean assassinate her?"

"Precisely, sahib. Others may want to force the numbers out of her for money. In any event, she has no possible retreat. She's in this to the end."

"You must realize that I've thought of these things, Hassan," said Emir. "My colleagues worry less than I do about taking human life, to say the least. But getting rid of her solves nothing and, even if they tortured her, she could give them false information which they wouldn't realize until it was too late. Besides, she may have a confidant in the States who has been instructed to release everything if they don't hear from her. No, she's a smart girl who would not leave herself exposed, not even for me. We'll have to rely on her cooperation."

The dinner party went well. Nick Mitropoulos was a consular official for the Greek government and the Frangos were in Lebanon on business. The social life in Beirut was bleak, so both couples were delighted to receive the dinner invitation. They weren't sure why June was in the city, but they knew that she and Emir were related and assumed it was for a family visit. At the last minute, Emir called to invite himself. All were delighted to have him. The food was outstanding, and, of course, there was a lively discussion of Middle East politics.

About ten o'clock, the guests started to look at their watches. Sophia Mitropoulos suggested that June must be very weary from jet lag and that they should be going. June protested but they muttered something about early morning meetings and graciously took their leave.

"I'm really not sleepy and I hate to have everyone desert me this early in the evening," said June. "You don't have to go, do you, Sal? Stay and let's talk about old times."

Emir agreed to stay for a cigar and a cognac. They saw the other guests to the door and strolled slowly back into the living room. They talked for a few minutes about the dinner, the departed guests, and the comforts of the villa. Neither was disposed to mention the reason June was in Beirut. She walked dreamily around the room, reminiscing about her playmates of the early days, most of whom Emir had forgotten. She called for the cognac, dismissing the servant for the evening after he had poured. Emir lit his cigar and leaned back on the sofa, enclosed in a cloud of blue smoke.

It began innocuously enough. June moved over on the sofa and sat beside him. She took the cigar from his hand and crushed it out in the ashtray. "You know you shouldn't smoke. An athlete like you. How are you ever going to win another swimming meet?"

"It's my only indulgence. One cigar a day."

"It seems like old times. I feel as if I should be sitting on your lap. Tell me a story."

She leaned over and kissed him lightly on the forehead.

Out of the depths of the past, he remembered one that had been a favorite of hers, full of kings and princes and beautiful young ladies, all of whom lived happily ever after.

He pulled back his head and looked into her half-closed eyes, soft and dreamy with reminiscence.

June was suddenly aware of the masculinity of the cigar smoke and conscious of his stirring beside her. A little embarrassed, she shifted slightly. They sat for a moment in silence. She started to get up, but his arms held her softly. She sat still.

"I'm afraid it would be a different kind of story now, June," he whispered. He pulled her to him and kissed her hard on the lips, her breasts crushing against his chest.

Her eyes opened wide with surprise and alarm. She struggled slightly to release herself, but he held her firmly until he felt her sigh and go limp.

They rose, her arms tight around his neck, his hands searching softly from her shoulders to her thighs.

"Oh, Sal, Sal. Yes, yes, yes."

They went wordlessly to the bedroom, his eyes mesmerized by her unfolding beauty as she shed each garment, hers conscious of his finely proportioned, lithe body.

When he entered her she was frenzied with the need for emotional release. He had all he could do to exercise restraint until they could both be brought to a peak. She climaxed with a series of screams. As he collapsed with his own release, he heard her whisper as from a distance, "My darling, my sweet. I'm afraid this was part of it."

# 5

---

KANE FLEW TO WASHINGTON ON SATURDAY AND
played golf with his two Washington office vice presidents and
Senator Tim Sullivan early Sunday morning. He wished he
hadn't made the date. Sullivan had to play early because he was
scheduled to be on a TV panel in the afternoon, but to Kane,
with his biological clock on California time, an eight o'clock tee
time meant getting up in the middle of the night. He had invited
Sullivan to play at a course where his company had a member-
ship, but the senator had refused.

"No, me bucko," he had shouted over the telephone, "I'll not
have it in the *Washington Post* Monday morning that Senator
Timothy Sullivan was golfed, wined, and dined by three members of the military-industrial complex. It's bad enough to be
seen at all with you spalpeens, especially when you're testifying
before my subcommittee Monday. We'll play at my course, the
Congressional."

Kane and Sullivan had been classmates in college. Kane had
been the big man on campus as quarterback of the football
team, good enough to be selected in the professional draft. But
a knee injury in his first year ended his career, so he went back
to school to earn a Ph.D. in physics. His roommate, Brad
Appleby, had been baseball captain, but he went right into the
foreign service after graduation. Sullivan had been the golfing

star, and he was the only one who went on to a successful career in sports. Tim was good-looking, with a blond cowlick that was a natural for TV. When he quit the tour, his smooth Irish wit put him in high demand as a color commentator. Politics was a natural follow-on. After two terms in the House, he was elected to the Senate on his first try.

Kane played poorly and lost five dollars, even with the ten strokes Sullivan spotted him. He slumped in the chair in the clubhouse grill room and threw a worn bill on the table. "You should have given me more strokes on your home course," he grumbled.

"You bum, I gave you full handicap . . . You should only get eighty percent, you know. Will you sign this for me? I think I'll save it for posterity." He pushed the five-dollar bill back across the table.

"If you're not going to spend it, give it back to me and I'll write you a check," Kane countered. "Don't forget, winner buys the drinks," he said as the waiter hovered over them.

"I can't have a drink," Sullivan said. "I've got to be on this TV show. But I'll buy you one."

The two vice presidents took their cue from Kane. When he shook his head, they shook theirs in unison. Sullivan got up to leave.

"Before you go, Tim," Kane said, "tell me what the hell I'm doing testifying before you tomorrow. I don't mind doing it when you ask, but plant security is a little out of my line."

Sullivan sat down. He explained that the prime subject of the hearings was nuclear terrorism. One of the members of his subcommittee, Senator Bill Bronsky, was a rabid anti-nuke who was having reelection problems and was looking for an issue that would get him some publicity.

"He has a hair across his ass and I know he'll give the government people a hard time," Sullivan said, rising again. "I needed a witness from industry and I figured he wouldn't dare to take a shot at a big wheel like you. Don't let him get your goat. I've got to run. See you in the dock."

Kane shook his head and slumped further in the chair. "With friends like you . . ." he shouted at the retreating senator, but Sullivan waved his arm and kept on going.

The Subcommittee on Strategic and Theater Nuclear Forces met at 10:00 A.M. in room 4232, Dirksen Senate Office Building, Senator Timothy X. Sullivan presiding, with Senators Thompson, Wilkins, and Bronsky in attendance. Sullivan announced that the subject of the hearings was nuclear terrorism. They would focus on the possible fabrication and detonation of clandestine nuclear explosives. They would bring out the extent of the nation's exposure to nuclear blackmail or harassment, and the extent to which the nation could take preventive measures and countermeasures.

The first witness was Dr. Sherman T. Bidwell, assistant secretary of Energy. He stood, professorially, pointer in hand, while assistants scurried to remove charts and put up new ones during the presentation. He explained the difference between nuclear weapons and nuclear power plants. The fuel in a nuclear power plant is not concentrated enough to be used in a weapon, he pointed out.

"What about terrorists blowing up a nuclear power plant and spewing radioactivity around for hundreds of years?" asked Senator Thompson. She fingered the bow on her blouse. "What about our children? What about Chernobyl?"

Bidwell explained that the plants are designed to withstand earthquakes, hurricanes, and a direct hit from a 747 aircraft and that they would be very difficult to blow up. "As for Chernobyl, Mrs. Thompson," he said, "that was not sabotage, that was obsolete design, a different kind of problem."

She pursed her lips and sat back, looking unconvinced, but deferred to the next questioner.

Senator Wilkins wanted to know if a terrorist could fabricate a nuclear weapon if he had stolen material, since the information on how to build one had been made public. Bidwell replied that it was theoretically possible but would be too difficult for an individual or a small group. "After all," he said condescendingly, "I know how to build a bicycle, but it's not likely that I could build one in my basement."

He did agree that a well-managed terrorist organization with time, money, and resources, operating in a country friendly to its cause, could be successful.

"What about the ayatollah?" Senator Thompson asked.

"Oh, yes, he should be able to do it," replied Bidwell, walking away from his charts. "The shah had a very ambitious nuclear power program before he was deposed. There are thousands of American-trained scientists and engineers now under the ayatollah's command in Iran. On the other hand, Qaddafi has been trying to build, buy, or steal one for years, without success."

Bidwell went on to point out that the most straightforward action a potential nuclear terrorist could take would be to steal an existing weapon. He described the Department of Energy's program to maintain a secure physical control system for the fissionable materials and the assembled weapons under its control.

"Mr. Chairman," Bidwell said, gesturing to a crew-cut, beribboned naval officer sitting ramrod straight in the front row, "Vice Admiral Parsons of the NATO staff is present today to brief the subcommittee on the physical security aspects of our custodianship of fissionable devices in other countries, and Dr. William Kane, chairman of the board of Kane Industries, will brief you on plant security. Admiral Pars — "

Senator Bronsky broke in, raising his beefy arm toward Sullivan. "Just a minute, Mr. Chairman. I am well acquainted with Admiral Parsons; he is an outstanding and patriotic naval officer and I am proud to have served under him during my days in the military service." He nodded to the admiral. "I will say as much for Dr. Kane. I have followed the good doctor's career since his days of football prowess through his marvelous inventions in the computer field and magnificent accomplishments in building a Fortune 500 company." He smiled unctuously at Kane, who stared warily back. "It is not through any lack of respect for these gentlemen's magnificent accomplishments that

I ask you, Mr. Chairman, to move this hearing forward to more substantive matters. While we have them here, I'd like to get down to fundamentals."

He leaned into the microphone, lowering the pitch of his voice to a growl, but raising its intensity. "There are more than fifty thousand of these devices strewn all over the world — we have twenty-five thousand, the Russians have twenty-five thousand, the British have some, the French have some, the Chinese have some, and God knows who else. Sooner or later, no matter how good your security systems are — and most of these are not under your control — some terrorist is going to get hold of one. Suppose he does. What can he do with it? Could he smuggle it into this country? How much damage can a single weapon cause?"

Bronsky pounded on the table, his florid face getting redder. "And finally," he demanded, "is there anything we can do to desensitize it or to keep it from going off? These are the things we should be talking about."

Tim Sullivan winced, then cocked his head and turned his palms up off the table. Kane could see the words "Oh shit" form silently on his lips.

Sullivan agreed that although these were important questions, they were afield from the subject of the morning's discussion.

But Bronsky would not budge. "These people are the experts," he said. "We don't need any fancy charts. Let's just get their offhand opinions."

Bidwell, an experienced bureaucrat, took the chairman off the hook. In answer to the first question, he stated that a low- to intermediate-yield weapon would fit into a large suitcase. There would be no problem moving one around anywhere in the United States. Furthermore, it would not be at all difficult to smuggle one into this country. He pointed out that the government couldn't stop drugs from coming into the country.

"I don't want to be facetious, Senator," Bidwell said, "but all he'd have to do is hide it in a bale of marijuana. How much damage would such a weapon cause?" He paused, his demeanor became very serious, and he looked intently at each member of the subcommittee in turn.

"A single nuclear device would wreak havoc. It could easily be brought in on a boat right here on the Potomac River." He pointed out the window. "A time clock could be set to explode it when the President was in the White House and the Congress and the Supreme Court were in session. Washington would be demolished. There would be no President, no Congress, no Pentagon, not even any radio or TV antennas left standing to inform the world of what had happened. The radioactive waters of the river would flood the city, rendering the area uninhabitable, even for rescue crews. What would happen next? Would a panicky silo commander or submarine captain unleash a salvo at the Soviet Union, initiating full-scale thermonuclear war?" He paused again and threw up his hands. "Who knows?"

Senator Thompson was shocked. "My goodness," she said. "We've had these things explained before, but I've never heard it expressed so bluntly. Isn't there anything we can do?"

Bidwell shook his head. He explained that there was no magic wand they could wave to desensitize or neutralize a nuclear explosive but that, if it was a device stolen from the U.S. stockpile, it could be detonated only by an authorized agent.

Bronsky, upstaged for the moment, bore in again. "How do you do that?" he asked.

"By devices called Permissive Action Links, commonly known as PALs," said Bidwell. He described them as switches, deeply embedded in the weapon, which control the firing circuits. They can be made operative only by a code controlled by the President. The code is in the so-called football that a military aide to the President carries near him at all times. The aide can be seen occasionally on television, following the President down the steps from an aircraft or in the background when he is making a speech. In a national emergency, should the President decide to put our arsenal on readiness alert, he would open the "football," read the code, and transmit it through the proper channels.

"What if someone got hold of the code?" asked Bronsky. "You can't hope to keep it secret forever, can you?"

Bidwell did not know the answer, but he suggested that Kane might be able to supply it, since he had invented the memory chip that controls the PAL and his company manufactures the hardware. The chairman turned to Kane.

Kane was hesitant. "I didn't expect to testify on this subject either," he said, "but I'm generally familiar with it. The code is made up by what is known as a random number generator. When people make up codes for their office safes or their bank withdrawal cards, they tend to use numbers that they can remember, like their mother's birthday. Cryptographers don't do anything that simple. They generate codes from tables of random numbers, using a computer."

Bronsky glared at Kane. "That wasn't the question I asked. What are you trying to do, put me off?"

Senator Sullivan tried to lighten the tension. "Did you hear the story of one of them cryptographer fellows who woke up dreaming of the number five. He looked at his watch and it was five A.M. It was the fifth day of the fifth month of the fifth year of the decade. He took the day off, drew five thousand dollars from the bank, went to the racetrack, and bet it all on horse number five in the fifth race."

"Okay, Tim, I'll bite," said Senator Wilkins. "What happened?"

"The horse came in fifth."

Bronsky did not join in the laughter. He continued to glare at Kane, who glared back and stated that of course it was necessary to change the code from time to time.

"What do you do, go around and change all twenty-five thousand of them at once?" asked Bronsky.

Kane kept his calm. "Senator," he said, "my company is just a contractor to the government. It is not for me to say whether there are twenty-five thousand or twenty-five hundred. When the controls were first installed back in the sixties, it was necessary to change one at a time. Now there is an automatic changing mechanism built into the system."

"Will you explain that to me, please."

Kane was not going to be drawn in any further.

"Senator, I'm just pinch-hitting on this subject," he said. "If the chairman would like me to do so, I can bring our expert, June Malik, from the design laboratory in California to give you more details."

Bronsky agreed to a forty-eight-hour delay to await the expert. Sullivan took the opportunity to hastily gavel the hearing into recess.

Kane, followed by his two vice presidents and other members of his Washington staff, stormed out of the conference room.

Arriving at the company office, he threw his coat on the chair and immediately dialed Senator Sullivan's private number. "Tim, what the hell's going on? Who does that guy Bronsky think he is, refusing to hear Parsons and bypassing the testimony you wanted me to give. I thought you said he wasn't going to take me on. I don't have to take that kind of crap."

"Calm down, calm down," said Sullivan. "It's a good thing you never went into politics. He is kind of crusty, but he's having trouble with his Polish constituency. His opponent claims that Bronsky should have raised more hell about the Communists. He's just grandstanding."

"Well, he doesn't have to push me around. It makes me furious that I got sandbagged into talking about Permissive Action Links. That means I'll have to bring June Malik back here to testify. The last thing I need is to spend a week in the same town with her."

"Hee, hee, hee," said Sullivan. "Now I see your problem, me bucko. You're more worried about your old girlfriend than you are about Bronsky. Hell hath no fury like a woman spermed, they say. I don't know why you broke up with that beautiful creature, anyhow."

"Oh balls," Kane said and hung up.

"Get June Malik on the telephone," he barked at the office receptionist.

Kane spent the next fifteen minutes rearranging his schedule;

he looked angrily at his watch. "Where the hell is my telephone call?"

"I'm sorry, sir, but Miss Malik is out of the country," the receptionist said. "We're checking to see where she can be located."

"Out of the country? Impossible. She can't be out of the country. Let me talk to her secretary."

The flustered secretary was almost in tears. Friday, just after he had left for the East Coast, June had told her to get a ticket for Paris the next morning and make a reservation for her at the Intercontinental. She had just called the Intercontinental and found that June was a no-show. So she called a friend of hers who worked at the Ambassadors Club. The girlfriend had seen Miss Malik. She remembered it distinctly because Miss Malik had taken pains to avoid talking to her. The secretary felt that she must have changed to some other flight without telling anyone.

"Did you check with Security?" Kane asked. "She'd never leave the country without checking with Security."

"That's another strange thing." The girl's voice quavered as if betrayed. "I was going to inform Security like I always do, but she said she was going by there and would fill out the papers on her way. Now they tell me they have no record of anything."

Kane whistled. He had completely forgotten his conversation with Herb Goldstein on the previous Friday. June must have gone out of the country after she left his apartment that night. Had she decided to go before they had their argument? Must have. But why?

His orders to the secretary were crisp. "Call Security and tell them to alert the FBI immediately. Call Personnel and give them the story. Call Travel and see if they have any ideas. Then call Legal and tell the general counsel he's in charge of the investigation."

This time Schultz made his plans and assembled his associates with great care. He moved out of the basement room he had been renting in Frankfurt, telling the landlady that he was going to Berlin but leaving no forwarding address. He took a train for Bonn, where he bought a secondhand Mercedes van for cash, using one of his several forged passports for identification on the registration. A used-clothing store was the source of two dark business suits and a raincoat. He even bought a hat because he wasn't sure what clothes a conservative businessman should wear. Then he drove to Munich, discarding his old clothes in a dump on the outskirts of Bonn.

He rented a small furnished apartment in a blue-collar neighborhood in Munich and set up the regular schedule of a clerk, leaving the apartment every morning at eight and returning at five-thirty. Every evening, sitting over a beer in the Vogelhof Restaurant down the street from his apartment, he went over his list.

He ruled out anyone from the Baderhofs on the grounds that any concentration from West German terrorist groups would be looked on with suspicion. He also eliminated the Italian Red Brigades. The storage site was too close to the Italian border and such people might be recognized. What he needed were mercenaries, not ideologues. He wanted people who knew nothing of the politics of nuclear weapons and who would therefore be less likely to disobey his instructions or double-cross him.

He needed six associates: one to drive the van, two to handle the package, one for each of the two American military officers, and one to be available for cover or for emergencies. He decided that they should all be German and, to make it easier for him to maintain absolute control, that they should speak little or no English. He went to Hamburg to do the recruiting.

The van driver, recruited directly out of a Hamburg prison, was a convict who had served three years for knifing his girlfriend when he caught her in bed with another man. The package carriers were twins, massive, dull brutes whom he had encountered in a bar. The guards were soldiers recently dishonorably discharged from the army of the Federal Republic after serving six months for beating up a military police officer in a drunken brawl. His cover man, Otto Drucker, was the only one to whom he told the whole plan. Drucker, thin and nervous, was a small-time bookie and pool shark, always on the edge of a big deal or a new scam, but never quite able to carry anything off. He had harbored Schultz for two months when the police were looking for him after one of the Baderhof strikes.

When he told Otto the plan, they were again seated in the tiny room that had been a home in hiding for Schultz. Drucker smoked one cigarette after another, his eyes gleaming at the audacity of the concept.

"This is it, Ludwig," he said, coughing violently in his excitement. "This is it. This is what I've been waiting for. I'm with you. We can pull it off if anyone can."

Except for the twins, each man was recruited and briefed separately. Schultz gave each of them one thousand deutsche marks from the cash advance Emir had given him. The plan was for each to arrive in Munich four days before the protest; Schultz arranged for lodgings in different rooming houses where they were to remain until he summoned them by telephoning the rooming house managers. He would deliver the following message: "The boxes have arrived." Then he would hang up.

They would drive together in the van to the storage site, where they would carry out the duties assigned to each of them. Upon disposition of the package and the officers at the Nuremberg airport, they would each be given one hundred thousand deutsche marks in small bills and embark in separate taxicabs that would be waiting to take them to destinations of their choice.

Schultz gave a great deal of attention to the van. He had purchased a five-year-old surplus army vehicle with the original insignia still on it. He took the van to the main Mercedes maintenance center on Wilhelmstrasse and had it fitted out with a new engine, new brakes, and four new heavy snow tires in case there should be mud at the storage site. He made five round trips from the vicinity of the site to the airport, traveling at the highest possible speed on the autobahn, where he knew he would not be stopped, but keeping well within the speed limits off the main highways so as not to draw attention to himself. When he was satisfied with the performance of the vehicle, he took it to a canvas shop.

"We're having a parade as part of a fund-raiser for the Munich General Hospital," he told the proprietor. "I'd like to have snaps installed on the sides and hood of the van. We will have a Red Cross tableau, so I would like large canvas red crosses for the sides and smaller ones for the hood."

The proprietor looked at Schultz quizzically, but said nothing and did his bidding. Schultz then went to a hospital supply store where he purchased a quantity of surplus military stretchers, khaki blankets, pillows, and white surgical gowns.

He had accumulated his armory over a period of six months. His cache, which he kept hidden in a large commercial storage locker, consisted of knives, two rifles, and seven military-issue .35-caliber, eight-cartridge Luger pistols, one for each of his associates and one for himself. In addition, he had an AK47 rifle, which he had owned since his days in the Italian Red Brigades.

Schultz was ready.

# G

HERB GOLDSTEIN HAD BEEN SEARCHING FOR June all week. Now he wanted to call in the FBI immediately. Kane was reluctant, but he finally gave in and agreed to fly back to meet with the FBI the next morning.

Kane was impressed by the amount of information the agency had accumulated when he, Goldstein, and John McDonald, his general counsel, met with the local agency chief at corporate headquarters.

McDonald brought him up to date. They had picked up the trail to Athens. She had boarded Kuwait Airways flight 436, leaving for Beirut and Riyadh. They didn't know who had met her, but she was only ticketed to Beirut. Furthermore, there was a Scotland Yard man on the plane who noticed that she was not on the flight to Riyadh. She seemed to have made no effort to cover up her tracks.

"Maybe she's just taking a trip to Lebanon. There's no law against that," said Kane.

"No. We wouldn't have asked you to hurry back if that was all the information we had," continued the general counsel. "She withdrew all her money from the savings plan two weeks ago — "

"That was before she knew she wasn't going to get the manager's job," Goldstein said.

"But the most damaging thing is that she has subleased her apartment and asked the building management firm to put her furniture into storage," McDonald said. Then he nodded at a man who had accompanied him. "Henry Osborn here, chief of the Los Angeles branch of the FBI, would like to ask you some questions about possible breaches of national security."

"Shoot," said Kane.

"Dr. Kane, did Miss Malik work on classified projects at Kane Industries?" asked Osborn.

"Yes, she did."

"At what level did she have access to classified material?"

"We have had only one classified project in the company in the last several years. As you may have read in the press, I have been concerned about the complexity of the latest weapons systems. I believe that complexity and reliability are mutually exclusive, so I have chosen not to bid for government weapons systems contracts in the past few years. They are too complex and too difficult to build reliably. I am not anti-military. It has been a simple business decision. Of course, if the government comes to us because they believe that we are uniquely qualified, I will accept the program. Such was the case for the contract I mentioned. The contract was on a 'top secret' level. However, June had access only at a 'secret' level."

"Can you tell me what the work was about?"

"Oh, sure. The contract documents themselves are unclassified. The hardware and software are classified 'secret'; the codes themselves are 'top secret,' or 'eyes only' for the President and a few members of his staff."

"The codes?"

"Yes. The contract was to design and build a new set of hardware and software for electronically locking and unlocking nuclear weapons to prevent unauthorized access. The specifications and techniques are 'secret.' The actual codes to the locks have the higher classification. The reason I am so concerned about Miss Malik is that the specifications and techniques could be very important to a potential enemy."

"But without the codes, what good would they be?"

"Maybe no good at all." Kane shrugged. "Nothing's perfect. The devices are supposed to be tamperproof, but who knows?"

"Dr. Kane, I think I've asked you enough questions for now. I share your concern. I assure you that this matter will get the highest priority in the bureau."

When Osborn left, McDonald turned to Kane and Goldstein. "What about it, you technical experts. If somebody tries to get information out of June, is there any way they can get access to the codes?"

"Not that I can think of," Kane said. "The PALs change programs every three months, and the President can always direct that the codes be changed. There's provision in the software for that, isn't there, Herb?"

"Yes, but it's tricky. Software programs are complex animals; you never know what bugs are in them. Depending on the intent of their creator, the programmer, they can be infected with what we call viruses. These are bugs for which there is no known cure. Viruses can resist all attempts at correction, and they can pop up in different places at different times. Sometimes they can destroy the program completely, just like viruses in humans."

McDonald shivered visibly. "My God, that sounds eerie," he said.

Kane couldn't sleep that night. His feelings for June ran the gamut, from loving concern for her safety and well-being to white-hot anger. He got up and walked into the living room, pouring himself a drink from a crystal decanter June had given him. He then sank onto the couch and gulped down his first shot of scotch.

Kane had met June at a computer show in Las Vegas. He was staying at the Desert Inn but decided to walk the two miles to the Convention Center. The glitz of Las Vegas had always fascinated him. To many, it was a turnoff, offensive in its hedonism. To Kane, it was funny, a caricature of all that was superficial in the United States. Energy and sex and money oozed from every particle of its flashing lights, its seductive billboards, its invitations to unmitigated greed and depravity. To Kane, the hype and the hoopla intensified as he walked into the Convention Center, where the blinking lights of the counters merged with the strobes of the show ads, and the steady green glare of the cathode ray monitors gave an underlying pastiness reminiscent of the stares of the pit bosses.

He stopped to glance at a new software program a well-endowed young woman was demonstrating, assuming that she was a model trained to do booth duty. "Is one of your engineers around?" he asked politely. "I have a technical question."

"Yes?"

"I'd like to ask him if this program is compatible with PASCAL or FORTRAN, the main computer languages," Kane continued.

"It's not a him, it's a her," she purred.

"Who?"

"Me."

Startled, only half thinking about the question he had asked, Kane raised his glance from her figure to her mocking brown eyes.

"Oh, I'm sorry, I didn't think —"

"I'm sure you didn't." The brown eyes hardened and the creamy brow knitted into a professional frown. "PASCAL and FORTRAN are the names of computer languages, of course, but they are for two completely different applications."

"I know but —" For the first time he could recall, Kane was completely flustered. "I guess — well, actually, I was thinking of simultaneous different applications." He dug himself in deeper. "You know, in order to get computers to run faster, we are going to have to run several programs at the same time. It's called parallel processing. I was really, uh, wondering, uh, whether this logic would be adaptable to using two different programs at the same time. It's probably not a fair question to ask, since the application hasn't hit the market yet."

She didn't let up on him. "It's a perfectly fair question, and the answer is yes. It's compatible with all applications of the TI3204, the HP7182, and the new KA9090."

It was his turn to become professional. "But the KA9090 won't be available for another three months."

"I understand that." She was still in command. "The company released design specifications to software designers six weeks ago, and we small outfits have to move fast to keep ahead of the big boys."

"That's fine," he said. "Can you tell me who designed this program?"

"I did," she replied, her eyes blazing.

"Wow, I sure do owe you an apology," he said, with a sweeping bow.

June, savoring the victory, moved on. "Parallel processing is an absolute must for artificial intelligence, especially if we expect to compete with the Japanese. I'm convinced that the KA9090 is the answer to a maiden's prayer and I've been working my buns off since the specs came out to be the first on the market with appropriate software," she said proudly. "Are you familiar with the KA9090?"

"You don't look any the worse for wear," he said, sticking his hand out to her. "I'm Bill Kane."

She gasped, looking at the name on his badge for the first time, then broke into a giggle. "Touché," she said, reaching for his outstretched hand. "I'm June Malik. We're even."

The evening went well. They discovered that they both liked escargots, abalone salad, and red meat. And both happily sipped dry white wine with their rare beef, to the consternation of the sommelier. June had never been in Las Vegas and inquired about the odds at the gambling tables.

Kane rattled them off in statistical jargon. "Keno and the slot machines are impossible — they're for the potbelly and polyester crowd," he said. "The cut is at least ten percent and you don't last long taking numbers to the point nine power, as you know."

She smiled acquiescence.

"Craps is a lot better, because they bar boxcars, or double sixes. This makes the cut less than one in thirty-six, split between the Come and the Don't Come. It amounts to a little more than one percent, which isn't bad. Blackjack is pretty good, but you have to count the cards. That's too much trouble."

"It certainly would be for me," she said. "I'd never play more than a dollar at a time, anyhow. I've read about betting systems, but I can't even conceive of a computer code which could touch those odds."

"Right on. They have a saying in this town — 'Show me a guy in New York with a system and I'll send a cab for him.' "

"You seem to know a lot about Las Vegas. Have you spent a lot of time here?"

"Sure have. But not to gamble. In the early days of the company, we made instruments for the nuclear weapons tests at the Nevada Test Site, up the road apiece. And when my wife was living, we used to come here occasionally for some golf and a show."

June murmured her regrets but pursued the subject no further.

The rest of the evening was exciting. The difference in their ages and positions vanished in the glamour and excitement of the crowded casinos. With their technological backgrounds offsetting the artificiality of the teeming city, the shouts of the gamblers, the computer executives nodding deferentially to Kane, the women looking enviously at June, she felt like Cinderella when she glanced at her watch and found that it was midnight.

"I hate to break up the evening, but I do have early booth duty tomorrow. The eastern crowd will be breaking down the doors at the crack of dawn with their three-hour time difference and I have to be on my toes because most of them don't believe that a woman can answer their questions," she said, teasing him. "I really must go."

The second night was more serious. They dined at another magnificent restaurant on the Strip. This time he ordered for both of them — chicken liver pâté with caviar, a clear consommé, Caesar salad tossed at the table, roast rack of lamb very rare, and a California white wine. The decision was made when the captain came to inquire about the after-dinner drinks as they finished the soufflé and sipped a thick café noir. This was the time to suggest a nightcap at his suite or at her hotel and the evening would progress from there. He had held off so far and the urge was strong within him. He could sense that she was waiting for his move, but he was hoping for more and felt that she was, too. Their eyes met in a flicker and broke. He looked up at the captain, nodded his assent, and ordered brandy in a snifter with more coffee.

"Tell me about you," he said.

"There's not an awful lot to tell," she said ruefully. "I'm just a big-busted girl with a knack for mathematics. The two things keep getting in each other's way, literally and figuratively. Sometimes I wish I were just a mousy little flat-chested creature with skinny legs and horn-rimmed glasses. I think it would make my life easier. You're laughing. I don't want to rub it in anymore, but look at the way we met. And I've had other problems. My father was born in Greece. His parents became naturalized citizens. My mother is Lebanese. They were never able to shake the old country completely. That's why he went to work for an oil company right after he got his geology degree, so they could get back to the Middle East. I spent most of my youth roaming around the Mediterranean.

"People in this country don't understand the problems of the Middle East. They fight and kill and die over problems of religion. They fight and kill and die over ethnic problems. They fight and kill and die over who owned what land two thousand years ago. What the hell's the difference? I'd like to see someone come along and stop the fighting. I don't care on what basis because there is no real answer, just stop the fighting and the killing and the dying.

"When we came back, my English was kind of rusty. People talk at you when you don't speak well, as if you didn't know what they were talking about. And the innuendos from the boys. When I was a cheerleader in high school, they used to sing, 'June is busting out all over,' so I quit."

"You do have a chip on your shoulder," Kane commented. "You have a beautiful body and you know it."

"I'm sorry. I've never talked to anyone like this before. I guess I just wanted to get it off my chest. Oh, my God, there I go again." She giggled. "Anyhow, thank you for not maneuvering to pop me into bed right away. You made the right decision."

"I hope so. Let me make you a different kind of a proposition. Could you be persuaded to come to work for Kane Industries?"

"Why?"

"You have to realize that I haven't been smitten only by your personality and physical charms. In the design of the new chip, we are just now getting around to doing application engineering. You've jumped the gun on us by designing a parallel processing application with two different assembly languages. We could use you. There I go, screwing up a romantic evening by talking business."

"Let's put romance on hold for a while. I don't want to mess up my life by falling in love with the guy I work for. Even worse, I don't want to go to work for the guy I've fallen in love with. Give me some time."

"I'm nervous about it, too," he confessed. "I've always heeded the old adage that says, 'Keep your pecker out of your pocketbook.' Let me have my personnel people contact you when we get back. In the meantime, let's have a nightcap — here — and I'll take you home to your solitary bed."

"I'll drink to that," she said softly.

Back in his office in Los Angeles, the first thing Kane did on Monday morning was call in Herb Goldstein. "How's it going, Herb?" he asked.

Goldstein wiped the imaginary perspiration from his furrowed brow and sprawled on the comfortable divan in a simulated gesture of weariness. "Not bad, boss. Inquiries are coming in all over the place; we're just getting started on the applications. It looks super. We're going to leapfrog the Japs on this one, for sure. We need more help, though."

He rose and strode over to stare out the picture windows of

the corner office, unable to see to the ground forty stories below. "Goddamned smog," he said. "The guys are working every night and getting a little groggy. How was the golf? You needed a few days off."

Kane ignored the question. "Have you ever heard of a woman named June Malik?"

"Sure have. She works for some software house in Palo Alto. They've been knocking down the walls trying to get hold of our specs. She's a juicy-looking broad, and smart as hell, but she's kind of a testy bitch," Goldstein replied.

"What do you mean, 'testy'?" Kane went on the defensive, rising from his chair behind the mahogany desk and walking over to spin the large illuminated globe in front of the bookcases.

Goldstein turned away from the window and faced Kane. "My brother Aaron went to Stanford with her; she was always championing some weird cause. I've only met her a couple of times. Aaron says she's into all the women's lib stuff, Equal Rights Amendment, comparable worth, the whole nine yards. She's a big fan of Papandreou in Greece. I think he's a pompous shithead, myself. She's big on the Palestinians, too. Aaron thinks she's a little anti-Semitic."

"Oh, balls," said Kane. "You guys are always seeing ghosts. Is she any good? Her work, I mean."

Goldstein smiled. "Top-notch. She ran away with everything in math, and Aaron's no slouch. He's already a full professor at Stanford. Why?"

"I ran into her at the show in Vegas. She has a program for using the 9090 with two different languages simultaneously."

"Really?" Goldstein whistled. "We've been so busy we haven't gotten around to that problem yet. She just got the specs."

"Would you hire her?"

"Shit, yes. I wouldn't care if she was Carrie Nation or the queen of the Ku Klux Klan if she can do that kind of work. You got to expect these bimbos who are math majors to be some kind of oddball. Aaron gets a little spacey himself sometimes."

Kane ignored the comment, walking back to his desk and

picking up his pen to conclude the discussion. "Good," he said. "I'll put the headhunters to work on her right away."

He had intended to wait a month after she had come to work, but after two weeks he couldn't stand it any longer. When she answered the phone, it was as though it had been yesterday.

"June?"

"Hi, boss," she answered merrily, not waiting for him to identify himself.

"We have some unfinished business in Las Vegas."

"I know."

"Friday night at the Flamingo?"

"I'll be there."

They picked up where they had left off. They went to the same restaurant. He ordered the same meal, but this time refused the after-dinner drinks. They had them in the suite.

It was all they both knew it would be. He tried to be slow and gentle with her, but her eyes shook him off.

Kane tried to recall it all as he poured another drink of scotch, but his memory could not tie it together. It came back to him in bunches, in incongruous, discontinuous scenarios. He remembered her lips seeking his, her tongue overpowering him with sensuous pungency. He remembered her mouth all over him with an eagerness which brought him quickly to the edge, then pulling back with a tenderness that said, "Tarry a while, my darling. Not yet." He remembered her taking command, forcing his rhythm to hers with such a rising crescendo that he could feel Symphony Hall in the background, the walls reverberating to the clamor of "The Hall of the Mountain King." Then, as he drifted back down the mountain, there came to him, oddly, the image of the last panel of the comic strips of his boyhood, the indescribable sensations of confusion and delight and bewilderment: %##$$$%%%***(()))(((**$#(*!))) ++?>?>^:::&&&%###!!!!!!!

The second time was slow and unhurried. The urgency, the uncertainty, the awkwardness, the tension, the sensation of the sin of violation of their mutual creed of noninvolvement had been expiated in those few minutes — or was it milliseconds? — of passion. Now he was in complete command, gentle but deliberate, she a different person, pliant, submissive, and cuddling. This time there were no discontinuities, no gaps which could not be recalled. This time they made all the stops along the way.

He rose, drink in hand, to put Grieg's *Peer Gynt* Suite on the CD. This time it was not the "Mountain King" that poured from the speakers, but the doleful laments of "Solveig's Song" and "Ase's Death." He slammed the switch off and gulped down the double shot. His body shuddered from the shock of the alcohol and the foreboding of a tragic end to a delicate love.

It had been a beautiful world for the better part of a year; then it started to slip away from them. She was in Silicon Valley, he at the Los Angeles headquarters. She became more deeply involved in the myriad of software applications for the KA9090, he withdrawing from technical matters to attend to the overall management of the rapidly expanding company. The usual gossip about a company love affair affected them both and made their liaisons more infrequent. It was the call from the secretary of Energy that brought them back together again, he remembered.

He'd objected to the whole thing from the beginning. It had seemed too complicated. But a call from the secretary was a command, so he, Herb Goldstein, and June dropped what they were doing and set off for Albuquerque the next day.

There, at the airport and to the east, Kane could see Sandia Mountain and its namesake, Sandia Base, shimmering in the morning sunshine. As they had circled to land, they had passed over the Jornada del Muerto, the Journey of Death, where the first nuclear weapon had been tested at the Alamogordo bombing range. To the north, he could make out the Sangre de Cristo Mountains, across the Rio Grande Valley from where it had all started, the Los Alamos Scientific Laboratory.

Visitors' badges and an escort were waiting for them at the security office. The others at the meeting seemed to know one another, and the meeting had half started when they were ushered in. The names meant little to Kane, but he could almost tell the affiliation automatically by the dress.

The Sandia director, as chairman, wore a dark gray suit, a checked shirt, and a necktie a little too wide; the other Sandias wore slacks and sport shirts that had seen better days. The scientist from the hill wore the standard Los Alamos uniform — corduroy slacks, string tie with silver turquoise clasp, boots from Sears, and a pipe. His counterpart from the Lawrence Livermore Laboratory had the Berkeley stamp with slacks and tweed jacket, loafers, tan shirt, and no necktie. The man from the Department of Energy wore the Washington summer special — rumpled tan poplin suit with blue shirt and yellow tie.

The major general from the Department of Defense was decked out in full regalia — four rows of ribbons with command pilots wings and two-star pins everywhere they could be attached. The major and the captain were similarly attired. Kane and Herb wore summer-weight business suits. June's skirt was conventional navy, the white blouse high with delicate lacy collar, and the cut of the jacket designed to call attention from her femininity. She tried to be inconspicuous, but it was difficult. Kane glanced from her to the general; he struggled to conceal a smile as he recalled Mark Twain's famous compliment on seeing a lovely lady: "I would rather sleep with that woman stark naked than with General Grant in full uniform."

They had been discussing a new concept for Permissive Action Links. There was a requirement in DOD for a new generation of PALs that could change their own codes periodically and automatically. "I understand, Dr. Kane, that your people are not cleared," said the chairman.

"I still have my 'top secret' and a 'Q,' but my associates haven't worked on government programs before and they have no clearances," said Kane.

The general frowned. "Couldn't you bring someone who was cleared?" he asked.

"Not if you're thinking of using the KA9090. The secretary told me that's why he wanted us here. These are the experts — Dr. Goldstein on hardware and Miss Malik on software."

"Is there any way we could get a couple of quick clearances?" the Sandia director asked.

The DOE man shook his head. "You might be able to push through a military 'secret,' but the nuclear clearance, the 'Q,' is impossible to speed up these days."

"I guess that kills us," said Herb. "June's father was born in Greece. His parents were naturalized citizens."

"And my mother's Lebanese," came from June.

"Yes," Herb continued. "And my parents snuck out of Germany in 1933, just ahead of the gas chamber."

"Okay," the chairman said. "Let's see how far we can get on an unclassified basis."

He explained that the President had become concerned about terrorists' stealing nuclear weapons. A group of scientists affiliated with the Nuclear Control Institute had written a report claiming that there ought to be PALs on all nuclear weapons. This had upset the Navy, which had refused to use them, based on their traditional concepts of self-sufficiency at sea. "You know the Navy doctrine," he said. "Never take rudder orders from shore."

The resultant flap had bucked the issue up to the National Security Council. They persuaded the President to order PALs on all naval weapons, including submarines, and started to worry about the confidentiality of the codes. The Security adviser had recommended investigation of a system in which the codes changed periodically and automatically; the council and the President thought the suggestion was great and signed off on it.

"Typical of the goddamned White House," Los Alamos said. "There's no room for the additional circuitry. These warheads are as full of shit as a Thanksgiving turkey."

The chairman was patient, stating that this was why they had convened the meeting. There was an additional requirement which had been designed into some PALs, but not all. The President did not want warheads disabled by someone making an error inserting the code, which could easily happen in a period of high tension. The circuitry should have allowance for two erroneous codes before disabling the warhead. There was also a political problem. The NATO allies were clamoring for access to the codes on missiles that were deployed in Europe, but American law required complete control of the warheads.

Livermore and Los Alamos groaned in unison. They argued that even if the circuitry could be designed for these additional requirements, anything added would affect reliability or lead to some other uncertainty. Furthermore, they pointed out that if the codes were made available to NATO, they might just as well be published in the *International Herald Tribune*.

The military men disputed the scientists' arguments. They had their orders and intended to carry them out.

"Look here," said the two stars, rising. "If you can't do it, we'll get someone else."

Los Alamos's smiling face emerged from a cloud of smoke. "Who you going to get, Gorbachev?"

"Knock it off, knock it off," ordered the Sandia director, slamming his fist on the table. "These are obviously tough problems. Arguing with each other is not going to help. Does anyone have any suggestions?"

"Excuse me," said June. "I do have something to suggest."

"There you go, gentlemen." Two-Stars sat down, leaned back in his chair, and spread his arms wide in a gesture of finality. "This little lady is going to take care of all your woes. She never heard of this problem before, and she's not even cleared, but she'll show you how easy it is. Go ahead, young lady, give us the good word."

"You have the floor, Miss Malik," said the director.

June smiled demurely at him, ignoring the major general. "Thank you, Mr. Chairman," she said. "I think that this would be a good application for a set of cryptographic systems called trapdoor functions."

"What the hell are trapdoor functions?" Two-Stars came back up in his seat.

"I've heard of them," said Livermore. "Shoot."

"I'm not sure how technical to get . . ." June began. "They constitute a very secure cryptographic system which has the added advantage that there are two keys to the code. One can be a public key, the other a private key.

"We start out with two prime numbers; let's call them $P$ and $Q$. They have to be pretty big numbers. I'll get back to that. We multiply these numbers and let's say we call the product $N$. We then subtract one from each of the original primes; we'll call the new numbers $R$ and $S$. Of course, having subtracted one from a prime number makes it no longer a prime, so we can find their greatest common denominator, or GCD. Then we multiply the GCD by the product of $R$ and $S$, and for reasons I won't bother to go into, this number can turn out to be the product of another pair of prime numbers, which we'll call $D$ and $E$. One of these numbers becomes your private key, $D$. The other number and $N$ make up your public key."

"What is this, some kind of a parlor game?" asked the major. "What's the point?"

"The point is that you can give out the public key to your NATO allies or, as someone said, publish it in the *Herald Trib*. But you keep control of the private key. You give that to the President or to the officer who follows him around with the 'football.' "

"So?"

"The 'so' is that if you make the numbers large enough, it is practically impossible to calculate the private key from the original primes, even though the public keys are known."

"Look, little lady," Two-Stars snapped back at her, "I may not have heard of your trapdoor functions, but I've been around cryptography long enough to know that any code other than a one-time tape is capable of being decoded if you work hard enough."

"Yes, sir, you are correct. But the beauty of this technique is that to calculate the private key you would have to factor one of the original primes, a process that would take over three million years on a Cray-One computer. That's why they call them trapdoor functions, because in cryptographic jargon, anyone following that path would effectively fall through a trapdoor into a large black hole."

Kane had a hard time to keep from chuckling. He could see the smiles on the faces of Livermore and Los Alamos. She had just opened up her own trapdoor for the general and he fell right into it, he thought.

"How come we've never heard of these things?" asked one of the Sandia scientists.

"Oh, the basic concept is an implementation of the process called the sieve of Eratosthenes, based on that ancient Greek's observation that the multiples of prime numbers cannot themselves be prime numbers." She was hitting her stride now, talking more aggressively and leaning forward to emphasize. She smiled. "Maybe it takes a young Greek to understand an old one. It's been in the public domain for a couple of years, but the CIA or somebody has been trying to classify it and they've managed to keep it out of the professional journals lately. If you can separate what you want from your classification and from theirs, I am sure we can do a job for you on an unclassified basis. That is, except for the private key," she added, almost as an afterthought.

"This sounds pretty complicated," said the director, his chin cupped in his hand. "How much memory would you need to store all this coding and change it automatically, say once every three months for five years?"

"The clock is no sweat. Four changes a year for five years is only twenty changes. That's nothing. It's storing the numbers and manipulating them that gets a little hairy. I think that we could do all the multiplication, the exponential functions, and the modulation with a couple of KA9090s. If so, and I can't be sure offhand, the memory becomes manageable. We should be able to squeeze the whole ball of wax onto a standard plug-in circuit board. What do you think, Herb?"

Goldstein had his head down and was scribbling on a lined yellow pad, looking up only to punch a few numbers into his pocket calculator. He scratched his head, paused for ten seconds to run through the calculations again mentally, then shook his head, an admiring grin on his face. "You may have something."

"I hate to say this in front of my boss, since he invented the damned thing, but you couldn't touch this problem without the KA9090. You'd run into a dozen microprocessors; the interconnections and resultant memory would get you into minicomputer size. I don't know anything about your warheads, but I doubt that you'd have that much space sitting around empty."

"Amen," said Los Alamos, tapping his pipe into an ashtray.

The director was delighted. "Let's see if I understand what you are proposing. Miss Malik is saying that circuits can be designed, using the KA9090 chip, to set up Permissive Action Links which will have two codes, one public and one private, and that the private code, using trapdoor functions, will be, to all practical purposes, undecodable by an intruder. Miss Malik is also saying that the codes, public and private, can be programmed to change automatically every three months for five years, and will fit into a standard plug-in circuit board, the whole thing being mil spec'd of course."

"Not so fast," Kane admonished. "We are already committed out the kazoo for commercial applications of the KA9090. I just can't go repudiating contracts. The best we can give you is a set of electrical signals which are generated if there are more than two incorrect input codes. Somebody else will have to take it from there."

"We can take care of that," said Livermore. Los Alamos raised his pipe in agreement, and the Sandia scientists nodded assent.

"How do you want to proceed?" asked the director.

"I'm not sure I want to proceed at all," replied Kane. "Under the new procurement rules, I'll lose money. Well, I'll tell you what I'll do. Give me a couple of hundred thousand for a study contract, and I'll come back in a month and tell you what I can commit to."

The tan poplin suit grinned. "You are both generous and resourceful, Dr. Kane. Make it three weeks and you've got a deal."

"Sold."

*

It was much later when the question came.

They hadn't been able to avoid the dinner invitation. Two-Star and his aides had pleaded official business, and for Goldstein, there was a brother in town whose twin daughters had a birthday. Kane had told the Sandia group that he and June loved real Mexican food and that they agreed the Old Town in Albuquerque was better than anything in Mexico City. The hot food hadn't set well with either of them, but what could he do with adjacent rooms and Herb gone for the night. He sensed that she was groping for an excuse to say no, but she had made the mistake of telling him that she was going swimming in the morning, and a sudden headache would have been too obvious.

Room service had closed at ten, so she uncapped a couple of miniatures of an unnamed bourbon from the room refrigerator and hacked out enough ice from the tiny half-filled ice trays to take the tepid taste out of the whiskey.

"To Mexican food."

"Olé!"

The lovemaking had been as uninspiring as the conversation, both realizing that it had been the least satisfying since they had met.

"Goddamned twin beds," he said.

"I'll move."

"No, not yet. What the hell ever made you come up with that idea, right out of a clear blue sky? It was a damned good one, but it must have taken a lot of thought and you never mentioned it to Herb or me before you sprung it on us at the meeting. They would have given us a production contract on the spot. Then we would have lost our ass or gone to jail for defrauding the government, depending on whether we were lucky or not. Those things look good, but they are lose-lose situations. I barely had a chance to switch the thing to a study contract, to give us a little breathing spell."

She made no apology. "I got thinking about it when you called me. You remember, I did my thesis on trapdoors, so it was a natural line of thought."

"But you're such a goddamned peacenik. When you're not

bellyaching on women's rights, you're spouting off on nuclear freezes and test bans and all that kind of crap. Now you're suddenly in the middle of one of the biggest problems in U.S. military policy. It doesn't wash."

"But, honey, this isn't an idea to use nuclear weapons. It's to prevent people from using them when they shouldn't. It's a completely different thing. Let's forget about it. I'm going over to the other bed."

He was already sinking into sleep and didn't answer. When she tripped on the bedclothes as she left his side, her soft Lebanese-accented Arabic curse hardly registered on the memory cells of his unconscious.

Pyotr was lost in thought as he and Anna were finishing breakfast.

"More tea?" she asked as she rose to turn on the radio and close the draperies, sensing that he had something on his mind which required privacy from listening microphones or watching cameras.

"*Pazhaloosta,*" he replied. "A half cup," he continued, switching to English. "I'm still thinking about that Arab the other night."

"It was a tiny incident, Petroshka. He set out to deliberately confront Appleby without any provocation, but the Americans seem to be used to that. It didn't bother Brad as much as it bothers you. I just pulled you away before he made a scene. I don't understand what's important about him."

She poured the tea, placed the teapot on the counter, and turned down the heat under the kettle. Returning to the table, she stooped to pick a bread crumb off the floor, then leaned over to kiss him lightly on the cheek. "Why don't you ask Brad. Aren't you having lunch with him again today?"

Later, as he entered the screen room, Rostov was greeted by his deputy and three intelligence officers. The deputy was all business, professional KGB, selected by the General Secretary to offset criticism of Rostov's unusual assignment by the system. "We find additional buildup of PLO troops on the Israeli border. The buildup is disturbing in itself, but the makeup of the deployment is perplexing."

The deputy explained that there was no heavy artillery and no tanks, nothing to support an attack. There were four regiments, all drawn from reserves, not a combat company in the whole contingent. So far as his people could determine, there were no indications of liaison with air units for close-in air support. In fact, the PLO army and the regular Lebanese armed forces seemed to be ignoring the buildup completely — no leaves canceled, no supply buildup. It almost seemed like a covert operation, but he couldn't see how they could ever expect to send four lightly armed covert regiments into Israel without being discovered and wiped out overnight.

"What do the other countries have to say about this — the Syrians, the Iranians, the Iraqis?"

They hadn't talked to them. They discovered it only through some very good intelligence work in Beirut. They were watching a detachment of electronic counterintelligence specialists there to pick up some of their techniques when they suddenly disappeared. This detachment had never left the city before, so they thought it was pretty peculiar. One of them apparently sneaked out a letter to his girlfriend explaining his absence. He didn't say where he was, but they were able to identify the postmark. They located the detachment but they disappeared again. However, in following the trail, they discovered the four regiments. He doubted that any of the other intelligence services had noticed them. Moscow decided not to mention it to anyone else until they could find out some more about the activity.

"Fascinating, Boris Alexandrovitch, but it seems pretty remote to us here." Rostov turned to the briefing officer from the Far East desk. "What's new in the People's Republic?"

"Deng Xiaoping's man seems to be moving too fast for his own good. Beijing is swarming with Europeans and Americans and Japanese, but nothing seems to be happening. The Chinese want their partners to loan them money, but the capitalists are not about to do that. Everything is at a standstill. The Chinese bureaucracy is enjoying the situation."

Rostov's mind wandered while the specialist rattled on. The PLO buildup did not make sense to him. Rostov had found out that the new Lebanese president was the Greek athlete he had beaten in the 1948 Olympics. Although that connection seemed coincidental, it did give him a further interest in Lebanese developments. Al Emir must know about the PLO activities, but Russian intelligence had not yet been able to establish the direct link between him and the PLO. He suddenly realized that the specialist had stopped talking.

"Thank you, Captain." He concluded the briefing. "Anything in South America or Central America?"

The deputy decided to give the briefing himself. "The Americans averted the crisis of the finance ministers for a couple of days in their usual manner, by offering to pour in some more money, but we don't think that's going to work. There are a lot of objections in the Congress."

"Have you had time to collect anything on the Arab, Assim Mahmoud?" he asked casually.

"A little. He's a Syrian, a hard-liner, and close to Assad. We talked directly to Assad's chief of staff. Part of the compromise which settled on al Emir as president of Lebanon was that he accept staff assistance from other countries, particularly Iran and Syria. The agreement is that they will be given specific, responsible assignments in the new government. Al Emir is not too happy with the arrangement. The chief of staff didn't say so directly, but reading between the lines, we believe that Mahmoud and al Emir didn't hit it off well together. Al Emir has shipped him off to New York to be his special representative to the United Nations, probably to get him out of his way."

"I judge that Mahmoud is not too happy with the assignment."

"No, and he's been complaining that he has virtually nothing to do. It appears that he's right. We've monitored his phone calls for a week. There is practically no local traffic. In fact, he had only one outgoing call yesterday. That was to an American diplomat. He talked to the man's secretary, but she brushed him off and the call was not returned."

"Who was the diplomat?"

The deputy looked at Rostov intently.

"Bradford Appleby."

# 7

SCHULTZ RECOGNIZED THE FACE IMMEDIATELY as the woman stopped hesitantly in the middle of the sidewalk, oblivious to the bumping of the crowd, lips moving to pronounce the unfamiliar letters on the sign. It was an eager, trusting face, pale with the Nevada sunburn faded, fragile in contrast with the stolid features of the Germans eddying around her.

Penelope did not have to exert herself to look like an American tourist as she walked through the sidewalk café toward the rear of the Bavarische Brauhaus on Friedenstrasse in the central district of Munich. The heavy shoes, the coarse woolen knee socks framing her knees from below, the Bermuda-length khaki shorts reaching down to cover her thighs, prepared his upward-sweeping gaze for the Abercrombie and Fitch leather jacket and the jaunty red-feathered Bavarian fedora, which sat askew on her blond hair. At an American costume party, she would have looked attractive, but here the exaggerated outfit looked sufficiently out of place to enhance the role she was playing. A heavy Minolta camera slung from her shoulder and a large gunnysack handbag gave her whole body a tilt as her eyes, adapting to the dark, sought out Schultz through oversize mirrored sunglasses.

He came as close as he could to having a pang of conscience

when he recognized her naiveté. He was accustomed to strong adversaries, not people like those attracted to Makepeace, whose innocence and gullibility prepared them poorly for the harsh world they had entered. Her very vulnerability attracted him to her in a way he had never felt before. Maybe he shouldn't have made the first contact with her. Maybe he should have waited for Foster Martin. Maybe if he could get her away from Foster Martin . . .

It wasn't exactly a James Bond entrance as she stumbled into a small coffee table, sending a near empty beer bottle skidding across the shiny surface, just missing an annoyed couple as it crashed to the floor. Her *"Verzeihung, bitte"* was lost in the confusion as she backed into a buxom waitress carrying three large steins of lager in each arm. The waitress, with the long experience of a broken-field runner, anticipated the action. She leaned to the left and stuck out her right hip, bouncing Penelope off onto a stanchion as she protected the six glasses without ruffling their heads, not looking back as she proceeded imperturbably on her way.

The rendezvous was to have been covert. The red feather in Penelope's hat was to signal that all was clear and she was not being followed. Schultz's signals were with ashtrays. A single ashtray meant "Go away, I'm being watched." Two ashtrays stacked meant "Caution." Three ashtrays stacked with two marks in the top one meant that all was clear and she could proceed to the table. Schultz was sitting quietly sipping a Pernod with three ashtrays and two marks prominently displayed in front of him. He rose quickly, strode across the tiled floor, and caught her arm. Steadying her, he half dragged, half steered her across the floor and onto a hard wooden chair, conscious of the amused stares of the patrons.

"For God's sake, you couldn't have been more conspicuous with a brass band," he muttered in a low voice, his indignation burying all thoughts of sympathy. "Let's get out of here. Turn to the right as you go out the door. On the corner there is a rathskeller. Go down and take a small table in the back of the room. I'll join you in about ten minutes."

Penelope, blushing with frustration, turned and ran out of the café, the camera and handbag cutting a swath through the patrons as she departed.

Schultz again sat at the table until the stares had disappeared. Then he lit a cigarette, took a few puffs, and reached into his pocket to find coins to pay the bill before strolling off in the opposite direction. After two blocks, he crossed the street, walked back as far as the rathskeller, then crossed again and entered the building.

Subdued, she was sitting at a small table in a dark corner at the rear of the bar. A waitress was flirting with a customer near the entrance, but they were not within hearing distance.

"I'm sorry, Ludwig. Coming out of the bright sun —"

"Penelope, this is serious business. You are not in the United States now, waving flags for television. You are in a foreign country where you are not under the protection of your American laws. You will have to be careful about exposing your actions to people who might be unsympathetic to our cause. You have been in touch with Eva Spengler?"

"Yes, I've spoken with her on the telephone. Foster Martin arrives tomorrow. We decided it would be better to travel separately. Foster and Eva and I will meet on the day after tomorrow."

Schultz looked up, wary. "You have not spoken to Eva about me?"

She raised her hands to reassure him. "As you requested, no. I don't understand why not. Didn't you work with Eva and her Greens Party when they organized the first nuclear protests?"

He explained to her that in West Germany, things were different now. Eva had been a radical then, but the Greens were badly beaten in the election when they protested the NATO decision to base Cruise missiles and Tomahawks in Europe. The opposition propagandists labeled them Soviet sympathizers. Now they were trying to project a milder image, a nonviolent image, one which would identify the interests of the Federal Republic as separate from those of NATO or the Soviet Union.

"How does that affect their relations with you?"

"Oh, it doesn't really." He lied. He lit a cigarette and looked toward the front of the room. The waitress had finished talking and was glancing inquiringly in their direction. He beckoned her over and ordered two coffees. He was silent until the coffees arrived, trying to decide what to say to Penelope.

"I'm a nonviolent person, Penelope. But Interpol and the CIA object to my previous associations in Italy and Spain and have falsely accused me of being a terrorist. I'm not. I'm merely a freedom fighter like you and Foster. But the capitalist propagandists have been successful in propagating their lies. If I play too prominent a role in this protest, the Greens Party is afraid of receiving bad publicity. I will be there. But don't mention it to Eva. She has enough problems on her mind, poor soul."

Schultz knew that Eva Spengler was a clever politician, using these protests to strengthen her party's position for the next election. She would not object to his participation when the time came, but she would be suspicious of his attempts to become involved in the early planning. Much better that he should work through the American Makepeace group. If questioned, he could pass off his role as that of an old friend and interpreter.

"You're so thoughtful, Ludwig," Penelope said, smiling up at him. "When shall we get together again?" She laughed. "The next time I'll try not to be so clumsy."

He felt confident that she would not divulge his involvement to Eva Spengler. His next move would be after their meeting.

"I'll leave a note in your mailbox. The usual code." He motioned to the waitress for the check, then, to his own surprise, stood up to kiss her hand before she carefully picked her way out of the restaurant, this time unnoticed by the patrons.

Three days later, Schultz met with Penelope and Foster Martin at the Bavarische Brauhaus. They came in separately, first Penelope, in the identical outfit she had worn on the previous visit, then Foster, matching her completely. They reminded Schultz of the boy and girl in the cuckoo clock. They advanced together, red feathers prominent, toward the rear of the restaurant, circling the table at which Schultz sat and surreptitiously eyeing the three ashtrays with the two marks in the top one. They sat down on either side of him and proceeded to express their mutual surprise at running into their old friend in this out-of-the-way restaurant in a strange city. After the appropriate philosophical comments on the smallness of the world and a dialogue with the waiter as to the variety of their coffee, they lowered their voices and adopted a conspiratorial tone.

"We're all here, all six of us," said Foster, showing great satisfaction at this logistical achievement.

"Have you talked to Eva yet?" Schultz asked, getting to the point. These amateurs made him nervous.

Penelope took over. "Yes. Foster and I met with her yesterday." She explained that Eva wanted them to be particularly prominent in this demonstration to point out to the world the firm linkage between the American and West German peace movements. She wanted little advance publicity, but had arranged through her own public affairs department that tapes would be prepared for the following day's TV. She would have at least fifty experienced demonstrators available on the day of the demonstration. There would be a number of strong speeches protesting missile deployment in the area, so she would be assured of plenty of television coverage. Her game plan was to stress local fears rather than national fears so that she could bring out the crowds from the surrounding towns and villages.

"You were very perceptive in warning us not to mention your name," said Foster. "She wants no connection with either Soviet sympathizers or any group proposing forceful means of overthrowing the government." He looked apprehensively at Schultz, embarrassed to have to tell him this. "We believe that people like you have gotten a bum rap from the media, but we can understand her concern. I hope you won't let this opposition bother you, Ludwig. We believe you are very important to the cause and would hate to lose you. After all, you have been part of the system. We know you worked at Eniwetok and Bikini in the days of atmospheric testing and that you spent a year at the Nevada Test Site. There are very few people active in this movement who have seen a nuclear weapon explode in the open, who can testify at first hand to the horrors and destruction they cause. Stay with us, please."

Schultz had difficulty maintaining an impassive face. If they ever suspected . . . Yes, he knew the horror and destruction nuclear weapons could cause; he knew it better than these innocent protestors would ever understand. There flashed across his mind the vision of Braun's legs disappearing from sight into the hole in the tower cab, frantically pumping like a fish out of water in a vain attempt to reach the firing cables only a few feet from his grasp. He could still sense the flash that had almost blinded him, that had burned the spots on his retina, that had caused the cataracts which would leave him sightless within a decade. That's why he needed money — to support himself in that helpless old age. Strange that no one had ever mentioned, had ever inquired about, Braun or Wagner or Miller or Kramer. That was the fate of undercover operators. When they went under cover, they were already dead as far as the rest of the world was concerned. If he disintegrated tomorrow, who would remember, who would mourn? The bile built in his throat and his stomach knotted in anger that the Communists and capitalists should possess this enormous power. He didn't know what Emir would do with the weapon, but he knew what he was doing was right.

But it was not easy for Schultz to play the role of a martyr. He managed a weak smile and bowed his head modestly. "You won't lose me," he told the Americans. "I'll stay with you."

Schultz obtained his primary logistical information from the Makepeace group. He knew the background well. Through the 1970s the United States had deployed a variety of short-range, tactical nuclear devices throughout Western Europe. They ranged from land mines to large howitzers. Over the years they had become obsolete.

When the Soviet Union began its accelerated conventional force buildup, the NATO countries were reluctant to assign the necessary resources to match it. Instead, they called upon the United States to deploy new Cruise and Tomahawk tactical nuclear missiles. During the Carter administration, the United

States built the devices but would not make the decision to deploy them. The Reagan administration decided to deploy the missiles complete with propulsion systems, but held back the nuclear warheads. After the Intermediate Nuclear Force treaty was negotiated, the NATO countries put renewed pressure on the deployment of tactical warheads, which the new President authorized.

Since the main bodies of the missiles and all their support structure were already in place, the warheads could be transported without attracting much attention. Schultz's plan depended on this. Each warhead fitted into a two-foot-diameter canister four feet long, weighing only seventy pounds, easily transportable in an armored van. Each canister was outfitted with handles so it could be carried by two men without cranes. The canister was sealed and tamperproofed, with an alarm system that would be triggered by an attempt at illegal entry. Kane Industries had done their job well, stepping up their development and production to meet the accelerated schedules. The warhead itself contained the latest in Permissive Action Links, the design by which the detonating system was rendered inoperative if an improper code was entered more than twice. The code changed automatically every ninety days and was matched to a master code contained in the President's "football." Each shipment was accompanied by four armed military officers, two to carry the canisters and two to stand guard.

The deployment of the warheads had gone without incident. Of 162 warheads to be deployed, 121 were already in place, with the remaining 41 to be installed in the next ninety days. Schultz knew that this information was classified "top secret," but with warheads being deployed in Holland, Belgium, Italy, and Turkey in addition to England and West Germany, security was a farce. In Holland and Belgium there was so much opposition to deployment and so many intelligence leaks that the basic information could be obtained by an inquisitive high school student and was well known to every terrorist and protest group throughout Europe.

What was kept well under control was the time and location

of each deployment. The warheads left the United States one at a time by special military transport under continuous fighter support. The crews were given sealed orders not to be opened until the aircraft was in flight. But someone always has to have advance information. Since the shipments had to be met and transported on the ground, NATO and the defense officials of the receiving country had prior notification. Eva Spengler, through her Greens Party sympathizers, had access to the deployment plans and schedules well in advance. She even joked to her campaign manager that if she only knew what to do with it, she would steal one of the damned things. Eva's plan was simple. She would conduct a demonstration while a deployment was in progress.

The particular shipment would arrive at the Munich airport about five in the evening. It would be met by a special van similar to a Brink's truck with extra armor around the cab and the back. It would be driven by an Army master sergeant stationed in Germany. Four U.S. military officers would accompany the warhead from the assembly area in Amarillo, Texas, to final storage in the vault. Two Federal Republic armored vans would also meet the shipment, one to precede the nuclear van and one to follow it. The convoy was scheduled to proceed from the airport to the storage site in a remote area thirty miles from Munich between Ingolstadt and Landshut.

Schultz picked up the details of Eva's plan in successive daily meetings with Penelope. Foster came to the first one but was concerned primarily with overall publicity plans, leaving the specifics to her. She loved the secret meetings and felt so important delivering the information to Schultz that she never once questioned him about why he needed it.

Eva had selected this specific deployment with great care. She did not want the authorities to be aware of the demonstration more than a day or two in advance. The site was not far from three major cities. Munich was thirty miles away, Nuremberg forty miles, and Stuttgart only seventy miles distant. Her headquarters was in Munich, with subgroups in the other two cities. Rallies were scheduled the night before in Ingolstadt and Landshut.

She had picked the month of May for its good weather and because it was the campaign kickoff time for the September primaries. The protest would be completely nonviolent, but she wanted to embarrass the authorities. She felt that she could draw at least five thousand people. The police and local civil authorities always took a couple of days to react to a suspected protest, and since it would erupt simultaneously in Nuremberg, Stuttgart, and Munich, they would not be able to pinpoint the location. Few local authorities knew the location of the storage site. This absence of liaison between local authorities and the NATO command was the essence of her surprise. The NATO people would not pay much attention to local protests. Besides, the missiles were already in place, and they would not expect that the transportation of a warhead would attract attention. Indeed, that was the main reason for keeping the convoy small.

Eva's main plan was to bring the shipment to a halt for several hours, long enough to get good press and TV coverage. She would do this through sheer force of numbers. With five thousand protestors, they should easily be able to bring three armored vehicles to a halt. She was sure that the German soldiers would not fire on unarmed civilians from the local community. Besides, they knew that the Americans were ordered not to leave their van under any circumstances.

Schultz was feeling very good about his plans as he checked his post office box for the last time. Leaving the building, he was accidentally jostled from behind as he entered the revolving door. He stumbled into a section already occupied by a woman he immediately recognized. The two were spun around together, not catching their balance until they were deposited on the slippery top step of the rain-swept entranceway. The woman turned around angrily.

"Schultz," she shouted. "What are you doing in Munich?"

He tried to pass it off. "Everyone has to be someplace, Eva."

"They told me you were in Milan," she said. "I don't want you here."

Schultz moved to descend the steps. "As you say in your speeches, Eva, it's a free country. I have every right to be where I want. I might ask you the same thing."

"You know very well why I am here. I want you out of this city by tomorrow morning." He saw her motion with her closed umbrella to a man standing at the bottom of the steps. "If you're still here, I'll have you picked up on suspicion of subversion; you'll be a month getting out of jail, if you ever do."

Schultz cursed her, turned up his coat collar against the rain, and dashed down the steps. As he crossed the street, he could see the man following him, insolently making little attempt at concealment.

He was shattered. He knew that Spengler could have him picked up by the police and detained indefinitely, especially since all he had with him was forged identification. For a person who had been on the run most of his life, the man following him was no problem. A dash through a building, a short bus ride, and two taxi rides did the trick. He was sure he would have no difficulty evading the police for a few days, but he dared not make contact with Penelope again. Spengler might make the connection and have her followed. He left Penelope a message saying that he had to go away for a short time but would be at the demonstration and meet her afterward. Then he turned his attention to his accomplices.

He had planned one dry run for just before the events started. He felt that he must still take the chance, so he called in his messages. He and Otto Drucker paced the floor of his apartment nervously when the rendezvous hour approached, cigarettes littering the ashtrays from the thin man's chain-smoking. They were relieved when Karl Brandt, the van driver, arrived ten minutes early.

The knife scar on his face and the multiple tattoos on his arms gave Brandt a menacing appearance, but his demeanor was relaxed and pleasant, almost nonchalant. He went to the refrigerator uninvited, poured himself a glass of beer, and gave strong opinions on the forthcoming championship boxing match as he threw his leg over the arm of his chair and sipped the brew. When the two men who would serve as guards, Adolf Wald and Leonard Kellman, came in, he offered cigars all around. "The real stuff. Picked them up from a Cuban in the can," he explained. "He was a little guy. Needed protection. Still have a couple of boxes."

They waited three quarters of an hour for Heinrich and Hermann, the twins, who were to carry the package. Drucker was so nervous that he couldn't finish his cigar. Then there was a commotion in the hallway and the two massive brutes burst through the door, dead drunk. They were also dead broke as it turned out, having spent all their advance on liquor. Schultz was furious. What more could happen to his beautifully conceived plan? The twins demanded more money and when Schultz refused, Heinrich dealt him a blow on the side of the face that sent him sprawling, half unconscious, across the room. Heinrich stood swaying, ready to take on all comers. The next thing he knew the beer hit him in the eyes, blinding him momentarily. Brandt came out of the chair like a cat. He swung the empty beer bottle against the back of the other brother's head, felling him on the spot. Before Heinrich could clear his eyes, he felt his arm twisted painfully in back of him and a knife point at his neck. The others stood without moving. Brandt kicked the fallen Hermann and waited for him to recover from the blow. Schultz, in the meanwhile, had gotten to his feet. There was silence.

Brandt looked around calmly. The only sign of emotion was the pulsing of the purple scar that ran from the tip of his chin along the lower jaw and up behind his right ear to disappear in the close-cropped hair line.

"*Sie Schwein*," he said to the twins. "There's a hundred thousand marks in this thing for me, and you *dummkopfs* are not going to spoil it. If you do, you're going to end up in the gutter with your throats slit ear to ear. Understand?"

The twins nodded dully. Brandt asked Schultz to repeat his instructions to the group and to give the twins another ten marks each. "Not enough to get drunk on," he warned. They took the money and left.

"Do you think they'll give us trouble?" Wald asked. "Why don't we get rid of them right now."

Schultz's head had cleared. He was back in command. "No, we need assistance. It's too late to get anyone else. They're not very smart, but they understand power. I've checked them out. They'll be meek as lambs when they sober up." He turned to Brandt. "Thanks for the help, Karl," he said.

"Nothing to it, boss." The pulsing in Brandt's scar had subsided. "I need another beer. I never did finish the first one."

# 8

---

THE PROTEST BEGAN ON SCHEDULE WITH GENER-
al anti-nuclear speeches in Hamburg, Bonn, and Frankfurt.
These did not pinpoint any specific demonstration area, they
merely protested deployment in general. The kickoff speech was
given by Eva Spengler from the Munich town hall. There had
been a high-power publicity buildup for several days previous,
with media ads, television and radio spots, leaflets, and minor
demonstrations in public parks and meeting places. Schultz
paid no attention to the balmy spring evening with the almost
full moon, which lent a festive air to the crowd pouring into the
town hall. His face was still sore from the blow delivered him
by Heinrich. He had sent Drucker to check on the twins the
next day. Otto found them docile and penitent as predicted,
vowing not to have another drink until the exercise was over.
Schultz felt better about them, but he was still wary of running
into Eva or the Makepeace people. He stood behind a column
on the steps to the building, where he could scan all three
entrances without being observed. His stomach muscles relaxed
when he saw the two red feathers in the hats of Penelope and
Foster standing out in the crowd as they pushed their way into
the center entrance fifteen minutes before the speeches were
scheduled to begin.

Eva was a handsome woman, tall, well-sculpted, her blond

hair pulled neatly back into a bun. Her blue eyes and quick smile attested to her mother's Irish ancestry, while her strong brow gave evidence of her father's Prussian forebears. The combination of aggressiveness and wit had served her well in life. She had been an antiwar activist for almost as long as she could remember, starting in high school and continuing as editor of the student newspaper at the University of Berlin. She was not old enough to remember the war, but she was quite conscious of the struggles of a divided Germany. Her four years in Berlin were enough to convince her of the superiority of the capitalist democracy over its Communist neighbor on the other side of the wall. For this, Schultz considered her and her party another of his enemies and was prepared to use her to his advantage.

"My countrymen and countrywomen," she began softly and smiled. "Our nation has been a battleground for two major wars in this century. The causes of those wars are behind us, buried with the bodies of the dead and healed with the scars of the living. We have become a nation at peace with our neighbors to the west and tolerant of our brothers and sisters to the east.

"We, in our Greens Party, have no quarrel with the United States or our NATO allies. They are acting in their own interests and think they are acting in ours.

"There are more than fifty thousand nuclear warheads in the world. Half of them face us with the morning sun, threatening that each day will be our last. Half of them reassure us with the setting sun, consoling that they will protect us in the hours of darkness. Any one of these weapons would wipe out all of us here tonight. A single weapon detonated on the storage site at Landsruhe would wipe out the neighboring towns of Ingolstadt and Landshut. That site is only forty kilometers from this hall. A nuclear explosion from an enemy at war, deliberate from the terrorists who are in our midst, or accidental as in the Chernobyl reactor, could send us deadly fallout, with burns and lesions and marrow-sucking cancer the result."

Schultz entered just before the speeches started and made himself inconspicuous in a corner of the hall. He could see

Penelope, seated in the front row with a "No Nukes" placard hand-lettered in English. She looked around from time to time, perhaps expecting to see him.

"*Hund! Schwein!* Communist! Marxist! Bloody Russian-lover! Bring back Stalin! Leave us defenseless!" The shouts came from the back of the hall.

A scuffle broke out. Two guards came rushing over, broke it up, and led the shouting man, kicking and biting, from the hall. Schultz recognized him as one of the Baderhofs whom he had separately recruited to agitate at the rallies in Nuremberg and Stuttgart as well as this one in Munich.

Several of the Makepeace group stood up in front, waving their placards. "Go on, Eva, go on. Don't let them shout you down."

Eva paused and held up her arms for silence. "They tell us that these missiles are here for our protection. What kind of protection is this, that we can be obliterated by our enemies or by our well-meaning friends? Friends? No friend would emplace these monstrous horrors in our midst. The missiles are for their protection, not for ours, placed here to localize a conflict, so that our allies can sleep peacefully in their beds in London and Paris and New York and San Francisco."

Another scuffle broke out. This time the police had to use nightsticks to break it up and were pelted with fruit and beer bottles. Someone threw a pie onto the stage; it narrowly missed Eva and landed against the white background, where it seeped down in syrupy rivulets for all the television audience to see. The crowd was murmuring. It became more difficult to hear.

"The Americans will save their own shores at any cost. Remember this village in Vietnam." The television cameras swiveled as she pointed to a large black and white photograph of a burning, smoking rubble of tropical tents and huts, with arms and legs and bodies grotesquely protruding from the debris, no living soul in sight. " 'We had to destroy the village to save it' was the callous explanation from the American officer who ordered the destruction. Will we be destroyed to be saved? Never! We want no part of this salvation."

The crowd was at a fever pitch. Schultz could feel the pulse of the counterprotest. His agitators had done their job well. Tomorrow's events would be exciting and well attended. Eva's voice rose to a shout. Arguments broke out all over, many no longer listening to the speaker. Foster Martin was calling for quiet, his arm around Penelope to shield her from the bottles and cups and cartons that were flying in all directions. Schultz felt it was time to escalate to the next stage. He reached into his coat pocket and balanced a tear gas bomb in the palm of his hand.

Eva was screaming, trying to get in her last remarks before pandemonium broke out. She spoke primarily for the television cameras. The noise was too loud in the hall.

"Join us, my friends. March tomorrow, bring your automobiles, take your school buses, your bicycles, yes, your wheelchairs. Come with us to Landsruhe, come from Munich, from Nuremberg, from Stuttgart, from Ingolstadt, from Landshut, from your villages, from your farms, from wherever you are. March, march peacefully so that the world will know that we want this canker removed from our breast, this smoldering tumor torn from our innards, that we may live in peace among ourselves."

Schultz tossed the tear gas bomb high into the air, landing it in the middle of the crowd, momentarily encompassing the protestors in an impenetrable cloud of vapor. As the cloud dispersed, he could see men and women screaming and flailing, digging at their eyes, shielding their mouths and noses against the noxious vapor.

"The police," Schultz shouted, tears pouring from his own eyes. "They're tear-gassing us. Pigs, pigs," he yelled as he slipped out a side entrance, ducking down a back alley to evade the riot squads pouring toward the hall with engines racing, blue lights flashing, and sirens screaming shrilly into the night.

The riot had its effect. Everyone in the region was aware of the demonstration scheduled for the next day. And they came. They came on motorcycles, in automobiles, in vans, in trucks, on bicycles, on mopeds, on farm wagons pulled by stout Bavarian horses, and one or two on tractors. From the neighboring farms and villages, whole families came on foot, carrying sausages, thick loaves of pumpernickel bread, and half kegs of beer on their shoulders. They came in suits, they came in sweaters, they came in workclothes identifying them as painters or artisans or students or farmers or housewives or clerks. They came in faded uniforms from bygone wars, in Tyrolean dress from the mountains, in clerical collars and nunnery habits, and in the hats of Hasidic Jews. And they came for many reasons. The peace groups, led by Foster Martin and his Americans, came as professional demonstrators, from Holland and Belgium and Denmark and Sweden, greeting one another warmly like old friends as athletic competitors from international ski or soccer matches do.

The politicians from the Greens Party stuck together for the media and the television cameras, alert to any possible exposure and well aware of the importance of this demonstration to their broader political aspirations. The thieves came to pick pockets or to rob, the agitators came to cause trouble and incite to riot, the local farmers came for relief from boredom, the students came for excitement, but most came from curiosity and good fun, as they would come to a county fair.

The weather was ideal, a soft, sunny May day, warm enough for shirt sleeves and dresses, but not too hot for hiking and bicycling. The apple trees were in bloom, the rhododendrons still held some color, and late-blooming tulips framed the foundations of the stuccoed farm buildings and town cottages. There was an aroma of picnic and holiday in the air. Schoolteachers, unable to keep the attention of their students, finally gave up in midmorning to declare a half holiday, satisfying their own curiosity by marching along with the excited throngs.

Schultz, looking at the driver beside him in the front seat of the van, could not keep his eyes from the tattoos and knife scars on Karl Brandt's face and arms. The facial scar was not so prominent now. But there was another that ran the length of his forearm, which was also covered with tattoos. Just below the elbow the raised legs of a woman on her back straddled the scar to give it the crude appearance of a woman's genitals with a flowery FÜCKEN inscribed below the buttocks. A man to be reckoned with, Schultz thought, reflecting on his handling of the drunken twins. The other five were in the back, dressed in white surgical gowns, playing cards as best they could, while the khaki-colored vehicle with the Red Cross markings made its way in the congested traffic of the autobahn.

Schultz had started off at noon. He needed plenty of time. It took him an hour and a half to inch through the crowds to the main gate in the barbed wire fenced storage site. He found a parking spot in a grove of trees about five hundred yards from the gate and settled down to wait. He could see the television trucks two hundred yards away, one for each major network, studded like porcupines with shortwave antennas and with the familiar aluminum concave dish of the satellite antenna pointed skyward like some shallow bowl beseeching manna from heaven.

Carpenters were finishing a makeshift but sturdy platform big enough to hold about forty people, electronic technicians were putting the finishing touches on a public address system with large powerful-looking speakers, and a crew of electricians were trying to move their truck through the crowd after installing floodlights on tall aluminum tripods. Schultz could see the carpenters' hammers flashing in the sun; the fractional-second interval between the sight and the sound of the hammers was a reminder that he was still some distance from the center of action. He decided to move a little closer. After half an hour of horn blowing and shouting, they had moved only fifty yards against the flow of the crowd, so they pulled over to the side of the road to relax and watch the show. About four o'clock, a three-man brass band, dressed in traditional Bavarian jackets, shorts, and long hose, climbed onto the tower and began to play folk songs and martial music to the delight of the crowd. Schultz could see that the demonstration was well organized. Eva knew her business.

Eva Spengler arrived early to get exposure for the six o'clock news. She made a short speech, expressing her gratitude to the people for the size of the demonstration and emphasizing the peaceful nature of the protest. The crowd was now large enough that it was difficult to hear her words even with the powerful public address system she had had installed. There was some polite pushing and shoving; a few steins of beer were spilled to the amusement of the good-natured onlookers.

Schultz got out of the van and opened the rear door. Heinrich and Hermann were sleeping on the benches, the others playing a desultory game of cards on the floor. They seemed calm, except for Adolf Wald, one of the dishonorably discharged soldiers he had recruited as a guard. Wald was noticeably jittery, complaining about the stuffiness in the van and the inactivity. He wanted to get out and move around, but Schultz vetoed the idea, saying that they were going to move the vehicle another hundred yards closer to the platform. His friend Drucker glanced at Schultz with an "I'll keep an eye on him" look. Schultz closed the rear door, securing it from the outside as a precaution.

"How are they holding out?" asked Brandt when Schultz slid back into the front seat.

"Okay. You sure put the fear of God into the twins. They'll do as they're told. Wald is feeling the strain. Otto will keep an eye on him."

"He's been complaining about money when you are not listening. He thinks we can get more if we put up a united front against you," said Brandt.

"I know. Otto has warned me. We'll have to keep an eye on him. One slip and none of us will get anything. Let's move a little closer. There's another grove of trees up about a hundred yards."

"Will do, boss," said Brandt, starting the engine and shifting into low-low to inch against the thickening mass of demonstrators.

The guards at the gate near the barbed wire fence were getting nervous. A sergeant came out of the compound behind the fence and detailed five additional soldiers to the four on duty. The guards were young West German conscripts barely out of their teens, awed by their NATO commanders, cowed by the enormous power and size of the missiles they guarded, and clearly uncomfortable with the rifles they carried on their shoulders as they paraded back and forth along the gate.

Eva and her party members were not worried about the guards. She had sat in the German Parliament only the month before and participated in the debate on the use of deadly force in the protection of NATO installations on Federal Republic soil. The Parliament had overwhelmingly voted against such use except in clear life-threatening situations. The experienced demonstrators, sensing their nervousness, looked at the soldiers with obvious scorn and a few began to taunt them, shouting insults from battery-operated bull horns in the middle of the crowd. By 4:30, as the American transport plane was landing at the Munich military airport, the crowd was getting unruly.

Through Penelope, Schultz had obtained the shortwave frequencies used by the local police, the civil defense authorities, and the NATO transport crew. There was no traffic yet on the NATO channel, but the police channel was alive with increasingly nervous conversation between base security and local police forces.

"Landsruhe to Ingolstadt. Landsruhe to Ingolstadt. Come in, please."

"Ingolstadt here." Schultz put his hand up to stop the van so he could hear better.

"Ingolstadt, we are getting a much bigger buildup of demonstrators than was predicted. Estimate three thousand outside gates already."

"We are surprised also. Estimate more than one thousand already passed through. Mainstrasse is filled with people and the beer halls are jammed. We begin to smell trouble."

"Landsruhe and Ingolstadt, this is Munich militia headquarters. We verify your concern. Nuremberg police report heavy traffic on Route two-sixty-two south, Stuttgart has similar report for Route one-forty-three east. Be advised that at sixteen hundred hours, Commandant Munich Militia recalled all personnel on leave and all off-duty officers. Expect to have force of one hundred, repeat one hundred, riot troops assembled by twenty-two hundred hours, ready to dispatch your area if requested."

"Landsruhe here. That may be a little late. They are building up pretty fast. Can't you speed it up?"

"Munich here. District headquarters screwed up again. They didn't raise the threat level until an hour ago. We're balls-out to collect people and equipment, but we're not miracle workers. We'll do our best."

"Landsruhe here. Thanks a lot, Munich. We understand your problem. We were warned on the same time schedule. Those bastards in headquarters have had their fingers up their asses for years."

The transmission was coming in a little more clearly now. Brandt smiled as Schultz motioned him to go forward.

"Landsruhe to Munich. I think we'll be all right except for one thing. There is supposed to be a shipment in here this evening but we haven't received word on a definite time. Do you have anything on it?"

"Munich here. Wait one. I'll check.

"Munich here. Yes, we do. Aircraft landed sixteen-thirty hours, ten minutes ago. That's another screwup. Those NATO bastards never tell us anything in advance. Them and their goddamned security. We didn't get anything on it until they requested permission to land. No flight plan, no nothing. They say they're self-contained, they don't need any help. That's okay by us, but we should know where they are, especially on a night like tonight, when there may be trouble. Screw them."

"Landsruhe here. That's the story of our lives. We don't hear from them until they're practically ready to roll up to the gates. If you want to listen to them they should be coming up soon on ninety-eight megahertz. Landsruhe out."

For a time they could only hear occasional bursts of static on ninety-eight megahertz as the convoy from the airport drew closer to the storage site. Schultz kept switching back and forth between the two channels, cursing himself for not having had the foresight to bring enough coaxial cable to mount his antenna on a tree or a pole in the vicinity. Suddenly the transmitter came in loud and clear. It must have come over a hill. The Americans were commenting on the amount of traffic on the autobahn but didn't seem particularly disturbed by it.

"Munich Airport, this is Green Dragon again. There seems to be a fair amount of traffic building up here — heavier than the usual rush-hour traffic. Anything going on that you know of?"

"Airport here. The previews of the six o'clock news are talking about some kind of a demonstration at your destination, but we've had nothing official. Do you want us to check with the police?"

"No, we should be able to pick up destination soon. I'll check with them directly when they come up on this frequency. Thanks again. Green Dragon out."

Schultz could hear the convoy trying to communicate with the storage site. Brandt had backed the van into the trees and shut off the engine before they could hear a reply.

"Landsruhe, this is Major Atkins checking in. We're seeing a lot of traffic here, about twenty miles from destination. Anything going on?"

"Atkins, this is Colonel Gibson. Where the hell have you guys been?"

"What do you mean, sir? We landed on schedule, picked up the transport van and two West German escort vehicles, and are on our way to your site without incident. Our orders were to maintain radio silence until close to destination. I couldn't pick you up until we cleared the last hill. Anything wrong?"

"I don't know that there's anything wrong. And I don't know who in hell writes your orders. The last shipment was in touch with us from the time they were picked up by the British air controllers. With your kind of cargo, you shouldn't expect to drop in like you are coming for a cup of coffee."

"Sorry, sir. This is a new security procedure so nobody knows where we are until the last minute. What's up?"

"What's up is that there's a full-scale peacenik demonstration going on here. That's what's up. The goddamned security people get my ass. Every air controller in Europe knew who you were and where you were going. So did the people who provided air support at Munich and the transportation battalion that supplied your escort. Everybody knows where you were except the people who are responsible for your safety. I'm sure the peaceniks knew you were coming and they've told the television crews parked outside the gate."

Schultz smiled as he heard the American colonel give a sigh of frustration.

The colonel continued. "I shouldn't be beating up on you, Major, but it drives me nuts how stupid these headquarters people can be. I want you to proceed with caution when you get within five miles of here. Is your escort up on this frequency?"

"No, sir." Atkins's voice sounded worried as it came over the radio. "They're just on a short-range intercom between the three vehicles. Security thought —"

"Security, shit. Keep them informed and tell them not to leave their vehicles no matter what. If you get bogged down in the crowds here, let me know and we'll come out and get you. Understand?"

"Yes, sir, Colonel. Green Dragon out."

Schultz sensed a mounting excitement in the crowd as the newcomers attempted to get closer to the speaker's platform. He saw men and women with walkie-talkies. They were apparently plotting the progress of the convoy. Penelope hadn't told him about the walkie-talkies and he had nothing to pick up that frequency. He cursed but felt better when one of the demonstrators mounted the platform and started to announce the convoy's progress over the loudspeakers. It was two miles away, moving slowly but making deliberate forward progress.

Ten minutes later, Schultz could tell from the announcements that the convoy was about to come into sight. It was time to make his move. A woman was making an impassioned speech from the platform, but he couldn't tell who it was or what she was saying.

"This is it," he said to Brandt, putting on a white surgical gown. He slipped out of the vehicle, unlocked the latch on the rear door, and ducked behind a tree. The AK47, the rifle with the telescopic sight, the Luger, and the three tear gas bombs suspended from his belt were bulky under the gown, but no one was paying attention to him. The crowd was either looking at the woman on the platform or craning to see the convoy approaching on the road. He moved off about twenty yards to the edge of the clearing and fired two short bursts into the air from the AK47. There was an electrifying silence in the crowd. The woman who was speaking paused in confusion, looking around to see where the shots were coming from.

Schultz moved back about ten yards toward the van. He put down the AK47 and raised the rifle to the platform, his eye at a slight angle to focus away from the burned spots on his retina. He could see the woman now, stretching up on her toes to reach the microphone and resume her speech. It was Penelope, with the same skirt, the same hose, the same hat with the red feather, the same leather Tyrolean jacket she had worn the morning they had met in the Brauhaus. He focused on the Tyrolean jacket, just below the left breast. The pang of remorse lasted only a fraction of a second. Her breasts aren't very large, he thought as he squeezed the trigger firmly.

The single shot rang out, breaking the shocked silence of the crowd. Schultz saw the blood burst out, the redness staining the brown and white of the jacket as Penelope was thrown backward by the force of the .44-caliber projectile. Her knees gave way and she crumpled to the deck of the platform, dead before Foster Martin, standing beside her, could reach out to break her fall. Schultz leaped back into the truck.

There was a roar from the crowd. They assumed that the shots had come from the compound. A wave of humanity surged against the barbed wire fence, shaking fists and shouting at the guards within. The convoy was almost opposite him, but the sound of the volley from the AK47 and the rifle shot that had killed Penelope had infuriated the mob in the path of the vehicles. They turned and pounded on the hoods and sides of the three vans, stopping their forward progress. Schultz could hear the radio conversation as he closed the front door of the van.

"Green Dragon here. What's going on, for Christ's sake?"

"Colonel Gibson here, Green Dragon. Some agitator is shooting from the crowd. I believe he's just shot someone on the platform. I'm assembling a squad to come to your assistance. Be there in about ten minutes. Remember your orders. No deadly force except in self-defense. Don't leave your vehicles."

"We ain't going no place, Colonel, believe me."

Schultz opened the door of the truck and stole out, warning the driver to have the others stay put. He took one of the tear gas bombs from his belt and pulled the pin. He threw it at the speaker's platform, where Eva Spengler and her people were trying to come to the aid of Penelope and Foster Martin while using the public address system to call the crowd into order. He was too far away to reach the platform, but the wind blew the gas in that direction. Utter confusion reigned as the vapor spread from the platform to the open doors of the television trucks. He pulled the pin on the second bomb and heaved it as far as he could toward the gate. Again, it was too far away to reach, but the mob, undulating from the spot where the tear gas hit, like ripples from a stone thrown into a lake, stormed the barbed wire gate and overwhelmed the squad of soldiers trying to form ranks to come to the aid of the convoy. One of the soldiers panicked and shot into the crowd, felling two men. Schultz could hear the screams of women and children.

He turned and pushed his way toward the stalled convoy, discarding the rifle but clutching the AK47 under his gown. The crowd made way, sensing a person of importance.

"Tip them over, tip them over," he yelled, pushing against the side of the first military van. With a roar, the crowd did his bidding, tipping the vehicle on its side, the wheels spinning in a vain attempt to seek traction in the empty air. Another group turned the third vehicle on its roof. The occupants crawled out with their hands up, seeking mercy. The warhead transportation van was a sturdier vehicle, built to survive high-speed crashes or direct gunfire. The occupants refused to budge, but the crowd, concentrating on this one vehicle, managed to turn it on its side. Schultz moved to the bottom of the van, unarmored because its designers never anticipated an attack from that direction. He saw the opening where a large electrical cable fed power in from the engine's generator. A burst with the AK47 demolished the cable and enlarged the hole. He armed his last tear gas bomb and stuffed it into the opening.

Then he ran back to his own vehicle and banged three times on the rear door.

"Let's go," he yelled as he opened the door. Otto Drucker came first. He gave Schultz a thumbs-up. The others followed. Then the five men, wearing their white surgical coats, rushed out. Hermann and Heinrich carried a stretcher piled with khaki blankets. Wald lagged behind. Schultz gave him a shove and told him to get his ass moving.

"Red Cross, make way, Red Cross," he shouted. The crowd, seeing the white coats and the stretcher, made way for him to move easily toward the rear of the overturned van. It had taken a minute for the tear gas to seep up through the electrical cable duct, but by the time he returned, the Americans had realized that they had to open the door or suffocate. The door opened and the crew emerged, wheezing and coughing and digging at their eyes. With the odor of the tear gas, the crowd fell back to form a half circle twenty feet away. Schultz and his associates drew their pistols, holding wet towels to their faces to ward off the effects of the tear gas seeping slowly from the truck.

"Drop your guns," Schultz ordered. "Line up there." He motioned to an area away from the seeping tear gas. The four American officers lined up and stood at attention.

"Identify yourselves," he barked.

"John Atkins, major, United States Army, serial number 5763423."

"I don't give a shit about your serial number. Speak up."

"Joseph Curtiss, captain, United States Air Force."

"James Curran, captain, United States Army."

"Paul Murray, first lieutenant, United States Air Force."

"Major, how many warheads do you have in that vehicle?" Schultz asked.

The major was silent.

Schultz raised his Luger and shot the major between the eyes from a distance of two feet. The major's brains blew out of the back of his head and splattered on the door of the van as the impact knocked him down. He twitched once and lay still.

"Captain Curtiss, how many warheads do you have in that vehicle?"

"Three."

"Curran and Murray, go back in and bring one of them out," he ordered, tossing each of them a wet towel, "and don't forget the keys." They said nothing as they put the towels over their heads and went back into the van. They returned quickly, gasping from the fumes, carrying one seventy-pound canister between them and placing it on the ground in front of them. Curran also threw a small locked briefcase to Schultz, who caught it deftly.

"Put it on the stretcher and cover it with a couple of blankets," he commanded the twins. Hermann and Heinrich looked at him dully and did what they were told.

Wald seemed to be hanging back, but Schultz noted that Drucker was watching him carefully. Wald moved forward to object: "*Mein Gott,* Schultz, there's three warheads in there. They're each worth a fucking fortune. Let's take them all."

"I said one," Schultz shouted. There was a strange hush around the van, although a great clamor could be heard from the platform and the compound.

Wald raised his pistol and pointed it at Schultz. "Screw you, I'm going in to get the other two. What do you say, guys, are you with me?"

Schultz said nothing but gave an almost imperceptible nod. Before Wald could move, Drucker, off to the side, rattled three shots into his back.

"Curran and Murray" — he pointed to the two junior officers, still gasping from the tear gas fumes — "you're coming with us."

Leonard Kellman, Schultz's second guard, stepped over the body of his former companion and herded the two with his gun, motioning them to follow the twins.

"Curtiss" — Schultz spoke to the remaining American officer — "turn around." As he turned, Drucker calmly fired the remaining three rounds in his revolver into the back of Curtiss's head. The crowd pulled back in horror.

They stumbled against each other to give way as Schultz strode purposefully but unhurriedly back to his vehicle, followed by the twins with the stretcher, then the two American officers, Kellman, and Drucker. The demonstrators who had witnessed the events were too dumbfounded and frightened to make any moves, while those in the rear of the crowd parted politely for the white-coated Red Cross ambulance men, completely unaware that the stretcher contained a twenty-kiloton nuclear warhead, not an injured demonstrator.

Once back at the van, they strapped the warhead container down carefully and bound and gagged the Americans in the rear while Schultz climbed into the front seat. Brandt skillfully worked the van back in the direction of the autobahn, the crowd gradually making way for the insistent siren and the Red Cross markings.

## 9

K ARL BRANDT HAD SAT THROUGH THE WHOLE melee impassively smoking a cigarette as though he were watching a movie at a drive-in theater. "Which route, boss?" he asked, weaving around parked vehicles and forcing oncoming cars off the road by driving straight at them.

"The Nuremberg autobahn," replied Schultz. "When you get out of this crowd, shut down the siren and cut your speed to ninety kilometers per hour. We don't want to be too conspicuous going through these villages. They'll be looking for us as soon as the Landsruhe troops get to the weapon van."

"Got it," he replied, aiming straight for an oncoming Volkswagen, lights flashing and siren wailing. The Volkswagen and a BMW following it swerved off into a ditch as the driver cut back into the right-hand lane, ticking the bumper of the truck he was passing. Schultz could see the truck driver cursing and slamming on his brakes as he disappeared in the distance.

"*Verdamptes,* don't get us all killed. We have work to do."

"Relax," said Brandt, grinning. The scar on his face made the grin appear to spread ghoulishly to the hairline in back of his ear.

Schultz turned his attention to monitoring the two radio frequencies. On 98 megahertz, Colonel Gibson was trying to raise the transportation van. "Green Dragon, Green Dragon, hold fast. Reinforcements are on the way. Should be at your vehicle in two or three minutes. Do you read me?"

Silence.

On the police channel, the base commander was raising a general alarm. "Mayday, Mayday, this is Landsruhe. Situation out of control here. We need help."

"Landsruhe, this is General Richter, Munich headquarters. Describe your situation."

"Herr General, Colonel Kemper, base commander, Landsruhe. Massive demonstration organized by Greens Party to coincide with receipt of classified shipment has turned into a general riot. Several people have been shot. Tear gas has been used by demonstrators to incite confusion. Rioters have broken through gate and assaulted our guards. We have been forced to open fire in self-defense. Rioters have been beaten back and security of storage vaults has not been breached. Transportation convoy has been stopped by rioters and all three vehicles have been overturned about five hundred meters from the gate. I can see them from here. We have regrouped and detached a squadron to their aid. I assume vehicles are still secure but cannot raise them on radio."

"Don't assume anything, Colonel. Get to those vehicles as quickly as possible. You have my orders to use deadly force if necessary. Police assistance is coming from all towns in vicinity. Military will proceed immediately from my headquarters. Understand?"

"Yes, sir."

The other radio receiver suddenly came alive. Schultz could hear a Lieutenant Cooper describe the situation at the weapons van to Colonel Gibson. The lieutenant told him that the two escort vans had been overturned and that the occupants had been disarmed and beaten. Brandt remarked to Schultz that the beatings must have been done by the protestors since they had not beaten anyone. Schultz was pleased that the crowd was in such a frenzy. It would give them more time to get away in the confusion.

The report continued. "The security of the transportation

van has been breached and tear gas introduced into the interior. Two American officers and one German civilian have been shot at close range and killed. Personnel from a Red Cross vehicle removed an object on a stretcher and have departed, accompanied by two American officers. Reports here are confusing. Some say the personnel are paramedics who carried away a wounded bystander. Others say they did the shooting and have carried away an object from within the van."

The colonel cut in abruptly. "There was no Red Cross van requested in this area. Assume it is a ruse. Can you get a description of the vehicle?"

"Wait one, sir. There's a lot of confusion here. I'll try."

There was a pause.

"Colonel, no one seems to have noticed it very carefully. The best I can get is that it is a four- or five-year-old Mercedes van with Red Cross markings. Nobody can tell me in which direction it went after it pulled out of here."

"Thank you. I'll put out an all points bulletin to pick it up."

Schultz cut off the radio and turned to Brandt. He told him to turn into a side road and stop once they drove through the next village. As they turned off the main road, they heard the *thomp, thomp* of helicopter blades approaching noisily from the south.

"Pull into that grove of trees. Quickly."

He held his breath as the driver pulled up against a large maple just before the chopper passed directly over them at about fifty meters' altitude. As the noise of the blades receded in the distance, he darted out of the van and yanked the canvas Red Cross markings off the sides and the hood without bothering to undo the snaps. He stuffed the canvas on the floor of the front seat and instructed Brandt to proceed at reasonable speed toward the autobahn. "No more acrobatics and no more siren," he snapped.

"Okay, boss," Brandt replied, obviously disappointed.

Schultz went back to monitoring the radios. The story gradually unfolded. The men in the white coats had shot the two officers and the civilian, stolen one of the three warheads and carried it off at gunpoint with the other two American officers. There were reports of a Red Cross van speeding north, but the trail ended at the village of Eichstätt. As they pulled onto the Nuremberg autobahn, Schultz heard the general conversing with the base commandant.

"Richter, here. It looks like he managed to cover up his Red Cross markings or change vehicles outside of Eichstätt. I have ordered an expansive sweep for an abandoned vehicle in that area. I have also ordered roadblocks to stop any old Mercedes van they encounter on all branches of the autobahn."

"Only twenty kilos to the airport cutoff," Schultz said. "We should be able to make it before they organize the roadblocks. Besides, it's getting dark. Another ten minutes and they won't be able to recognize one van from another from the air."

He lit a cigarette and leaned back to relax. The muscles in his shoulders were aching from the tension; he was quietly and luxuriously rubbing them against the back of the seat when he heard the helicopter coming back from the north.

"Pull off to the side of the road under the next bridge and stop," he ordered.

They sat quietly under the bridge, the engine idling, while the helicopter whirred overhead, traveling at about forty meters' altitude in the gathering darkness. Twice more they hid under bridges as the helicopter swept over them, Brandt making the stops on his own initiative. Under the third bridge, they got a break. A late-model Mercedes van sped by them at 120 kilometers per hour, unaware of a police car a short distance behind. Schultz ordered the driver to follow the police car, which had also sped by, intent on the car ahead, not noticing the parked vehicle in the darkness. When the police car turned on its lights and siren, cutting off the surprised driver in the late-model Mercedes, Schultz's van passed quietly by at a moderate 80 kilometers per hour.

They were only one stop away from the airport cutoff when they ducked under another bridge to let the helicopter sweep by again to the north. Intent on the noise from the departing helicopter as they pulled out from under the bridge, they did not hear or see the second one darting in at twenty-five meters' altitude from the west. The pilot whirled and angled back for another look. Schultz could see his cutoff one kilometer in the distance and a police roadblock forming just ahead. He decided to go for it.

Brandt agreed. He put the gas pedal to the floor as the helicopter positioned itself overhead and boomed out instructions from a bullhorn for the van to pull over to the side of the road. By the time the van reached the roadblock it was traveling at 160 kilometers per hour and accelerating on a slight downhill grade.

"*Dummkopfs,*" Schultz said, "to set up a roadblock on a downhill grade." The door of the helicopter opened and a trooper leaned over the side, firing a warning burst from a submachine gun in his hands.

The police were not ready. They had had no warning from the helicopters of an approaching van. Two patrol cars were parked by the side of the road, the drivers smoking and chatting. One officer was setting out sawhorses when the van and the pursuing helicopter suddenly burst into view. The van smashed into the stack of sawhorses, knocking the officer sprawling across to the side of the road and showering the cigarette smokers with a hail of splintered wood. The trooper in the helicopter held his fire to avoid hitting the police in the roadblock, and when the impact with the sawhorses slowed the van down momentarily, the helicopter overshot it and had to come around. The van was only 200 meters from the cutoff by then, and by the time the helicopter returned and the patrol car officers had gained their composure, Schultz was out of sight down the ramp.

There was a stoplight at the bottom of the ramp, with a green arrow pointing to the right for Nuremberg to the east and a red light for those going west under the autobahn to the airport road. Brandt went through the red light, forcing an oncoming car to swerve wildly to avoid a collision. Under the bridge, he brought the van to a screeching halt. He had obviously been in chases before; Schultz was happy to let him take control.

Brandt, his face red and his scars and tattoos gleaming fluorescently in the near darkness, grinned at Schultz. "We'll wait under the highway for thirty seconds to confuse the helicopter pilot but not long enough to let the police cars catch up."

He hit the gas pedal in exactly thirty seconds and ran the van up to speed, keeping it in first gear until the engine screamed for mercy. Schultz looked back to see the patrol cars come careening down the ramp, where they split up, one going to the east and the other to the west. The helicopter was not in sight although he could hear the *thomp* of the blades and knew it must be close by.

Schultz was exultant. "They've lost us," he said.

"Not for long," Brandt said, intent now on the empty road as he sped along without headlights. "I'd just as soon have some traffic to follow. It's easier to follow their taillights."

Schultz looked back to see the cruiser gaining on them one kilometer back. A Mercedes 380 SEL pulled out of a side road and erased his view of the patrol car. The 380 speeded to catch up with them, blinking its headlights to warn the van that its lights were out.

"The turn into the airport is just ahead," Schultz said.

Brandt nodded and yanked the steering wheel to the right, the left wheels almost leaving the ground.

The 380 stopped blinking as the van took the right turn to the freight terminal and continued straight ahead to the passenger gates. Five seconds later, the police car followed the 380. Schultz gave a sigh of relief. Only another few hundred meters.

But the *thomp* of the helicopter grew louder. A powerful searchlight pierced the darkness as it swept across the access road. There was another burst of fire as it picked up the van in its beam. The van swerved off the road and onto the tarmac as the chopper overshot. Brandt hurtled down the tarmac, saw an empty hangar open, and pulled into it, leaving the engine idling. The helicopter swept up and down along the runway approach, the searchlight beam darting in all directions, but obviously it had lost its prey. After the second sweep the chopper went back to retrace its path along the airport highway.

Brandt switched his headlights back on and backed slowly into the approachway. He picked his way carefully down the tarmac toward the freight terminal, where Schultz had been told to look for a DC-9 with Kuwait Airways markings. Their vehicle was now indistinguishable from the other meal and fuel trucks that bustled along the busy service runway. The driver found the DC-9 facing the runway, but in complete darkness. Schultz reached over and flashed the headlights four times.

Headlights and interior lights came on in the plane. The passenger door opened and the internal stairway slowly unfolded. A smiling Hassan appeared in the doorway. Schultz got out of the van and walked toward the aircraft, hand outstretched.

There was a roar as the helicopter burst over the freight terminal, spotlight illuminating both the aircraft and the van. Schultz bolted back to the vehicle and pulled the AK47 from the front seat. Hassan stood immobilized, an easy target framed in the illuminated doorway of the aircraft. The helicopter settled quickly, its blades still rotating rapidly as the door opened and three men with submachine guns leaped out. They were obviously not experienced helicopter troops, because they instinctively ducked their heads under the whirling blades as they ran toward the van.

That was all Schultz needed. In the split second that they took their eyes away from him and ducked their heads under the helicopter blades, he opened up with the AK47. Hassan watched in horror as Schultz mowed them down with a single sustained burst.

The helicopter pilot, feeling the bullets rip through the skin of his aircraft, didn't even look around. He engaged the blades, gunned the engine, and took off for safety over the freight terminal.

Hassan, followed by six armed men in civilian clothes, came running down the steps. "What have you done?" he asked Schultz.

"No time to argue. They'll be back with reinforcements as soon as the pilot can get the word out. We'll have to get out of here. Do you have the money? Not mine. The money for my men?"

"Yes. Six packages, each with one hundred thousand deutsche marks. It's right here."

"One of them we won't need. Let's get the back of the van open."

As the men piled out, they were pale and shaken from the sudden starts and stops and the gunfire. The American officers were turned over to Hassan's armed guards and marched quickly up the steps to the DC-9. Two of the guards lifted the canister and disappeared into the aircraft behind them. Schultz's men took off their white coats and stood waiting anxiously. Schultz took the packages of money from Hassan and handed them to the men. To the grinning Brandt he handed the extra package meant for Wald. "Here's an extra one. You earned it," he said, and he shook the man's hand.

As the taxis drew up, each man ripped open his package and riffled greedily through the small bills. Schultz did not wait to see them drive away. He grabbed Hassan by the arm and hustled him up the steps to the DC-9, its starboard engine already purring smoothly and the port engine starting with puffs of smoke as they secured the door. Schultz followed Hassan to the cockpit as the plane taxied down the runway. There were no other aircraft waiting to take off.

"Hurry," said Schultz. "Can't you go faster?"

The pilot and copilot ignored him as they made their turn into the open runway. There was no other traffic in sight. The pilot switched his radio to flight control.

"Kuwait 654 requesting clearance for takeoff."

There was no reply for fifteen seconds; then the voice of the flight controller came in, hesitantly. "Wait one, 654. There seems to be some confusion here."

"I can't wait, tower. We have royalty aboard and they're raising hell. Let us go or you'll probably hear from Bonn in the morning."

"Okay, go ahead. We're getting requests to close the airport, but I'm not going to do anything until I get it through channels."

Schultz could hear sirens over the noise of the aircraft and see police cars flashing blue and red lights as the DC-9 picked up speed and passed the abandoned Mercedes van. As they became airborne and banked back over the airport, flashing lights came from all directions and the control tower closed the airport to all incoming and outgoing traffic. But they were free.

"How come you are in a Kuwaiti aircraft?" he asked Hassan.

"We leased it through an agent in Turkey. The crew is ours. We felt it was safer than stealing one or using one of our own. But never mind that. What about the troopers you shot? You were under instructions not to use violence. President al Emir will be very angry."

Schultz remembered Emir's saying the same thing when they had first met. It was hard for him to believe that they felt this way. Don't they realize that terrorism is inherently violent? he thought.

"It was us or them, Hassan. You'd have been a dead man as soon as they came out from under those blades. We've got the warhead. I don't understand why we had to take along the Americans. That was very dangerous."

Hassan didn't answer but turned and walked back into the main cabin. The Americans were still bound and gagged.

He addressed the guards in Arabic. "Take out the gags and take off their leg bindings. Make them comfortable. They can use the toilet but do not close the door. If they make a false move shoot them through the shoulders or legs, but don't kill them. We need them alive."

He waited until they were untied, then addressed the Americans politely in English. "Your names, please."

The red-haired officer with the freckled face answered sullenly. "James Curran, captain, United States Army, serial number 3754612."

The younger man — Schultz guessed he was in his early twenties — squared his shoulders, held up his head, and stared straight ahead. "Paul Murray, first lieutenant, United States Air Force, serial number 1648573."

Hassan leaned on the seats in front of them and smiled. "We are not interested in your serial numbers, gentlemen. Relax. If you do what you are told, you will not be hurt. In fact, you can do your country a great service. That canister contains a nuclear warhead for a Cruise missile, does it not?"

The officers were silent.

Hassan continued. "That canister is in your custody while you are with us." He reached back and took the briefcase with the keys from Schultz and placed it in Curran's lap. "You probably won't believe this, but we only want to borrow your warhead for a short while. You are not to let it out of the sight of one of you at any time. One of you must stay awake and guard the canister while the other sleeps, eats, showers, or uses the toilet. Do you understand?"

The officers, puzzled, dubiously nodded assent.

"In fact, gentlemen, if you cooperate and do what we ask of you, you will have the privilege of returning it and yourselves unharmed to your superiors in the United States government."

It was only a two-hour flight. Schultz settled back in a first class seat, hoping to get some sleep. As he dozed off, he wondered why Emir had been so insistent that he come along instead of having him paid off in Germany, which he would have preferred.

For all the commotion raised about Lebanon through the centuries, it is difficult to realize how small a country it is, with the distance between Beirut and the Israeli border no more than fifty miles and the distance to Damascus about the same. The camp was nestled in a barren area of the otherwise fertile Bekáa Valley, between the Lebanon and Anti-Lebanon mountains. To the east, the legendary Mount Hermon looked down on it from nine thousand feet, while the Golan Heights loomed ominously to the south. For Emir, it was ideal, virtually uninhabited, close enough to the capital, with mountains cutting off the line of sight to the major cities of Tyre and Sidon.

June had wanted to talk in the helicopter on the way from Beirut, but it was too noisy. She started in earnest as soon as they left the helicopter and climbed into the back of the jeep. She attracted everyone's attention. She was wearing light blue slacks and a cashmere sweater over her shoulders. Her dark hair was tucked into a single elastic band, and she wore a bandanna on her head, like a movie star on location, as well she might be to these rough construction crews, many of whom had not seen a woman in weeks. She held her head and her shoulders high, occasionally tossing those shoulders away from Emir in a gesture of disdain and frustration. Emir, dressed in khaki shirt and pants, looked more like her lackey than the president of the country.

"I shouldn't have let you —" she started.

He interrupted. "English, please, speak English. The driver does not understand it."

Annoyed, she switched languages. "Damn it, Sal, aren't you ever going to let me speak. I said I never should have let you talk me into this. I feel as if I'm doing something dangerous and traitorous. It sounded like the right thing to do when I was back in the States, but now that I'm here, it seems wrong. Can't we call it all off?"

"June, it's too late. The warhead will be here in an hour. The deed is done." He hoped he wasn't going to have trouble with her. When he had talked to Hassan from the helicopter, he detected a note of worry in Hassan's voice, but since the circuit was uncoded and they wanted to keep the transmissions short, he did not ask for details. He hoped Schultz hadn't gotten out of hand. When you hire a man like that, anything can happen. It was a chance he'd had to take. He glanced at June, whose bandanna was blowing in the wind.

"I know it seems strange and foreign to you, but, believe me, it's the only way to do it. We want our homeland back, June.

Your ancestors and mine fought for that land, were born on it, lived and struggled and died on it. Now they've taken it away from us and two wars have been fought over it already. The Americans don't care. Ninety percent of them believe that the Jordan River exists only in the Bible. Your American politicians would like to forget the whole thing. Even in Israel, the moderates are embarrassed at this failure to live up to the terms of the peace treaty. Peace cannot come to the Palestinians or the Israelis until this issue is settled. There will be bloodshed for another generation under the present stalemate. I don't want that bloodshed on my hands, nor on yours. I want peace for my country and for the whole Middle East."

"But what if the President doesn't agree to your terms?"

"He will. He has no choice. He has a sworn constitutional responsibility to protect the citizens of the United States. Everything else is secondary."

"Oh, Sal, I'm out of my depth. I may be making a terrible mistake. I'm just a mathematician. I'm not an international politician. I trust you. You'll have to help me do the right thing."

"You are. When this is over, you will give them the numbers and nothing will be changed. You will be a heroine."

"But why did you keep me a virtual prisoner in Beirut? The villa was beautiful, and you were wonderful. I loved every minute that we were together. But when you left, it felt as if I was in a jail. Now look at me, in a hellhole at the end of the earth. I don't like it."

The wind was blowing her hair and the sand from the unpaved road was stinging her face. "Slow this damned thing down, will you, please," she shouted. Emir tapped the driver on the shoulder. The jeep slowed.

June looked around at the desolation of the site and shivered in the warm sunshine. She thought of Kane and how she had deceived and betrayed him. Would this get him in trouble? And Herb, too. She hadn't thought of that. Would the government hold them responsible for what she had done? And could she ever go back, even if Emir was right? She felt Emir tugging at her arm for attention.

"June, everyone is looking for you. As long as you are the only one who knows the numbers, you are literally the most important person on the face of this earth. I can't take the chance that anything could happen to you." He gave an involuntary shudder at the thought of anything happening to her in the next six days. "Everything will be revealed to the American President tomorrow. He will know that you must be protected. Otherwise, they could send bombers and blow us to kingdom come."

The jeep stopped a mile from the technical area at the air-conditioned plywood building that would be her home for the coming week. It had been put together quickly but not hastily. Emir showed her around, pleased that he had made extra provision for her personal comfort. There was a living room, bedroom, bath, and even a small office with a personal computer and a printer, identical to the equipment she had at home. There were drapes on the windows and oriental rugs on the floor. A large bouquet of spring flowers sat in a delicate Irish cut glass vase on the cocktail table.

"Look at these," he said. The closets were stacked with casual clothes, slacks, blouses, and robes. A young Moslem girl, scarcely more than seventeen, her face veiled, opened the door and announced in broken English that she would be June's personal maid. She introduced the cook, an older woman in her forties, similarly dressed, who apologized for speaking only Arabic. June assured her that this would be no problem. "My own Arabic is almost back now," she said.

"I'll leave you to rest and clean up," Emir said, smiling proudly at this oasis of comfort in the crude desert construction camp. "If you feel up to it, I'd love to have you dine with Hassan and me and some guests at six-thirty."

June accepted and Emir left. He was worried about her doubts, particularly if she expressed them to Hassan and the others. Perhaps he shouldn't have asked her to dinner. On the other hand, she would have to associate with them eventually. If there were going to be any surprises, he felt that he would prefer to cope with them sooner than later.

He was driven in the jeep to a similar building, fifty yards away. Guards were in evidence at both buildings, trying to look languid and inconspicuous for June's sake but, from long training, unable to resist coming to attention in Emir's presence. Two more helicopters landed in the distance, one met by trucks and a large contingent of guards. This group drove off toward the technical area. The other helicopter carried only a single passenger, who climbed into a jeep and was driven to Emir's building.

"What is this, the Ritz Hotel?" Assim Mahmoud asked as he looked around the Lebanese president's comfortable quarters.

"Hold your lip, Mahmoud." Emir's eyes flashed. "You are here to meet some people and receive instructions. We are not interested in opinions. Your instructions are these. At dinner tonight, in addition to Hassan and myself, there will be an American woman named June Malik and a German man named Ludwig Schultz."

Mahmoud stood in the center of the room with his arms folded. "And they are —"

"Patience. I will tell you. I will tell you what you need to know to accomplish your mission. Ludwig Schultz has managed to procure for us a nuclear weapon with the explosive force of twenty thousand tons of TNT. That weapon has just been brought to this site. You will see it before the evening is over."

Mahmoud whistled. His eyes grew wide with surprise and curiosity, overcoming, for the first time in Emir's experience, his sour composure. "*Allah akhbar*. So that is what it is. Tell me about it." He walked up to the edge of the desk.

Emir shook his head. "You will be told in due course." Emir could see Mahmoud's sour expression return as he continued. "June Malik is an American mathematician who has some very important information about that weapon. She must be treated very delicately until we can obtain that information."

"Delicately . . . Women . . . You Lebanese are too soft. Why don't you just torture the American cunt until you get what you want and then shoot her. In Syria —"

"You are not in Syria. After dinner, you will be taken to the technical area one mile from here, where you will see the weapon and meet two American military officers. It is very important that you are able to identify Schultz, Malik, and the two officers to the American authorities.

"I will deliver to you, when you are leaving, a sealed document addressed to the President of the United States. Then you will be taken by helicopter to Beirut Airport, where a Boeing 747 will be waiting to fly you to New York City to meet with Bradford Appleby. You will deliver the sealed document to Mr. Appleby, verifying to him the whereabouts of the individuals you will meet tonight."

Emir stood up, reading Mahmoud's objection in his eyes. "Is everything clear?"

"No, it is not clear." Mahmoud was furious. He moved forward with his fists clenched. "I want to know what is going on. It is beneath my dignity to become a simple messenger boy. I am a senior envoy of the president of Syria himself. I demand to know what this mission is all about."

"Demand, shit." Emir leaned forward, forcing the surprised Mahmoud to step back. "You are under my orders. If I give you any further information about this mission the Americans may torture it out of you. The CIA does that, you know, and they do it well. My agreement with Assad was to put you in a senior position so that you could report back to him that the mission was carried out as agreed between us. I don't need you. If you refuse to carry out my orders, I will contact President Assad and get his permission to put a bullet between your ears, after which I will use one of my own people. Dismissed."

Mahmoud was speechless. He glared at Emir, almost reaching across the deck to grasp him by the neck. Then he remembered that, after the Washington incident, he had vowed to Allah that he would never again lose his temper. He unclasped his fists, nodded once, then turned and walked out of the building.

The second helicopter contained Hassan, Schultz, Captain Curran, Lieutenant Murray, two guards, and the weapon. Hassan politely helped the handcuffed officers out of the helicopter while extra guards picked up the canister. Schultz looked around in bewilderment at the bustle and the openness of the camp. He had expected to arrive in some secluded hideaway. Instead, dozens of people could see him, the canister, and the captured officers. Furthermore, none of the construction workers seemed to be paying any attention to them.

One truck carried them the two miles to the technical area, a cluster of four plywood buildings surrounded by a high barbed wire fence. One of the buildings was square, about a hundred feet on a side. The plywood was unpainted. Inside, the windowless building one wall was tastefully decorated, with oriental hangings and crossed flags of Lebanon and the United States. The other three walls were bare. Schultz could tell that the officers were astonished to see the Stars and Stripes hanging on the wall. In front of the flags was a platform, three feet high and twenty feet square, covered with a magnificent oriental rug, and accessible by four carpeted steps. In the center of the platform was a cradle designed to fit the cylindrical shape of the weapon canister.

The guards placed the canister on the cradle, then retired to the other sides of the building, armed but at ease.

In front of the platform were a half dozen comfortable chairs, and to one side, a cot. The rest of the building was full of lights, cameras, tall tripods, and television-type moving camera platforms.

Hassan motioned to a guard, who removed the handcuffs from the two officers. "Gentlemen" — he spoke softly, and it seemed to Schultz almost deferentially — "we regret the inconveniences you have been exposed to. We had hoped that the operation could be carried out without violence, but, alas, that was not to be."

He glowered at Schultz for an instant, then composed himself and smiled at the perplexed officers. "You will be our guests for the next week, after which you will be returned, unharmed, to your homeland. We would appreciate your cooperation in our mission. Such cooperation will not only assure your own safety but will contribute to the security of your country and to peace in the world.

"One of you will be in attendance at this weapon at all times. There is a comfortable bedroom and toilet facilities over there." He pointed to a closed door. You can set your own schedules for resting and dining. If you prefer to dine together, we will be happy to set up a table in front of the platform. You will not be allowed to touch the canister, only to observe that no one else does. For the present, I will retain possession of the keys.

"Please do not attempt to escape or cause bodily harm to anyone. You are in a military camp surrounded by desert, and you will be heavily guarded at all times. I realize that you have had a difficult experience. If one of you would like to rest, please notify the sergeant and a guard will go with you to the bedroom. Gentlemen, good evening."

Hassan bowed to the astounded officers, motioned to Schultz, and walked out of the room. Hassan and Schultz rode in the jeep to Emir's headquarters.

"What's going on here?" Schultz asked. "Why did you bring me here? I've finished my job."

"You will be told in due course," Hassan answered. "I can assure you that all that will be required of you is your presence. President Emir will tell you the rest."

Schultz fell silent. He felt nervous, not knowing what to expect. Nevertheless, he strode into the office smiling, extending his hand to Emir. "Good to see you again. We had a few rough spots, but we pulled it off successfully."

Emir ignored the extended hand. "Here are deposit slips for ten million deutsche marks, two million each in the five banks where we set up accounts for you — Münchner Reichsbank, Crédit Suisse, Banc de Paris, Citicorp, and the Bank of London. If you prefer, each bank has agreed to honor the deposits in local currencies at the prevailing rate of exchange." He threw the deposit slips onto the desk and turned his back.

"You had strict instructions that there was to be no unnecessary violence." Then he whirled around. "Why did you shoot the American woman? Wasn't she a friend of yours?"

Schultz shrugged. "I had to create some confusion. I didn't know who it was until I had her in my sights."

"And the American officers?"

"You only wanted two. I could see the soldiers coming from the compound and didn't have time to tie up the others. Besides, one of them wouldn't cooperate. I shot him as an example. But why do you bother me with such trifles. You have your weapon. When can I go?"

"In about a week you will be flown to the country of your choice. Until that time, I will need your presence to verify that we have the actual weapon you borrowed. You will have dinner tonight with my messenger, Assim Mahmoud, and a Lebanese-American girl, June Malik."

"Who is she?"

"You will find that out. I want you to tell them your story but leave out the shootings. After that, you will remain in your quarters until we are ready for you."

The dinner had been Emir's idea. Hassan had tried to talk him out of it. Emir wanted Mahmoud to meet the other two, so he could describe them to the Americans if necessary. Also, since all three would be in view of the television cameras eventually, he felt that they would be more relaxed if they had spent some time together. He had not expected the dinner to be a pleasant one but thought that he and Hassan could pass it off with casual conversation and a few pleasantries.

They were not successful. June was nervous, uncomfortable in these strange surroundings, and more and more filled with remorse over what she had done. Mahmoud was still seething from his earlier confrontation with Emir. Schultz was sullen and disinterested, remaining silent and drinking several glasses of wine before he was asked to speak.

Schultz told the story of the hijacking in a dull, emotionless tone, leaving out the shootings, as instructed. But when he came to describing the chase on the autobahn, he became more and more animated, gulping down another glass of wine as he spoke. When he described the final attempt of the helicopter to storm the DC-9, he forgot himself.

*"Gott sei Dank,"* he exclaimed, "those soldier *Schwein* had probably never been in a helicopter before. When three of them came out with machine guns, I felt that we were dead men. But you know what?" He laughed uproariously. "They ducked their heads when they went under the helicopter blades. *Dummkopfs.* That was all I needed. I stood up and blew their brains out with the AK47. They lost their heads anyway."

He raised himself unsteadily and swept an imaginary machine gun around the table. "That helicopter pilot, he was a smart one. He knew what to do. He got the hell out of there in a hurry."

June was frozen in horror. "But, Sal, Sal, you said there'd be no violence. This monster —" She could hardly get the words out.

Schultz looked at her malevolently before sitting down. "Fräulein, you can't have terrorism without violence. That's crap."

At a signal from Hassan, two guards came in quickly and removed Schultz, still muttering, from the room. June began to cry softly, as Emir tried to smooth things over. Mahmoud tried to keep his temper in check, but he couldn't help leaning over to Hassan and whispering, "I told him he shouldn't put up with women. He ought to kick her ass and put her out in the kitchen."

June heard the remark. She looked around the table. "You're all monsters, all of you." She pushed her chair back and stalked out of the room.

An hour later, Mahmoud entered Emir's office for final instructions. Hassan sat silently in the corner. Emir was tense.

"The helicopter is ready for you. Here is a sealed package to deliver to Mr. Appleby. We have established that he is in New York and are sending him a telegram stating that you will be arriving with an important message early tomorrow. He is to open it in your presence. Inside are pictures of Miss Malik, Schultz, Hassan, you, and me. These were taken at dinner. I felt that informal photographs of the group would look more authentic than posed pictures. There are also photographs of the weapon canister and of the two American officers. Also inside is a sealed message for the President of the United States. If Mr. Appleby has any doubts about the importance of your mission, they will disappear when he sees the photographs that were taken tonight. The 747 will wait for you at Kennedy Airport. You will return here immediately to report to me on the meeting with Appleby. You have diplomatic immunity, so I doubt that the Americans will attempt to detain you. If they do, you can honestly tell them that you have no knowledge of the situation other than what you heard at dinner tonight. If you don't show up at the airplane by noon, we will immediately begin proceedings to effect your release. Any questions?"

"Why can't I deal directly with the American President?" Mahmoud asked, almost petulantly.

"First, because he would probably refuse to see you," Emir replied. "Second, because I want no direct connection to us until after he has read the message."

Mahmoud grunted and turned to leave. "I will obey your orders explicitly," he said. "But I insist on a personal meeting with President Assad when I return."

# 10

In washington, all hell broke loose. The first message came from a CIA agent who had infiltrated the Greens Party and participated in the protest. The garbled report indicated only that a warhead had been stolen and that an American woman, two German soldiers, and possibly an American officer had been shot. Verification soon came in from Munich, Brussels, and satellite monitors of German police radio. The clincher was German TV. The technicians had momentarily been blinded by the tear gas, but the cameras kept grinding away. Once recovered, the crews zoomed in on the convoy, and the whole Federal Republic audience, as well as many East Germans who surreptitiously turned on their television sets, watched from their living rooms as the vehicles were overturned and the Red Cross truck sped away from the scene.

There was no covering up this one.

The President was on his way to Chicago to deliver a speech when the first reports came in. He would be back in less than an hour. The Vice President was in Denver. Fred Billings, the chief of staff, took command until the President returned.

The secretary of State, Harold King, arrived in the Situation Room first. The windowless room in the basement of the White House was dominated by a heavy mahogany conference table that accommodated eight on each side in comfortable worn leather chairs. Three of the walls were lined with smaller wooden chairs for staff. The fourth wall held a blackboard, in front of which was a pull ring for a screen that could be lowered to show slides from the projector recessed in the back wall.

The chief of staff waved King to a chair. "Jeff Slocum will be here any minute," he said. "If you don't mind waiting, Harold, I'll brief you both at the same time." King, containing his curiosity, nodded and settled into his chair.

As Billings finished speaking, the secretary of Defense burst in. A burly man, wearing a disheveled brown herringbone tweed suit and with a head of hair that looked perennially uncombed, he contrasted sharply with the impeccable, thin, unruffled secretary of State.

"What the hell's going on?" He spit out the words like an accusation. "Reporters followed me down the hall from my office. They'll be all over my ass when I go back."

The chief of staff did not answer but proceeded directly into the briefing. He calmly informed them that a nuclear warhead had been stolen in Germany. One of the three Cruise missile warheads being delivered to the Landsruhe storage site had been taken. Two American officers had been shot and two others kidnapped. He described the getaway in the DC-9.

Billings went on to explain that there was no trace of the aircraft after it left Nuremberg. Their only clue was an Athens report of an unidentified aircraft that had been traveling southeast at a thousand feet over the Aegean Sea. The aircraft had not replied to queries, and because of the low altitude, the radar had lost it pretty quickly.

They all scrambled to their feet as the President burst into the room. His long stride carried him rapidly across the floor to the armchair at the end of the table. His face was handsome, but not movie star handsome; the features were too strong, the chin a little too jutting. But it was a face that radiated power and self-confidence into the television cameras. Now the face had lost its usual calmness, a flush of red in his cheeks deepening the color of the blue snapping from his eyes like an arc of electricity.

"Sit down, sit down. This is no time for ceremony. Jeff, Hal, Fred." He nodded to acknowledge the presence of the secretaries and the chief of staff. He had been briefed by secure radiophone on the helicopter from Andrews and was enraged.

"Who the hell was stupid enough to send three atom bombs into a crowd of five thousand nutcakes staging a protest? You can't help but have trouble. Somebody's going to pay with their ass for this one, I'll tell you."

"Apparently a new security procedure left a link out of the communications process, Mr. President," Billings said.

"Look, Fred, I'm not angry at you, but these security people drive me nuts. They have so goddamned many secret procedures that they end up screwing themselves — and me, too. Spengler knew that shipment was coming. Every nut in West Germany knew it was coming. That's why they showed up. The hijackers knew it was coming. They weren't just sitting around waiting for something to happen. Everybody was told about it but the men transporting the warheads. Why? Because it's too secret, because it violates security? What kind of security is this? What we have now is two men dead, two kidnapped, and a twenty-kiloton nuclear warhead roaming around loose somewhere in Europe. Where is it?" He looked around the room. "Do we have any idea where it is? Do we have any idea who is behind this? It has to be an organized effort."

"No, sir, not yet," said the chief of staff. "Senator Matthews was just on the tube saying that the Russians are behind it —"

"The Russians. They have twenty-five thousand of them. Why in the hell would they want another one? Any reaction from Moscow?"

"Not yet. They're probably waiting to find out who stole it, if they don't already know."

The Soviets were as much in the dark as the Americans. That morning Rostov was up for an early briefing in his screen room, digesting the news from all over the world. The KGB had supplied a complete report on the hijacking, including background on Schultz. (One of the KGB infiltrators in the Greens Party had been standing beside Eva Spengler during the hijacking. "It's Ludwig Schultz," she exclaimed. "I should have had him put in jail.")

Rostov sat alone in the screen room for a long time, trying to piece out the puzzle. There were too many things that didn't add up. Who was behind Schultz? It was clearly an organized effort. The Syrians came to mind, but they would never have done it without checking with Moscow. On the other hand, they could know who stole it and deny knowledge afterward. That was possible. He thought of the Palestine troop buildup, of the disappearance of the electronic counterintelligence specialists from Beirut, of the new Lebanese president, Salom al Emir. If Schultz was the swimmer from the 1948 Olympics, he and Emir could have met there or at one of the many swimming meets in Europe thereafter. It couldn't be just a coincidence that the two names had suddenly come up after all those years. Maybe we're going to have another competition, he thought.

Appleby received a telegram, hand-delivered from the Lebanese United Nations embassy, at ten o'clock that night. It was from his friend the Lebanese ambassador in Washington, courteously requesting that he receive a special messenger from the president of Lebanon, one Assim Mahmoud. Mr. Mahmoud would deliver to him a message of utmost importance. Appleby remembered Mahmoud well after their encounter, reflecting that the man may have been so offensive just so he would be remembered. He sensed that the message would have something to do with the stolen nuclear weapon. As a precautionary measure, he phoned the President's chief of staff, who had the head of the New York bureau of the CIA call him immediately. The agent stated that he would check Mahmoud's whereabouts, send a detail to Appleby's office, and have an airplane at Appleby's disposal first thing in the morning. The CIA quickly determined that a chartered Boeing 747 had filed a flight plan from Beirut, giving an estimated time of arrival of eight o'clock the following morning.

Appleby slept fitfully and was in his office by 6:00, just in case. At 8:15, he received a call stating that the 747 had arrived at 7:50, with just one passenger, a man answering to Mahmoud's description. The man had been met by a limousine with a driver and a uniformed guard. The caller estimated that the limousine would arrive at Appleby's office by 9:00 A.M.

Appleby pressed the button on the tape recorder in his top desk drawer when his secretary announced the visitor, who pompously announced that he had the honor to deliver to Mr. Appleby a personal message for the President of the United States.

"The President of the United States is a very busy man, Mr. Mahmoud," Appleby said calmly. "Can you tell me the nature of the message?"

"Open the package," said Mahmoud.

Appleby slit the sealed envelope and looked at the pictures. He immediately recognized June Malik, whom he had met several times with Bill Kane, but was puzzled by her presence. With her, having dinner, were Salom al Emir, Mahmoud himself, another man he did not recognize, and an athletic-looking German whose countenance he recollected, after more than four decades, as Ludwig Schultz. The White House had informed Appleby that Schultz was the suspected hijacker of the Cruise missile warhead. Appleby did not recognize the pictures of the canister or of the two young officers in American uniforms.

"Jesus," he muttered, trying to hold his excitement but unable to remain calm any longer. He looked at the other sealed envelope, addressed personally to the President of the United States from the president of the Republic of Lebanon. "You want me to deliver this?"

"If you will be so kind, please," came the reply.

"Where will you be, if the President has any questions?"

"I have no further information to offer you, Mr. Appleby. I am under orders to return to Lebanon immediately after delivering this package," said Mahmoud. "I bid you good day."

As soon as Mahmoud, tailed by two agents, left Appleby's

office, Appleby called the agent in charge of the detail from the adjoining room. "I will need a police escort to LaGuardia," he instructed the agent. "Call the White House and tell them that I'm coming with important information. Have your plane stand by for immediate takeoff to Andrews Field. Get me a helicopter pickup from Andrews to the White House lawn. And by the way" — he turned to the agent as he hurried out the door — "find some way to hold that 747 for two or three hours. If you don't hear from me by noon, let him go."

The President was waiting in the Situation Room with all the members of the National Security Council when Appleby rushed in with the pictures and the envelope. Emergency or no emergency, the chief of the Secret Service insisted on taking the envelope out to the lawn to look for explosives before the President could handle the message. While waiting, the President looked at the photographs and handed them around one by one as he finished.

"Bastards," said Slocum. The others said nothing, but the hushed silence was punctured by soft whistles of amazement.

The President, expressionless, read the first two pages in silence, then handed the complete document to the chief of staff to be read aloud.

The letter was long and rambling. It began with an apology for the violence attendant to the "borrowing" of the nuclear warhead and assured the President that the officers would be unharmed. It went on to mention Permissive Action Links, reminding him that the codes were scheduled to change automatically on May 31.

Then came the clincher.

As you can see from the photographs we sent you with this message, the person who designed the software for these codes has joined us in the interests of world peace. She has modified the software for the Permissive Action Links so that the code which will unlock the devices after May 31 has been changed from that which is in the code manuals in your possession. If you attempt to detonate any of the weapons in your arsenal after May 31 without obtaining the new code, you will be unsuccessful and the weapon will be rendered permanently inoperable.

There was a gasp from the men around the table.

The tone of the letter changed as it went on to describe the hardships suffered by the Palestinian people since the foundation of the Israeli nation and to demand the withdrawal of all Israelis from the West Bank of the Jordan River.

Then the threat.

Should you, or the Prime Minister of Israel, refuse to comply with our terms, we will inform the government of the Union of the Soviet Socialist Republics that all your nuclear weapons are inoperable. We trust, Mr. President, that your constitutional responsibility for the safety of the American people will prevent you from allowing that unfortunate state of affairs to come about.

It is possible that you are not convinced that your entire arsenal of nuclear weapons will be inoperable at the announced time. It is to demonstrate to you the accuracy of our statements that we have arranged to borrow one of your weapons and two of your officers to guard it. You will be allowed access to that weapon by your secure classified VHF satellite channel 91 to attempt to insert the proper code after midnight on May 31. You will also be allowed access to television coverage of your attempt on channel 86.

I suggest that you designate a personal envoy to meet with me in Beirut within twenty-four hours to discuss the details of the Israeli withdrawal from the West Bank. We are peace-loving, nonviolent people and trust that the evacuation can be carried out without bloodshed.

> May Allah give you peace,
> Salom al Emir,
> President of Lebanon

The President broke the silence. "Can it be possible . . ." He paused. His voice was quavering, the pitch plaintive. Several heads lifted to see who was talking.

"Can it be possible that one person with one act can disarm the United States of America? Can it be possible that at one moment we are the strongest nation on the face of this earth and, on the stroke of midnight, all of those thousands and thousands of bombs and missiles upon which we base the security of our nation become useless pieces of metal? become pumpkins? Can it be possible that one sentence of computer software, like a diabolical writing on the wall, can render us helpless before our enemy? Can it be possible that with all our billions and billions of dollars and the cleverness and complexity of our designs, we have become so clever and complex that our own skills can turn back against us and render us powerless? Can it be possible?"

He slumped in his chair. His head hung low, his strong fingers twitching slightly as they covered his eyes, blotting out the room so that his brain could concentrate and comprehend the consequences of this sudden, horrible revelation.

No one answered.

A minute passed in silence. Then the hands came down from his face, firming as he pressed them flat against the table, gaining strength from its rigidity. The shoulders straightened, the head lifted, the voice resumed its familiar strong baritone. "What about it, Jeff?" He turned to the secretary of Defense, who was just regaining his own composure. "Can this be true?"

"Obviously I will have to check with the experts, Mr. President," Slocum replied. "But it is true that we have just finished refitting all our old weapons with the new design of Permissive Action Links after the attempt to steal one of the weapons from a destroyer last year. It is also true that for security reasons the codes change automatically every ninety days —"

"Security reasons, security reasons," the President almost shouted. "What the hell kind of security do we have? People don't talk to each other in Germany for security reasons and some nut steals a weapon. We change codes for security reasons, one lone programmer pulls a switch, and bingo, we're disarmed. Who would know?"

"Let's get hold of the scientific adviser. He's next door," said the chief of staff. "And Jeff, why don't you get your experts over here from the Pentagon, pronto. Let's see if this is some wild idea dreamed up by a whacko in the Middle East. We don't really know much about this guy Emir. He may be off his rocker."

The President turned to Appleby, who had been standing since delivering the package. "Sit down, Brad. It looks like it's going to be a long day. All right. If this is for real, and we'll have to assume that it is for now, we have a lot to do and not much time to do it in."

He told the Vice President to get ready to take Air Force Two to Israel. He was to tell the Prime Minister the story in the strictest confidence. It was clearly not possible for the Prime Minister to evacuate the West Bank without the approval of the Knesset even if he were willing to, and the President was not about to divulge this scheme to the Knesset.

"Ask the Prime Minister to make some moves that will make it look as if he's preparing to evacuate. I don't know what. Maybe send some transport vehicles there or something. You stay with him as long as you feel is necessary."

He continued giving instructions around the table. He told the director of the CIA to verify the movements, insofar as possible, of Emir, Schultz, Hassan, Mahmoud, and Malik. After checking with Appleby, he told the FBI to release Mahmoud's airplane to return to Beirut and instructed the CIA to keep tabs on him after he landed.

He gave further instructions to the director of the CIA to locate and estimate the strength of the Palestinian troop buildup and to ascertain the location of the site where the nuclear weapon was being kept.

"Brad, it's a good thing you're here," the President said. "Somehow we've got to keep the Soviets from feeling that anything is wrong. I've been in touch with the General Secretary about a joint effort to locate the missing warhead on the basis that a terrorist might well decide to detonate it on Soviet territory as well as ours. He has designated Peter Rostov as his contact. Since you are already working with Rostov, I'll designate you as mine. You'll have to play a cat-and-mouse game with him until we know more about this situation."

The chief of staff came into the room with Don Horton, the President's scientific adviser, and two colonels from the Pentagon. One of the colonels gave the President a briefing on the operation of the latest model Permissive Action Links. The electronics had been designed and built at the Palo Alto plant of Kane Industries. The principal software designer, June Malik, the President was told, had mysteriously disappeared ten days earlier. The brain of the PAL was in a master clock, which accepted new codes from the White House and programmed them to take control at ninety-day intervals. The electronics package was sent to the weapons assembly plant at Amarillo, Texas, where the package was attached to the mechanical portion of the PAL, the codes inserted, and the complete assembly integrated with the weapon.

The scientific adviser asked whether anyone at Kane Industries had access to the codes and was assured that they did not. The colonels were dismissed and a heated discussion broke out among the NSC staff members about how the codes could be tampered with, some of the staff insisting that the whole thing was a hoax. The scientific adviser insisted that the June Malik involvement was the key to the mystery and recommended that Dr. Kane, principal guru of Kane Industries, be contacted at once. Two phone calls to California elicited the information that Kane and his chief engineer, Herb Goldstein, had flown to Washington that afternoon to discuss Malik's disappearance with the CIA and were currently sitting in the deputy director's office at McLean. They were contacted and told to report to the White House immediately.

Escorted into the Situation Room, Kane was astonished to see both the President and his old friend Brad Appleby sitting at the table.

"Mr. President, Brad, what's —" He had met the President

many times at social functions and business meetings, but to suddenly come upon him with his jacket off and his tie loosened was a shock to Kane.

"Sorry to bother you at such short notice, Bill." The President tried to put him at ease. "We have a very serious problem. You may be able to help us. Don Horton here will explain it to you." He turned away to give some instructions to a staff member.

The scientific adviser brought Kane up to date, then handed him the letter from Emir. A sickening feeling began to build in Kane's stomach. When Horton showed Kane the photograph of June Malik having dinner in Emir's quarters, perspiration broke out on his face. He began to feel dizzy. Keep control of yourself, he admonished himself. He needed time to think. He reached for a glass of water and hoped that the others would not notice his hands shaking.

Words came out of his mouth, but he felt disconnected from his voice. "Wow," said Kane. "I knew that she was close to Emir and that her mother's family had come from the West Bank, but I never would have believed that she could be talked into something like this."

The scientific adviser said that the important question was not why she did it, but whether and how she did it. As he understood it, no one at Kane Industries had access to the codes. "If no one had access, how could she have modified them to a code of her own?"

Kane had to have time to think. He asked for fifteen minutes to converse with Herb Goldstein, who was waiting in an outer office. Permission was granted and Kane left the room. He felt lightheaded and didn't want to talk to Herb until he could compose himself.

He saw a men's room a few steps down the corridor. Its two stalls and three urinals were unoccupied. He entered the farther stall and locked the door. He lowered his trousers and sat on the toilet. His head was in a whirl. He knew exactly what had happened, and he had caused it.

His mind went back to a dinner he and June had had in San

Francisco, a few months after the Albuquerque meeting. June had been harping on her favorite subject, injustice in the Middle East. The issue bored Kane, so he tried to bring the conversation back to a topic of mutual interest. He told her about an item that he had seen in the newspaper that day. A software designer, assembling a payroll program for a major corporation, wrote into the instructions a command that one penny from every weekly paycheck be accumulated in a special account. When the sum reached five hundred dollars, the account would clear and deposit the total in his personal bank account. Since there were thousands of employees on the payroll, he had embezzled a large sum of money over several months, until one parsimonious employee complained that his paycheck was one penny short each week, and the scheme was uncovered.

"It took them two weeks to find it, at that," he said.

June laughed. "Software programs are difficult to analyze," she said. "It can take me a couple of weeks to find one of my own bugs. It could take a lot longer to find a bug — or worse, a virus — someone else put in." She signaled for another glass of wine.

He remembered his next words exactly. "Don't go messing around with that PAL software you're designing," he said. "We don't want atom bombs going off in our faces when they're not supposed to."

June's dark eyes had glittered sharply for an instant but disappeared from view as she brought the wine glass up to her face. She took a long drink, then lowered the glass and touched it to his. The glitter was gone from her eyes. In its place was a look of softness, of sadness, of remorse. He sensed a change in their relationship, a change that would not bode well for either of them.

"Here's to us," she said, taking another long swallow.

Kane shook his head. How could he be so stupid. How could he remember such things as the Arabic curse in Albuquerque and the look in her eyes when he joked about changing the software in the PALs? They had stuck in his mind all this time, but he had not connected them. There had probably been other indications, but his love for her had overwhelmed them. Fool.

Now he was paying for his stupidity. He, Bill Kane, who had been complaining for years about technology run rampant, about simple glitches that could force large systems to fail, was now part of the most serious technological blunder of all, one that would render the nation's complete nuclear stockpile impotent. His mind cleared and he realized where he was — sitting on a john in the basement of the White House while the President of the United States waited for him to come back. The ridiculousness of the situation struck him and counteracted the remorse. His muscles relaxed and he took control of himself. Recriminations would solve no problems. He pulled up his trousers, straightened his clothes, and left the stall.

He had no need to consult Herb but decided to do so anyway. Goldstein confirmed his fears in a few minutes and Kane dashed back to the Situation Room.

"I had an idea how she could have done it, but I wanted to double-check it with my chief engineer first," he said, sitting at the conference table again. At the President's suggestion, he went to the blackboard to explain. He was still nervous. The eraser went spinning from his hand when he tried to clear the board. Harold King picked it up and helped him erase. He reminded his listeners that all computers are very dumb beasts, doing only what they are told to do.

"The function of the software in a Permissive Action Link is to operate a master clock which accepts a new code into its memory every ninety days and to open an electrical gate if that code is subsequently fed into the circuitry. When a signal is fed in through a connector on the surface of the warhead, the software compares it with its memory. If the two are identical, the PAL opens the gate and allows the firing signal to feed through. If incorrect numbers are fed in, the software rejects them. It will tolerate two errors. If a third incorrect set is fed in, the software activates circuits which permanently disable the weapon."

He looked around. Some of the faces were blank, but the President seemed to be following him. In his excitement, he pressed too hard on the chalk. The piece broke. His fingernail scraped against the blackboard, its high-pitched squeal sending shivers down the spines of several of the listeners.

"What the software designer did was to tell the software to accept all codes fed into its memory until midnight of May 31. When the new code for the subsequent ninety days was fed in, the software was told to reject it, but not give any rejection signal. By design, no PAL tested before May 31 will give any indication that all is not well. The software was then told to substitute on May 31 a code that the designer had fed in."

Kane went on to explain that it would not be possible to disassemble a PAL to determine the substitute code or to determine from it the matching key which would unlock it. Only the designer has that. Until that key was obtained, no weapon using the new design could be detonated.

"Then it's true that at midnight on May 31, our whole nuclear arsenal will be disarmed?" asked the President.

"Yes, sir, unless we can obtain the key."

Jeff Slocum smashed his fist on the table and bellowed his disbelief at this statement. Harold King shook his head from side to side without making any comment. The room broke out in a buzz of astonishment and dismay, every man having a different idea of who was at fault and how to correct it.

The President raised his arms for silence. "But, Bill, how could this happen? We're supposed to have so many checks and counterchecks," he said.

"I don't know, sir. Apparently no one thought of this loophole when the concept of automatic code changes was introduced. I hate to say it, sir, but modern weaponry is so complex that it's impossible to determine in advance all the things that can go wrong."

"If we ever get out of this mess, I'll convene a full board of inquiry," said the President. "But for now, the big problem is not how we got into it, but how to get out of it. What do you suggest?"

"I'd suggest you convene a few software experts to check out our analysis and to determine how difficult it will be to decipher the code. It is now six P.M. on Monday the twenty-sixth. We have five days."

# II

*Tuesday, May 27*

JUNE KNEW THAT EMIR WOULD COME TO HER that night. He had called her twice during the day on unimportant matters, testing her, trying to soothe her, explaining that Schultz and Mahmoud were not the kind of people he liked to deal with. "They are the kind of people we will be rid of when my approach is understood," he said.

She was cool and noncommittal, neither rejecting nor encouraging him. Listening on the phone, she knew it would never be the same; the ardor had cooled, the spell was broken. She must put a stop to it all. But she needed him still. He was her only hope of getting away, of getting the code to the American authorities and stopping this mad plan. After hearing Schultz, she knew that there would be violence in the future, violence that Emir would be powerless to prevent. But she had the ultimate weapon, the code.

She had gone to Athens on a vacation while working on the PAL software. Emir had arrived to visit her parents for a couple of days. She was entranced. He was older of course, more mature, shorter than Kane, but with that electric athletic bounce she remembered from her childhood.

And his politics. She responded enthusiastically to his ideas — ideas that shallow Californians could never understand. She knew that he had fared well in Middle Eastern politics, but when her cousin told her that he would likely be the next president of Lebanon, she was dumbfounded. She had followed him around with the awed deference she had felt as a child.

He had visions of nonviolent solutions to Palestinian problems. They were a little vague, but his sincerity convinced her. One fragment stood out in her mind all the way home to San Francisco.

"June, if I could control the world for a day —"

In the succeeding months that remark had lingered in her mind, recurring frequently. One day she coupled it with Kane's statements about inserting bugs in software. She plugged in an innocuous variation to see if any of her subordinates would discover it. They didn't. Perhaps, she thought, this would be the way to give her revered Palestinian the power he needed to carry out their ideas. If it didn't work, there was no harm done. If she was discovered, she could put it down to an error in development. If she wanted to cancel the idea at any time, a single line of instruction would do it.

She had telephoned Emir when she was ready, asking him to meet her again in Athens. As she told him the scheme, they could feel the electricity of mutual attraction. He almost took her in his arms in his excitement, but he restrained himself and merely bowed to kiss her hand.

"My dear," he said, "you will be remembered by generations of our people. In their name, I express to you my gratitude."

The phone rang. It would be Emir.

"June, I'd like you to look over the plans for the television presentation." His voice was businesslike. "Could I stop by about nine?"

She told him that she was a little tired but that nine o'clock was all right if it didn't take too long.

His mind was not on the television plans. He insisted on fixing them both drinks and motioned her to sit beside him as he spread the plans on the coffee table. After fifteen minutes, he reached out to put his arm around her.

She moved away. "Sal, I'm going crazy in this godforsaken place. I've been cooped up in this building for two days and now you tell me that it's going to be almost another week. I've tried to walk around outside, but the trucks and the noise and the dust make it worse than staying in. Can you let me have a car so I can take a drive up Mount Hermon? It's only a few miles and it looks so green and cool."

"June, that would be impossible. It's too dangerous. There are all sorts of people roaming around that mountain. Army deserters, Shiite extremists. You don't know what you might run into."

She moved back again and patted his cheek lightly. "You command the whole army. Can't you protect one little civilian girl? Please."

He reached out for her again. "Let's talk about it later," he said.

"No, I want to talk about it now."

"I just couldn't let you leave this camp alone. Even if you only went a few miles."

It was time to compromise. "If you're so worried, I can take someone with me."

"Well, maybe, if you're willing to take a couple of guards along."

She nodded and pulled him to his feet. She kissed him lightly and shook her head. "It's time for you to go."

Anna rose from the breakfast table, crossed the room, and closed the kitchen draperies, sensing by the abstract expression on his face that her husband had something to talk about.

"I drew a blank with Appleby the other day when I brought up that Syrian, Mahmoud," he said, "so I put a tail on him. He did nothing here, but last week he went to Beirut. He had a helicopter waiting, so we lost him. Suddenly he shows up in the airport again, and gets in a chartered plane for New York, a Boeing 747, no less. I'll find out more in my briefing."

Rostov was reluctant to share his curiosity about Mahmoud with his deputy. He sat through an hour of routine briefings before he could get to the news he wanted. Mahmoud had been met by a limousine that took him directly to the office of Bradford Appleby, where he remained no longer than twenty minutes. Appleby was then taken by police escort to LaGuardia Airport, where a waiting military aircraft flew him to Andrews Field. From Andrews he was ferried by helicopter directly to the landing platform on the White House lawn.

Rostov was impassive. "What happened to Mahmoud?"

"The strangest thing, Comrade Rostov. He went right back to Beirut on the chartered 747. We'll track him from there."

Dismissing his deputy, Rostov went over the information in his head. Mahmoud was obviously a messenger, and an important one, to have Appleby go directly to the White House. The message must be connected with the missing weapon, to have such urgency. Was it connected with the troop buildup on the Israeli border? Would the Lebanese be stupid enough to use a nuclear weapon? If so, why did they steal only one? And what was in the message?

It had been a harrowing night for Bill Kane, inwardly berating himself while trying to show a calm demeanor. The scientific adviser had hurriedly assembled a panel of six computer systems, software, and hardware professionals in the Washington area. Kane felt good when the President appointed him chairman. It would give him an opportunity to make up for what he had done. By dint of prodigious effort on the part of the White House switchboard, they were able to meet in the Situation Room at midnight.

The members of the panel all knew the concept of trapdoor functions, but Kane gave them a basic briefing so that they began at the same point. Starting from the technical definition of a prime as a number that can be divided only by itself and the numeral one (1, 3, 5, 7, 11, 13, 19, 23 . . .), he pointed out that if two large prime numbers are multiplied together, they can be manipulated in such a manner that they can be converted into the product of two other prime numbers, one of which can be made public and the other kept private. It is almost impossible, he pointed out, to decipher the private number even if you have the public number and the product.

"It can't be impossible, because the number exists." The voice of the physicist from the Naval Research Laboratory was both disdainful and skeptical. "There has to be some probability that it can be discovered randomly, like the old chestnut of the ten thousand monkeys with the ten thousand typewriters who eventually must type out the complete works of Shakespeare. What is the probability of discovering it by brute force if I had ten thousand computers with ten thousand operators?"

Kane explained. "This was the first thing the panel was charged to estimate. I've heard it might take two million years on a Cray One computer to have a reasonable probability of deciphering the code. If you had ten thousand Cray Ones, then you might be able to do it in two hundred years."

A young mathematician from the Energy Department cut in. "But the Cray One is the most powerful computer there is. There certainly are no more than fifty of them in existence."

"That's the problem, buddy," said Kane.

He proceeded to lay out the plan of attack for the remainder of the night. A group at the Amarillo assembly plant was already dissecting the latest model PALs ready to be installed in weapons. They would be able to determine the public number that had been inserted into the program to substitute for the now useless number in the President's "football." From that information, a better estimate of the probability of deciphering the private number could be calculated.

The members of the panel were to get on the phone to consult with any of their colleagues anywhere about suggestions for solving the general problem. The panel would reconvene at three. They should be ready to suggest a course of action to the President by six o'clock in the morning.

By the time three o'clock rolled around, Kane was pleased with the accomplishments of his impromptu panel. Among them, they had managed to speak with more than sixty mathematicians, theoretical physicists, software engineers, and hardware manufacturers in a few hours, revealing nothing of the crisis, just feeding them the general problem of how to go about finding the private number in a trapdoor function problem if you have only the public number. The experts were puzzled by being questioned in the middle of the night, but they were too experienced in government consulting to ask why.

The panel's consensus was that there was a 50 percent probability that the number could be found on one large mainframe or on a group of parallel-processing minicomputers in about 1.6 million hours of operation. With one hundred computers, this reduced to 16,000 hours, or about two years, allowing 10 percent downtime for maintenance.

"What chance does that give us of solving the problem in the next four days?" Kane asked the mathematician from the National Security Agency.

"It's not linear, of course," came the reply, "but roughly, with setup time, one in a thousand."

"That means that the chances against breaking the code before Saturday midnight are a thousand to one?"

"That's right, but we might just get lucky and hit the jackpot. It's worth trying, and maybe when these hotshots get going, they can find some more shortcuts."

Precisely at six o'clock, the President, looking grim but fit and well refreshed, walked into the Situation Room. His tall figure was ramrod straight, his full shock of gray hair neatly combed, his chin firm, and his blue eyes piercing. He motioned to the occupants of the room to sit down as he went to his accustomed seat. He did not sit, but stood with his hands gripping the back of the chair.

"Okay, men, let's have it," he said, managing a tight smile. "Where do we stand?" He looked at Kane.

Kane picked up his briefing papers and rose to his feet. In the next few minutes, he explained that although the probability of success was low, there was a slim chance that the code could be broken in the next four and a half days. He estimated that with a strong personal appeal from the President, he could have the equivalent of one hundred large-frame computers working on the problem by noon. He recommended that the President requisition one hundred PALs from the Amarillo inventory and have them delivered to the operators of the computers.

"We recognize that the devices are classified," he said. "If you prefer, mathematical equations can substitute —"

"Forget the classification. Go on."

Kane completed his report by saying, "If all goes well, we estimate that there is one chance in a thousand of success."

The President frowned. "That low?"

"Yes, sir. But we think that it's worth doing."

"Okay. Sounds like the only game in town. What do I have to do?"

Good. Kane knew how to take charge. With a firm voice, he proceeded to lay out a plan. First, the President should requisition a hundred PALs from Amarillo and rustle up couriers to deliver them posthaste. Next, he should issue a directive to all government agencies and associated civilian installations to provide staff and hardware on a twenty-four-hour basis. Then he should telephone the presidents of the major universities and ask them to devote all their capabilities to this problem. Also the heads of the major computer companies. By then the panel would have staff available to tell the computer centers how to go about the search and what to do until they got the PALs.

"We recognize that an effort of this magnitude will immediately be picked up by the press. We recommend that you tell everyone that the work is related to the stolen nuclear weapon but give them no details. Ask the press to sit on it for a few days. Maybe they'll cooperate and maybe they won't, but it's doubtful that they can guess the real story. We recommend that you do not contact the Soviet Union, at least until we get organized. A crash program on a nationwide basis is too susceptible to sabotage."

The President nodded, then faced the chief of staff. "Did you get all that, Fred? Good." He turned back to Kane. "Consider it done. Good work, gentlemen. Get some sleep now."

When Mahmoud's plane touched down at the Beirut airport, three groups of people were waiting for him: a KGB colonel

185

and three captains, three CIA agents, and Hassan with two Lebanese officers. The colonel, in civilian clothes, was posing as a West German business executive, and the three captains were dressed in the uniforms of a flight crew of a South American airline; one of the CIA agents was handling baggage while the other two were operating a refueling truck; and Hassan and his aides were wearing Arab robes. Hassan had instructions to bring Mahmoud back to the camp, where he would essentially be in custody with Schultz and June. Emir didn't trust either Mahmoud or Schultz. Neither knew the full story, but they did know where the hijacked weapon was and should not be left unguarded.

Hassan met the Syrian at the bottom of the stairs to offer him transportation back to the camp. When Mahmoud protested that he had some business to attend to in Beirut, a signal from Hassan brought the two Lebanese officers to either side of him, their weapons outlined by the creases in their lightweight robes. Mahmoud went quietly.

Both the Americans and the Russians had helicopters waiting at the airport, but Hassan went by limousine to the other side of the city. He was trailed by two American agents in a Saab and the Russian colonel in a Fiat. The compacts had difficulty keeping up with the large vehicle.

The limousine pulled off the main highway to a cleared field with a waiting helicopter, and the others were caught flat-footed. It was almost a Mack Sennett chase scene as the Russians and the Americans frantically called up their aircraft by radio, the Lebanese aircraft taking off due south and the others barely able to hold it in their radars.

When Hassan's helicopter put down at a small pad close to the Israeli border, those in the two others could see armed troops surround the vehicle as the passengers were loaded into waiting jeeps. They decided to keep their distance, hoping to follow. Sporadic gunfire from the ground kept them far enough away to lose track of their quarry. The two pursuit vehicles, long since conscious of each other, almost saluted as their tail rotors swung around to head dejectedly for the Beirut airport.

None of the three parties was pleased with the result, but the trail was beginning to unwind. Hassan expected to be followed by the Americans and was prepared to shake them, but he was distressed to have another group, almost certainly the Russians, involved. The Americans, who had recognized the KGB colonel, were unhappy that the Soviets had picked up the scent of Mahmoud, but pleased to pinpoint the location of the PLO troop buildup. The KGB colonel, expecting the wrath of Moscow to settle on his head, could counteract his failure by establishing a connection between Mahmoud's mission and the PLO troop buildup. He was sure that Moscow would be pleased at that.

Neither Rostov nor Appleby was aware of any of this when they met at noon. Because of the urgency and secrecy of their new missions, they had decided to abandon the practice of meeting in hotel dining rooms, settling instead on a Manhattan apartment formerly used by the FBI as a safe haven for defectors. The tone of the meeting was set before it started, when Rostov called for permission to check the apartment for bugs before they met. Appleby agreed on the condition that his own man accompany the Russian technician. He didn't want any Russian bugs set in his own safe haven.

The building was in the garment district. It had been a warehouse, converted a few years before to small condominium apartments, generally occupied by working couples who had no interest in or curiosity about their neighbors. The apartment was clean enough, but spartanly furnished. Old brass beds, cheap mahogany tables, and a few scatter rugs filled the bedroom. The other room had a stove, a refrigerator, and a wooden kitchen table covered with a red-and-white-checked tablecloth. Appleby was irritated when he saw it, thinking that even the FBI should be able to do better than that.

Appleby arrived early, Rostov exactly at noon. They tried small talk, but it didn't work. Appleby could see that Rostov had questions to ask. He decided to take the offensive and ask his first. "Pete, how much part did your people play in Eva Spengler's demonstration?"

"Not much," Rostov replied. They had kept the demonstration well infiltrated but played no specific part. They had a good file on Schultz, which he offered to furnish.

Appleby felt pleased with this offer and accepted with profuse thanks.

But Rostov came right back. "Why did Schultz take only one warhead, and why did he take the two officers?"

Appleby was prepared for the first question, but he had to move carefully. He informed Rostov that the accomplices picked up in Nuremberg each had one hundred thousand deutsche marks, proving that the theft was for money. Schultz's payoff was probably hundreds of times that. He may have figured that, with the payoff agreed upon in advance, he wouldn't get any more money if he delivered a dozen warheads. The second question was trickier for Appleby, since he knew the answer. He fended it off by saying that the officers were merely couriers and that he probably took them along merely as evidence that the warhead was the stolen one, in the event that it was to be used for ransom or blackmail.

Rostov seemed satisfied. "The next question. Did this warhead have a lock on it to prevent unauthorized detonation? You call them Permissive Action Links, I believe."

"Yes, it did."

"Do you think they will be able to bypass it or decipher the code?"

Appleby chose his words carefully. "We are confident that they will not be able to bypass it. Any attempt to mechanically breach the integrity of the device sets off a very small explosive charge which destroys the symmetry of the implosion lenses and makes it a dud. Understand?"

Rostov nodded.

"As for breaking the code, who knows? The experts tell us that any code can be broken eventually. It depends on how sophisticated the thieves are."

Rostov pressed harder. "My people tell me that one of your principal code designers has disappeared and is suspected to be in Lebanon. Would she have the current code, and can these two events be connected?"

"The procedure is that the code is inserted at the weapons assembly area and is known only to a few high government officials. As to a connection, the only report we have on the DC-9 is from Athens, stating that the aircraft was headed southeast at low altitude to escape detection. We think it flew over Yugoslavia or Hungary to get there, but those countries refuse to give us any information. Can you get it for us?"

Appleby felt relieved at turning the question. He stood up and went to the refrigerator, where he found a six-pack of Diet Coke. He pulled the tab on one, drank directly from the can, and placed a second on the table. Rostov's face was impassive as he pulled the drink toward him but did not open it. He was weighing his response. "I'll have it for you tomorrow," he replied.

"All right. Let's assume a couple of scenarios." Appleby changed the subject. The discussion was going his way. "This device is about twenty kilotons. That's about the size of the Hiroshima or Nagasaki explosion. It will pretty well knock out any major city. There are two classes of probabilities. One is that it was stolen by a national group to use on one of its enemies, say, Iraq on Iran or Libya on Israel. In that case, neither of our countries is in immediate danger. We each have satellite networks which can unambiguously identify a nuclear explosion. There will only be one and we will know what it is. I think that communication with each other over the hot line will be adequate, don't you?"

"Agreed."

"My President proposes an immediate joint communiqué condemning the perpetrator, imposing sanctions, and offering military assistance to the victim nation."

Rostov went to a cabinet, took out a glass, and held it to the light to be sure it was clean. He sat down and poured the Coke into the glass.

"That's going a little fast, Brad, and you know it. Don't try to put my man on the spot. He has a very conservative element in the Politburo and has to be more circumspect than you. After all, it was your device and your deployment that caused the problem. If you kept all your warheads in your country the way we do, you wouldn't be in this mess. Let me say that we would look favorably on such a proposal and let it go at that."

Appleby ignored the barb. He pressed on. "We accept. Now, what if the weapon is used on one of our cities, particularly Washington or Moscow. Our President is prepared to have the Vice President establish headquarters in a remote location during the crisis and to furnish you information on the location of that headquarters. Will you reciprocate?"

Rostov was cautious. "I have only been able to communicate with the General Secretary by telegram. I will cable him that question. If he reacts favorably, I will ask that the details be sent by special courier. I should have an answer for you by Saturday. But you have left out the big question. What if one of us is threatened by blackmail?"

Appleby had already discussed that with the President, who had directed him to be circumspect. "It would depend on the nature of the blackmail threat. If the security of either nation is involved, it is natural that each of us act in our own best interests, unencumbered by oral agreements."

"What does that mean?"

Appleby could feel the Russian boring in. "It means, uh, well, there are so many kinds of blackmail threats that it's difficult to generalize. They could be against us, against an ally of either of us, against a neutral nation; there are so many possibilities."

"Why not say that neither of us will submit to blackmail and will notify the other if a blackmailer comes forward?"

"We do that all the time, Pete. Our Nuclear Emergency Search Team has investigated hundreds of threats and we have refused to negotiate with nuclear terrorists. We notify you if it's important. So far, all the bomb threats have proved to be hoaxes, thank God. But this is different. There's an actual warhead out there. The people know it, the press knows it, the Congress knows it. I can't guarantee what the reaction would be to a threat of blowing up New York or Washington, nor can you about a threat to Moscow."

"Yes, I can," said Rostov. "We would still refuse to negotiate. Brad, you are not leveling with me. The whole concept of our relationship was that we would be open with each other. Now I sense that you are holding back. What is it?"

Appleby felt the discussion coming apart. He decided to try to bull it through. "I resent your accusation that I'm holding back on you. I was willing to compromise on the question of sanctions and the location of headquarters in the event of a catastrophe. This isn't a one-way street. You have to make some compromises, too."

"Those concessions are minor, and you know it," said Rostov. "This thing smells of blackmail, and you refuse to get specific."

"I'm sorry, Pete, this is as far as I want to go."

Rostov's eyes hardened; his shoulders stiffened. "If that is the way you are going to act, Mr. Appleby, we shall have to call these meetings to a halt until I can communicate with my ministers and ask for further instructions."

Appleby realized his error and changed his tone, but it was too late. "Trust me, Pete. Give me a couple of days to get back to you."

Rostov stood up, glared at Appleby, then turned away. "I'm sorry, Mr. Appleby," he said. "Good day."

# 12

---

JUNE WAS EXCITED AND NERVOUS ABOUT HER ride to the mountain. She had no specific plan, only somehow to entice the guards away from the car and make a dash south for the Israel border. Emir had insisted that she take the limousine with two guards, that she not get out of the automobile, and that she be back by two in the afternoon. She went to the box of tampons on the back of the toilet seat and removed one with a scratch mark on the applicator. She separated the two halves of the applicator and removed a small piece of parchment wrapped around the tampon. Typed on it was the assembly code, the method of assembling the small primes she had memorized into large prime numbers. She had memorized the assembly code also, but did not trust her memory under stress.

She looked at the code for a moment, then replaced it, reassembled the applicator, and put it in her purse.

June put on a long-sleeved tan shirt, slacks, and the heavy shoes she had been furnished for walking in the stony soil of the campsite, but when she stepped out into the morning sun, it was so pleasant that she went back and changed into a light blouse and shorts, carrying the heavier clothes with her in case she needed them. She took along a set of binoculars that were on the living room mantel. The maid had packed a lunch and the limousine had a small refrigerator stocked with soft drinks. Her worries, even the thought of escape, fell away from her for a few minutes as they climbed the gently rolling hills at the foot of Mount Hermon. She convinced the guards that she could not use the binoculars properly from the back seat, so they stopped periodically to let her walk around the car to view the scenery. Every fifteen minutes she could hear one of them reporting to base camp on the radio.

Abu Nidal's man, Yusuf, paid little attention to the limousine as it passed through the gates of the site. Limousines and helicopters had been going back and forth for the week that he had been observing the activities. It wasn't until the vehicle left the main road to Beirut and turned north on a dirt road up the mountain toward him that he trained his high-powered binoculars on it.

Nidal had been furious with Emir since his dressing-down after the airplane hijacking. He had suggested recruiting Schultz, who he felt would be useful to him, but had refrained from contacting him until Emir's intentions became more clear. The theft of the warhead had caught him by surprise. He knew of the existence of the test site and assumed that it must have some connection with the theft. The arrival of the American girl at Emir's headquarters and her transfer to the test site only confused him further. Somewhere in this complicated scheme must be an opportunity for some gain for himself and revenge on Emir. He had placed his lieutenant at a strategic point overlooking the site, with instructions to observe carefully and, if possible, to abduct someone who might be interrogated. The limousine, thought Yusuf, might contain just what he was looking for.

Yusuf lost sight of the vehicle several times as it reached the wooded part of the foothills, but there was only one road on this part of the mountain and the limousine was coming directly at him. Just before noon, it stopped in a clearing a few hundred yards below the large rock he was using as an observation post. He decided to go down and take a closer look.

June had been using her charms on the guards. She inquired

about their jobs, their families, and their interests. She realized that the reason they were letting her out of the car against orders was that they could get a better look at her than when she was cooped up in the back seat. At lunchtime, they pulled into the clearing, where there was a good view of the campsite and the desert at the foot of the mountain.

She received their permission to set up her picnic lunch about fifty yards away. She invited them to join her, but they refused politely, saying that they had to stay close to the vehicle to hear the radio. She toyed with her salad, wondering how she could entice them far enough away to make a dash for the car, when she heard a gurgling scream from the woods.

One of the guards had wandered away in the trees; the driver stood leaning against the front door of the limousine, the engine running, the window down to hear the radio turned up to full gain. When he heard the scream, he looked up, startled, at first thinking it might have come from the radio. He called to his associate. Receiving no answer, he ran into the woods, pistol in hand.

Yusuf had bungled the garroting. When the man stopped to relieve himself, Yusuf had plenty of time to steal up in back of him and reach the thin cord around his neck. But the guard was a foot taller than he, and the rope caught in his beard for a fraction of a second before the assassin could pull it tight, leaving time enough for the scream, which started out shrill but ended in a breathless gurgle. Yusuf cursed, let the lifeless body sink to the ground, and stepped behind a tree, not visible to the driver stumbling toward him. This time it was easy. When the guard knelt to turn over the body of his companion, Yusuf needed only a downward thrust of the hunting knife into the back of the man's neck to dispatch him silently.

June heard the scream and saw the driver run into the woods. This was her chance. She dropped her fork, stood up, and began running toward the limousine. Halfway there, she was astounded to see an unfamiliar short figure, carrying the slain driver's pistol and running directly at her. She could see that he was as astonished as she was.

"You are Emir's woman. What are you doing here?" he asked in Arabic.

She could see the leer in his eyes and the tongue darting between his lips. She must buy time.

"*Manish Araba.* I speak only English," she replied.

"You . . . come . . . me," he said, stringing out the English words and beckoning her toward the upper road, where his car was parked.

He looked intently at the light blouse and revealing shorts. "But first, you goddamned whore," he rattled off in Arabic, "I'll teach you that you shouldn't be running around naked to attract men. Come here, you bitch."

He reached out and tore her blouse, knocking her to the ground. He then pulled off his belt, dropped his pants to his ankles, and straddled her on his knees. He wore no underwear.

She could smell his coarse breath and see his arousal as he reached to pull off her shorts. She had to stop him now, she thought. She shouted a string of Arabic curses into his ear that made him pull back in confusion. As she did, she pulled up her knees with all her strength into his groin. He was off balance, and the desperate strength of her thrust pushed his slight body over her head, sprawling him ignominiously on the ground behind her. She rose quickly and turned. He was on his side, his knees drawn up almost in a fetal position. She drew back her heavy walking shoe and kicked again, as hard as she could, into his exposed testicles. He screamed and rolled over, hands clutching his groin.

She ran for the limousine. The motor was running and the radio was blasting. She turned once and saw him, clutching his groin with one hand and trying to pull up his pants with the other. She got into the car, slammed it into reverse to change direction, then spun the wheels against the dirt road to speed past him down the mountain.

Yusuf dropped his pants and reached for the pistol he had thrown on the ground. As she went by, he put two shots each into the rear tires of the speeding limousine and ran up the road to his own truck, hidden in some small evergreen bushes.

June felt the tires flatten and realized that she would not be able to control the vehicle at high speed. She pressed the radio transmitter button and shouted. "It's June Malik. Help, help. The guards have been murdered." Then she had to drop the transmitter to keep both hands on the wheel.

She went careening down the mountainside, feeling that he must have a vehicle and that she would not be able to control the limousine well enough to stay ahead of him, but hoping to get out of the trees and onto the main road before he caught up. She went only a mile before she could see, in the mirror, a vehicle coming toward her at high speed. It disappeared as she went around a bend, but reappeared much closer as it came around the corner. She could wait no longer. As she traversed the next bend, she pulled the limousine sharply off the road into a gully, braked to a stop, opened the door and ran off into the woods. She looked back to see the truck come around the bend and speed past her, then screech to a halt and back up toward the limousine. She knew she could not run fast enough to keep ahead of him. The trees were sparser now; it would not be easy to hide. A huge beech loomed in front of her. She climbed it as fast as she could, skinning her legs as she climbed. She stopped, panting, about twenty feet up.

She could hear him coming, thrashing through the brush, stopping every once in a while to listen to the sound of her movements. He went by, about ten feet away. She considered climbing down and running in the opposite direction, but she had no energy left. In a few minutes, he returned, walking stealthily, looking up into the trees, the pistol in his hand. She moved to get out of his field of vision, but a branch cracked. He looked up and pointed the pistol at her.

"Come down, you whore." He cursed her in Arabic. "I'm taking you with me, you bitch, but before I do, I'm going to give you the —" He never finished the sentence.

The bullet hit him between the shoulder blades. He went down from the force of the impact. Three PLO soldiers came running toward them, machine pistols at the alert.

As June reached the ground, Emir himself came running up.

She threw herself into his arms, sobbing with exhaustion. He would never know that she had intended to escape.

It was a hot, dry afternoon when Air Force Two landed at the Tel Aviv airport. The Vice President, aware of the Israeli officialdom's predilection for informality, had discarded his coat and tie and rolled up his shirt sleeves as the aircraft stopped at a portable landing platform at the far end of the airstrip, heavily guarded by armored vehicles and troops carrying AK47s. No time was wasted on greetings. A minor functionary led him and one aide to a waiting limousine, where a motorcycle escort led them to the Prime Minister's residence. The Prime Minister and the minister of Defense were waiting, clad in light slacks, loafers, and bright sport shirts. They were stolid, swarthy men, the Defense minister prominently hawk-nosed, the two in marked contrast to the slim red-haired Irishman in his early forties who had risen from the back streets of Boston politics to the second most important post in his nation.

The Vice President took only fifteen minutes to relate the chronology of the defection of June Malik, the hijacking of the weapon, and the letter from al Emir, with its onerous demands on the nation of Israel.

"The man must be mad," the Prime Minister said. "We have broken no treaties. We are prepared to work out a mechanism to live in harmony with our Arab brothers on the Jordan River. As you must know, Mr. Vice President, we are often hindered rather than helped by our friends in the United States. They are more alarmist than we, and they stir up people like al Emir. Even if we were willing to evacuate, I would have no authority to make these decisions. I would have to go through the Knesset. That could not be done on this time scale, and could not be done at all with a gun at our heads. Nor could it be done without publicly exposing this wild scheme. What he demands is impossible."

"I understand, Mr. Prime Minister, but we do have a gun at both our heads, a very large gun indeed, and our own guns are being rendered useless. We must buy time to either reason this man out of his wild scheme, search for a record of this code, or decipher it. We are doing all three. I must ask that you take steps to partially evacuate the West Bank or to appear that you are doing so over the next four days. Perhaps he will relax the time schedule if we appear to be cooperating with him. As you know, this is the standard procedure with all terrorist groups — buy time, negotiate."

"We have noticed troop movements near the border," said the Defense minister. "But we have not been concerned because of the absence of heavy armament. You have told us that the Syrian was taken by jeep to an area close to this troop buildup. We have the area thoroughly infiltrated and should be able to pinpoint the location of the proposed demonstration within a day, now that we know what we're looking for. We can put in a surgical strike and wipe them all out in a matter of hours."

The Vice President patiently pointed out that such an action would be counterproductive. The code key would be lost forever. Furthermore, Emir would certainly leave a secret message for the Russians, to be delivered in the event that he was killed or captured. "That is why he is not concerned about our finding the location of the weapon and why he is willing to broadcast on coded TV. We expect to find the location ourselves shortly. He is enjoying this twisting of our tails. He is baiting us, almost goading us, to try something. Clearly, gentlemen, whether he is mad or not, he has the upper hand."

The Defense minister would not let go. "Why don't we try to capture the girl. She is an American citizen who has probably been duped. If we could get hold of her, we could surely persuade her to talk."

The Vice President explained that there would be considerable risk in such an effort. If it failed, the result could be catastrophic for Western civilization. He departed within the hour, leaving behind two agitated and skeptical Israeli officials.

When the Prime Minister returned from ushering the Vice President to his limousine, the Defense minister was already on the phone, demanding an immediate briefing on the troop buildup on the Lebanese border. "Yitzhak," he said when he had finished, "the hell with the Americans. They're too cautious. They're not going to talk this lunatic Emir out of anything. If the Russians wipe out the United States, we'll be the next to go. Even if the Americans capitulate and negotiate, you know that we'll be the first ones thrown to the wolves. The weapon and the girl must be only a few miles from our border. Let's go in and grab her. We'll make her talk."

At that moment the director of the CIA was receiving a briefing from his deputy about information that had just been received from one of the Big Bird intelligence satellites. The satellite had picked up bursts of carrier on classified intelligence VHF channel 89. The signal, originating from an unauthorized location in the Middle East, had only the carrier with no modulation or coding. The bursts were at one-minute intervals, one minute on and one minute off. The location of the unauthorized transmitter was thirty degrees, twenty-eight minutes north latitude, thirty-four degrees, fifty-one minutes east longitude, about forty miles southeast of the Lebanese city of Tyre. The station was on for one hour just as the satellite was positioned directly overhead. It was the duty officer's opinion that whoever was transmitting was trying to get their attention. The United States transmitting station in northern Virginia responded but there was no reply. The director then instructed the deputy to contact the head of the Middle East mission for covert operations, headquartered in Cairo. Cairo was ordered to dispatch secret agents to the location of the transmitter immediately.

A strong argument developed in the National Security Council about sending an envoy to Beirut. Fred Billings felt that the President should send a high-ranking official. Harold King volunteered. The CIA director objected that sending the secretary of State would be interpreted as overanxiety to negotiate.

Jeff Slocum wanted to ignore Emir's message. He pounded on the table, shouting his objections. "We should never deal with terrorists. If we refuse to deal with this scum, he will eventually give up. I would like permission, Mr. President, to dispatch the complete Mediterranean fleet to the Lebanese coast and to alert Special Forces for a rescue mission as soon as we know the location of the weapon. Two American officers have been kidnapped. There should be no deals until they are returned."

Harold King forced himself to remain calm. "For God's sake, Jeff," he said, "this is no ordinary terrorist threat. You've seen the pictures. They have the hijacker, they have the code designer, they have the officers, they have the weapon. If Emir carries out his threat, the Russians could control the world."

The President raised his hand. "Get George Yacobian in here," he instructed Billings. "We'll send him."

Emir was not happy to see the President's Middle East negotiator; he had expected to deal with a cabinet officer. When Yacobian was ushered into his office, Emir waved him to a chair.

The envoy wasted no words. "I am instructed to demand that you return the stolen nuclear warhead and the kidnapped American citizens. These actions are in violation of all tenets of international law."

Emir was unruffled. "I did not steal a nuclear warhead. I merely bought it from the person who was able to steal it because of your utterly confused security practices. Allah forbid that it should fall into other hands, those who would use it to kill and destroy. No one will die, no nuclear weapon will be detonated, if you and your Israeli puppets agree with my most modest proposal."

"And if we don't?"

Emir smiled. "Then the decision will be up to your enemies. I hope that they will be merciful to you in your weakness."

"But you don't leave us enough time," said Yacobian. "Four days is insufficient to talk to our allies and begin a withdrawal. A week would be the minimum to agree on a plan and set up the mechanics —"

The smile left Emir's face as he put his hands, palms down, flat on the table. "Let us not mince words or play games. I know that the standard ploy with what you call terrorists is to buy

time and negotiate needlessly. I will have none of that. Your
Vice President is already in Tel Aviv talking to the Israeli Prime
Minister. He should know by now what the Israeli position is.
The code switches at midnight May thirty-first. At half past
twelve we will arm the device so that you can attempt to detonate it with your code. Up to that time it will be guarded by
your own officers and you will be able to observe it on your
classified television channel. I will be standing beside it, and so
will Miss Malik. If the device does not detonate, we will open
the channel for all nations to monitor, and the world will realize
that the United States nuclear arsenal has been disarmed, not
by any action of mine, but by your own electronic circuitry. If
you and your allies cooperate, the weapon, the code, and the
officers will be released to your custody."

Yacobian got up to leave without speaking.

Emir raised his hand. "I should like to ask one thing of you,
Mr. Yacobian, in our mutual interests. Our transmitter is already broadcasting the carrier frequency on satellite VHF
channel 89. We will need one of your scrambling modems so
that we can transmit on a secure basis for the next four days.
Should you refuse to cooperate, we will have to operate on a
clear channel immediately."

"You will have a scrambler modem plus a spare within
twenty-four hours," said the envoy. "I bid you good day."

The President had spent the day on the telephone talking with
university presidents, computer manufacturers, service companies, research laboratories, and independent government agencies. His message to each was simple. He wanted immediate and
complete access to their large computers to solve a mathematical equation. Unfortunately, the approach would have to be
"brute force," that is, trying a great many numbers in succession, hoping to find the solution by sheer persistence. He told
them that it was of the utmost national importance and that it
was related to the hijacking of the nuclear warhead. He di-
vulged no further information. A direct call from the President
of the United States was too compelling to be argued with. By

evening eighty-five large computer systems were taking their orders from Kane and his panel. By 10:00 P.M. there were one hundred and five. The President had one more task before he was scheduled to talk to the press.

At 7:00 P.M. the congressional delegation was ushered into the Cabinet Room. It was a grave and perplexed group who had come in by back and side and basement doors to avoid reporters. There were the Speaker of the House, the Senate and House majority and minority leaders, the chairman of the Foreign Relations Committee, and the chairmen of the Armed Services and Energy committees. The President was waiting for them as they arrived, standing with a sheaf of papers in his hand. To these experienced politicians, the fact that he did not make the usual dramatic entrance after they were assembled was the strongest indication of the gravity of the moment.

He warned them that the nation was in dire peril and that there could be no political partisanship or leaks to the press. He gave them the story straight, with nothing left out. The members of his party slumped in their chairs as the story unfolded. The opposition listened at first with little half smiles, which gradually turned into frozen grimaces. By the time he finished, any thought of political advantage had been wiped from the heads and the faces of the group.

The Speaker of the House, a wrinkled veteran of many political and fighting wars, promised complete cooperation and support. The others nodded in stunned silence.

"What are you telling the press?" the Senate majority leader asked.

"That the calculations are part of the search process to find the hijacked warhead."

"What are we telling our allies? What about the United Nations, Western Europe, NATO?" asked the chairman of the Foreign Relations Committee.

"Except for Israel, nothing," the President replied.

After the first polite speech, the Speaker of the House had been quiet and reflective, taking no part in the discussion, puffing on his cigar, lighting it twice as it went out. He shook his massive frame, stubbed out the cigar, and prepared to speak, the others deferring by force of habit.

"Mr. President, we now have twenty-five thousand functional nuclear weapons, right?"

"Approximately, Mr. Speaker. Go ahead."

"At midnight Saturday, we may not have any, right?"

"Yes."

"Well, at eleven-thirty Saturday night, if we haven't found the code, why don't we push the twenty-five thousand buttons and blow those Russian bastards off the face of the earth before they get a chance to do it to us?"

# 13

BY SIX O'CLOCK WEDNESDAY MORNING, THE SIT-
uation Room in the White House had been transformed into a
command center. Gone were the coffee cups and the Danish
pastry, the flags, the extra chairs around the periphery of the
room. Two six-by-eight-foot TV monitors had been installed on
the wall facing the President's chair, with a blackboard on one
wall and an easel holding a large paper pad on the other.
Additional telephones had been installed; the red one was for
direct connection to the hot line TWX to Moscow. A twenty-
circuit intercom had been placed in the center of the table. A
small dining area was set up outside the door, with tables
containing pots of coffee, regular and decaffeinated, hot water,
tea bags, juice, soft drinks, regular and diet, pastries, sand-
wiches, and fruit.

A section of living quarters in the West Wing had been set
aside for Security Council members and key officials. Kane was
assigned a large bedroom with a double bed and private bath.
The President, a stickler for orderly working habits who had
great respect for the dangers of fatigue, picked up during his
military experience, had ordered that everyone get a minimum
of four hours' sleep a night and at least one meal a day in the
dining room.

Kane spent the first hour staring into the darkness, recalling his many hours with June. They had been in love, so although her preoccupation with Middle East affairs sometimes bored him, it generally only added to her charm. And how excited she had been after her vacation in Greece. He had put that down as pleasure at seeing her relatives. But he cursed himself for talking to her about bugs in software. Maybe she would have thought of it on her own, but he would feel responsible until he had deciphered the code. From sheer exhaustion, he fell into a deep sleep.

He woke up refreshed at five minutes to five, anticipating the call from the switchboard, showered, and settled for juice and coffee from the tables. His activities had been moved to a large conference room two doors down, where his panel could keep in touch with their nationwide computing network without interference from the general bustle of the Situation Room.

One hundred and ten systems were now on line. All of these were feeding into PALs, the disabling circuits disconnected, so that if the correct numbers were found, a switch would close and a light come on. The numerical spectrum had been divided into one hundred distinct parts, each computer assigned a portion of the spectrum to investigate. The other ten systems were designated as spares. Kane had decided not to shut down computers for routine maintenance, but to work them twenty-four hours a day, filling in with the spares if breakdowns occurred.

There was an aura of adventure in the air. Typically, the scientist was able to detach himself from the purpose of the operation, concentrating only on the technological problems involved. All were aware of the complexity of the search process, but none had an inkling of the short time available for solution. In addition to the computer managers themselves, dozens of engineers and scientists at each location were seeking shortcuts and more efficient processes, so that by early morning, several thousand of the best scientific minds in the nation were actively working on the project.

A mathematician called in from the Idaho National Engineering Laboratory to suggest an application of the theory of finite differences, in which the computer could be fed every second number to be analyzed, retracing if the answer looked promising. This theory was assigned to a spare at the Jet Propulsion Laboratory in California to be investigated. An MIT theoretical physicist called in from home, suggesting an application of the concept of successive approximations, in which the computer would skip around randomly until a reasonable-looking path was located, then try to bracket the solution, much as artillery theory provides optimum solutions for homing in on targets. The physicist lived in Lexington, Massachusetts, so he was directed to the MIT Lincoln Laboratory in his hometown for further work on the project. Gradually, they were chipping away at it.

Jeff Slocum asked for a short meeting with the President. He walked into the Oval Office accompanied by the undersecretary for Research and Development.

The Defense secretary came right to the point. "Dr. Cranston, here, is one of the nation's best statistical analysts. He feels that this guy Kane is on a wild-goose chase. I agree with him. The computer search isn't going to work."

The President was cool. "Oh?"

The owl-eyed scientist was deferential. "Mr. President," he said, "the actuaries give the probabilities of success at one thousand to one. I think that's optimistic. He's not going to make it in time."

Slocum cut in. "I'd again like to ask permission to send the Mediterranean fleet to Lebanon. We need a show of force to impress this nut. If that nuke is where I think it is, we can go in and take it out with a few helicopters from an aircraft carrier. You can't win wars with computers."

The President sighed. "Okay, Jeff, I'll allow contingency preparations. Dispatch one aircraft carrier under secret orders. No action without specific orders from me. No publicity, and you can deploy a couple of helicopter squadrons with it."

At noon, Kane called a staff meeting to review progress. The staff, now broken into three shifts, were alert and confident.

"Have we cut down the odds at all? That's the key question," Kane said.

An actuary from a Washington insurance company, filling in as the staff statistician, was pleased at the progress. "I estimate that this morning's ideas have cut the probabilities from one in a thousand to one in five hundred," he announced.

"Shit, that's still only two tenths of one percent," said Kane.

"Depends on how you look at it," said the scientist from Naval Research. "As I see it, we've improved our chances by a factor of two."

In Tel Aviv, the Prime Minister was reading the headlines in the morning papers while casting occasional glances at the television news, shaking his head at the newspapers while wrinkling his nose at the TV. The previous evening he had put out a feeler, quoting an anonymous but usually reliable source, to the effect that the West Bank buildup was going too rapidly. The source said that the administration was considering halting migration generally and perhaps pulling back in areas of maximum tension. The reaction from the press and from members of the Knesset was devastating. Hard-liners accused the administration of indecision and cowardice; even the moderates and members of his own party felt that no such action should be contemplated without full national debate. The Palestinians' demands could not be carried out in the time scale available. He called in the special envoy the Vice President had left behind and convinced him to ask for more time to consult with national leaders, knowing that it would not do much good. He then called the minister of Defense and told him to proceed with the contingency plan.

General Berman was in the minister's office when he received the call. Berman was an old hand at counterintelligence and antiterrorist tactics. The best plan, he cautioned, since the camp was so close to the Israeli border, was not to storm it, but to infiltrate it. He would keep a helicopter squadron, ready to be loaded with commando troops, on the Israeli side of the border, where they could reach the encampment within thirty minutes if a frontal attack were ordered. He had already dispatched four covert agents to the campsite to determine the layout of the area and the location of the woman.

He had three plans in mind. The first assumed that the agents would be able to locate the woman, overpower the guards without raising an alarm, and get back to the Israeli border. The second assumed that they would be able to locate the woman but not be able to free her without danger that she would be killed. In that case, the commandos would land on the base, spray the area with tear gas, and hope to make off with her in the confusion. The third was the most risky all around. The commandos would storm the area, disarm the warhead, wipe out the whole contingent guarding the bomb, including, if necessary, the American officers and the woman, in the hopes that, without a demonstration, the Russians would not believe Emir's story.

The Defense minister balked. "I can't go for that one. The Americans would be furious. The old man would have my ass."

Berman laughed. "Don't tell him. Then he'll have what the Americans call 'plausible deniability.' Sometimes we have to rise above principle."

"What happens if the Palestinians detonate the weapon during the attack?"

"Our analysts don't think they can. We don't think Emir has access to the present code. If we are wrong . . ."

Rostov walked out of the screen room and took the elevator to the living quarters with a grim look of concentration on his face. Anna looked at him quizzically. "Anything wrong?"

"Yes, a lot of things don't add up. I need to do some thinking. It's a beautiful day. If you're not doing anything special, let's go down to the World Trade Center for lunch."

"Oh, Petya, what a wonderful idea. I'm delighted."

As the chauffeur drove by Battery Park, Rostov tapped on the window. "I've changed my mind. Let's do something crazy. Let's take the boat ride out to the Statue of Liberty instead."

Anna's eyes widened. "Whatever you say."

They purchased their tickets and pushed their way to a hard bench in a corner of the upper deck with no one near them.

"Whom are you trying to get rid of?" she asked.

"No one in particular, but I'm sure that with this new assignment the KGB has someone tailing me, if only for my own protection. I want to talk to you, but I wanted to be sure we are not overheard. I think we're safe here."

"I think so too," she said, smiling. "Look."

As the boat pulled away from the dock they could see two stocky men in ill-fitting suits and felt hats arguing with the dock crew, who shook their heads and walked away.

He told her of his concerns that his deputy was asking too many questions. In his opinion, the hard-liners in the Kremlin thought he was too soft on the Americans and were putting him under special surveillance — witness the men on the dock. This was worrisome, not for his own sake, but because they were willing to take the risk that the General Secretary might find out. It would make it more difficult for him to work with Appleby, who was holding back information from him.

"What kind of information?"

He was convinced that Mahmoud was connected with the hijacking of the warhead and had delivered a message about it to Appleby. He related his meeting with Appleby and the whole story of what they had found by trailing Mahmoud. He had just received a briefing on a strange transmission that their satellites had picked up from a location in Lebanon.

The boat was approaching the dock with the magnificent torch to American freedom rising majestically in front of them. "It's beautiful," said Anna, recognizing the irony between the symbol of freedom and the subject they were discussing. "Do you want to get off?"

"No, we can talk here. We've obviously shaken them."

He continued. "I'm positive that Mahmoud, the transmitter, and the warhead are all in the same place, and that the Americans did not know where it was until the transmissions began. The Palestinians must intend to transmit something about the hijacked warhead. But in the clear? Aren't they worried that the Americans will send in troops to recover the warhead? Nothing makes sense."

"It sounds as though they're not intending to detonate the weapon," said Anna. "It would make no sense to detonate it in Lebanon, for goodness' sake. Do you think they're going to start an invasion of Israel and want the weapon for some sort of protection, or do you think, Petya, that it's for some sort of blackmail?"

"I think blackmail."

June slept almost until noon after her ordeal on the mountain. When she awoke, she was depressed. No only did she hurt all over from the abuse she had taken, but she was sure she would not get another opportunity to escape. Toying with her breakfast, she decided she had better have it out with Emir. He was polite, almost unctuous, when she called, and said he would send a car for her right away. She dressed quickly, replacing the tampon from her purse in the box in the bathroom.

She made no attempt to smooth over her concerns. She was afraid of Schultz and Mahmoud and horrified by the violence she had heard about. Why didn't he get rid of those people?

"June," he said, "you know that Mahmoud is primarily here as a spy for Assad. As for Schultz, I need him for the televised demonstration. His presence removes any doubt that we actually have the weapon. It's for the same reason that I want you here, so that the Americans will realize that the software designer is on our side."

June rose and began pacing the floor. "I'm not on your side, goddamnit, and I'm sorry I ever got into this mess. I'm an American citizen with Palestinian roots. You convinced me that you could solve the Palestinian problem without violence by having the United States put pressure on Israel. Now I'm beginning to doubt it. Please have me taken back to my quarters."

*

Mahmoud and Schultz were quartered in different buildings, but Mahmoud was able to come and go freely, so he decided to visit Schultz that morning. As he waved away the guard in front of Schultz's door, he saw Emir's car pick up June and take her to the office.

Schultz was wary and jittery, not about Mahmoud, but about the events of the upcoming days. He hated to admit it to himself, but he was literally frightened of the prospect of appearing on television. After a lifetime of moving from one hiding place to another, the thought that millions of people would be able to recognize him filled him with fear. He would rather face a gun battle than a television camera.

Mahmoud knew the whole scheme. Before he had left Beirut for New York, he had gone to the Syrian embassy and had an expert remove the seal from Emir's letter. He had read the message and had the expert reseal the envelope. Needing an ally in the camp, he decided to tell Schultz everything.

At first Schultz was not interested. All he wanted was to get his money and get away. Mahmoud paced the floor while Schultz languished, with his leg over the arm of a chair, half listening. Mahmoud stopped pacing and stood by the window, his back to Schultz, while he collected his thoughts.

"*Allah akbar.* Look," he shouted, pointing to the entrance to Emir's office.

Schultz jumped up and dashed to the window.

June came storming out of the building, not bothering to close the door, and ran toward the waiting automobile.

Mahmoud was elated. "She's only been in there fifteen minutes. They must have had an argument."

"I'll bet that bitch would be a tigress in bed," said Schultz.

"Maybe you can find out," replied Mahmoud.

"What do you mean?"

Schultz was more interested in hearing the story now. When Mahmoud concluded, he had only one question: "What about the woman?"

"As I told you, she's the only one with the code. She either has it hidden somewhere or she's carrying it with her. The next time she goes out, we'll search her quarters. If we don't find it, we'll have to force it out of her."

"What do you mean, we? And what are you going to do with the code, give it to the Americans?"

"That's right. The Israelis and the Americans are never going to go along with this crazy scheme. I could have told Emir that if he had confided in me. Assad doesn't think so either. He has no love for the Americans, but he feels comfortable with the present balance of power. The Soviets need him as an ally. If they become the dominant power on earth, he's afraid that Syria will be occupied within six months. He wants to get the code and give it to the Americans before the Russians find out what's going on. The Russians wouldn't dare retaliate against the man who saved America. He'll be the king of the Middle East."

"What's in it for me?"

"Twenty million deutsche marks and the protection of Assad."

"I don't need any more money. I have ten million deutsche marks already. What I'd like is a chance to spend it."

"Exactly. Have you thought about what is going to happen to you? If the Americans win, you'll be hanged. If the Russians win, they'll shoot you. They won't want someone as dangerous as you running around loose. If Assad gives you asylum, nobody can touch you."

Schultz pondered for a moment. "Tell me more."

Mahmoud explained his scheme. He had already found two guards he could bribe. They have relatives in Syria, he explained. The next time the woman went out, they would search her building. If they were not successful, his plan would come into effect.

Mahmoud pointed out that as an emissary from a friendly government, he had a considerable amount of freedom. He had arranged for Assad to send him a message by Syrian armored vehicle. While Mahmoud was pretending to prepare a reply, Schultz would bribe the guards and abduct the woman. The three would be taken into the armored car and have a good head start toward the Syrian border before anyone could raise an alarm.

"Then maybe you can find out what kind of a tigress she is."

The CIA agents had no difficulty locating Emir's demonstration site and reporting back its configuration. They slipped across the Israeli border during the night and, in possession of the coordinates, were on a small hill three miles away by dawn. Since it was designed to communicate primarily with satellites, the tower was low, not more than twenty feet high, just enough to get above ground cover. The VHF dish was standard, about six feet in diameter. It was pointed north at a very shallow angle to beam toward the American satellites passing over the Soviet Union, although it was on a swiveled mount that allowed it to change angle to point at other orbits. The tower was surrounded by four plywood buildings, unpainted. One was larger than the other three, square, about one hundred feet on a side, the others half that size. They guessed that the weapon was located in the larger building. The complex was surrounded by two high, heavy barbed wire fences, one inside the other. They could count a dozen guards patrolling inside the innermost fence. In the middle of the west side of the complex were two high barbed wire gates, each wide enough to allow entry of an oversize truck or flatbed.

From the gates, a two-lane macadam road led west for about ten miles, with light barbed wire fences paralleling it on each side. At the end of the road, a cluster of ten buildings was enclosed in a light wire fence. This looked like a typical construction camp. Four of the buildings, close together, appeared to be VIP accommodations. There were two long, barracks-style buildings, a dining hall, a motor pool with a dozen trucks and miscellaneous construction vehicles, and two maintenance buildings. There was little activity in the area, indicating that the construction work was practically finished. A half dozen guards listlessly patrolled the VIP buildings, but the rest of the area was unguarded. The agents were back across the border by noon.

When the information arrived at the White House, the agent in charge had sent along the opinion that the secure area would be difficult to penetrate but that the base camp could be overrun with very little difficulty.

The secretary of Energy was bubbling with excitement as he asked for a meeting of the full NSC at three o'clock. He wanted the President there. He'd be bringing a Dr. Carruthers from Los Alamos.

Carruthers was trying not to look ill at ease as the President strode into the Situation Room at three-thirty on the dot. After the introductions, Carruthers walked to the blackboard, his rumpled tan slacks, herringbone jacket, and boots looking out of place among the neatly attired staff members around the room.

Carruthers started off with a simple explanation of computer memory circuits and the concepts of reliability and redundancy. He assured the audience that computer memories were very reliable, usually affected only by stray cosmic radiation. Generally, that radiation was so random that an average computer memory cell had a lifetime of a million years. "That seems like a pretty long time," he said, smiling, as the nontechnical audience shook their heads. "But when you have a complicated piece of circuitry like a PAL, which has fifty million cells, one of those cells gets put out of business by a cosmic ray every week, on the average. So you have to have plenty of spare memory. We call it redundancy."

He went on to explain that the trick in keeping the device small is to put in just enough redundancy, but not too much. In a PAL there is another problem. It gets additional radiation from the nuclear core of the weapon, so that the designer has to put in still more redundancy to compensate. If a code that uses too much memory is put into a PAL, the device will reject it. His calculations showed that the additional complexities put in by June Malik for her code might be too much for a PAL assembled in a weapon and there would be a high probability of a rejection.

The President was leaning forward in his chair. "What happens then?" he asked.

"The device automatically reverts back to the previous code."

Carruthers then pointed out that this phenomenon could not be checked out in the laboratory, because it would occur only in a device that had been subject to the additional radiation from a nuclear core. The longer the device was in a weapon, the higher the probability that the code would be rejected. The hijacked weapon had been assembled four months previously, which gave a high probability that the new code would be rejected.

"How can we test this?" asked the President.

"We could simulate the phenomenon by giving a PAL a much higher dose for a shorter period of time or try to detonate a weapon which has been exposed to the same amount of radiation."

"The hell with simulation. We've had enough technological shenanigans already. Get a real one."

"The trouble is, sir, that all the warheads in that batch have been deployed," the secretary of Energy announced.

"Well, get one back. Bring back one of the other warheads that were in the same shipment. Get it to Las Vegas by tomorrow night. They can check it out and try to detonate it when the code changes Saturday night."

"Won't that be the same time that we're trying to detonate the one in Lebanon?" asked the secretary.

Fred Billings answered the question. "No. We've just gotten another message from Emir. He has delayed the time by two hours. Somebody over there must have figured out that he had better allow a little more time in case the clock has drifted. He'd be in a hell of a state if he opened up the firing circuit to us before the code changed. His zero time is now ten in the morning local time. There's an eight-hour time difference."

The President addressed the secretary of Defense. "Tell your guys to bring back one of that batch from Germany, pronto."

He then nodded to the Energy secretary. "And you tell your guys in Nevada to drop everything they're doing and get ready to test this thing Saturday night."

"Yes, sir," the two secretaries replied in unison.

# 14

KANE LEANED BACK AGAINST THE WALL OF THE computer room with the satisfied look of a man who has just finished polishing his automobile. Ten operators sat in front of consoles, the pale green of the images on the cathode ray tubes flickering and wiggling in endlessly changing patterns as the information fed into the computers was analyzed and modified for visual presentation. Headphones on their ears and microphones jutting out over their chins provided for the reception and transmission of speech to augment, clarify, or question the volumes of information fed into the computers. A telephone sat at the right of each operator for communication with those not on the main circuit, an intercom box stood on the left for conversations within the room, and a switching panel attached to the top of each keyboard provided for channel selection.

He had recruited three more actuaries from local insurance companies to analyze data and calculate probabilities. They spelled each other every four hours, as did the console operators.

Kane's desk, flanked by those of two secretaries typing data as it came from the actuaries and the operators, was in the back of the room. Kane walked back and sat down, his smile registering pleasure at what he had wrought so far, his brain in turmoil contemplating the magnitude of the tasks still before him.

The computer room had become the nerve center of a techno-logical world that lived in the major computational facilities of the nation. There were now one hundred fifteen calculating centers tied together in a parallel processing network, the like of which had not even been considered a week earlier. It was as though the science of data processing had been advanced one hundred times in two days. The scientists had little inkling of the project they were engaged in, but they were aware of the magnitude of the effort and were thrilled and fascinated to be a part of it.

In computer technology, the basic processing function is the turning on or off of a transistor, the opening or closing of a switch, the lighting or extinguishing of a light. This basic func-tion is known as a "bit" of information. The bits of information are correlated inside the machine to form characters or num-bers. Eight bits of information are combined to form each of these characters or numbers, known as alphanumerics. Origi-nally termed "bites" of information, their name was later changed by some wag to "bytes." Computer processing power is generally expressed in bytes per second or megabytes per second, which are millions of bytes per second.

As computer speeds increase, the velocity of light becomes a limiting factor. Although light travels at 186,000 miles per second, it is still not fast enough. At the incredible speeds at which modern computers operate, light travels only a few inches.

Computer designers, well aware of this problem, have de-veloped a technique known as parallel processing, in which problems are worked on simultaneously in several parts of the computer, with the results brought together at the output. In some major processing centers, equivalent speeds of five hun-dred megabytes per second had been reached, a major exten-sion of the state of the art. Here, for the first time, most of the nation's major computer centers had been brought together in a single massive paralleling process, on a scale one hundred times more powerful than had ever been achieved before. Ef-fectively, a transistor was being switched in the time it took light to travel a quarter of an inch.

Kane watched the operation in the early morning hours. The ten operators in the basement of the White House were quietly controlling the network, trading a shortcut here and there, eliminating duplications when investigators came too close to working on one another's problems, deftly switching in minutes to a spare computer in San Diego when a facility in Butte, Montana, went off the line during a power outage. The actuary was already at work, poring over sheets of data, plotting average rates of calculation as results showed up on the wall-mounted monitor, getting up to walk over and whisper to an operator for an up-to-the-minute check, beaming as he made summary calculations.

"How do the odds look?" Kane asked.

"A lot better, a lot better. We've improved from one chance in five hundred at this time yesterday morning to one chance in two hundred this morning."

"But that means that there is still only a half percent chance that we'll succeed," Kane said.

"I know, but we're making progress, we're making progress." The actuary beamed.

My God, thought Kane, the man even talks in redundancies. To the actuary, this is a technical problem, having a reality all to itself, as it did to the many thousands working together in this vast, electronically integrated system. The ultimate objective was not important to them; many of them were not even curious as to why the network had been put together. It was the excitement of the chase, the ultimate culmination of their scientific acumen, that provided the stimulus.

It was shortly before 8:00 A.M., the hour at which the President had scheduled an all-day meeting of the National Security Council, congressional leaders, the Chief Justice of the United States, and a few technical experts such as Kane and the directors of the weapons laboratories. Its purpose was to consider alternate modes of action in the short time left before Emir acted.

There were about twenty people in the room. The senior officials seated around the large conference table chatted nervously to relieve the tension. The junior aides and the technical experts seated in chairs around the wall were silent unless asked a question.

Kane looked around the room from his corner chair against the back wall. The first thing that struck him was that no women were present. Here we are, he thought, about to decide the fate of the world, with no representation from the sex that represented half its occupants. The men were drab, their suits about equally divided between blue and gray. Most wore black shoes, a few had chosen dark brown. Their shirts were universally solid color. White prevailed, with only the secretary of Defense and the secretary of State wearing blue; their neckties were blue, except for that of one young staffer who had probably read that yellow ties signified power. It was as though someone had prescribed the dress code for a funeral.

The informality and bustle of the last few days had vanished. Water pitchers, glasses, pads, and newly sharpened pencils sat in front of the chairs at the conference table; there were no coffee cups or ashtrays. The contents of briefcases were inversely proportional to the person's rank, the senior officials carrying none, the juniors balancing their pads on top of bulging ones.

At precisely eight o'clock, Fred Billings, the chief of staff, opened the door and walked in. The President, accompanied, to Kane's surprise, by Brad Appleby, was three steps behind. The two had obviously been talking before the meeting. The President looked fit and refreshed, as did most of the others in the room, since instructions to get the required four hours' sleep had been followed. Everyone stood silently until the President had taken his seat after pausing briefly to shake the hands of the Chief Justice and the Speaker. Appleby, uncertain, stood at the door, until Kane waved to him to take a vacant chair beside him. Appleby, smiling his gratitude, hurried around the table to take the seat.

"Gentlemen," the President said, "you've all been briefed.

We are here to consider the various options open to us. There are half a dozen paths we can take in the next two days, some of which we have to decide on immediately, some of which can wait until we see how the situation develops. Fred will present them to you."

Billings explained that the first option was to depend on the computer network to break the code and find the numbers. He introduced Kane as the head of the panel conducting the search.

Kane walked up to a series of charts on a tripod at the front of the room. On the way he received an encouraging pat on the rump as he passed Senator Tim Sullivan. He explained the nature of the network and how the search had been divided among the various investigators. He pointed out that with one hundred fifteen computer installations, several thousand of the best scientists and technicians in the country were already putting their minds to the problem. He estimated that the probability of breaking the code was about one in two hundred. With improvements in the system, he estimated that the probability at zero time would be reduced to one in a hundred.

Kane watched as the President's brow knitted. Kane paused.

"But you might come upon it at any time, right?"

"Yes, sir, that's what the odds mean. Right now the odds are two hundred to one against that happening, but it could."

Jeff Slocum objected. "Don't forget, Mr. President, statistics go both ways. It might take them a month."

The President wrinkled his brow in annoyance but ignored the comment. "Suppose you had more time. Would that improve your chances?"

Kane brightened. "Yes, sir, quite a bit. If we had five days, we'd have an even chance."

"How much time would you need to be certain?" asked Senator Sullivan.

Kane had the answer ready. "Tim, with the kind of talent we have out there now, we'd have it for sure in a week."

There was a murmur of excitement around the table. The

President leaned over to speak to Harold King, the secretary of State. King nodded his head.

The President turned back to Kane. "So if we can get Emir to delay his demonstration, our chances will improve dramatically, is that what you're saying?"

Kane picked up his pointer and referred to one of the charts. "Every minute brings us that much closer."

"Thanks, Bill, we'll get you as much time as we can."

Kane walked back across the room to smiles of approval from those around the table. As he took his seat, Brad Appleby silently held up two fingers in a victory salute.

Billings continued with the second option, which was to place heavy emphasis on the test being performed at the Nevada Test Site. He pointed out that the new code which June had inserted was considerably more complex than the normal codes and that for reasons having to do with the radiation coming from the core, it might be rejected by the PAL. Unfortunately, this could be ascertained only by testing a weapon similar to the one hijacked. He related that a warhead had been brought back from Germany and was being prepared for a full-scale test on Saturday night, as soon as the code was scheduled to change.

"What are the chances of that happening?" asked the secretary of State.

"That's not easy to calculate, but simulations are going on at Los Alamos and the Lawrence Livermore Laboratory. The experts are divided on these things. Let's ask the laboratory directors."

The directors of the weapons laboratories had opposite opinions. Los Alamos felt that the memory circuits would be overloaded and the device would revert back to the previous code. Livermore was less sanguine, feeling that there was plenty of spare memory. The two scientists got into a heavy argument on the radiation sensitivity of silicon when the President broke in. "Let's go, let's go," he said, annoyed. "We have a lot of ground to cover."

Billings continued. "A more cautious alternative is to storm the compound and try to take out the officers and the woman and maybe even Emir himself. This way we could treat it as a minor incident and gain time with the Soviets, who would be left with a high degree of uncertainty."

"I assume that we are preparing to use this option if we decide upon it," Senator Sullivan said.

"Yes sir, Tim," replied Billings. "We have CIA agents in the area and workmen in the compound who have access to arms. We'll be prepared for this if we decide to use it."

"Why don't we just blow the damned thing up while we have the code?" asked Slocum.

Sullivan looked at him derisively. "Obviously Emir won't connect it up until after midnight," he replied.

Kane looked around the room. Harold King was composed, displaying his only sign of tension by fingering his mustache lightly. Jeff Slocum was glowering. The Speaker sat quietly, his politician's poker face showing no emotion, his hands perfectly still. The Chief Justice looked bewildered; Kane felt that the man of deliberation was out of his environment.

He glanced to Appleby at his side. Brad had an appearance of anticipation, of forewarning. Brad knows what the President is going to say, thought Kane.

Billings turned to the President. "Sir?"

The President straightened up, threw his shoulders back, placed his hands flat upon the table, and took a long, slow glance around the room. "I have authorized an all-out program to remove Permissive Action Links from stockpile weapons and from weapons in the final stages of production. Our experts tell us that it will take about three days before we can have more than a dozen cores modified. The Soviets will be well aware of our course of action and of our efforts to break the code. Their tendency will be to act quickly before we can recover."

He paused to look around the room, his face paler as he made the statement. "They may demand immediate surrender. There will be precious little time for debate. I must be prepared."

Faces went white and heads shook. Even Appleby, forewarned or not, was visibly shaken as the statement was made. Kane had never even thought of such a possibility.

The Speaker was the first to regain his composure. "Surrender, Mr. President? I would never have believed that you could use that word."

"I do not use it lightly, sir."

"But you couldn't surrender, even if you wanted to," the president of the Senate interjected. "Any such action would certainly be classified as a treaty and would require the consent of the Senate."

"We would not have enough time for consultation, Senator. I would have to act on my own authority."

The secretary of State stopped fingering his mustache and stepped in to relieve the awkwardness of the moment. With his characteristic smoothness, he offered the opinion that the Soviets would require some immediate action on the part of the President, the least of which would be renunciation of NATO and assurance of complete troop withdrawal from Europe and Korea, the most likely, turning over our stockpiles before we could modify any warheads.

Kane watched Jeff Slocum, who was not about to let his rival take command of the debate. Slocum leaped to his feet for attention. "But, Mr. President," the secretary of Defense cried out, "what if the whole thing turns out to be a technological scam or if we figure out the code the next day? Are we going to give up our independence without firing a shot? It's against our whole tradition. I say don't do it. The American people would rather be dead than red."

The President refused to be stampeded. "What do I say when the General Secretary calls me on the hot line and gives me an ultimatum? I can't just say no and have a hundred million people dead in an hour."

The Chief Justice spoke up. "This is too horrible to contemplate. Don't we have any alternative?"

"Yes, we do." It was Slocum, still on his feet, glaring around the table. "We can order a preemptive first strike before our weapons become inoperative."

The room was pin-drop still. The President was expression-less, giving no hint of his own thoughts.

The Chief Justice's breath exploded as he gripped the arms of his chair. "My God, you mean blow up the world before we even negotiate with the Russians? Two minutes ago, I thought all of you were going chicken. Now I think you're crazy."

Slocum sat down without further comment, a look of deter-mination on his face.

The room buzzed with subdued conversation, each politi-cian and bureaucrat looking for a sign from his neighbors be-fore committing himself to an opinion. To Kane, it was a moment made for the military. The stars and the ribbons glittered as the chairman of the Joint Chiefs of Staff mois-tened his lips in obvious pleasure at this statement from his civilian superior.

"It makes sense, sir," said the general. "If we think that they are going to strike us as soon as our weapons are deactivated, we should strike them first. It would mean a large loss of life in this country, but if we can knock out their counterstrike capability, we can save fifty million lives.

"You mean we lose fifty million lives instead of a hundred million?"

"Precisely, sir. We save fifty million lives."

Tim Sullivan stepped into the silence that followed. "What kind of madness is this? That a small change in a computer software program can lead to the end of the world? One woman changes a few numbers in a code. She is picked up by a Pales-tinian zealot who uses her to his advantage. And then, *bingo*. We find ourselves with the most promising action being a first strike which will destroy civilization. Every argument I ever hear of, whether it's civil defense, 'Star Wars,' defense of Europe, or what have you, ends up with the conclusion that we should strike the enemy before he strikes us. We piously state in public that we would never consider a first strike, but I can see in the eyes of every military person who appears before my committee that he does not trust our retaliatory capabilities, that if he is charged with the defense of our country he must strike first. And the other guy probably feels the same way. That's not an alternative, that we should solve a problem by bringing about the end of the world. Is there no logic in this nuclear age, no reason?"

Billings rose from his chair and walked around the room, collecting his thoughts. The President stared straight ahead, thinking, listening. Kane's heart went out to the troubled man, alone in this crowded room. Billings returned to his chair and stood gripping the back so that the whiteness of his knuckles was apparent to all.

He spoke gently. "Logic or no logic, Tim, we have to be prepared. If our intelligence tells us that the Russians have caught on and are preparing a strike against us, it makes sense that we be prepared to strike before they do, and before we lose our ability to retaliate. I don't know if this qualifies as logic, but it sure as hell qualifies under the principles of self-preservation."

"But can't we feel that the Soviets have the same instincts of self-preservation?" Sullivan asked. "Can't we pick up the telephone and tell them of the ridiculous predicament we've gotten ourselves into? Can't we tell them we're about to solve the problem momentarily and that it would not be in their best interests to mobilize for a first strike?"

The director of the CIA spoke up. "You can't trust them, Tim. You know that."

Kane was proud of his old friend. Sullivan would not give up. The senator pushed his pad away from him and sighed. One more try.

"I know that you can't trust them in little things, but in major matters they have shown commendable restraint. They can blow us up in an hour, whether we have the counterattack capability or not. For half a century we have trusted that in their cold, calculating hearts they have chosen not to push the doomsday button. Will they believe Emir that he has not chosen some con game if he informs them of our weakness? They don't trust him. They don't trust us. They don't trust anybody. They understand the paradox that the only value of nuclear weapons is that they not be used. Can't we talk with them, level with them, and wipe this madman off the map?"

The President held up his hand. "What do you think, Brad?" he asked. All heads turned to Appleby, sitting unobtrusively in the corner of the room, next to Kane.

The President had been a longtime admirer of President Kennedy, particularly in his handling of the 1962 Cuban missile crisis. Kennedy, in setting up his committee to advise on courses of action, had found an appalling lack of knowledge of the Soviet Union on the part of his advisers. He added Llewelyn Thompson, former ambassador to Moscow, as his Russian adviser. "Tommy Thompson was our in-house Russian during the missile crisis," Dean Rusk later recalled, supporting Robert MacNamara's assertion that Thompson was the "unsung hero." When Appleby had delivered the message from Emir, the President asked him to sit in on all meetings. "I want you to be my Tommy Thompson," he said.

Appleby realized that this relationship would not sit well with many of the President's advisers and was careful not to participate in the discussions until requested to. He first pointed out that the Soviets wanted desperately to improve their economy. The General Secretary would like to cut down on military expenditures, he explained, but there was not unanimity in the Politburo. Appleby did not believe that the General Secretary would want to see the United States destroyed, even if it could be done unilaterally, because it would seriously destabilize the world economy and put his own recovery off indefinitely.

He went on to say that the Soviets had seen their country devastated twice in this century, which made them well aware of the consequences of mass destruction. He felt that the General Secretary would listen to reason, but that he would not hesitate to launch everything they have if there was threat of attack.

Jeff Slocum laughed. "I think you've been brainwashed by Rostov, Brad. Neither I nor any of my senior associates have ever believed in that kind of one-on-one negotiations, Mr. President. Now you're seeing the consequences."

"I take exception to that, Jeff," Hal King said. "The Appleby-Rostov discussions have gone on with my approval and that of the whole State Department. And I think Brad's opinions are right to the point."

Appleby decided to sit back and let the two secretaries argue, but Tim Sullivan wouldn't have it. "This is a hell of a time for you guys to be battling for turf," he said. "You sound to me like you should be over with us in the Senate. You're fighting for deck chairs on the *Titanic*."

"Look here, Senator," said Slocum, "You know we can't trust —"

The President raised his hands from the desk. "In my heart, Tim, Brad, Hal, I thoroughly agree with you, but I can't take the chance. It's too soon to talk to the Russians. Here's what we'll do.

"Dr. Kane, you and your panel will continue the attempts to break the code at maximum effort. The Energy Department, Mr. Secretary, will place top priority on the attempts to detonate a warhead after the code has changed. He nodded to the Vice President. "You will maintain liaison with the Israelis and investigate mechanisms to delay the demonstration and gain time. The Central Intelligence Agency, Mr. Director, is empowered to coordinate interdepartmental efforts in planning to storm the compound. The Secretary of Defense and the chairman of the Joint Chiefs of Staff will present to me as soon as possible a plan to mobilize for a first strike against the Soviet Union, taking maximum precautions not to make any moves which would incite the Soviets to similar action. Are there any questions?"

Silence.

The President stood up and left the room.

# 15

---

FOSTER MARTIN WAS ROUSED FROM A DEEP
sleep by the insistent pounding on his motel bedroom door. He
looked at his watch; it was 4:30 A.M. He jumped to his feet with
a start as a key turned in the lock and the angry face of the
manager's wife appeared, disembodied in the dim light.

"Mr. Martin, are you there? There's a phone call for you in
the office. The lady says it's from Germany and it's very important. She has a funny accent and I can hardly understand a
word she says."

Foster pulled on his jeans and stuck his arms into a heavy
shirt, apologizing to the woman and grumbling to himself at
having to stay in a motel that had no phones in the rooms,
but it was the closest one he could find to the Nevada Test
Site.

Under the disapproving glare of the manager's wife, he
picked up the phone from the office desk. It was Eva Spengler,
brimming with exciting news. The Greens had continued to
monitor the Landsruhe storage base since the hijacking. Infor-
mants reported that the Americans had removed one of the
Cruise missile warheads which had come with the hijacked
weapon and were sending it back to the United States on a
special shipment.

Foster was wide awake now. The dingy motel office had

taken on a mellow glow as the first stirrings of the new day began to outline the mountains to the east and south of the little mining town of Beatty. He stared back at the manager's wife, who dropped her eyes and self-consciously tightened the sash on her shabby robe. He felt a surge of power in his bones as Eva continued.

"Two hours ago it was loaded onto an American transport plane which has just taken off from the Munich airport with an escort of two NATO fighter planes. We have an agent in the airport dispatcher's office who tells us that the flight plan of the transport calls for a final destination of Nellis Air Force Base in southern Nevada. As we understand it, this is the closest airport to the Nevada Test Site. We knew you were somewhere in the vicinity and that you might be engaged in a protest. Foster, we know that you must have even stronger feelings against nuclear weapons since Penelope's death. I hope that this information may be of use to you."

Foster cringed at the mention of Penelope, but the thought passed quickly in his excitement. He cradled the receiver against his shoulder and began to button his shirt as he talked, anxious to take advantage of every minute. He mumbled his thanks for the mention of Penelope and expressed his condolences to Eva over the Greens Party's defeat in the recent national elections, attributing it to bad publicity after the hijacking. He was in Nevada on an antitesting protest, he explained, but was having difficulty stirring up interest.

"I've been talking to a California group who claim they can deliver two major Hollywood stars to the protest if I can assure them of enough press coverage. Obviously the government is bringing this device to the test site for something connected with the hijacked warhead. We don't have to know the connection, just that it exists. I can get the whole Hollywood crew over here in a few hours with the press on their heels. We can cook up a major demonstration with full press coverage by evening. Thanks a lot, Eva. With good luck, you'll be reading about it in Friday morning's newspapers."

\*

The reception group lined up to meet the incoming KC135 at the Nellis Air Force Base was imposing. It was headed by the secretary of Energy and the deputy secretary for Military Applications. Accompanying them were the manager of the Nevada operations office, his technical deputy, scientists from the major weapons labs, and senior officials from EG&G and REECo, the site's major operating contractors. The manager of the operations office was reviewing the schedule put together in the last few hours.

Under the 1963 Partial Test Ban Treaty, no tests could be carried out that vented nuclear radiation to the atmosphere. The radiation was contained by exploding the nuclear devices in large tunnels dug into the sides of mesas on the periphery of the site or in ten-foot-diameter holes dug deep into the dry lakebeds that formed much of the basins. These tunnels and holes took weeks to prepare; it was impossible to ready a new one in the time available. The warhead would be placed in a canister that usually contained diagnostic instrumentation and lowered into the hole, trailed by the connecting firing and diagnostic cables to communicate to the surface. The manager explained that there was an experimental device being lowered into a twelve-hundred-foot-deep hole in preparation for a test scheduled for the following week. Orders had already been given to bring up the test device to make the hole available for the emergency test.

The manager raised his voice to be heard over the gusty winds blowing the tumbleweed like large soccer balls across the runway. The sand stung their faces as they huddled to hear the briefing.

"The schedule is tight, but doable," he told the Energy secretary. "If we can get the test device out of the hole by morning, we should be lowering this one by ten o'clock and have it at depth by six o'clock tomorrow evening. We'll start backfilling the twelve-hundred-foot hole immediately and have it finished by Saturday morning. Checking the firing and instrumentation cables will take a few hours, giving us enough time to evacuate the area and have a couple of hours to spare before the deadline, nine o'clock, our time.

"A lot of things can go wrong," he warned. "The big thing is the weather. This wind is so strong and the dust so thick that you can hardly see the aircraft that's waiting to take off at the end of the runway. That plays hell with the operation of the large cranes we need to raise and lower canisters in the hole. Also, it has been raining for two days at the site and there's half an inch of water on Yucca Lake, where we have a runway for small planes. That's why we decided to run it up to the test site by ground transportation."

"Won't that cost time?" asked the deputy secretary.

"No, because the other device is still in the hole. We should have enough time to truck it the ninety miles from here to the site and install it in the canister before the hole is ready. One problem does exist. A small group of demonstrators from Make-peace is protesting the test program in general. They could cost us some time, but they've been here before and usually give us little trouble."

"We don't want another Landsruhe," said the secretary.

"Don't worry. We have the area well guarded."

"What is your biggest problem with the schedule?" the deputy wanted to know.

"Lowering the device in these strong winds. When you have a thousand-pound canister hanging on a twelve-hundred-foot cable in a hole only ten feet in diameter, it's not exactly a yo-yo. It's pretty tricky going."

By the time the warhead and its accompanying entourage passed the town of Indian Springs, halfway to destination, there was word of increased activity on the part of the demonstrators. Security had received a report that a plane had come in from Los Angeles, containing two Hollywood movie stars, one of the Berrigans, Ellsberg, and twenty newspaper and television reporters. As the convoy approached Camp Mercury on the edge of the test site, it was obvious that they had another full-fledged protest on their hands. But this time it was not to steal nuclear material; it was to gain publicity.

The convoy pulled up to the guardhouse, a simple two-man post with only railroad-crossing retractable barriers extending on either side. A dozen private contractors' guards stood on either side of the road, pistols at the ready but not drawn. Six state of Nevada sheriffs stood off to one side, leaning on their two patrol cars and holding the brims of their caps low across their faces against the blowing sand. Foster Martin and three of his associates had stationed themselves twenty yards in front of the guardhouse, holding a symbolic chain across the road. Several of the reporters recognized the secretary of Energy in the lead khaki Government Services Agency sedan, and when the Makepeace demonstrators blockaded the road, he decided to get out to talk with the press while waiting for security guards to clear his path. He denied any connection between his presence and the missing hijacked weapon, but could not conceal his astonishment when asked about the weapon removed from stockpile.

"Better get it out of here," he whispered to the manager. As a diversion, he agreed to a taped television interview while the manager strolled back and ordered the last three vehicles to turn and head back toward Las Vegas. He jumped into the lead car, waving to the others to follow him.

Foster noticed the vehicles turning and ran toward the reporters, yelling to them to follow the departing convoy, but he was neatly tripped up and sat upon by a burly Nevada sheriff. By then the Hollywood actors started to perform, insisting on being dragged out of the road while the cameras whirred. With the warhead safely out of range, the secretary stood calmly by while the protest ran its course and the guards escorted him into the site.

Looking back to see that he had a good head start, the manager decided to bring the weapon-carrying vehicle back to an intermediate airstrip at Indian Springs and to fly the warhead into the site from there. Since the airstrip was still under water, the manager could not fly it up by small plane; they were reluctant to risk a helicopter trip in the darkness and the strong winds, so they had to delay the transfer until daylight. By the time the canister package was ready to be lowered into the hole, they had used up five hours. Although Foster Martin didn't realize it, the protest had served its purpose of delay and confusion. They were now three hours behind schedule and in serious danger of not being ready to test by midnight eastern time on the following day.

Rostov had spent practically the entire day in the screen room, being briefed by his staff and receiving messages from Moscow. He had a number of isolated pieces of information which he was sure added up to something big, but what?

This much he was sure of: the hijacked warhead was in Lebanon under the control of Salom al Emir. Mahmoud was also at the site, as was the woman who had disappeared from California. Emir had made no serious attempt to hide his actions. In fact, he seemed to be flaunting the fact that the warhead was under his control. Rostov was also sure, from Appleby's evasiveness, that the Americans knew where the warhead was but were not prepared to take any action. The audacity of transmitting from the camp on the frequency of an American security channel with no attempt to hide the transmission from Soviet satellites was particularly puzzling.

He also knew that the American Vice President had made a hurried trip to Israel, and, according to the Russian agents in Tel Aviv, seemed to be unhappy with his reception. Then there was the massive computer effort that had been set up in the United States in the past few days. A series of reports from agents in six different areas of the country testified to the magnitude of these efforts. It was all very confusing.

He picked up the phone and called Anna. "What are you doing this evening?"

"At your service, Mr. Ambassador."

"How would you like to have dinner and spend the night in a hotel?"

"You came to the right woman."

He reserved a suite on the fifteenth floor of the Park Lane, overlooking Central Park. They had a leisurely dinner in the main dining room, talking of family trivia and reminiscing of Russia and their children. Then they went up to the suite, broke out a bottle of brandy, pulled chairs up to the picture window, and looked out at the lights of the tall buildings framing the darkness of the park. It was a clear night with no moon. They could see all the way up to 125th Street.

He poured a little more brandy into his glass, signaling with his eyes for her to drink up. As she did so, he leaned over and kissed the back of her neck. She responded by standing, removing her robe, and, silhouetted against the lights of the city in her bra and panties, pulling him gently to his feet to undress him. They embraced silently and, arms around each other, proceeded to the shower. They soaped each other, giggling and touching like teenagers. He reached around her from the back, cupping her firm breasts proudly in his hands and pressing himself against her perfectly rounded buttocks. As she turned to meet him and reached down to encompass his hardness, he noticed that neither the tresses peeping out from her shower cap nor the pubic hair with the water dripping from it in rivulets had lost a shade of the deep black sheen or their seductiveness in the decades of their marriage. They dried each other silently and moved toward the bed.

Their lovemaking was prolonged and sensuous, moving toward its crescendo with the steadiness and artistry of many years of experience, until they lay sated and satisfied in each other's arms. Only then did he begin to talk, picking up at their conversation of the day before and filling it out with his information and deductions of the day's briefings.

"There are only two things you can do with a nuclear weapon," Anna began. "Detonate it or not detonate it, right?"

"Correct."

"Obviously, Emir does not intend to detonate this weapon. It would do him no good to blow up his own country. He seems to be using it as some kind of hostage, daring the Americans to do something about it. Yesterday, we agreed that the purpose was blackmail. Now it seems certain that the blackmail is against Israel and that the Israelis either can't or don't want to agree."

"That seems to be the case."

"What puzzles me is how you enforce blackmail by not exploding a nuclear weapon. Maybe they are daring the United States to try to explode it. That could somehow explain the preparations for the television broadcast, the presence of the girl, Mahmoud, Schultz, and the kidnapped American officers. Is there some reason the Americans couldn't explode it, given the opportunity? Is there some lock or something where Emir may have stolen the key?"

"Well, there are electronic devices the Americans call Permissive Action Links, which prevent access to anyone who does not have the code."

"Code? Code? Wouldn't the Americans have their own code? Help me, I'm not very good at these things."

"They would, unless somebody changed it."

"Or it changed itself. Could that happen?"

"It's possible that the devices could be programmed to change codes periodically and automatically. Our people have considered such designs but have discarded the idea as too complicated. We don't need such devices. We keep control over our own warheads."

"Yes, but the Americans are so cocky, you know that. They think they can do anything technologically," said Anna. "The massive computer program you have explained to me . . . It seems that they may be searching for some kind of code."

Rostov jumped out of bed, naked, and dashed into the living room, where he paced up and down, deep in thought, for several minutes. He then strode purposefully back into the bedroom where Anna lay, bewildered, the covers still thrown off her body.

"Honey, you've done it again. You've found the answer. A code — I don't know what it is. But I don't have to know.

They'll get the details in Moscow. Our man in Damascus will be able to pry them out of Assad, now that we know what we're looking for. Get dressed. We're going back to the embassy."

Passengers scheduled to depart for Moscow on Aeroflot flight 365 at 6:00 P.M. Thursday night were chagrined to find that it had been canceled due to lack of available aircraft. They were not informed that the aircraft had left at five o'clock that morning with a single passenger.

# 16

*Friday, May 30*

AT 7:00 A.M., THE TELEPHONE RANG IN JUNE'S
bedroom. As she opened her eyes, the sudden noise and the
bright sunlight streaming into the room sent a pang of pain
across her temples. She responded with a grunt but the voice
on the other end of the line was unctuous and friendly.

"June, it's Sal. Did you have a good night's sleep?"

"No, I didn't. I'm tired and I have a headache. What do you
want?"

"I thought we might talk a bit. I have some good news. How
about joining me for breakfast? I'll send the car around."

She sighed, debating with herself whether another meeting
would do any good. She paused for a moment, then shrugged
and closed her eyes against the pain of the headache.

"Give me twenty minutes to get dressed," she answered curt-
ly and hung up.

Mahmoud watched as June climbed into Emir's car and was
driven the short distance to his quarters. He waited fifteen
minutes, assigned Schultz the task of watching for her return,
signaled to the guard he had bribed, then slipped to the back
of her building, entering through the door that had been left
unlocked for him. The guard had informed him that June did
not allow the maid into her bedroom, so he assumed that if

anything was hidden, it would be there. He cursed as he noted that June was a fastidious housekeeper. She had made her bed and arranged her belongings in a manner that would make it difficult for him not to leave signs of his search. The bathroom was spotless. He carefully unscrewed the lids of various cosmetic jars and, finding nothing, replaced them as nearly as possible in their original locations. As he was searching, he knocked a box of tampons onto the floor from the back of the toilet. Frowning with disgust, he picked up the box, holding it at arm's length as he replaced it. He found nothing in her closet or dresser drawers. Frustrated, he decided that the only feasible approach in the time frame was to capture the girl herself. He rearranged everything as carefully as possible and slipped out the back door just as he heard the returning vehicle pull up to the front of the building.

June, recognizing the need to conserve water in the desert, had taken a quick shower, rubbed herself down quickly, and swallowed two aspirin before dressing and straightening up the bedroom. Except for the headache, most of the aches and pains from her ordeal had gone away. Without makeup and with hair pulled back severely, she looked composed and reserved as Emir led her to the breakfast table, his face beaming with excitement.

She waved away the sumptuous foods offered her, silently settling for juice and coffee as he spread English-language Israeli newspapers in front of her.

"Look, June, it's working," he exclaimed. "The Israelis are getting ready to move out of the West Bank. The Americans are putting pressure on them, just as I predicted. We may not even need the demonstration after all. I'm inclined to give them a couple of more days if they continue this kind of progress. We've won. We'll get back the West Bank without violence."

June looked at him with astonishment. This was a side of the usually pragmatic Emir she had never seen before. The man must be mad, she thought. Doesn't he realize that this is an obvious ruse to gain time, or is he so immersed in his plan that he blinds himself to reality?

The pain shot through her temples again and she shivered as a cold chill went through her, realizing that this man was living a delusion, a delusion that could lead to incalculable catastrophe.

She took a sip of coffee with shaking hands, trying to look calm, hoping that he would not notice the tremors. "What does Hassan think?" she asked, not knowing what else to say.

"Oh, Hassan, he has no vision, just like all the others. He distrusts the Israelis so much he can't conceive of their doing anything sensible. But you believe it, don't you, my dear?"

June stood up, thoroughly confused. She knew he was wrong, but if she agreed with him he might be willing to delay. She needed time to think. "I don't know what to believe, Sal. I have a terrible headache. Let me go back to my room and rest for a while. I'll call you in a couple of hours."

"Of course, my dear. Rest and think about it. I'm sure that you will agree with me."

Colonel Dmitri Velikhov, commander, Lebanese Surveillance, Intelligence Division, KGB, USSR, was bewildered. He had been bewildered since he first noticed the absence of the electronic counterintelligence technicians from Beirut, tracing them first to the troop buildup on the Israeli border and then to this construction camp in the southeastern desert. Having been commended by Moscow for this intelligence feat, he was preparing to leave for the seashore on a weekend of celebration with his Syrian mistress when he received instructions to proceed immediately, under cover, to the construction site for observation purposes. He was miffed, not only at losing a pleasant weekend, but also because such tasks were usually delegated to lower-ranking officers. He had taken out his irritation on the only two lieutenants he could find to take with him on such short notice.

They had rented an old Volkswagen pickup truck and filled it with plumbing supplies; they borrowed hobnailed boots and wore the oldest clothes they could find. The only hard hats they could locate were two sizes too small for the colonel's massive cranium, much to his annoyance and their own chagrin.

They found an abandoned shack on a hillock five miles to the north of the campsite, where they could conceal their vehicle under tree branches and set up the tripods for the three pairs of high-powered binoculars. The colonel was grateful for the modern communication systems that allowed him to set up a small dish antenna and talk directly and clearly to the Middle East headquarters of the KGB. As soon as he was camouflaged and operational, he called in for a briefing.

They informed him that there was considerable activity by foreign powers in the vicinity of the campsite. It was highly probable that the hijacked nuclear warhead was located in the camp, which must account for the considerable interest by powers.

"Comrade General, can you tell me which foreign powers I am to observe and how I can recognize them?" Velikhov asked.

"I'm coming to that. Have a little patience, Colonel," the general snapped. "This is what we know. Two American CIA agents, dressed as construction workers and driving a blue American Ford pickup truck, slipped across the Israeli border about midnight last night. When last seen they were headed in your general direction. About twenty miles east of the Americans, two Israeli personnel carriers containing a dozen Israeli Mossad commandos also went across the border into Lebanon about the same time. The personnel carriers are American make, General Motors. They are painted standard Israeli khaki with army engineering insignia and registration plate numbers 769LXV and 532LXV. The detachment commander is a Colonel Benjamin Shapiro. He is considered a very able officer. He distinguished himself by breaking up the attempted hijacking in Beirut recently.

"The Syrians are also involved. For the last three days a black Mercedes with Syrian markings has left President Assad's headquarters in Damascus and been passed through the Lebanese border without incident. It has proceeded in the general direction of the campsite. It would seem that the vehicle was bringing messages to and from the camp. About an hour ago, the Syrians detached three vehicles instead of one, all black Mercedeses; they are currently crossing the border. A Syrian named Mahmoud, an aide to Assad, has been traced to the campsite, so it's most likely that the Mercedes has been passing secure communications that the Syrians prefer not to have sent through Lebanese channels.

"It is very important that all information you can pass on to us be forwarded immediately. This station will be monitored constantly. Is all this clear?"

It was.

For about an hour, the waiting Russians could hear or see nothing. They could look down into the camp, which was bristling with communication antennas, but there were no emissions to pick up. Velikhov could see the main satellite communication dish, which headquarters had told him was set to operate on an American secure communication channel. Using the height of a man as a range finder, he could calculate the diameter of the dish, which corresponded with the wavelength of the channel he had been given. He aimed his most sensitive directional antenna on the satellite dish hoping to pick up some radiation from the side lobes, which always spilled out from the most efficient transmitter, but could find none.

He estimated that the camp housed about a thousand people, all of whom seemed to be scurrying around with great haste, but there was no traffic in or out of the base, no supplies coming in, no people going in or out. It was eerie, as though the camp existed by and for itself, with no connection to the outside world.

About ten, the Russians spotted the blue American Ford pickup moving slowly toward the camp from the south. It pulled off the road and disappeared into a grove of cypress on a small hillock. Almost simultaneously, they observed the two Israeli personnel carriers approaching from the east and seeking cover on a hill only two miles from them.

Fifteen minutes later, they could see a cloud of dust ten miles or so to the north of the camp. It quickly resolved into the three black Mercedes sedans. Five miles from the camp, two of the vehicles pulled off into a clump of scrub pine, one on each side of the road. The third vehicle moderated its pace and headed for the camp. Velikhov followed its progress into the camp, where it stopped in front of one of the dormitory buildings. Both the Americans and the Israelis were in a position to follow the progress of the three Mercedeses.

June didn't get much chance to think. As she was driven back to her dormitory, she was more certain that she had made a horrible mistake and that somehow she must get the code to the Americans. But whom to turn to? How could she escape? She kicked off her shoes in the doorway, then walked into the bedroom to turn down the sheets on the bed.

Something was wrong. All her cosmetics were out of place on the dresser. A check of the bathroom showed the same disarray. The box of tampons had been moved but not opened. She looked in her briefcase. The papers were out of order. The room had been ransacked. A feeling of panic came over her. Could it have been Emir? No. Misguided though he was, he couldn't have been that crude.

She stood with her hand on the phone, trying to decide whether to call Emir. In the silence, she heard a rustle behind her. Before she could turn, a hand reached around her back and clasped over her mouth while the cold hardness of a pistol barrel plunged into her back.

"Don't make a sound," said Mahmoud softly. "I'm not going to hurt you. I want to talk. If you are willing to listen to what I have to say, nod your head and I will release you. Otherwise I shall have to gag you while I talk."

June nodded and backed away, glowering. "I have no interest in what you have to say. You are all alike and I want nothing to do with any of you."

"You will if you hear me out," said Mahmoud. "As you

realize, I am the personal representative of President Assad of Syria, assigned to monitor the actions of Salom al Emir. I am no friend of Emir's."

June was frightened. She backed away until her knees hit the side of the bed. Involuntarily, her legs collapsed and she sat down heavily. Mahmoud stood three feet from her, looking down, his legs spread wide apart. His face relaxed, and, with a slight bow, he addressed her. "I can see that you are frightened of me, but you needn't be. I apologize for the remark I made about you at dinner. I was very upset that night; as you will see, I had good reason to be.

"Three weeks ago, Emir came to Assad with a scheme to remove the Israelis from the West Bank of the Jordan by putting political pressure on the United States. He asked for Syrian support but refused to divulge the details of the scheme. My president is a pragmatic man who has little trust in Emir, considering him a visionary who feels that his troubles can be resolved without bloodshed. Such visionaries often cause more problems than they solve; we Syrians are wary of them. Assad would make no commitments but agreed to go along if Emir would accept me as a special observer to be kept informed of the details of the scheme as it developed. President Assad and I have been quite upset that Emir has not kept his promise. It was only yesterday that I was able to deduce the whole plan and your part in it. You, as I understand it, are the only person who has possession of the code that will go into effect on the Permissive Action Links of all American nuclear weapons at midnight tomorrow night."

June kept her face frozen, hiding her surprise. She had no idea that Mahmoud had not been familiar with the plan all along. She was beginning to see the Syrian in a new light.

"Without the code, the complete United States nuclear arsenal will be useless. If Emir notifies the Russians, the United States will be helpless before them. It is completely impossible for the Israeli administration to get agreement to withdraw from the West Bank in so short a time, even if they were willing to do so."

June began to nod her head in agreement. This was the conclusion she herself had come to.

Mahmoud continued. "Naturally, we would have tried to talk Emir out of this wild scheme if he had consulted us. He chose not to do so. My country has no concern for Israel. The Zionists are our enemies and will continue to be. But our differences with Israel pale before the consequence of world domination by the Soviet Union. If we seem to be more friendly with the Soviet Union, it is because we are so close to them geographically. We exist as a free nation only because of the balance of power between the superpowers. If that balance is destroyed, we will lose our independence within six months and become a puppet nation like Poland or Hungary. So will Lebanon, of course, a point Emir has not the good sense to realize. We must obtain that code and give it to the Americans in the next thirty-six hours."

My God, thought June. Can this be my deliverance? Here was this man she had considered a monster talking sense, while her beloved Sal had fallen victim to his own delusions. She rose from the bed and pulled over a stool from her vanity, motioning to Mahmoud to sit on the chair beside it. She leaned forward to encourage him to continue, making no pretense of hiding her interest. "How do you propose to do that?"

"The simplest way would be to find where you have hidden it, assuming that you have done so. It was I who searched your room this morning. I assume you were about to call Emir to tell him. I'm sorry I had to be so forceful in preventing you from making that phone call."

June nodded and then shook her head as he proceeded.

"The second way would be to convince you to release the code to me, and I will pass it on to the Americans."

"I'm sorry." June shook her head and pushed back. "I'm beginning to believe you, but this information is the only thing which makes my life valuable. Under no conditions will I release it to you."

His expression softened. He made another slight bow and smiled slightly. "I understand completely. What I recommend is that you go immediately with me to Damascus, where you can hand it over to the American ambassador. Will you cooperate with me? You must realize by now that your actions, however well motivated in the beginning, have put your own country and the prospects of world peace in dire jeopardy."

June put her hands to her face and began to cry. "I don't know what to say or what to think. Up till ten minutes ago, I considered you a monster and Sal as a person who could free my mother's people without any more fighting. Now I'm confused."

She stood and walked to the other side of the bed, wiping her eyes. Could this be another trick? This is the first person who has talked sensibly since I arrived here, she thought.

"We don't have much time, June." He spoke to her softly.

She looked at him intently, then made up her mind quickly. "No, I'm not confused. If you can put me in touch with a representative of the United States government, I will release the code. But how can you do that? We're both virtual prisoners here. I have already tried to escape once. Emir is suspicious of me and will have me watched carefully. How can you escape?"

"June, forget how I have acted up until now. That was a role for a specific purpose. I am not a prisoner. There is a vehicle about to arrive here from Damascus, ostensibly bringing messages to me from President Assad. If you will trust me and cooperate, we can be in that vehicle when it leaves and on the way to Damascus in half an hour. I will have to take Schultz with us because I don't trust him out of my sight. I have already convinced him to cooperate."

"But won't Emir's guards see us and stop us?"

"This camp is full of spies and mercenaries, June," said Mahmoud. "I have bribed the guards surrounding this house and mine to look the other way. If Emir gets suspicious and comes after us, I have two other armed vehicles in ambush five miles down the road. They should hold up the pursuit long enough for us to get to the border. You must decide quickly. Every minute counts."

June put her hands over her eyes and thought for a full fifteen seconds. Trick or no trick, what Mahmoud was saying made sense. Besides, what other choices did she have? She took down her hands and stared at him intently again, her lips quivering. "I'll go."

"Good. I'll leave now and return to my quarters. If everything is in order, I will raise and lower the shade in the room across the way twice. When I do, walk quietly across the way. Take nothing with you except the code information."

He put away his pistol and stole quietly out the door. Within five minutes, the shade went up and down twice. June picked up her purse, transferred the copy of the assembly code hidden in the tampon, and stepped out the door, blinking in the bright sunlight.

The black Mercedes pulled up to the front of Mahmoud's dormitory; the driver and three passengers, dressed in flowing robes, alighted and went into the building. Once inside, the passengers took off their robes, revealing Western construction attire. Two carried strings of grenades, the third a Kalashnikov machine pistol. There was a whispered conversation between Mahmoud and the driver, but otherwise silence. June, Schultz, and Mahmoud carefully donned the discarded robes. When they were ready, the driver inspected the costumes for appearance, nodded, then strolled out the front door, nonchalantly smoking a cigarette, and patiently held the back door of the vehicle open. The three new passengers bowed politely to an empty doorway, then turned and entered the back seat of the automobile. The Mercedes proceeded slowly to the gate, where the driver handed his papers to the guard, joking as he waited for them to be returned, then turned north, driving slowly.

June kept her face covered and her head turned until they were clear of the gate, then looked back apprehensively. "What if they discover that we've gone?" she asked.

"They will, quickly enough," replied Mahmoud. "They've certainly been watching us. They will be wondering why it took four people to deliver messages, but they will be afraid to inquire before the vehicle leaves for fear of antagonizing me or the representatives of Assad. There will be some activity in the next few minutes."

As soon as the Mercedes cleared the gate, the phone rang in Mahmoud's bedroom. The Syrian with the Kalashnikov let it ring eight times before answering.

"Mahmoud?" Hassan's voice was uncertain.

"Yes?" replied the Syrian.

"Mahmoud?" Hassan's voice was suspicious now.

"Yes?"

"By Allah, you are not Mahmoud. Where is Mahmoud?"

Silence.

Hassan turned from the phone and looked at Emir. "We have been tricked, sahib. Mahmoud is not there. We should sound a general alarm. I'll check on June."

Emir yelled for an aide while Hassan listened to the phone ringing in June's quarters.

"Get a detachment down to buildings ten and eleven as quickly as possible. Sound a general alarm and be prepared to follow the Mercedes that just went through the guard gate."

The Syrians moved quickly to their assigned tasks. Mahmoud had left them a diagram of the location of the main nerve centers of the camp. Before the Lebanese troops could react to the general alarm, one of the Syrians had strolled over to the power distribution transformer, placed a grenade under it, and walked quickly away. The transformer exploded with a roar, sending streaks of burning oil one hundred feet into the air and setting fire to two adjacent buildings. There were screams of pain from construction workers scalded by the oil or struck by the flying metal fragments of the transformer iron.

While the attention of the camp was on the exploding transformer, the second Syrian walked calmly over to the telephone switching center, opened the door, and threw two grenades over the tops of the telephone racks while the operators looked at him in shocked amazement. He closed the door and ran quickly away, following the crowd in the direction of the fiery debris from the transformer explosion. He had not gone more than fifty yards when the switching center also blew up. The crowd milled about, bumping into one another in their haste, but with no one certain which way to run.

The third Syrian pulled the pin from a grenade and tossed it into Mahmoud's bedroom before dashing across the short walkway to June's quarters. A guard, obviously alarmed by the explosions and the confusion around him, stood up and pushed out his rifle to impede the Syrian's progress.

"Halt," he yelled, his voice pitched high in fright. "Where do you think you are —"

The Syrian never paused. Without breaking stride, he swung the Kalashnikov around and mowed down the soldier with a three-second burst. Then, opening the door to the dormitory, he threw in two more grenades. By the time he reached the rendezvous with his two companions, both buildings were burning fiercely.

The camp was in complete chaos, with workers running in all directions and petty officers trying to rally their troops into some kind of order. The sirens on the camp's two fire engines wailed and their lights flashed in all directions, adding to the general confusion, but they were unable to cope with the burning buildings, the fires now spreading to engulf all the wooden dormitories.

The three Syrians had intended to discard their weapons and blend into the crowd of construction workers, but the disorder was so great that they decided to make a break at once. Trotting along with the crowd, no one paying any attention to the weapons they were carrying, they reached the gate of the motor pool, where they could see a dozen or so unattended vehicles. They found a truck with keys in the ignition and piled in. The only attendant left to challenge them was also cut down by a burst from the Kalashnikov. They pushed along in first gear, blowing their horn and shouting to part the crowds running along and across the main road. They could see troops assembling at the main gate, so they drove to the other side of the camp. Their last two grenades blew a wide gap in the wire fence. They drove through the hole and across the desert, climbing into the foothills of Mount Hermon, where they could hide out until it was safe to make a dash for the Syrian border.

The Syrians had done their job well. When the lights went out, Hassan was picking up the phone to call for air support to pursue the fleeing Mercedes. The phone rang twice, a calm voice answering, "Major Awad here."

Hassan barked instructions into the transmitter, but soon realized that the line had gone dead. He threw the transmitter to the floor, yelling to an aide to establish radio contact with the helicopter squadron, but realizing that he might not have time to dispatch aircraft before the Mercedes could reach the Syrian border. At Emir's insistence, he also rounded up two personnel carriers, loaded them with six of the president's crack Palestinian commandos, and sent them in pursuit of June and Mahmoud.

June continued to look back in awe at the flames coming from the campsite. She began to lose some of her apprehension as the Mercedes sped along the road with no vehicles emerging from the guard gate as it began to disappear in the distance; only the flames and smoke were visible against the clear sky. She could see that Mahmoud was jubilant, although Schultz sat silent and expressionless beside him.

"Are we safe? How long will it take to get to the border?" she asked, looking all around to see that the Mercedes was alone in the desert.

"You'll see" was the mysterious answer. It was the first time she had ever seen Mahmoud grin.

As they approached a wooded area, the Mercedes began to slow down. The driver pulled off the road, traveling a quarter of a mile across the rocky desert, then coming to a stop in front of a large clump of trees.

"Why did he do that?" June started to get nervous again.

This time Mahmoud broke into a broad smile. "Land mines," he said.

June was able to make out two carefully camouflaged automobiles, identical to the one they were riding in, one on each side of the road. A uniformed officer stepped out and returned the driver's salute as Mahmoud rolled down the window.

"We have a good start on them, Major," he said, replying to the officer's inquiry. "Your men did an excellent job of creating confusion in the camp, and I shall see that they receive appropriate commendation. But we must hurry, because they will certainly be pursuing us by now. If you can hold them for thirty minutes we will be safely across the border."

He motioned to the driver to move on and rolled up the window, waving triumphantly to the major's salute as they pulled back onto the road and picked up speed.

Again, the Syrians did their job professionally. Ten minutes after Mahmoud's departure, the two personnel carriers came roaring down the road, one hundred yards apart. When the first hit the land mines, it went twenty feet in the air, limbs and torsos flying in all directions. The second managed to pull off the road, mowing down saplings and underbrush like a threshing machine, coming to a halt only ten yards from one of the hidden Mercedeses.

The Palestinians were professionals also. One burst from a bazooka completely demolished the Mercedes and its occupants, while heavy machine-gun fire took care of the Syrians on that side of the road. The Palestinian captain in command realized that he had no chance to catch Mahmoud. With no radio contact, he dispatched four of his soldiers to cover against the Syrians on the other side of the highway, backed his vehicle out of the grove of trees, and roared back to camp to announce that Mahmoud had gotten away.

The three foreign groups observed the action at the camp with different degrees of comprehension. The Americans to the south were thoroughly befuddled. They had not seen the Syrian vehicles coming from Damascus and had no indication of what was going on until they heard the gunfire and grenades exploding inside the camp. They took advantage of the confusion to edge closer to the camp and noticed that the building which had been June's quarters was aflame and that two heavily armed personnel carriers came out of the camp, speeding north.

"What do you make of it, Jim?" the taller CIA agent asked his companion.

"Well, we're sure as hell not going to be able to capture the girl," was the reply. "Someone's gotten ahead of us. If she was in the building, she's dead. It's unlikely that she could have caused all this commotion by herself. Someone's tried to capture her. If they blew the attempt, she'll be under heavy guard, but from the looks of those personnel carriers barreling down the road, they've probably been successful."

"But who would do it? Who would know she was there, besides us?"

"The Israelis, most likely. They know the whole story. There's nothing we can do here now. Let's get back in the woods. The satellite will be over us in a couple of hours. We can talk to Washington and see what they want us to do next. We're going to catch hell for missing the boat."

"I know. Maybe they'll get mad enough to send us home."

The Israelis were in a better position to see and understand what was going on. They also had better communications than either the Americans or the Soviets. They were close to their own border and did not have to wait for satellites to come overhead for transmission. Tel Aviv had advised them that the daily messenger service had been augmented by two other vehicles, and to be on the alert for possible action on the part of the Syrians.

Colonel Shapiro watched the three vehicles come into sight with only one proceeding to the camp. He also saw the others laying the land mines.

"They are obviously going to ambush somebody," he said to his lieutenant. "It's got to be something connected with the Malik woman. We can't do any good here. Let's split up and go down there, on either side of the ambush. Then we'll be in a position to react to whatever happens."

"Yes, sir. But don't you think you had better check with General Berman?"

"No. Those assholes in Tel Aviv would shit their pants if they thought we were going to get in a fight with the Syrians. They'd probably have to get an act of the Knesset and a blessing from the Americans before they'd let us shoot off a popgun. We're in the field. We're in command. We have to act. Let's do our job and tell them about it afterward."

As the driver set out at full speed for Damascus, Mahmoud began to make plans for their arrival. He explained to June that they would be met at the president's headquarters by the American ambassador, who would arrange to have the code immediately transmitted to the United States.

June didn't like this idea. She still didn't trust Mahmoud. She knew that if she gave up the code she would be at his mercy wherever she was. "But I don't know the American ambassador," she said. "How do I know this isn't another trick?"

"June, you can speak to the American President if you want, or to Jesus Christ if he is available." Mahmoud's exuberance gave way to impatience. "You have to get that code to the Americans, don't you understand?"

Schultz was less tolerant. "What are you screwing around with this bitch for? Give me a pair of pliers. I'll get hold of one of those pretty red fingernails and pull it out by the roots. She'll talk then."

June was appalled. All her old fears came back and she drew away from the two others in horror.

Mahmoud drew a pistol and put it to Schultz's head.

"You're in my power now," he warned. "I've promised you your safety, but only if you cooperate with me. Do you understand?"

Schultz seemed about to spring at Mahmoud when he felt the car slow down and looked up to see the driver leaning back with a massive .45-caliber revolver in his hand.

June screamed and pointed to the road where the Israeli personnel carrier loomed up broadside in front of them. A burst of machine-gun fire from the Mossad commandos went streaming over their heads.

"Duck, June, get down low. The car's armored," shouted Mahmoud.

"Back up, turn around, quickly," he said to the driver. "I know another road. They won't be able to catch us. We're too fast for them."

The driver shoved the Mercedes into reverse, but before he could turn, the other Israeli personnel carrier came up at high speed in back of them.

"Stop, for Christ's sake," yelled Schultz. "We can't get away. No sense getting killed."

Even as he spoke, bullets slammed into the front tires. The Mercedes veered wildly as the driver tried to maintain control, then came to a stop in a small ditch off the side of the road.

"Come out, one at a time, your hands up. No firearms, or you'll be shot on the spot." Colonel Shapiro spoke through a megaphone.

The driver was first. He was frisked expertly by one of the Mossad, then pushed out of the way after his hands were tied behind his back.

Mahmoud came next, cursing as he slipped his way up the side of the embankment.

"My name is Assim Mahmoud. I am a personal representative of the president of the Syrian Socialist Republic, with diplomatic immunity. Who the hell are you, and why are you stopping us?"

"I am Colonel Benjamin Shapiro — as you can see from my uniform, an officer in the sovereign nation of Israel. And you know damned well what I want — the woman."

"You have no right to stop us. This is an act of piracy. I will not stand for it." He lunged at Shapiro.

He had not moved six inches when his head snapped back as though he had been hit by a sledgehammer as a shot rang out from in back of Shapiro. Mahmoud's eyes widened in surprise, his knees gave way, he slumped to the ground, twitched once, and lay still, the blood beginning to ooze out from the neat hole in his forehead.

"Next," said Shapiro, not even turning his head.

The German came out quietly, trying to hold his balance with his hands in the air as he negotiated the slippery slope.

"You must be Herr Schultz, the hijacker," said Shapiro with a smile. "I recognize you from your photographs. You have been getting more publicity than the queen of England recently."

Schultz was sullen. "I have nothing to do with this. Mahmoud forced me to come along. As you can see, I am not even armed."

"Herr Schultz, I could shoot you now and save the Americans the inconvenience. However, I think they may want to ask you some questions when your customer comes to trial. We will spare you as long as you do everything we tell you to do."

He turned to one of the troopers. "Tie him up. We'll take him with us."

In the meanwhile, June was scrambling up the side of the bank, clutching her purse and stepping on the hem of the garment she had put on back at the camp, forgetting the instructions to hold up her hands. She was almost in a state of shock.

She looked at Mahmoud lying dead at Shapiro's feet and recoiled in horror. "Who are you? What are you doing?" Her voice was almost a whisper.

"I am Colonel Benjamin Shapiro, Israeli Army. You are Miss June Malik, I believe."

"I am."

"Miss Malik, it is my understanding that you possess the key to the code for the Permissive Action Links on American nuclear weapons. I am to take you to Tel Aviv, where you will be asked to reveal that key to our Prime Minister for transferral to the proper United States authorities. If you cooperate with us you will suffer no harm. If you do not . . ."

"What did you do to Mahmoud?"

"I am sorry, but he tried to attack me, and one of my men shot him."

"Oh, my God. What have I done? All this violence —

I was promised that there would be no violence, but it gets worse all the time. When will it end?"

"It will end when you give us the key to that code."

June's anger began to build in her. Her cheeks flushed. She looked at the Israeli contemptuously, knowing that in his zeal he had seriously undermined his own cause.

"You fool," she screamed. "You've screwed up everything. Mahmoud was taking me to Damascus where I was to turn over the key to the American ambassador. If you hadn't interfered, I would be out of this accursed country now, ready to correct the mistakes I've made."

"I know nothing of that. It was probably some Arab trick. My orders are to take you to Tel Aviv. We must hurry. The PLO will be looking for you, but we can be across the border in an hour."

He grabbed her roughly by the arm, while she was still protesting, and shoved her into the front seat of the personnel carrier next to the driver. He then climbed in beside her, shouting orders to proceed to the Israeli border at top speed. Schultz was tossed into the rear of the other vehicle.

Halfway to the border, Shapiro decided to break radio silence.

Sitting between the two men in the cramped front seat of the personnel carrier, June subconsciously felt the driver's thigh press against hers more firmly than necessary, but she ignored the move, placed her purse between them and listened to the conversation. A jubilant Shapiro raised his commanding general on the radio and explained to him the details of the interception of the Syrian vehicle with June in it.

General Berman was cautious. "You should have called in to us before taking matters in your own hands, Shapiro. Is Miss Malik all right? Were there any casualties?"

"Miss Malik is unscathed. She is sitting here beside me. We have also captured Schultz, the German hijacker. We did have to shoot one Syrian who would not cooperate."

"What about the envoy, Mahmoud?"

"Unfortunately, sir, he was the casualty."

There was a pause on the other end. "The Prime Minister will not like that," said General Berman. "What about the woman — will she talk?"

June reached over to seize the microphone. "You're damned right I'll talk. Give me that microphone."

"I'm sorry, Miss Malik," said Shapiro as he tried to pull the microphone away from her. "You'll have plenty of time — "

June decided that she had better not hold back any longer. "If I'm going to talk, I'm going to start right now." She grabbed the microphone out of his hand.

"General, whoever you are, the dead Syrian, Assim Mahmoud, was taking me to Damascus to talk to the American ambassador. If you people had not interfered, we'd be there now. But we can discuss that later. Listen carefully to me. I am going to give you the numbers of the Permissive Action Link code. Are you ready?"

"Ready."

June started to reach into her purse for the formula that would serve as a memory aid, but her brain was so alert with excitement that she could see the numbers in front of her eyes. She began to recite them.

"The first number is three hundred seven — three zero seven. Please repeat."

"Three zero seven. Go on."

"The second number is one hundred one — one zero one."

"One zero one."

"The third —"

In their concentration, they had not heard the helicopters until the roar of the engines blanked out the radio transmission. The first helicopter swept over the roof of the personnel carrier. Bullets rained on the road in front of them as a warning to stop.

"Keep going." Shapiro thrust out his arm as a signal to the driver. "They won't dare to shoot. They don't want to kill the woman."

The first helicopter pulled a hundred yards in front of the two personnel carriers and hovered, the other two moving along behind the Israeli vehicles. A rifle with a telescopic sight peered out from the window of the aircraft and expertly shot the two front tires of each of the personnel carriers.

"General," shouted Shapiro into the microphone, "we are being attacked by PLO helicopters. Can you send us air support?"

"Yes, but it will take half an hour to get to you. Whatever you do, don't let anything happen to the woman, or the Prime Minister will have both our hides."

The personnel carriers pulled to a halt, surrounded on three sides by the helicopters. The Mossad commandos poured out, guns at the ready.

Hassan's voice boomed out on a bullhorn from the lead helicopter. "Israelis, you are heavily outgunned. Release Schultz and Malik to us and we will allow you your freedom. If you do not comply in the next five minutes, you will all die."

Shapiro walked out ahead of his vehicle and shouted, "If we die, she dies with us."

Hassan's voice was calm and contemptuous. "We don't need the woman. We want her only for show purposes. If she dies, you will never know the code. Release her quickly."

Shapiro went back to have a hurried conversation with General Berman. He emerged and shouted to the lieutenant in the other vehicle. Schultz's bonds were cut and he and June ran to the helicopter. Three minutes later, the helicopters took off and headed toward the campsite, leaving a chagrined and chastened Shapiro standing morosely in the middle of the roadway, surrounded by Palestinians.

Colonel Velikhov had watched the unfolding of the whole scene with complete amazement. He watched the tumult in the campsite, the belated chase of the Syrian vehicles, the ambush of the Syrians, and the dash of the Israelis toward the border. He saw the three helicopters as they came from Beirut to intercept the Israelis. The interception was too distant for the Russians to make out what was going on, but they watched one helicopter return to the campsite where Schultz and Malik were removed under heavy guard. Colonel Velikhov did not understand what it all meant, but he dutifully reported everything to Middle East headquarters of the KGB, to be passed on to Moscow immediately.

# 17

M Y  G O D ,  T H O U G H T  K A N E ,  O N L Y  A N O T H E R  D A Y
and a half. He walked down the hall to the Situation Room,
which was occupied only by junior officers and White House
staff. The President had dismissed all the senior people at nine,
with the admonition to have a good dinner and get as much
sleep as possible. The meeting was to reconvene at 6:30 A.M.

At 4:30 A.M., Kane woke with a start. Jesus, he thought,
maybe we've been going at this ass-backwards. He let his mind
drift for a moment, knowing that early morning was the time
he came up with his best ideas, his brain fresh and clear of the
encumbrances of the previous day. Instead of working by analysis, maybe we should be working by synthesis. Instead of randomly analyzing these squindillions of numbers, maybe we
should be thinking of how June would have generated the numbers.

He sat bolt upright in the bed, remembering the first meeting
at Sandia laboratory. What was that she had said about its
taking a young Greek to know an old one? She was referring
to Eratosthenes' observation that large prime numbers can be
assembled out of combinations of small prime numbers. But
how small? One digit, two digits, three digits? He had no clue.
He spent the next hour looking over a table of prime numbers

and mulling over the problem, but he told no one about his idea.

The President opened the meeting at exactly 6:30. He was dressed in a navy blue suit with a white shirt and red necktie. The civilians were conservatively dressed as though attending some formal diplomatic occasion. They were clean-shaven and looked refreshed, having obeyed the President's orders about sleep, although it was questionable how many had gotten any sleep at all.

Kane could feel the tension in the room as the members took their places. With the excitement of the computer search he had lost most of his remorse of the previous day. At least he was accomplishing something while many of the others, unable to communicate with their associates, had looks of helplessness on their faces.

He could see who the key players were going to be. The President was clearly in command, decisive, but uttering little pleasantries to the others as they came in, sometimes with a half smile. The Vice President, as usual, took his position from his superior, saying little and betraying no expression. The politicians grouped together, taking their cue from the poker-faced Speaker of the House. Brad Appleby walked unobtrusively around the table, nodding only to Kane as he took his seat in the corner beside him. Fred Billings looked around alertly, much as a referee might before an athletic match. Harold King came in unattended, outwardly cool and relaxed, speaking politely to those around him. Jeff Slocum was the only one whose tie was loosened and collar unbuttoned. His face was flushed, and before taking his seat, he took off his jacket and draped it on the back of his chair. The chairman of the Joint Chiefs of Staff, impeccable in his five-star uniform, followed Slocum and took a seat directly behind him.

The President turned to his chief of staff for a situation briefing. Billings stated that the two-way secure television linkage between the Lebanese camp and the White House was now operating and that the Lebanese president would come on the air at 8:30 A.M. eastern time. The basic strategy in dealing with

Emir would be conciliatory, with the hope of having him modify his demands or grant another time delay.

He brought the meeting up to date as to the whereabouts of June Malik. An attempt to take her to Syria had been ruined by an ill-advised Israeli ambush. The failure had caused relations between the two countries to deteriorate and lessened the probability of further concessions by the Israelis. There was little likelihood that June could be reached in the time remaining. The disappointment in the room was tangible. Tim Sullivan raised his hands above his head in despair, while Slocum shook his head and cursed.

The other two attempts to solve the problem still looked promising, Billings stated. The second Cruise missile warhead had reached the testing area in Nevada in spite of a well-publicized protest at the gates. Technicians would begin lowering it into the hole within the hour. The experiment was now expected to be ready one hour before the automatic code change at midnight. He called on Kane to explain the status of the computer search.

"The statisticians tell us now that we have a fifty-fifty probability of finding an answer in the next forty-eight hours. The system is going all out and I know of no way to further improve these odds. It's simply crunch, crunch, crunch, with the equipment and people we have. The most important element is time. Every hour, every minute, we can delay this demonstration helps us enormously. Any questions?"

As he looked up, Kane could see that an aide had come into the room and was waiting to pass a message to the President. Billings motioned to the aide to bring the message to him. When he read it, his face broke into a smile. It was from Israel, reporting that June Malik had transmitted two numbers before she was recaptured.

"My God," said Kane, "why didn't they send this immediately?" He rushed down to Billings and almost tore the piece of paper from his hand. "They're low numbers, too. That supports my thesis."

"Mr. President, may I be excused?" Kane pleaded. Hardly waiting for the President's nod of approval, he dashed out and ran down the hall, the puzzled meeting members staring after him in astonishment.

Kane rushed into the computer room, calling the staff around him to explain what had happened. Within two minutes a message went out to the network, telling the operators to start building primes with the numbers 307 and 101.

Kane had been gone only twelve minutes when he was back in the Situation Room. The President held up his hand to halt a diatribe by Slocum, who was castigating the Israelis, when Kane burst in.

"What can you tell us, Bill?" the President asked calmly.

"The fifty-fifty probability point is now eighteen hours. If you can get us a few hours of delay, we should be there," Kane replied. "What's even better is that if you can get them to hold off until Sunday morning, we should crack it, for sure."

There was a round of spontaneous applause. The President held up his hands again. "Thank you, Bill," he said. "We'll buy you every minute we can. But we can't take any chances. We must look at our other options. Let's look first at the least desirable alternative, surrender."

Looks of anguish could be seen on faces around the room; there were mutterings of "Never, never."

"We must face facts, gentlemen," said the President. "If our nuclear arsenal becomes useless at midnight, and the Russians find out about it, there will be considerable pressure on the General Secretary to do something immediately."

"Wouldn't they be willing to negotiate?" asked Hal King.

Jeff Slocum snorted. "Negotiate what?" he asked. "They would have us by the balls. We would have no power to negotiate anything."

"But we do have some weapons without PALs, and as I understand it, we're rushing at Amarillo to turn out more."

"Unfortunately, Hal, that doesn't help us," said the President. "We're moving unlocked warheads to the ballistic missile sites as fast as we can, but will probably not have more than a few modified in time. The Soviets would interpret an offer to negotiate a treaty as simply a method of buying time.

"I have obviously given this matter a lot of thought. What I would do is offer myself as a hostage to fly to Moscow immediately. Once there, I would have to agree to do everything they demand. Before that, I'm sure they would insist on a disarming of our ballistic missiles, disabling of our bombers, and recall of our attack submarines."

Jeff Slocum stood up and pounded on the table. "We can't take this lying down. We can't abjectly surrender this magnificent country of ours to a group of godless Communist barbarians. I don't believe that we're better off red than dead. I'd rather die than live under their dominance. I come from the great state of New Hampshire, whose motto is 'Live Free or Die.' I believe in that motto and I'm willing to die for my country. We have an answer, and you all know it. We must prepare to strike while we have the capability."

"But, Jeff, that will make it certain that they will strike back at us," Fred Billings replied.

"I know, but if we strike first, their second strike will be much weaker and we'll have many fewer casualties."

Tim Sullivan broke in. "You can't be serious about such a proposal. What if the whole thing turns out to be a pipe dream or a hoax? What if we find the code after midnight? What if the Nevada test proves that her code has been rejected? These have high probabilities. If we strike before midnight, we'll find out too late. Hundreds of millions of Russians and Americans will be dead. It will mean the end of civilization as we know it. Mr. President, you cannot possibly consider so horrible an action."

"Mr. President, under your constitutional responsibility for the safety and welfare of the United States, you have a duty to consider this alternative," said Slocum. "I am not asking you to make such a decision now. I am merely asking you to hold it as an option."

"What does that mean?" asked the President.

"As you know, sir, the popular conception that you can push a button and fire our complete nuclear arsenal immediately is hogwash. Bombers have to be made ready; they require six hours' flying time to reach the Soviet Union. Submarines have to be alerted. Even the land-based ballistic missiles require preparation time.

"For us to be ready, I recommend that you put out an all points bulletin at noon, directing all military commands to proceed into condition DEFCON three."

"This does not commit me to any specific course of action?" the President asked.

"No, sir. It merely directs all military commands to take those steps that would allow them to go into action if you so order."

The President looked around the room, studying faces. "Does anyone object?"

Tim Sullivan felt that a warning was necessary. "I'm concerned, Mr. President, that you may be climbing onto a horse you'll have difficulty climbing off of," he said. "Soviet intelligence will soon be aware of what we are doing and may take action on their own."

"That's a chance we have to take, Senator," said Slocum.

"Are there any other comments?" asked the President.

Silence.

"Very well." He turned to Billings. "Declare situation DEFCON three, effective twelve hundred hours."

The Vice President rose from his chair, solemnly shook hands with the President, and walked silently from the room.

The readiness condition of United States defense forces is characterized in five stages. The normal peacetime condition is DEFCON 5, except for the Strategic Air Command, which is kept at DEFCON 4 in peacetime. DEFCON 3 orders troops on standby to await further orders. DEFCON 2 directs that troops become ready for combat, while DEFCON 1 orders troops deployed for combat.

Under DEFCON 3, the wheels of a massive defense effort were set in motion. The Vice President left for a secret location, which was changed from time to time, where he could be flown to rendezvous with the primary emergency airborne command post. He was on his way as soon as the President gave the order. In Minuteman silos throughout the country, sleepy off-duty crews were awakened to make checks on launch circuitry. SAC bomber crews were put on immediate alert and the aircraft fueled and prepared for rapid launch. The SAC Headquarters Emergency Relocation Team was assembled to stand by to depart for a secret location. Orders went out to increase readiness of the four national emergency command post aircraft normally stationed in Nebraska and Indiana and to generate to deployable status the special unit of the North American Space Command that serves as backup to the main communication center in Colorado.

Communications with naval nuclear ballistic missile submarines were upgraded by instructing them to monitor communications from higher authority continuously. Four additional TACAMO EC-130 submarine communication aircraft were launched to augment the two that are normally kept airborne over the Atlantic and Pacific ocean basins. Nuclear attack submarines in port were put on alert for immediate departure, while those returning were ordered to remain on station until further notice.

All these preparatory measures were made without attracting notice, because the troops were constantly put on alert for training purposes and had gone through these exercises dozens of times. Only at the highest level in the Pentagon did anyone know whether this was an exercise or the real thing.

The United States defense arsenal would soon be ready.

Rostov had slept well on the flight to Moscow. Although it was a daylight flight from New York, he knew he would get little sleep when he arrived. The flight attendants tried to ply their only passenger with vodka and food, but he resisted, piled cushions in the aisle, and was well refreshed when the aircraft landed.

A limousine with motorcycle escort was waiting to whisk him directly to the Kremlin, where he was promptly ushered into the General Secretary's office. The minister for Defense,

Dmitri Popov, a burly, thick-necked former military officer, and the minister for Foreign Affairs, Boris Kamensky, an urbane career diplomat with ten years' experience in the United States as ambassador, were waiting with the premier.

Rostov told his story succinctly. He concluded with the opinion that the Permissive Action Link code on all United States nuclear weapons would change at midnight eastern time and that the Americans did not have the code. All their nuclear weapons would be inoperative.

The usually stone-faced General Secretary emitted an uncharacteristic long whistle. The ministers were silent, but the glint of a smile shone on their faces and in their eyes.

"I have Professor Schnittke, chief of Nuclear Weapons Design, waiting outside the office, as you requested in your telegram," the General Secretary said. "Shall we call him in?"

"Please do," said Rostov. "I am not expert in these matters and may have come to the wrong conclusion."

The professor was an owlish little man, proud of his accomplishments as one of the leading experimental physicists in the world and disdainful of anything foreign, particularly American. He enthusiastically verified Rostov's conclusion about the American PALs.

"Do we have such devices on our own weapons?" asked the minister for Foreign Affairs.

"Yes, comrade, we do," answered the professor. "But we use far simpler devices. Since we keep all fissionable material in our own country, we have less of a problem with access. The Americans have active warheads strewn all over Europe in the NATO nations, hence they can run into trouble, as they did with the hijacked weapon in Germany. It is one of the fallacies of their foreign policy. Their nuclear forces are extended too far from their own territory. They would not have time to ship warheads from the United States in the event of imminent hostilities. If they would keep their warheads at home, as we do, they would not have this problem. Our policy of locating rockets on the soil of our friendly neighbors but keeping the warheads on our own land not only testifies to our peaceful intent but lessens the chance of accidental or unauthorized use of nuclear weapons.

"The Americans also tend to defeat their own purposes by making their weapons too complicated for their own good. They are now hoist on their own petard. They have made the system so intricate that they will be defenseless in a few hours."

"Comrade Professor Schnittke, we are grateful to you for your excellent analysis," said the General Secretary.

He now felt confident enough of Rostov's conclusions to bring them to the attention of the full Politburo, who had been summoned an hour earlier and were waiting impatiently in the main cabinet room. As he opened the meeting, there were resentful stares at Rostov for having caused them to get out of bed at this hour of the morning. What could be so important in the United Nations that an ambassador's arrival could cause such an unprecedented meeting as this?

When Rostov started to talk, the resentment began to disappear from their faces. As it dawned on them that the entire United States nuclear arsenal would be inoperative in a few hours, the entire Politburo rose to their feet and broke into spontaneous applause.

The premier felt that he should cool their enthusiasm. "You must realize, comrades," he said, "that all we are going on here is supposition. We do know that the warhead was stolen; we are quite sure that it is in Emir's control. We have also verified that the woman in Emir's camp was the software designer for the Permissive Action Links, and we are aware, from our NATO contacts, that the links are automatically programmable. We do know that Emir is beaming some sort of demonstration to the Americans on a scrambled satellite network, but we do not know exactly what it is. We have known for the past several days of a massive computer program to break a code of some sort. All these facts fit into the conclusion we have given you, but we cannot be certain as yet."

The oldest member of the Politburo, an octogenarian holdover from the Brezhnev days, stood up. "What are your plans, comrade, should Comrade Rostov's analysis prove correct?"

The General Secretary was brisk and to the point. He would

immediately contact the American President to demand the surrender of United States sovereignty to the Soviet Union. He would dispatch one hundred Soviet observers to Washington to oversee the disarming of intercontinental ballistic missile silos and the destruction of all intercontinental bombers. He would order the President to call all attack submarines to the nearest port and have them scuttled while Soviet observers were present. He would expect to complete the nuclear disarmament within twenty-four hours, before the United States had time to modify its warhead circuitry.

"What about the conventional forces and the troops in Europe?" he was asked.

"I feel that the most important action is to remove their nuclear threat so that they cannot solve their lock problem or continue to build additional weapons without locks. After taking away the initial threat, I would concentrate on dismantling their nuclear weapon production facilities at Oak Ridge and Hanford, then closing their research facilities, such as Los Alamos and Livermore. When that is accomplished, I would propose to turn our attention to American forces in Europe and to NATO. All of these actions, of course, will be subject to your approval."

"How do you feel about NATO, comrade?" Boris Kamensky wanted to know.

"Boris Vasilovitch, I am not going to worry about the NATO nations," he replied. "They will be helpless. We can deal with them in due course. The same is true for the Middle East. Israel without the United States is nothing. The Arabs will gobble her up and we will have no trouble controlling Middle East oil.

"I do not propose to use our own troops anywhere. I don't want another Afghanistan. With our nuclear superiority, we will be able to dictate policy in any country on earth. I do not intend to harm the American economy. It has been their strength and it will be ours. With the excess capacity available after the curtailment of military expenditures, they will be able to pay us reparations with no strain. We can relieve our agricultural shortages with their grain, and we can use their capital goods industry to build for ourselves the most modern and most powerful industrial economy in the world."

Rostov, looking out on the faces of these most pragmatic of men, could see that, for once, pragmatism was out the window. They were carried away, enraptured by their leader's vision of the future, visualizing the day when their motherland would take her proper position as the industrial and military leader of the world. He noted also that there was no mention of ideology, no talk of Marxism, no mention of Lenin. How far we've come, he thought, from the days of Brezhnev and Andropov and Chernenko. He bore no ill will toward the Americans, and he was happy to hear that the General Secretary was aware of the importance to his own country of maintaining the American economic machine. Rostov was lost in the reverie of his own dreams when he noticed that one man was frowning and scowling and shaking his head at the General Secretary's words.

Popov, the minister of Defense, finally raised his hand to get the attention of the group. He stood up. "Comrade," he began, "your vision of the future is an illustrious one. I certainly hope that it will come to pass. But before it can come about, we have to ask ourselves what the American President will be thinking. We all know that it is not in our self-interest to destroy America. But we have told the Americans over and over again that we will not carry out an unprovoked first strike against them and they do not believe us.

"Comrades, what would you do if you were the American President? You would not place your country's future in the hands of a stupid, ideological Palestinian. You would not allow your most potent military weapons to become useless. No. You would use that capability while you still had it. Comrades, I believe that the American President will order a nuclear strike against the Soviet Union before his weapons become useless and that we must be prepared to strike before he does."

Rostov's stomach sank. He knew that most of the members had a deep-seated distrust of the Americans and were instinctively of the Defense minister's persuasion. He rose to defend the premier's point of view, but he could see that the spell had been broken; the magic was gone. Others took up the cudgel. They pointed out that they should be ready to preempt a first strike by the Americans. If they decided not to do so, nothing was lost. Even the General Secretary could not argue against that.

Rostov looked again and saw rigid determination on the faces of all the members.

The premier saw it also. He rapped the gavel once, then spoke softly. "Comrades, I will order the armed forces into defense condition three, effective immediately."

Orders were dispatched within moments to put the Soviet ICBM forces on heightened alert. Intelligence units were instructed to monitor American troop units and military communications closely. All SS missile crews were ordered to their stations. Preparations were made to transport nuclear warheads to peripheral Warsaw Pact nations for insertion into missiles in those countries. Strategic ballistic missile submarines, most of which were usually held in port, were ordered to prepare to put to sea. Submarines on patrol were alerted for possible action. Bear, Blinder, Badger, and Backfire aircraft were ordered into immediate readiness.

The defense arsenal of the Union of Soviet Socialist Republics would soon be ready for war.

# 18

*Saturday, May 31*

SALOM AL EMIR'S GREAT DAY STARTED POORLY. Although repair crews had worked all night and the northern end of the camp where the warhead and satellite communications system were located had been spared, fires were still burning in the living section, there was no telephone service, and most of the camp was without electrical power. Emir was personally directing the repairs and had slept for only an hour. In the midst of the turmoil, he received a phone call from President Assad of Syria. To his chagrin, he had to drive to the gate house to talk on a noisy temporary phone line which was being patched in.

Assad was furious that Emir had allowed his personal representative to be assassinated by the Israelis. Emir's anger welled up in his throat as, tired and disheveled, he stood in the blowing sand. Didn't Assad realize that Mahmoud had kidnapped the American woman and that his Syrians had blown up half the camp? Assad brushed him off with a derisive *Maaleesh,* "So what?" Assad pointed out that Emir had kept him in the dark about the reason for hijacking the nuclear warhead. He had found it out from Mahmoud just two days previously. He felt that the scheme was thoroughly unworkable and dangerous and had agreed with Mahmoud that the quickest way to foil it was to capture the girl and release the code to the Americans.

"Don't you realize that the Israeli Prime Minister could not carry out the program of evacuation you desire in the given time scale," said Assad. "It is politically impossible, even if he wanted to do it."

"I beg to differ, Mr. President," said Emir. "Last night's Israeli television showed a strong tendency on the part of the press to go along with the concept."

"You fool, that's only propaganda to gain bargaining time. Do you realize what will happen to you and to me if the balance of power in the Middle East is suddenly changed by an American defeat?"

"Yes. It will allow us to run over the Israeli dogs when the Americans pull out."

"It will allow the Soviets to completely dominate the Middle East and make puppets of us all, that is what it will do."

"I am sorry to differ with you, sir," said Emir. "I am confident that my plan will provide a bloodless solution to our problems."

"Bloodless, in a camel's ass," retorted Assad. "By Allah, if you mess things up, you will have ten thousand Syrian troops surrounding you in Beirut two days from now."

While the session in the Situation Room was breaking up in preparation for the confrontation with Emir, the secretary of State was informed that the Prime Minister of Israel was on the phone, on a secure line in the Oval Office. The Prime Minister made no mention of the aborted kidnapping but stated that he had some encouraging news. He had taken a gamble and called in the heads of the major television and print media. He told them that he had a problem of the gravest national importance, which he was unable to reveal to them. They would have to trust him for that reason, but he wanted a favorable press reaction on the idea of withdrawing from the West Bank of the Jordan. The press moguls were astute enough to realize that this request was somehow related to the hijacked nuclear warhead. Even those who were violently opposed in principle had agreed to go along for forty-eight hours. The Prime Minister hoped that this would help in buying time with Emir.

At 8:20 A.M., the President seated himself in a straight chair close to the wall at one end of the Situation Room, facing the cameras and the monitors. The small table in front of him contained only a highly directional microphone, so that no sound but his voice would be picked up. His television makeup had been applied to give him a stern look, and the cameras were focused on his upper torso, allowing him to give prearranged signals with his fingers, concealed from the camera by the table. A tiny radio receiver, smaller than a hearing aid, was hidden in his right ear. He was flanked, out of the field of view of the cameras, by two men from the Washington Center for Strategic and International Studies, skilled negotiators in terrorist confrontation. Appleby was stationed beside one of the CSIS men to give political advice, if necessary, and Kane beside the other, to supply technical advice.

Promptly at 8:30 A.M., the television monitors bloomed twice, then steadied with a test pattern that the technicians used to peak up the reception. Five minutes later, the face of Salom al Emir scrolled across the monitors, settling quickly into a clear, sharply focused image. Dressed in flowing Arab attire, he was seated casually in an armchair on a foot-high dais. The television resolution was excellent, detailed enough to resolve the slightly bloodshot veins in his dark brown eyes.

Emir cleared his throat. "Good morning," he said, the microphones picking up a slight tremor in his voice.

The President said nothing.

Kane could hear one of the CSIS men whisper, "He's nervous," into the radio transmitter and saw the President's fingers signal agreement.

"Mr. President, thank you for your assistance in setting up this network. Because we can see each other face to face, it will be much easier to come to an understanding to reach our common goal, peace and justice in the Middle East."

"It is difficult for me, sir," replied the President, "to comprehend how we can reach an understanding for peace and justice under the threat of a nuclear holocaust."

"There need be no holocaust, nor indeed any bloodshed whatsoever, if you and your Israeli allies carry out the few requests I have made for the freedom of the rightful citizens of the West Bank."

The President stiffened, ready to make an angry response, but the CSIS man whispered calming words into his transmitter. The President collected himself with an effort, took a deep breath and answered without emotion. "Proceed, Mr. Emir. It's your meeting."

"My nickel, you might say, in the American idiom. Yes, Mr. President, let me show you what we have here, just so you will understand that this is no hoax. On this side of the room" — the cameras panned to a solitary, scowling figure — "we have Herr Ludwig Schultz, who borrowed this nuclear warhead for our demonstration."

Kane searched the screen for a sign of June. The accounts of her double kidnapping had been confused and fragmentary, but the numbers she had transmitted to the Israelis had been small primes, consistent with his theory. It could be a trick to throw him off course, but he was certain in his heart that she had changed her mind and that the numbers were genuine. But had she, and was there any way she could give him more information?

As the camera zoomed in on Schultz, he pulled his hand-cuffed arms over his face and averted his head.

"You will notice, Mr. President," Emir continued, "that Herr Schultz is handcuffed and under guard. And on the other side of the room, you will recognize Miss June Malik."

The image on the screen blurred as the camera swung quickly around the large room. Kane strained forward, sweating, needing to see the face of the woman he still loved.

"Miss Malik and her family have long been friends of mine. Her maternal forebears lived on the West Bank and have endured generations of suffering, which we will now alleviate once and for all."

Suddenly June came into sharp focus. Handcuffed, she sat silently, head turned to one side. Her face, devoid of makeup, was pale and she'd lost weight. Kane gasped at the sight of the handcuffs. He was right. She had changed her mind. June, speak to me. Send me a signal.

She was a tragic figure, sitting helplessly in the glare of the lights. She seemed to sense that her fate was sealed, that she would pay deeply for her mistakes.

But only Emir spoke. "We share common views on the problem and its solution, but the pressure of events and the cruelty of her kidnappers have temporarily upset her. She is restrained now for her own good, but soon she will be free to go."

At Emir's last words, June moved her head, looking straight into the cameras. Her liquid brown eyes were steady and unwavering, with only a hint of tears at the corners. She took a deep breath, deeper than Kane had ever seen her breathe, and slowly expelled it, her lips rounded. Then, in bitter contradiction of Emir's promise of freedom, she raised her handcuffed wrists in full view of the cameras. Light reflected off the cold steel as she made circles with the thumbs and fingers of both hands before dropping them again to her lap. Her face was expressionless. Kane was discouraged as he stared searchingly into her eyes. He saw no message for him — neither of love nor of hate.

"Miss Malik . . ." the President began.

"Let us continue the tour, so to speak," Emir said. "In front of me is the device you have been waiting to see."

June's face remained impassive as the camera turned away, focusing on the platform where the canister containing the warhead had been placed. It sat there in its cradle, with a rack of electronic gear containing a large cathode ray tube to one side. Two electrical cables fed out from the bottom panel of the rack, their free ends coiled loosely on the floor in front of the canister.

"First, I want to present to you the two gallant American officers who have been carefully guarding this canister for the last few days. They can assure you that the device has not been out of the sight of one of them since it was taken from the transportation vehicle in Germany. During that time the canister has not been unlocked nor the contents tampered with. Gentlemen, will you assure your President that my statement is correct, please?"

The camera picked up Captain Curran and Lieutenant Murray, standing rigidly at attention. Each man recited only his name, rank, and serial number.

The President smiled to ease their concern. "Gentlemen, I am pleased to see that you are alive and apparently well. You have my permission to make any statement you choose."

The captain spoke for the two of them, stating that they had been treated well. He verified the statement that they had guarded the canister at all times, taking turns eating and sleeping. He assured the President that no one could have tampered with the contents of the canister since it was taken from American custody.

Emir reappeared in view, now smug and confident, all traces of nervousness gone. He started to speak.

The CSIS man whispered into the transmitter. "Interrupt him. Don't let him take control." The President's fingers signaled assent. "How do I know that these officers are not drugged?" he asked before Emir could get started.

The Lebanese president looked pained. He sat up straight in the armchair and spoke harshly. "Sir, I am a man of honor. No one is playing games here. There is no hokeypokey, as you might say. I will ignore that question. Here is the schedule.

"At noon, your time, I will be broadcasting on this channel to discuss Israeli progress in meeting my terms. I will be available again at six P.M. If sufficient progress is not made, the demonstration will begin at midnight when the code changes. We will allow sixty minutes' grace for accumulated errors in clock settings, then begin the test. At one A.M., the canister will be unlocked and the warhead removed. The cables you see coiled on the platform will be connected to the warhead and, at precisely one-thirty A.M., switches will be closed so that you may send signals to the Permissive Action Link and to the firing circuit of the warhead.

"The numbers you insert will appear on the monitor in the rack on the platform. You know the circuitry. The lock will accept two incorrect inputs without rejection. If a third false signal is sent, the unit will not only reject it but will permanently disable the warhead. The Soviet Union will be trying to break the coded satellite transmission. You will have exactly one half hour to attempt to insert signals. At the end of that time, the transmission will operate in the clear and tapes of the demonstration will be repeated. The Soviet Union can then use the information for whatever purpose they choose. In this fashion, I will not be responsible for detonating any nuclear weapons, since the one in my possession will be inoperable. What others choose to do does not put any blood on my hands."

Then, with a sardonic expression on his face, he bowed his head to the cameras. "Mr. President, I bid you good day," he said.

Kane searched but in vain for another glimpse of June. The cameras remained fixed on Emir until the screen went blank.

"Jesus, this guy's really nuts," said one of the CSIS advisers as the lights were brought up and the tapes were being rewound for analysis. "He may be dooming half the people on earth, but he seems only to be concerned about blood on his own hands."

"That's the typical psychopath's urge for self-justification," said the other. "We are looking at a terribly warped but very strong ego here. He is deluding himself into thinking that he caused the change in Israeli press reaction. If we can get the Israelis to put out some more bullshit, we may get some delay out of him. It's the first delay that's important with these guys. If you can get them to put off the first deadline, you can usually count on more."

The President agreed. He directed the secretary of State to call the Israelis, suggesting that they reveal the whole plot in confidence to a group of reliable executives of the media to encourage them to publish another series of favorable press reports over the next few hours. "Now we're going to rerun those tapes."

Kane stood up to go. He wanted to consult with his computer panel, but something held him back. His feelings about June were in turmoil. One part of him was appalled at what she had done, another forgiving that she had realized her error. He decided to have one last look.

Kane sat down in his chair as the lights dimmed and once more the face of Emir dominated the room from the large television screen. Minutes passed as Emir's voice droned on.

And then a pale and drawn June was on the screen.

Is it really June? he thought. She looks so strange. Can she be drugged?

"Bitch," Slocum spat out, cigar smoke rising in the rays of the camera light.

Kane leaned forward. Why did she round her lips? That was unusual. For the first time, he glanced away from her face. He breathed in deeply, involuntarily, as her chest heaved. Then he noticed the handcuffs raised, and the circles she made with her fingers, gestures she had never made before. Both hands. It must be deliberate.

He sat gazing into the distance until the tape stopped, then moved quickly to the President's side. "I think June Malik's trying to tell us something."

"A little late, isn't she?" Slocum asked, his cigar glowing.

Kane ignored him. Urgently, he told the President that he wanted to review the tape with an associate who knew June. The President ordered the tapes rerun as Kane ran out the door. Minutes passed until the low drone of conversation stopped when Kane hurried back in with Herb Goldstein.

"There. Stop the tape there," Kane called out, excitement raising his voice to a shrill scream.

He and Goldstein studied the circles June made. She'd rounded her lips for a full ten seconds and made circles with her thumbs and fingers. Both concluded it must be a message. "Of course, she was signaling zeros," Herb yelled.

"You've got it," replied Kane. "The two primes she transmitted to the Israelis had zeros in them. I'm convinced now that she assembled her large prime numbers from small ones. One- and two-digit primes have no zeros. In three-digit numbers the zeros would have to be in the middle. There are only fifteen of them, which she could memorize. How brilliant! She built up a fifty digit series from only fifteen small numbers. This will cut hours out of the search. I'll get on the programmers right away."

Foster Martin stood at the gate of the Nevada Test Site and wept. The reporters and the television crews had departed as soon as the secretary of Energy had driven away. With the cameras gone, the Hollywood contingent had sped off to catch the next plane to Los Angeles. Foster had waved his associates away with the excuse that he would meet them back at the motel, with that harridan of a manager's wife . . . And where did he go from there?

At thirty-two years of age, he knew he was a total failure. He had started out to eliminate the nuclear arms race. Instead, he had intensified it and lost the only woman he had ever loved in the effort. Penelope: he could see her now, pert in her Tyrolean hat with the feather, as she rose excitedly to speak. Schultz. What a fool he was to have trusted Schultz. Tears of anger and mortification stung his face as he walked to his Jaguar, Penelope's pride.

The guards were relaxed, standing by the side of the road, joking with the state sheriffs. Only one was left in the guardhouse, drinking coffee and looking away from the flimsy wooden barrier.

He gritted his teeth. For Penny, he shouted, as he turned the car, floored the accelerator, and drove straight at the wooden barrier.

On Yucca Flat, the operation was going well. The Department of Energy and its contractors had picked up the time lost by evading the protestors. As the sun began to rise high over the desert mountains, Hank Reynolds, the construction foreman, took off the heavy jacket that had protected him against the nighttime chill. It seemed like another Washington screwup to have one device pulled up a hole and another substituted for it at the last minute. But we should make it now, he thought.

The device was about a hundred feet down the hole, suspended by cables from the drilling rig, when Hank noted the dust from a vehicle approaching from the south. That's peculiar, he thought. With a live device being lowered into a hole, all personnel should have been evacuated from outlying areas the day before. Whoever he is, he's coming like a bat out of hell.

He raised his binoculars to make out the vehicle. A sports car with the top down, it looked like a Jaguar. Trailing it by at least a mile were two General Services sedans with police markings. Hank could hear cackling on the radio circuits and noticed an uneasiness on the part of the special armed guards always assigned to cover fissionable material.

He strolled over to the guard shack, where the sergeant was talking with the Nevada operations office manager. Apparently one of the demonstrators had broken through the barrier set up at the north gate of the site and headed into the experimental area.

The Department of Energy has strict rules about the use of deadly force, but one of the stipulations was that it could be used when an intruder came within a hundred yards of a live nuclear device.

"What shall we do, sir? Shall we shoot when he comes into range?" the sergeant asked.

"I'd like to say yes, Sergeant. But if he's some cowboy who intended to veer off at the last minute, the department will have our hides. I don't have any authority to break the hundred-yard rule."

"I understand, sir. We'll wait."

Hank watched in horror as the Jaguar came straight at him. Three burly guards, whom he knew to be expert amateur huntsmen, tracked the vehicle as calmly as they might an approaching duck. As it reached the hundred-yard distance, all three fired their Winchesters once. Hank could see the driver's body slam against the back of the seat. The Jaguar went wildly out of control, veering from the road, careening off a large wooden cable reel, and slamming into the drill rig with a sickening crash. The rig teetered on two wheels, hovered in the air as though on a tight rope, and almost tipped over. Finally, after an agonizing ten seconds, stabilized by the long cable and the suspended warhead, it came back on all four wheels, rocked twice, and sat still.

The manager dashed toward the crushed Jaguar as the pursuing guards in the government sedans pulled up. They extricated the bleeding body of the driver from the collapsed seat of the two-passenger vehicle and laid him on a tarpaulin. The eyes of the slight, blond driver opened for an instant, tried to focus but could not, then closed. He uttered a single word, "Penelope," sighed once, and stopped breathing.

"For God's sake," said the manager, "who is he?"

"Foster Martin," said one of the pursuing guards, pulling the tarpaulin over the dead man's face. "He was the leader of the Makepeace demonstrators."

Hank Reynolds paid no attention to the dead man but rushed to the rig. It was stable, with the suspended cable oscillating slowly up and down and the stunned operator emerging from the cab. A quick inspection showed that the cable had sustained no harm, but that the gear train in the lowering assembly was badly damaged. There were no parts in the area to repair it, and even if he elected to scrounge parts from another rig, he would have to take the load off the gear train. After a hurried conference, the decision was made to bring in a substitute rig.

Unfortunately, the nearest rig was four miles away. Since the ponderous vehicles traveled at a maximum speed of two miles per hour, that meant a two-hour delay plus the tricky operation of transposing the cable with its load to the new rig. But they had no other choice.

While they waited for the new one to arrive, Reynolds and his crew fashioned a makeshift scaffolding around the damaged drill rig, snubbing the cable and picking up its weight. Two hours later, when the new rig arrived, they were ready to ease it in place in less than an hour. The manager congratulated the crew for a splendid job of improvisation, but the secretary of Energy had to report to the White House that they had lost three hours. It would be difficult to make up the time.

Brad Appleby sat in front of the desk in the President's office rereading the report that Aeroflot flight 365, New York to Moscow, had been canceled Thursday night and that the aircraft had left early with a single passenger, Ambassador Peter Rostov.

"Must be something big, Mr. President," Appleby said. "I've never heard of their commandeering a commercial carrier before."

"Stick around, Brad. I don't like the smell of this."

"Yes, sir," said Appleby. "I won't leave the building."

But he hadn't even left the room when Billings dashed in with another message: "CIA reports heavy military personnel movement around Moscow. The rumor in the diplomatic corps is that the Soviets have gone to their defense condition three."

"My God," blurted Appleby, "Rostov's on to us."

In Moscow, the General Secretary recessed the Politburo meeting for an hour and asked Rostov to come into his office. He was pacing the floor and remained standing after waving Rostov to a seat. Rostov's heartbeat quickened. Something was wrong.

"Pyotr Ivanovitch," he started.

Rostov's heart beat faster. In the name of Lenin, what's wrong? He has never used my patronymic before.

Rostov watched, fascinated, as his leader resumed pacing. Suddenly he wheeled and thrust out his arm. His hand held a bright red sheet of paper denoting a message of the highest urgency. "The KGB reports that the Americans have gone to defense condition three. What is most alarming is that they did it before we did. Do you know what this means?"

Rostov was sure that the American President had no intention of carrying out a first strike. He didn't think that it was the President they had to worry about, it was his advisers. Looking into his leader's eyes, he pointed out that the Americans have as many hard-line conservatives as the Soviet Union does.

The General Secretary nodded ruefully.

"When they find out that we have gone to our similar readiness condition, they will want to go on to the next stage," Rostov said. "The problem both of you will have is to stop the escalation before it is too late."

"Strangely, Pyotr Ivanovitch," said the General Secretary, looking drawn and staring into space, "in one sense I feel a kinship with that American President. Everyone thinks that we have unlimited power. But we both know that we must have political consensus to survive. I don't think I have mine."

When the General Secretary reconvened the Politburo meeting, he glumly announced the American action. The first question was whether the Americans had acted before he did. At his affirmative answer, there was pandemonium. Members milled about the podium, all shouting at once for attention. It took minutes to gavel the meeting to order.

The Defense minister spoke up. "I move that we mobilize our armed forces for the defense of our motherland."

Rostov tried to stem the tide. He had just come from the United States, he pointed out, and was certain that they had no aggressive intentions. He declared that such escalation could lead to mutual annihilation, that the Americans would immediately find out. They would be frightened and might escalate further. Couldn't they talk on the hot line? He was hooted down with shouts for a vote.

The General Secretary saw that there was no need for a vote. He turned to the chief of staff and instructed him to declare defense condition 2.

The ponderous Soviet military machine began to move into action. Ballistic missile submarines pulled out control rods on their reactors to bring the power plants to full readiness, liquid oxygen and rocket fuel were brought out of storage for the massive liquid-fueled SS-20s, Backfire and Bison bombers went to the end of their runways, and chiefs of conventional forces were put on alert for possible actions in Europe.

When the next meeting convened in the Situation Room, the arguments about Russian intentions continued. At the peak of the discussion, an aide came in and handed the President a note. The President read it, nodded wordlessly, then recessed the meeting for half an hour. He beckoned Appleby to come with him.

The President closed the door to his private office, motioned Appleby to a seat on one side of a small cocktail table, then sat wearily in an armchair opposite him, holding the message absently in his right hand. He was silent for a moment, then began questioning Appleby about the Russian premier's intentions.

"Frankly, sir," Appleby said, "I believe Rostov when he says that both of you are overly protected by your staffs and prevented from making the kinds of concessions you would be prepared to make to assure mutual understanding."

"I believe that, too, Brad, but you and I are going to have some strong arguing to do. Satellite reconnaissance tells us that the Soviets have just gone to readiness condition two."

"Oh, my God," cried Appleby. "I expected them to follow us into DEFCON three, but I didn't expect them to mobilize faster than we did. He must have his Jeff Slocums in spades."

If the announcement of the first Soviet action had caused heated discussion and consternation, the second announcement had the opposite effect. It was as though the doors had been opened and a chill Arctic wind blew across the room. Appleby could see hunching of shoulders and rubbing of hands and in some cases actual shivers down their spines. The secretary of State's head drooped. His argument had been demolished. The hawks, with Slocum as their spokesman, took over.

"There is no question in my mind," said the secretary of Defense, lighting up a cigar as though he had won a victory, "that they are not going to wait for us to surrender. They are not going to negotiate. If they were, they wouldn't have to mobilize now. They have figured out that we may strike before we lose our capability and are getting ready to strike first. We've got to be ready to beat them to the punch."

Appleby tried to stem the tide, to no avail. He referred to his recent conversations with Rostov and to the kind of caution Rostov was likely to urge upon his own countrymen, but the fear and the malice were too dominant. He looked at Kane. A slight shake of his head indicated that Kane had nothing to offer in the political arena. He turned and stared at Senator Sullivan.

Tim nodded and stepped into the fray, body forward and chin out with that look of belligerent determination familiar to all his television viewers. "Please remember that we have little data to make such a decision, and the Russians have less. We may find the numbers, the code may not change, we may be able to talk this Middle Eastern madman out of his demonstration, anything may happen in the next few hours. It was a mistake to go to the first stage. I believe the Russians wouldn't have alerted if we hadn't done so first. We can't bet civilization on so little information. I propose that we get on the hot line and tell them we are calling off our alert. Let's stop this foolish escalation while we can."

Slocum smashed his cigar into an ashtray, sending ashes and sparks skittering across the table. He declared that it was too late for anything like that. "Suppose we call it off and they don't. Then we'd be screwed. He turned to the chairman of the Joint Chiefs of Staff, who was sitting directly behind him. "How long will it take to mobilize the strategic forces in their present state of alert?"

The answer was that they had already started with DEFCON 3. For full mobilization, including submarine positioning and deployment of the Stealths and the BIBs, they needed another six hours. In an emergency, they would go with what was ready, but they would lose a lot of punch. He asserted firmly, with the stars gleaming on his shoulders and the ribbons shining in rainbow profusion, that if they were going to do this at all, they should do it at full strength to minimize the Soviet second strike capability. That was the best way to save the lives of their own people. To be ready before midnight, they should give the order at once.

"You see, Mr. President," said Slocum, "even if you wait only a couple of hours, you will be endangering our citizens' ability to ride out a second strike, which will cost millions of lives. If you act now, you will be assured of maximum strength whatever happens during the rest of the day."

We're losing, thought Appleby. He looked at Hal King, but the secretary of State still sat slumped in his chair. He had nothing to offer. The CIA director, the FBI director, and the general sat straight and alert, confident of their cause and sensing victory.

Tim Sullivan stood up to try once more. "That's suicide," he cried. "When the Russians see us mobilize, they will convince themselves that we are going to strike and could act immediately to preempt us. They may not even wait to see what Emir does."

"Sit down, Senator." Slocum was derisive. "By their mobilization, they have already made that decision. I don't trust the bastards and never have. We can't afford to deal with them without a full deck of cards."

The President was silent, but Appleby could see him watching the heads of the others as the secretary of Defense spoke. Hal King, Senator Sullivan, and Fred Billings were shaking their heads negatively, but the majority, including the Speaker of the House, the Chief Justice, and the majority leader of the Senate, were nodding their heads affirmatively.

The President had a pained expression on his face and sadness in his eyes. All heads turned to him as the secretary of Defense concluded. There was a moment of excruciating silence. The only motion in the room was the smoke still curling up from Slocum's extinguished cigar.

He decided to take no vote. He raised his hand, looked

around the room once, then spoke a brief sentence to his chief of staff. "Declare DEFCON two."

Only an hour behind the Russians, the Minuteman silos opened their doors, the Polaris and Poseidon submarines rushed silently to station, and the B1Bs and Stealths were positioned on their runways for takeoff.

# 19

JUNE WAS EXHAUSTED AT THE CONCLUSION OF the television exchange. She had gone through a number of experiences — her attempt to escape, the multiple kidnappings, the return to the camp, and now this exchange with the President of the United States.

When she had been brought back to the camp the day before and found her quarters burned out, she collapsed into tears. Although Emir and Hassan had monitored the radio transmission to the Israelis and knew that she had tried to pass on the code, they were solicitous. Emir felt that her defection was temporary, that when the Israelis evacuated the West Bank she would be back to her old self. Hassan, not so certain, kept his silence.

Hassan had evacuated his own quarters to give her some privacy, but surrounded the building with guards hidden from sight. He had borrowed a simple white dress from one of the maids so that she would look presentable the next day. She washed her own underwear in the bathroom. It dried quickly in the warm desert air.

Dead tired, she slept soundly and felt somewhat refreshed when the driver arrived to take her to the building with the warhead. She was fascinated by the small size of the container, having no idea how large a warhead would be. She was curious about the American officers, but they ignored her and refused to answer her greeting.

Hassan was polite, but firm. She was to make no attempt to communicate with the two officers and was not to move from her chair before or during the transmission. He warned her that if she made any attempt to signal the Americans, the microphones would be turned off and the cameras would instantly swing away from her.

"I am sorry, Miss June," he said, "but I must restrain your arms while the cameras are on you. It's a minor precaution against any misguided idea you might have to disrupt the proceedings. The handcuffs will not be uncomfortable, and we can hide them from the cameras if you would like."

"That won't be necessary."

She resolved to be withdrawn but civil, knowing that any obstructionism would cut down on her time on camera. Mahmoud had told her about the massive computer search, and she was certain that Kane would be involved in it somehow. She was also sure that he would be watching her carefully.

Kane knew that trapdoor functions involved prime numbers. She felt that he would also have reasoned by now that she had started with low numbers and built the large primes from them. If she could get the signal to him that the numbers contained zeros, he would know that there were no two-digit primes and that the three-digit primes had to have the zeros in the middle. This would give him the first fifteen numbers. Even with this information, it would be a difficult task, but it gave her some hope. If they could find the code soon enough, she reasoned, they would announce it and the demonstration could be called off. It had a slim chance of succeeding, but it was worth trying.

Schultz had not fared so well. They had separated him from June when they arrived at camp and she had not seen him since. When they brought him into the building, already handcuffed, he was wearing the dirt-stained fatigues from the day before. He was unshaven and his face bore scratches from one of the day's scuffles. He appeared sullen and refused to look in her direction.

Emir had arrived fifteen minutes before the scheduled time.

He did not glance at Schultz but walked over to June to greet her and apologize for any inconvenience. She was polite but cool. He looked trim in his robes, but she could see the fatigue in his eyes. He had probably spent all his time supervising the cleanup of the camp.

When she saw the face of the President of the United States, her whole body flushed and her palms began to tingle. This was her first contact with her previous life, the first visible indication of what she had cast aside in her ill-advised attempt to improve the world. When he tried to appeal to her and was cut off by Emir, her heartbeat quickened and tears came to her eyes. Somewhere behind that commanding figure sat her former lover. Had he gotten her message? He, who once knew her every move and gesture, had he recognized the unusual sigh, the rounded lips, the circles with the fingers? It was the only hope, the last hope she had.

She began to tremble and weep when the lights went down. Hassan came over to remove her shackles. Emir tried to comfort her, but she shook him off. In a daze, she watched the television crews leave the building, one technician remaining behind to rearrange cables, a cameraman to adjust a tripod.

Schultz stood while Hassan removed his handcuffs. A guard had a rifle in his back. Emir stepped over to them.

"Hassan," he said, "radio service is now restored to my office. Go raise our agents in Tel Aviv for a situation report. I want to talk to Schultz and June."

Emir glared at Schultz. He told him that the promise of freedom was nullified when Schultz teamed up with Mahmoud. He would be kept in custody until the Israelis conceded, then they would decide what to do with him. He warned Schultz that the final decision would be influenced by Schultz's behavior in the meantime. Emir, smiling and holding his arms outstretched, then turned to June.

He had not taken three steps when Schultz wheeled and knocked the rifle from the hands of the startled guard. It went spinning across the floor. Schultz reached inside his fatigues and drew out a folded hunting knife. With one motion he pressed the button and lunged toward the guard. As the blade snapped into place he drew it viciously across the man's throat, half cutting his head from his body. The guard's knees buckled, and he started to collapse, his heart still pumping blood through the severed arteries all over Schultz and the floor.

Emir's smile froze as he saw June open her mouth to scream. Before he could turn, the agile Schultz was upon him, a blood-spattered arm around his neck, the knife at his back. The American officers, the technician, and the cameraman stood immobilized.

"Arab *schwein*," his guttural voice grated into Emir's ear. "You thought you were passing my death sentence, didn't you."

He pulled back his head and shouted for the others to hear. "Americans, don't move from that warhead. I am acting in your interest. You, technician, turn on the broadcast equipment and make contact with the American President. Cameraman, focus your camera on Malik."

He spoke more softly to June. "This madman's plan cannot work. There is no way we can get out of here alive if it continues. The Russians or the Americans will wipe the camp out. Pick up the rifle and shoot anyone who moves. Be prepared to broadcast the code to the Americans when the technician contacts them. When he has the code, the American President will be willing to trade this dog's life for our freedom. Be quick, it's our only chance."

The technician's English was poor. He had difficulty raising anyone on the satellite frequency. Precious minutes were lost before the Goddard Communications Center in Maryland answered. The White House equipment had been turned off. More time was lost while they contacted Washington.

"Hurry, hurry" was all June could say in her anxiety.

When the picture came into focus, June could see a startled Signal Corps colonel staring from the White House Situation Room. He looked amazed to see her with one hand holding the bloodstained rifle, the other drawing a piece of paper from her blouse.

"Copy these numbers down, quickly," she said without introduction. As the colonel reached for a pencil, her attention was diverted when the door of the building opened and Hassan's head appeared. She turned back to her paper and began to dictate. Hassan's head disappeared. Before she could utter a number, the windowless room went completely black.

In the quiet, she heard a scuffle beside her — the two former athletes in combat. She knew that Schultz was strong, but Emir was quick. There was a curse in German. She could sense someone rush by her, headed for the door. She raised the rifle when she saw him silhouetted in the evening starlight. As she pulled the trigger, Emir's swimmer's legs pushed his slim body in a horizontal dive below her line of fire. He hit the ground, rolled once, and twisted out of sight. The building was dark and silent.

Within seconds, Hassan's voice boomed out of a bullhorn. "We have disconnected the main circuit breaker. Drop your weapons and raise your hands or you will be gassed out and shot."

When the lights came on, Schultz was standing with his hands in the air, the knife tossed in front of him. Hassan shot him on the spot.

June crumpled in a faint and lay on the floor, the rifle still held limply in her open hands.

# 20

HAROLD KING WALKED THROUGH THE UNDER-
ground tunnel to his own office and called the Israeli Prime
Minister. "You are doing a splendid job," said King, sitting
relaxed with his feet on the desk. "Emir seems to believe your
story. His comments were somewhat reserved, but we could see
on his face that he feels that you are going to get approval for
evacuation of the West Bank."

The Prime Minister was skeptical. He looked at his telephone
as though it were a person and shook his head wistfully. He
wished he could feel the same way. He had been getting irate
phone calls all night. So had the media people. The executives
were badly upset. He didn't know how long he could keep them
in line.

"If you can hold them through today's television programs
and tomorrow's early editions of the newspapers, that's all we'll
ask," said King. "If we can talk Emir into twelve hours' delay,
we have some things going for us that may get us out of this
mess. Do you think you can keep them with you that long?"

"I think so. I can hold the senior people, but some of the
reporters are beginning to ask difficult questions. I realize the
stakes; I'll do my best."

He hung up the phone and pondered for a moment. The
Americans. He would never understand them. Wearily, he rang

for his secretary, forgetting that she did not work on the Sabbath.

Hank Reynolds was holding his hand against the blowing sand in Yucca Flat at the Nevada Test Site. He was having a difficult time with his makeshift rig. The substitute equipment used a different type of cable. Even though he exercised the utmost precaution, the cable reel jammed twice, once at 500 feet and again at 750 feet. He went to his truck and radioed the secretary of Energy when the warhead reached the 1200-foot bottom, but stated that he might not have time to backfill the hole completely before he was scheduled to evacuate the area. The secretary consulted with blast experts at Los Alamos and Livermore, who calculated that he should have at least 900 feet of backfill; otherwise the gases might vent to the atmosphere in violation of the test ban treaty. Reynolds said he would do his best.

Just before his next scheduled conversation with Emir at noon, the President called for a progress report on computer operations. Kane stated that the entire system had switched to building large primes from the fifteen three-digit primes with zero as the middle number.

"Based on these assumptions, Mr. President," said Kane, "we conclude that with any luck at all, we should have the answer within eighteen hours, or roughly six o'clock tomorrow morning."

"You mean if we can get a six-hour delay out of this nut, we're in business?" the President asked.

"Nothing's certain in statistical analysis," said Kane. "But the odds would be in our favor."

When Emir appeared at noon, his face filled the entire screen. He made no reference to the struggle of an hour before, but Kane could see that his robe was pulled tightly against his neck, clasped by an ornamental pin, and several scratches showed on his forehead. Still, he seemed in excellent spirits.

He smiled broadly and commended the President and his allies for the progress they were making. It appeared that the Israelis realized that they had not only violated the spirit of the cease-fire agreements, but had also illegally breached the written treaty language. He apologized for having to choose such dramatic tactics, but he hoped the President understood. With a sweeping gesture of his arms, he leaned forward toward the cameras.

"To use your American idiom, sometimes people cannot see the forest for the trees."

"Thank you for the compliment," replied the President, bowing his head modestly. He paused and smiled his broadest smile. Kane had seen it flash on many television screens. The President had the ability to make the recipient feel like the most important person in the world.

"Sir," he said, "please take into account that we are all trying to solve long-term problems expeditiously. I suggest that you consider granting the Prime Minister an extra day to complete his preparations. Please think about it."

"Mr. President," replied Emir, "the advice of so eminent a personage as yourself does not fall on deaf ears. I will give you my decision at six o'clock."

The face vanished.

The Situation Room resounded with spontaneous applause, but the President held up his hand. He explained that some progress had been made in dealing with Emir but that the nation was facing a clear danger with both the United States and the USSR in a state of full nuclear mobilization. One mistaken move on the part of either country could plunge the world into a holocaust.

"Until now, I have refrained from using the hot line teletype because I did not want the Soviets to suspect what is going on in Lebanon. It is now clear that they have a good idea of our predicament, so it is time to see what we can do to cool down relations between us. I am ready to compose a message to the General Secretary."

The meeting in the Situation Room ran continuously, members occasionally leaving to answer telephone calls or explain to their families that urgent business would keep them into the night.

Appleby was talking to Kane, mostly reminiscing about college days, anything to keep their minds off the dreadful subject of escalation, when Billings returned to report on the exchanges with the Soviets. Appleby didn't like the look of distress on his face.

The President had informed the General Secretary that he had ordered full nuclear mobilization as a result of reports indicating that the Soviet Union had already gone to full nuclear mobilization. He would reconsider his action if the Soviet Union would do the same.

The Soviet response was blunt. They had taken action because the United States had not only gone on nuclear alert first, but had done so without consultation. After two exchanges of messages, the premier was adamant. The President broke off communications to consult with his staff.

"They have us by the short hair," the chief of staff glumly concluded. He paced up and down, his chin in his hand. "Maybe it was a mistake to go on alert in the first place."

"Nonsense," said Jeff Slocum. "We had no alternative. It's two o'clock now. It takes six hours to get aircraft airborne and effective over the target. We'll have to make the decision about launching the B1Bs and the Stealths damned soon."

Appleby explained to Kane the dilemma the President would face next: whether to launch his bombers soon enough to reach the Soviet Union before the weapons became inoperative and risk a preemptive ICBM attack by the Soviets or to hold back and risk the loss of one of the stronger legs of this three-part arsenal — bombers, submarine missiles, and land-based missiles.

The President walked in, face serious, brows knitted, holding his hands palms down in a "please be seated, let's not stand on ceremony" gesture. "Gentlemen, we are about to consider the most important decisions any of us will ever have to make. We have two hours to decide whether to launch our bombers if they are to arrive over target before midnight."

Harold King spoke first. He was not convincing. King was a diplomat, not a debater. He recognized that the order was theoretically reversible but pointed out that with hundreds of aircraft and thousands of excited crewmen in the air, anything could happen. The aircraft were to turn back without a definite order to proceed, but he warned that, in battle, men hear strange voices, not necessarily those of their commanders.

"And what of the Soviets?" he asked. "If they launched, could we trust that their crews would heed recall orders?"

Senator Sullivan tried next. He pointed out the arguments for delay, which everyone already knew. But the tone of the meeting had gotten away from him. The men were fidgeting, moving around in their seats. They were tired, angry, belligerent, not about to toss away an advantage.

The hawks took over.

Jeff Slocum was out of his seat, waving his cigar, before Sullivan could sit down. "Mr. President." His voice was hoarse now. "Mr. President, these arguments mean nothing. The Soviets are afraid that we will act before our weapons become impotent and are preparing to preempt our first strike. That's all that counts.

"If Emir postpones at six o'clock, the aircraft will only be an hour out, so they can be recalled easily. But the most important reason for launching is the old saying, 'If you don't use them, you're going to lose them.' It's cost us a lot of money to build this aircraft capability. Let's not waste it by leaving it on the ground."

It was all up to the President.

Inside the Kremlin, the same argument raged. Rostov watched the members of the Politburo take sides. Boris Kamensky, the minister for Foreign Affairs, took the case for not launching their bombers. He was a polished diplomat, smooth talking and wise in the ways of Americans after five years in Washington as ambassador.

"Time is on our side. By morning they will have disarmed themselves. We can take them over without firing a shot. We are only concerned about preempting a first strike by them.

"Remember that if we launch, they launch, and they have the stronger air force. If we stay on the ground, maybe they'll stay on the ground, and we will have neutralized a more powerful capability. Maybe they have no intention to preempt. We should wait to see what Emir's demonstration is going to show us."

A murmur of approval welled up in the chamber, but the spokesman for the hard-liners had not yet been heard from.

Pausing to light a new cigarette from the butt of his last one, Dmitri Popov, minister of Defense, rose to his feet. "That's all nonsense, Boris Vasilovitch," he countered. "The Americans are already provoked. They know more about whether their weapons are going to function than we do. If they are going to be locked out, they'll use them while they can. We have to be ready to move first if they make that decision."

In Washington, the President retired to his private hideaway to ponder. At 4:45 P.M., he sent for Appleby.

The office was small, with an old mahogany desk, a relic from a previous president, a comfortable desk chair, two matching armchairs, and a fireplace. The only window looked out on Pennsylvania Avenue. The President, holding a cup of coffee, was seated in one of the armchairs. He motioned Appleby to the second one.

"Sit down, Brad. Have a cup of coffee. I don't think you're going to like the decision I'm about to make, but I thought I'd give you one last crack at it. I simply can't afford to sacrifice this bomber capability by not launching. Their bombers are on the runways, ready to launch any minute. Obviously, they will be using a decapitation strategy, aiming first at Washington to cut off our communications. Since their airfields are closer to

Washington than ours are to Moscow, they can afford to out-wait us. Can you give me any new reason why I shouldn't launch?"

Appleby knew he was coming from behind, but he had watched this man for years and knew he was capable of changing his mind. He detected in the tone of voice a desire, almost a pleading, to hear good reasons for halting the escalation. He rose to pour himself a cup of coffee. He continued standing, putting the coffee cup down after one sip.

Appleby began his arguments slowly and carefully, picking his way by watching the intent face of the man who would make the terrible decision. He talked first about President Kennedy and the Cuban missile crisis. He reminded the President that decisions had been made with little information and understanding on either side.

Kennedy had escalated after a U2 scouting aircraft was shot down. Many years later, it came out that the U2 was shot down by a renegade Cuban crew not under Russian control. His advisers had voted unanimously for an air strike on Cuba. But it was Kennedy himself who made the final decision to offer the compromise, removing the missiles in Turkey in exchange for a Russian withdrawal.

The President smiled, stood up, poured himself another cup of coffee, then sat down again. "Staffs get pretty hawkish, don't they," he said. "It must have something to do with their pride. They don't want to be accused of being chicken."

Appleby walked over, sat down in the armchair, and leaned toward the President. He was ready for his big point. "Mr. President," he said, "I believe that the concept of having bombers as a primary striking force is obsolete. What happens if you do deploy them? As soon as they cross the Russian border, far from their targets, the Soviets will release all their land- and sea-based missiles, and we will do the same. Civilization will be destroyed before they can get to their targets. When they do get there, they will be bombing a devastated country. As Churchill said, 'They will only make the rubble bounce.' The same reasoning applies to the Soviet aircraft."

The President was startled. "Why do we have them, then?" he blurted out.

"Habit. Habit and politics," Appleby replied. "They are of no use to us on a first strike. The war will be over before they get there."

"I don't understand." The President was confused. "Why haven't I heard this before?"

"Because you've never considered a first strike before. All our planning has been based on the Russians' striking first."

The President grilled him for fifteen minutes. Appleby embellished his argument by pointing out that there was no need for invisible Stealth bombers or terrain-hugging BiBs in any event, since Russian radar capability would have been wiped out by the twelve thousand warheads already delivered by the land- and sea-based missiles. What you need for retaliation, he stated, was the simplest and most reliable design.

"By God, if we get through this crisis, I'm going to have a thorough analysis . . . But what you're telling me is that I lose nothing by calling off the aircraft deployment."

"That's right, sir," said Appleby.

The President clapped his hands and rose from his chair. "Let's get on the hot line and try again."

Appleby didn't move. He looked up at the President and said, "I have another suggestion, sir."

"Go ahead."

"Mr. President, Rostov is not as powerful as the hard-liners in the Politburo, but he is the person who figured this thing out and brought it to them. For now, he would have more influence than he would normally. Let me try talking directly to him, giving him the straight scoop, to see if he can influence the General Secretary to back off."

"You want to try the hot line again?"

"The hot line teletype system is too cumbersome. I want to pick up the telephone and call him directly on an open line. May I have your permission to talk freely to him?"

"You have it. There aren't many secrets at this stage of the game."

A message was sent out on the hot line that an open telephone call was being initiated from the White House to the Kremlin, that Mr. Appleby would like to talk to Ambassador Rostov. A flurry of teletype interchanges followed. At the Moscow end, there was suspicion and objection to the call, particularly from Popov, but this time the premier overruled the objections.

"Dmitri Gregorovitch, my old comrade," he said to the Defense minister, clasping him by the shoulder, "the future of our motherland and of world civilization is at stake. We must talk. Come, Pyotr Ivanovitch, we will take the call in my quarters."

Even at that, it took ten minutes to get the call through the cumbersome Moscow telephone system. When the connection was made, Appleby spoke in Russian. There were no words wasted.

"Pete, I'm not going to spar with you. I'll give you the whole situation so you can make your own decisions based on all the information available."

"Go ahead, Brad."

Appleby went over the status of the PAL codes, filling him in on June and Emir and the midnight deadline, the General Secretary listening to the Russian conversation on another extension. He pointed out that there were still three possibilities: one, that the whole thing was a hoax; the second, that the Nevada test might show that the codes had not changed; and the third, that the computer network might find the code before the deadline. Based on those practical considerations, he said, the American President was prepared to give his assurances that he would not launch his aircraft if the Soviet Union was prepared to keep its bombers on the ground.

There was a pause while Appleby verified these assurances with the President. In the meantime, the Russians discussed the proposal. Rostov argued forcefully that the American position made sense, that canceling out the two bomber forces gave the Soviet Union a strategic advantage, and if the Americans launched their bombers, he still had enough time advantage to launch.

The General Secretary took only fifteen seconds to make up his mind.

"Tell the American President," he instructed Rostov, "that we will not launch our bombers unless he launches his. He has my word on it. But if one American bomber goes into the sky, we will unleash our complete force."

Appleby put the President on the line. Rostov repeated the message in English. The President agreed to hold his aircraft on the ground.

"Good job, Brad," were his only words as he stood up to return to the Situation Room.

Appleby sagged and smiled. "To say we have just dodged a bullet would be a hell of an understatement," he mumbled weakly.

"That's just one bullet," said the President. "The missiles are still completely mobilized. They can wipe us out in twenty minutes."

In Nevada, Hank Reynolds called the secretary of Energy from his truck.

"I'm sorry, sir, but I don't think there's any way we can make up the three hours we've lost. I can't backfill the hole completely and keep the scheduled zero time. Do you want to delay or shall we take the chance and not backfill the hole completely?"

Blast experts were put to work estimating how much fill was needed to prevent large amounts of radioactive gases leaking to the atmosphere. The conclusion was that if 800 feet of fill could be achieved, the leakage would not be serious.

Reynolds informed the secretary that the best he could do was 700 feet in the time available. Another round of conferences put the decisions back to the President, who gave the green light for 700 feet.

Favorable reports kept coming in from Israel. The Prime Minister had called a special session of the Knesset at noon the next day to debate evacuation of the West Bank. Israeli television stations were predicting that the resolution would pass. The American press began to pick up the reports, skeptical at first, then incredulous that so momentous a national policy position could change so rapidly. The American Jewish community was caught flat-footed, spokesmen hemming and hawing while frantic phone calls were put in to Tel Aviv to determine what was behind this sudden change.

The White House had no comment.

While the President was being made up for the six o'clock conference with Emir, the psychologists from CSIS convinced him that he should ask Emir to call off the demonstration entirely. They pointed out that he should take the strongest possible position in a situation of strength.

It was a smiling President who sat before the television screen when communication was resumed. He was quick to take the initiative. "Mr. Emir," he said, "I have been watching the local television reports and am pleased, as you must be, that the Israeli Prime Minister is having so much success convincing the members of his Knesset to come around to your point of view. As soon as the motion is passed, I hope you will see fit to call off the demonstration."

It became apparent as the President talked that Emir was not pleased. His face, initially expressionless, became more and more contorted, until he angrily broke in on the President. "You lie in your teeth, American dog."

The smile left the President's face. He was not used to being talked to like that. His face flushed. The psychologists whispered into the microphones for calm.

Emir pressed on. "You put yourself forward as a man of honor, but you have been lying to me all along. You never expected the Israelis to take my suggestions. You and those pigs have gotten together and made up a story which you thought I would believe. But you are not dealing with a nomad from the desert who has just gotten off his camel. You underestimate me,

Mr. President, I am not naive. I have my own sources of intelligence."

"But, Mr. Emir." The President tried to regain control. "I have seen —"

"Never mind what you have seen. I have two impeccable sources who now assure me that the actions in Israel are a hoax. There will be no postponement. But I am a man of honor if you are not. The conditions of the demonstration will be exactly as I outlined them to you in our first conference this morning. Good day."

There was silence in the Situation Room as the transmission was cut short. They were stunned.

The deep voice of Jeff Slocum broke the silence. "God damn it. What do we do now? It's too late to activate the aircraft. We've pissed away our whole airborne capability on a phony set of press releases and we're right back where we started. If they start dumping missiles on us at midnight, we're helpless."

In Nevada, it was nip and tuck. All 1800 square miles of the test site had been evacuated by 10:30 P.M., except for the crews doing the backfill and the arming party. High-powered sedans were in readiness at the zero point to take the work crews and the firing party back to the safety of the control room, thirty miles away. The arming party did their final checks while the crews were still backfilling. With an hour and a half before firing time, the backfill was at 680 feet.

"We have a stretchy ruler down here that can read seven hundred feet, if you want to knock it off now," Hank Reynolds reported to the secretary of Energy.

"You got it. Head for the barn" was the reply.

It took forty minutes to load the vehicles, travel the thirty miles to the control point, and get the firing party set up for the one-hour check. They had five minutes to spare.

At fifteen minutes before firing time, it was midnight eastern standard time. All over the world, in submarines, in missile bases, in aircraft, in a 1200-foot hole in the ground at the Nevada Test Site, and particularly in a Cruise missile warhead on a platform in a remote camp in Lebanon, precise electronic crystal clocks, twenty-five thousand of them, instructed twenty-five thousand Permissive Action Links that the time had come to switch to a new Permissive Action Link code.

# 21

*Sunday, June 1*

THE SCREEN FLICKERED TWICE, ROLLED VERTI-
cally for a few seconds, then focused on a platform with a metal
weapons container, a cabinet full of electronic equipment, and
several electrical cables rolled neatly on the floor. The camera
panned silently at two American military officers standing at
attention in front of the platform. It paused for a few seconds
at a handcuffed dark-haired woman in khaki blouse and slacks,
then moved to close in on the visage of Salom al Emir, head of
the Palestine Liberation Organization and president of Lebanon.

"Good," said the General Secretary. "My congratulations to
the minister of Communications for breaking the television
transmission code in such a short time. We shall have a ring-
side seat at this performance. Let us hope that the Americans
are not as good at breaking codes. I assume that the woman is
Miss Malik and that the officers are the ones kidnapped in
Germany."

"That's correct, sir," said Rostov. "They don't look
very happy. Not as happy as the people in this room, certainly."

"If our assumptions are correct, the American weapons are
now disarmed and we are the only world power," Popov said.

*

In Washington, the atmosphere in the Situation Room was gloomy. The President sat expressionless as Emir berated him and the Israelis for fifteen minutes. Kane had rushed into the room just as the tirade started. He sat down beside the CSIS man with the transmitter and looked at the President, who was not paying attention to what Emir was saying but was listening to the countdown from Nevada being relayed into his earphone.

Kane tapped the CSIS man on the shoulder. He broke off the transmission, annoyed. "I have a message for him," Kane whispered. "One of our computer operators had an activation. He's checking for a bad PAL."

When the message was relayed, he saw the President hold up two fingers in a "V." Kane whispered that he was going back into the computer room.

As he dashed back in, a speaker in the computer room was blaring out the countdown from Nevada. *"In one minute, the time will be exactly minus ten minutes."*

"Turn that down, please," he yelled as a voice came up on the telephone repeater.

"Jack Winter here, Idaho National Engineering Laboratories."

"What the hell's going on, Jack. We heard you say that you might have something and were checking for a bad PAL. Then you went off the line."

"Sorry, I had to go find another PAL. We've been building up the primes based on the smaller numbers all day. When you gave us the clue about the zeros, we worked up from them as you suggested."

"Yes, yes, go on," shouted Kane. "What happened? Time is short."

But Winter, like a true scientist, was not going to be hurried into telling his story.

"When we built up to a couple of numbers starting with the fourth and fifth, we got a click in the relay of the PAL. Then we tried it starting with adjacent numbers, but got no click. We tried it ten times with the original numbers and got a click each time. I thought maybe we had a bad PAL, but the electronics guys checked it out and it seems okay. We just put in a new one and had the same result. Maybe somebody else should try these numbers."

"Send them over the line to me quickly," said Kane.

"Okay," said Winter. "I'll repeat them twice so there won't be any mistakes."

As a secretary was taking down the numbers, Kane could hear in the background the voice from Nevada relentlessly counting down. *"Six . . . five . . . four . . . three . . . two . . . one. Now. The time is exactly minus five minutes."*

In the control room at Nevada, the test director looked out at an unfamiliar scene. Usually, with a test conducted just before dawn, he could see the reds and pinks of the new day coming up in back of the mountains surrounding Yucca Flat and the contrails of cloud-tracking aircraft, aloft at thirty thousand feet to follow the path of any radioactive gases that might leak to the atmosphere. Tonight there were no pinks and reds of sunshine, no aircraft contrails. There was only darkness punctuated by the bright stars of a desert evening. Zero was 12:15 A.M. eastern time, 9:15 P.M. Nevada time. The stars were bright, but not bright enough for aircraft to track the cloud. They would have to play it blind, sending trucks with instrumentation down into the valley to measure from the ground and only guess what might be going on aloft.

He scrutinized the lights on the control panels as the countdown proceeded. As an exercise, this was an easy one. There were no diagnostic experiments. There was instrumentation to measure the yield of the explosive, should it detonate, but they would be able to tell that with their feet, when the shock wave arrived.

The countdown announced one minute before zero. The test director closed his eyes for ten seconds. He had found that this would give his brain relief from the tension of staring at the indicators and maximize his alertness as the clock proceeded toward zero.

*"The time is minus thirty seconds . . . Minus fifteen seconds
. . . ten . . . nine . . . eight . . . seven . . . six . . . five . . . four
. . . three . . . two . . . one . . . ZERO."*
Nothing happened. There was no crazy flickering of lights to
show that an enormous electromagnetic field had been created.
The yield meters registered zero. As much as he might strain,
the director could not see the telltale puff of dust that indicated
the shock wave breaking through the surface. The six men in
the control room stood immobile, not talking, hardly breathing,
mentally counting the seconds for the two minutes it would
take the shock wave to travel thirty miles to the control point.
When there was no shock wave at the end of three minutes, they
could hold off the conclusion no longer: The firing signal had
been locked out.

There were frantic calls from the White House during the
three minutes of silence. The test director could hold out hope
no longer. He turned to the secretary of Energy. "Mr. Secretary," he said, "please inform the President that the warhead
did not detonate."

Kane did not have time to pay attention to the countdown from
Nevada. As the secretary was copying down the numbers from
Idaho and verifying them with Winter, a call came in on an-
other line from computer operations at MIT.

"Bill, we've got it, I'm pretty sure," cried an excited voice on
the other end of the line. "I was trying all the primes you gave
me this morning. I had just gotten down to — "

"Never mind the story. For Christ's sake, just give me the
numbers," said Kane.

"All right already, here they come."

Kane copied them down himself. When he had finished he
walked over to the desk of the secretary who had copied the
numbers from Idaho. They checked exactly.

As Emir completed his speech, he rose from his chair, walked
over to the platform, inspected the warhead canister, then ad-

dressed the American officers, urging them to relax. They continued to stand at attention. Emir shrugged and walked back to his seat. He appeared to have regained his composure.

When he spoke, he was the Emir of old — suave, apologetic, and courteous.

"Mr. President," he began, "I am sorry that I became upset at the attempt of you and your Israeli allies to deceive me. I should not have been upset. It is completely in character with the pattern of deceit carried out by both your countries in the Middle East. We Palestinians have had to pay for that deceit in decades of misery and bloodshed. But no longer. By your actions, you have both rejected my plan for a bloodless solution to our problems, and now it is time to pay the penalty."

He paused, took a sip of water and looked around at June and the two officers. He then proceeded to tell the President that at the end of the demonstration, the Soviet Union would realize that the United States was helpless against their nuclear arsenal. He hoped that the President would show more sense in dealing with the Soviet Union than he had in dealing with him.

Whatever the President decided, the Palestinians would finally be winners. The Soviets would certainly eliminate the country of Israel by decree or, if necessary, by force. At that time, Emir stated, he would move his troops into both the West Bank of the Jordan and the Golan Heights. He promised to seek no territory that was not rightfully his and to treat the present interlopers with kindness and mercy so long as they did not oppose him.

"So you can see, Mr. President, that we will achieve our objectives without bloodshed. I had hoped that we would be able to achieve them with your cooperation, because I admire your country, but that is not to be. It was your choice, Mr. President, and you will be forced to live with the outcome.

"We will now go forward with the demonstration. My assistant, Hassan, will proceed to unlock the canister. Captain Curran and Lieutenant Murray, will you please verify that the warhead is untouched."

Hassan stepped up to the platform, unlocked the canister,

and exposed the warhead for inspection. Curran and Murray followed him, carefully inspected the weapon, and returned to their positions, saying nothing and standing at attention.

"Please speak up, gentlemen," said Emir.

The President cut in. "You may speak up, gentlemen, and stand at ease."

Curran reported for the two. "Everything seems in order, sir."

Emir thanked the officers and told them that their task was finished, since the remainder of the demonstration would be conducted in full view of their superiors. They would be escorted to their quarters, where they would remain for the next hour. When the demonstration was finished, they would be taken, along with the warhead, to whichever border point their President desired. There they would be released to be reunited with their families.

The officers stood at attention, saluted toward the television camera, then marched off to their room.

"The cable will now be connected to the warhead," said Emir. "It has been checked out for continuity by your officers and has not been touched since. To allay any suspicions you may have, we will perform a preliminary demonstration. On the adjacent cabinet of electronic equipment there is a receptacle identical to that on the warhead. The cable will be connected to that receptacle and you may send any arbitrary set of numbers as discussed with your technical staff this afternoon. Those numbers, unknown to us in advance, will flash on the monitor above the cable, so that you can be certain that, when the cable is connected to the warhead, any signal you send will be transmitted to the Permissive Action Link inside the weapon. Hassan, please connect the cable."

Hassan screwed on the ring of the firing cable and stood back. At a nod from the Signal Corps colonel, the technician in the Situation Room keyed the numbers 237, 596, 325, 687. Identical figures flashed on the monitor ten thousand miles away.

Emir was pleased. With a smug smile, he held out his arm, pointing to the numbers on the television screen. There was a buzz of conversation in the Situation Room, but the President remained immobile.

Beneath the table, his fingers drummed a question. He signaled the code for the letter *K*. The psychologist nodded, put down his transmitter, and went out to the computer room. He returned in a minute and spoke into the microphone.

"Kane believes he has a number. He is making a final check."

The President made the "V" sign again.

After a dramatic pause, Emir continued his monologue. "You see, gentlemen, that the circuits are complete. We will now open the switch on the front of the panel and connect the cable to the warhead. At one o'clock, that switch will be closed again so that you may transmit whatever signals you like directly into the warhead."

Hassan walked over to the panel and opened the switch. He then unscrewed the cable from the demonstration cabinet and screwed it into the receptacle on the warhead. He stood back.

Curran and Murray marched slowly into the room that had been their quarters for the last five days. The guard saluted them briskly and stood outside the door. Curran closed the door and slid the lock closed. The two dashed into the small bathroom.

The building had been hastily constructed, the bars on the bathroom window a last-minute addition. Curran had managed to hide a screwdriver, which a careless workman had left beside the platform as they were guarding it on the second day. Murray had found a piece of angle iron discarded by the technicians who had fabricated the support for the demonstration equipment. Using the angle iron as a hammer, they had loosened the frame holding the bars to the side of the wooden building.

They hastily discarded their jackets and caps. One drew a chair to stand on from the bedroom; the other stood on the toilet seat. Pushing on the bars from the bottom, they gave a desperate heave that sent the whole frame, bars and all, tumbling quietly into the desert sand below.

Curran dived through the opening, somersaulting once as he

hit the sand to get out of the path of Murray, who was directly behind him. They jumped to their feet and ran along the barbed wire fence for about a hundred yards until they came to a small motor pool with a dozen vehicles in it. The gate to the motor pool was locked but there was no guard and no barbed wire on the fence. They scaled it easily. Murray climbed into a massive eight-wheel truck and drove it through the motor pool fence. Curran followed him through the opening in a personnel carrier.

Murray jumped out of the truck and into the personnel carrier. The two roared down the length of the barbed wire fence to the gate, guarded by a single soldier who started to raise his gun to halt the speeding vehicle. But his reflexes were too slow as Curran drove directly at him at high speed. The guard dropped the gun and tried to get away, but Curran caught him with the left fender and sent him flying through the air.

The two went barreling down the road, not knowing where they were headed, hoping only to get as far away from the camp as possible before the startled guards could organize pursuit.

After Hassan had connected the cable to the warhead, there were still ten minutes before the enabling switch would be closed. The camera panned around the room, focusing for a few seconds on each of the participants in this momentous drama, as though it were doing previews to a movie. There was the canister, which had taken on a persona of its own, its soul the grapefruit-size sphere of plutonium, containing the energy of twenty thousand tons of TNT; there was June, calmly resigned to her fate, her mouth working wordlessly as she repeated to herself the numbers she hoped would soon flash on the monitor; there was Hassan, expressionless, waiting patiently to throw the switch; and there was Emir, smiling benignly at his costars, about to put on the greatest performance of his career.

The quiet at the campsite in those last few minutes was in marked contrast to the furor in the computer room in the basement of the White House. Kane was elated. Since the numbers that came in from MIT were exactly the same as those arrived at independently by Idaho, he knew he had the answer. He put out the word to all stations to stop their investigations and stand by for new input. He then put the Idaho-MIT numbers on the network with instructions to feed them into their computers and report back within five minutes. He ran back into the Situation Room to report.

As he entered, he saw the President signaling for his camera and microphone to be turned off while Kane delivered his message.

"Mr. President," he said excitedly, "we may have broken the code. I've had two stations independently arrive at a solution which works for their PALs. I need five minutes to check out with the complete network. How much time do I have?"

Fred Billings answered. "It's one-twenty-three. In seven minutes they will throw the switch to connect us to the warhead. We have a half hour to try whatever set of numbers we want."

Kane summoned the Signal Corps colonel who was directing the transmission. The colonel stood by the President's chair. Kane explained how the Permissive Action Link operated. He felt confident of his numbers but wanted to check one more possibility before feeding them in.

"Gentlemen, we have three tries at this design of PAL. It is programmed to prevent tampering, but it does make allowance for error. It will accept two incorrect inputs without reacting. If a third incorrect input is inserted, the device automatically renders the weapon inoperative.

"There is a small probability that the Nevada test failed for some other reason and that this warhead will still accept the old code. This design will allow us to check that possibility. Have the operator insert the old code into the transmitter when the circuit becomes available. If the new numbers check out, I'll be back with them immediately."

Kane returned, nodding his head. The numbers checked out. He glanced at the television screen.

Emir was looking at the clock on the wall in back of the

platform. "Gentlemen, it is exactly one o'clock. Hassan, please close the switch."

Hassan stepped up to the platform, reached out his right arm, and dramatically closed the open-bladed switch so that all could see it was activated. He then stepped back to his position and nodded to Emir.

The camera swung to the Lebanese leader. "Thank you, Hassan. Gentlemen, you have thirty minutes."

In the White House, Kane came up to the President's side as the Signal Corps colonel awaited permission to proceed. The President nodded, not breaking the silence in the room.

Kane listened carefully, checking his own papers as the colonel read the numbers of the old code, three at a time. The technician typed the numbers in groups of three as the colonel recited them. They flashed on the monitor in Lebanon as fast as he could type them. Ten minutes had passed.

When the technician stopped typing, the colonel asked permission to press the firing button.

"Proceed," said the President.

He pressed the button and nothing happened. The circuit was still locked out.

The silence on both ends of the line was broken by Emir. "Are you finished, Mr. President?" he asked, a self-satisfied smile tugging at the corners of his lips.

"No," the President replied. "We have some further input."

Kane handed the paper with the new numbers to the colonel, who calmly droned them into the ear of the technician. Again, the numbers flashed in groups of three onto the monitor. When he had finished, the colonel once again asked the President for permission to press the firing button. Someone in the back of the room could be heard praying quietly.

The colonel pressed the button. Again nothing happened.

"Gentlemen, are you ready to give up?" asked Emir. "You have eight minutes left."

There was no reply from Washington.

Kane was dumbfounded as all eyes turned to him. He

grabbed the paper from the colonel's hand and compared it with the numbers flashing from the monitor in Lebanon. "It's a typo," he screamed. "There's a typographical error in the second set of numbers. You'll have to rerun them. And mind you, no mistakes. This is our last chance."

The colonel reread the numbers, a little more slowly this time. Kane looked over the colonel's shoulder to be sure he was reading them accurately. Everyone else in the Situation Room watched the monitor, checking it against the numbers the colonel was reading, many of them moving their lips synchronously as they watched and listened.

As the last number appeared, the silence in the White House was broken by the shriek of a woman's voice from the speakers. "They've found it. It's the right code," June screamed. "You're beaten, Sal. You're beaten."

Hassan looked at her, startled, as the cameraman instinctively panned between them. Then, suddenly realizing the danger, Hassan stepped toward the platform to reach the warhead. June came out of her chair and rushed toward him, her handcuffed arms over her head. She crashed into him, the handcuffs slashing down to rip the flesh over his right eye.

They fell to the floor, Hassan rolling to get away from June, who kept pummeling with the handcuffs until, with a kick to her abdomen, he sent her sliding across the floor away from him. He crawled up onto the platform, the blood streaming into his eye, and reached for the locking ring of the cable connector.

He turned it once, twice. Four more turns and he could pull it away from the warhead to disconnect the circuit.

A bewildered Emir started to rise from his chair as the colonel again looked to the President for permission to push the firing button. The President nodded, himself transfigured by the scene unfolding at the other end of the transmission circuit.

The colonel pressed the button.

The action keyed the transmitter, sending a signal to a satellite five thousand miles from Washington and twenty-two thousand miles above the earth. The satellite received the signal and retransmitted it another twenty-two thousand miles down and five thousand miles across, into the antenna above the campsite, then down through the cable Hassan was trying so desperately to disconnect, through the now open Permissive Action Link, and into the firing circuit of the weapon, all in less than half a second.

The electrical capacitors charged and, in microseconds, sent the energy to the tiny bridge of wires of the detonators. The chemical explosive lenses imploded to compress the fissionable core, the initiator supplied the early burst of neutrons, and in a fraction of a millionth of a second, the nuclear equivalent of twenty thousand tons of TNT was released in that tiny sphere.

The television screen went blank.

Simultaneously, in Damascus, Tel Aviv, and on Mount Hermon, the sky lit up with a short blinding flash, dimmed for a fraction of a second as the shock wave formed, then came on again for several seconds before the colors of the fireball began to appear.

In Damascus, as the light poured into the window of his quarters, President Assad had a single thought: the fool.

In Tel Aviv, the Prime Minister was startled but elated. "We are saved," he said to his wife.

On Mount Hermon, Colonel Velikhov, just leaving his station, was almost blinded, but yelled to the lieutenants to drive north at full speed to escape the shock wave.

Curran and Murray felt the light and the heat hit them like a hammer as it poured onto the backs of their necks through the tiny rear window of the personnel carrier. Curran lost control in his surprise and the vehicle veered off the road. He screeched it to a stop. Both instinctively covered their eyes before they turned to the encampment, fifteen miles away.

When they were able to see again, they watched in horror as the fireball rose, turning green and yellow and purple in its majestic ascent, then flattening out as it hit the lower level of the stratosphere into the familiar mushroom shape they had seen so many times in photographs.

They were just beginning to regain their composure when the

shock wave hit them, a minute and a half after the detonation. It lifted the vehicle into the air. As the shock wave passed, the personnel carrier crashed down onto the desert sand, one tire giving way at the force of the impact. The vehicle rocked a few times, then settled down, its engine still running.

When their nerves had quieted, they climbed out of the personnel carrier to survey the damage. Except for the flat tire and some scorched paint, the vehicle was intact.

"We'll have plenty of time to fix this flat," Curran stated. "None of those people are going to come looking for us."

# EPILOGUE

I WROTE THIS PARABLE TO POINT OUT THE COM-
plexity of modern technology and to demonstrate how one
error, one misjudgment, or one act of sabotage could lead to
actions that would annihilate civilization.

The story is credible. Permissive Action Links exist and are
used on nuclear weapons. Some designs are more complex than
the system described. For example, in one variation, a sensing
device locks if the weapon is moved from a prescribed location.
The particular scenario could not happen today because PALs
are not yet installed on all weapons. But even simpler ruptures
in the command and control link are likely. It does not take
much imagination to conjure a plot wherein an enemy switches
the code in the "football" that accompanies the President. Even
an hour's confusion in a time of crisis would render us helpless.
Thousands of enemy missiles could be launched and detonated
in thirty minutes.

In designing a complex software systems, a skilled programmer can insert bugs that direct the system to ignore future
commands and act according to the designer's original wishes.
The industry is plagued today with viruses inserted by so-called
hackers who manage to break into software programs with
mischievous intent. These viruses are directed to lie dormant
through repeated checkouts, then break out and do damage

when the systems least expect them. Instructions such as those inserted by June Malik could easily be duplicated by a competent software designer.

It is an axiom of cryptography that any code can be broken. This is still true, but with modern encryption techniques, the time required to break a code can be extended almost to eternity. For codes using trapdoor functions, it can take more than a quadrillion years on the fastest computer in existence to analyze the product of two sixty-digit prime numbers. The encoding technique is commercially available.

Our society is rapidly becoming more dependent on complex computer software systems. But these systems have design limitations. They can handle only so much data and can take only so much time. It is annoying to lose an airline reservation because the computers are down, but our whole economy is becoming dependent on computers. When New York Stock Exchange trading became especially heavy on October 19, 1987, transactions were delayed so long that many automatic trading systems failed. The result was an exchange collapse that came very close to breaking down the complete financial structure of the free world. Such a potential catastrophe would have been inconceivable five years ago.

Dependence on computers in military applications is increasing at an alarming rate, especially in space. The Strategic Defense Initiative, or "Star Wars" program, is intended to provide for our nuclear defense by destroying fourteen hundred Soviet land-based missiles over the Soviet Union in the first minutes after launch. The hardware difficulties in designing optical systems, chemical and X-ray lasers, satellites, and sensing devices to act rapidly at such distances are staggering. But the complexity of the software for the computers is mind-boggling. Millions and millions of lines of software will have to work perfectly for a successful defense, but there is no way to test the systems in advance. The software will be especially susceptible to error or sabotage. One bug, one virus, one erroneous calculation, can spell disaster. The informed citizen does not have to be a technologist to weigh the pros and cons of these military applications.

The antagonists in the debates over escalation were deliberately conceived as near caricatures. There are Slocums and Popovs in every country. The model was the Kennedy-Khrushchev confrontation in the 1962 Cuban missile crisis. As history unfolds the events, it is apparent that participants on both sides advised the president and the premier to take the offensive with very strong opinions on and very little knowledge of the intentions of their potential adversaries. This should not be surprising because most of the intelligence and advice came from military officers. The military are dedicated by their training, their instincts, and their experience to the concept that preservation of their countries' liberty by force of arms is their ultimate responsibility. They also recognize that the best defense is a good offense. Small wonder that their advice should be to strike first. It takes a strong and prescient executive to resist such a recommendation in time of crisis.

The strategic nuclear policy of the United States is to rely on the concept of mutually assured destruction, appropriately acronymed MAD, to deter nuclear warfare. The policy assumes the ability of our weapons systems to survive a first strike. Our vulnerability comes, not in the inadequacy of our weaponry, but in our communication, command, and control systems, which are exposed to the tactic of decapitation. A deliberate nuclear attack would not likely start with the launch of thousands of enemy missiles. A more probable battle plan would begin with the detonation of a nuclear weapon smuggled into Washington, D.C., and installed on a barge in the Potomac River. Its detonation in a troubled time could wipe out our complete executive, legislative, and judicial organizations. There would be no television, no radio, no communication, to tell who was alive or who was dead. Bomb shelters would be useless, since the radioactive waters would render the city uninhabitable for weeks. Who would lead us?

An alternate strategy would be to detonate a single nuclear

explosive hundreds of kilometers above the earth. The only experiment on the effects of such a detonation, the Starfish test of 1962, lit the skies from Hawaii to Australia, knocked out satellite systems all over the globe, and seriously disrupted the Van Allen radiation belt. Exploded over land, the electromagnetic pulse would not only destroy satellite communications, but would be powerful enough to immobilize television and microwave systems and disrupt long-line telephones to a degree that we cannot predict.

Our high command is aware of this vulnerability. The government has refused to proclaim a policy of no first strike. Rhetoric to the contrary, many students of our strategy believe that the president's advisers would convince him to strike first in a showdown.

In the parable, the escalation stops when Appleby persuades the President that his Stealth and B1B bombers are useless to him, since they would only trigger a missile exchange and the war would be over before the bombers arrived at target. The same would be true of Soviet bombers. If the aircraft survived a first strike by either side, they would release their weapons over a country already devastated by thousands of missile explosions. Their only function would be "to make the rubble bounce."

Why do we rely on aircraft as equal to land-based and sea-based missiles in our triad of strategic nuclear weapons? The answer is habit, politics, and the tendency of military planners to fight the last war.

In the forties and fifties, bombers were our only means to deliver strategic nuclear warheads. In the sixties, land-based Minuteman and submarine-based Polaris missile systems were deployed. Aircraft were still of prime importance because of the vulnerability of land-based missiles to attack and the inaccuracy of the submarine-launched systems. In the seventies, multiple warheads were installed on the land-based ICBMs and the sea-based SLBMs, increasing the firepower of each launcher by at least ten times.

Today, there are more than four thousand ICBM warheads

and eight thousand SLBM warheads deployed or projected. Although the land-based missiles are vulnerable to a first strike, the submarine-based warheads are safe under the oceans. Furthermore, the submarine launches can now be corrected to pinpoint accuracy by celestial navigation after launch. In an age of missiles, bombers are as obsolete as battleships.

This susceptibility of technology to sabotage or error, this instinctive reaction of officials in high places to take the offensive, this questionable mix of strategic weaponry, should make ordinary citizens question the basic tenets of nuclear strategy.

We are currently engaged in a joint effort with the Soviet Union to reduce nuclear arms. The effort is highly commendable, but we must realize that it does not solve our fundamental mutual insecurity. In a time when a single submarine carrying twelve missiles, each with ten separately programmable warheads, can wipe out one hundred twenty cities, the safe limit is very low indeed. Neither side can afford to disarm completely, for fear that a Qaddafi or Khomeini could obtain a few weapons and blackmail the world. The solutions to our confrontations with the Soviet Union will have to be economic and ideological, not military.

We will have to live with the ideological differences for a long time. The Soviets look upon our Grenadas and Nicaraguas as we look upon their Angolas and Afghanistans. These differences are important, but no longer controlling.

It is in the economic sphere that we can see a glimmer of hope. The USSR economy is in desperate straits. We can help them improve it, but that is not our policy. With the threat of mutual annihilation hanging over our heads, a healthy Soviet economy does not increase our peril one whit. On the contrary, it should be an objective to improve our national security. We should help the Soviets to be fat, dumb, and happy, as we are. A healthy Soviet economy can reduce tensions, enhance free speech, and improve prospects for human rights.

We have fallen through our own ideological trapdoor and are groping for a way to climb from the abyss. We say we can't trust the Soviets, but we trust them every day, every hour. We trust that they have the instincts of self-preservation deeply enough ingrained in their souls not to push the button that will finish us all in thirty minutes. This parable shows how close we both can come. We can take the first step along the road to political reconciliation by economic cooperation.

We have time.

We have until the end of the world.